LHIND
THE THIEF

LHIND
THE THIEF

Sherwood Smith

This edition published through Book View Café
http://bookviewcafe.com/

Cover illustration by Sherwood Smith
Cover design: Amy Sterling Casil
Production team: Katharine Eliska Kimbriel, Hallie O'Donovan, Tamara Meatzie, and Patricia Burroughs, with text formatting by Vonda N. McIntyre

Lhind the Thief/Sherwood Smith
ISBN 978-1492387251

LHIND THE THIEF

ONE

"Stop the thief! Robber!"

A couple of stones thumped me in the back.

I enjoyed the angry bellows until my pursuers got close enough to hit me. The stones made me tuck my head down and run faster.

The street narrowed ahead. I scrambled around the corner of a dingy, crack-walled house, scattering poultry in a cackling wake, and found myself in a closed courtyard, high fences joining the three cottages that opened onto the court.

The closest fence stood about twelve finger-spreads high, made of thin, weather-beaten slats nailed together with warped rails. I risked a leap to the top, balancing on my toes, and from there another leap to the tiled roof of a cottage, crouching down as the first of the chasers bounded into the courtyard.

They stopped, confused to find the court empty, until those following behind ran smash into them. The hunt became a pushing, shoving crowd, everyone bellowing and nobody listening. I had to bury my mouth in the crook of my arm to smother my laughter. Then I raised my other palm and shimmered an image of myself disappearing over the fence on the opposite side of the courtyard.

"There," the blustering bully in the lemon-yellow smock howled, pointing in the direction of my shimmer. "He's crawled up the curst fence like a curst fly!"

"Around, you slow-footed slugs," someone in back yelled as Yellow Smock scowled up at the fence. Would he actually climb? I hoped he'd try, and bring the entire dilapidated rampart down.

One of the warped, iron-reinforced doors opened and a brawny woman appeared, a carving knife gripped in one of her mighty fists. "You're trespassing," she snarled. "Git!"

As quickly as they had gathered the mob scattered again.

The shouts faded away. The woman cast one last squint-eyed glare around the empty courtyard, then retreated inside and slammed the door. Whump! went the inside bolt.

I patted my stomach, where I'd stuck Yellow Smock's moneybag, the week's take from his so-called 'protection' service. That might buy me a corner to sleep in, even if it turned out the local Thieves Guild (which, I'd been warned by some young orphans who lived at the docks, was run by the harbormaster) wouldn't let me join.

Or maybe I ought to get something to eat first. I began the climb down, wobbling because my head felt light, as if it was about to roll off my shoulders and float away. Nothing but stale rain water, stolen from people's barrels, had passed my lips in nearly two days. No wonder Yellow Smock and his gaggle had almost caught me.

Breathing deeply until I felt steady again, I reached the filthy ground. And then, contemplating hot cakes with butter, I eased out into the street.

I stepped wide to avoid a foul mess in the street, then heard a scrape behind me, like boots against stone. A dark, heavy cloth flapped down over my head.

I fought as hard as I could, but I had two unseen foes, and both were stronger. I was thrown firmly to the ground. A knee thumped across my back and both my wrists were dragged behind me, and tied. Then someone picked me up, leaving the cloth still swathed around me, and I began to kick.

"Murder, he's a scrapper." The words were in a tongue I'd never heard before, but as always I got the sense of it right away. The speaker's voice was that of a young man, caustic and unfamiliar. "Aren't we in enough trouble? Are you certain we have to do this?"

He was answered by a younger male voice—also completely unfamiliar—in that same language: "I am bound by council rules."

The caustic one muttered (with difficulty, as I was struggling desperately), "You might allow another mage this pleasure."

"A servant of Dhes-Andis perhaps?"

Just then I got a foot free, and kicked hard at empty air. Mages? I thought, distracted. These two were definitely not Yellow Smock's blood-lusting friends.

The younger voice now addressed me, this time in Chelan: "Look you, boy. We have no quarrel with you. Stop fighting. We won't hurt you."

Naturally I fought harder. My toes walloped something soft.

"Oof!" someone snorted, and down I thumped onto the ground again. This time two heavy knees held me flat, and someone wound more cord around my feet and then around me and the sack, turning me into a kind of worm. It was getting chokingly hard to breathe, which forced me to give up. For the moment.

They held no further conversation for a seemly stretch. When they stopped I was unloaded onto wood, judging from the muffled thunk. The floor jounced as more thuds and knocks told me somebody else was climbing aboard, then the conveyance gave a jerk. I heard the clopping of horse hooves. I was in a cart, then.

The enemy started talking in low voices. Wrapped as I was in that dratted sack, it was difficult to hear them.

Caustic-Voice said, "We really don't need any extra trouble."

Light-Voice chuckled. "I have a plan..." And his voice dropped too low to make out individual words.

Alarmed—and puzzled—I lay quietly, to wait, plan, and gather my strength for the getaway.

A long time passed before the cart stopped. I heard a lot of shouting, and other noise that I was unable to recognize, but I was left alone. After another wait someone lifted me, and as I started to resist a voice said close to my head, "I'd advise you not to move, lad, or we might drop you and you'd drown."

Drown? Was I at Stormborn Harbor? The thought of all that water—and myself helpless in it—made me stiffen up, my heart thumping against my ribs, until I was dumped once more on a wooden floor.

The next wait seemed to stretch for three forevers, and I fell asleep. I woke up when someone began unwrapping the cord that bound the sack around my body. The cords binding my wrists and ankles were left alone, but at least that sack loosened, and someone pulled me up to a sitting position and propped me against a wall. Then the sack was, at last, pulled from over my head. Cool, tangy air ruffled across my hot face and I sucked it in gratefully, blinking against tears caused by the brightness of the light coming through a tiny, round window.

I shook my head, trying to clear my vision. Then I faced the enemy, scowling from habit.

Two of them sat side by side, both on low chairs. They were giving me as curious a scrutiny as I gave them, and for a moment no one spoke. One was a tall, brown-faced young man with long, braided black hair and the thin mustache of the warrior-lords west of the empire of Charas al Kherval. He was definitely a noble, complete with device stitched on the breast of his dark blue tunic, and both sword and knife at his belt. His long fingers sported several rings which I priced mentally, and decided to pinch before I made my escape. Fair exchange for being tied up and thrown in a sack when I hadn't done anything to them.

Because I hadn't—I'd never seen them before.

The other was shorter and slighter than the warrior-lord, fine brown hair just a shade or two darker than his flesh. It was tied back with the plain black band used by servants or clerks. He wore a simple, undecorated gray tunic, and no weapons. His only ornament was a ring of pitted, rough silver worn on the little finger of his right hand; the bumps on the face might have been age-worn, but the whole reminded me of something a bad prentice might have made. It wouldn't bring the price of two meals if I stole it.

This fellow had just begun to speak when the floor gave a pitch. Since my wrists were still bound, I nearly lost my balance, catching myself painfully on my elbow. The black-haired one grinned.

Then I realized why the floor had pitched: I was on board a ship. A ship? I changed my scowl to a slit-eyed glare, and the black-haired lord laughed. "Caught fairly, you are, young thief," he said in Chelan.

I scowled so hard my brow began to hurt outside as well as in.

He only laughed louder. "What a sight! And—are you sure you want to do this, Hlanan?—what a smell." He still spoke in Chelan, which meant he wanted me to hear and understand.

The one in gray frowned as he looked up at the black-haired Toad-brained Tick-Picker, then back at me. "Boy," he said slowly and carefully, "please believe we are not friends of that cross-looking man back in Tu Jhan. But we saw an illusion cast, while you were hiding behind that house. You did it, didn't you?"

I was sorry that my scowl was already at its most terrible.

"Answer him," the black-haired Son of a Scum-licker drawled.

"You got ale on the brain. Everyone knows no spell-casting's allowed in this land," I sneered. "And if you were thinking of trying same, they burn you for it in Thesreve." Then, so they would not think I was afraid of the threats of any Noble Pig-Wallowers, I spat on the floor in front of them.

Well, tried. I was too thirsty to work up any spit, but I gave it all my effort, knowing full well how rude a gesture it was.

The black-haired Night-Crawler reached down and gave me a cuff on the side of the head. It wasn't hard, but because I was sitting on a ship with my hands tied, I lost my balance and thumped my head against the wall with a hollow thok! that made him look surprised.

The other said "Rajanas," in reproach.

The black-haired Molester of Slime-eaters Rajanas (I memorized his name for adding to future curses) said, "I only meant to get his attention. And to discourage fouling the deck."

Hlanan said, "There's no need. He's obviously used to that sort of treatment, and he'll only mistrust us the longer."

Rajanas the Stink in Man Form shrugged. "He's a thief. Being tough with a thief is the only way you'll get any truth, instead of a lot more insolence. But very well. As I said at the outset, this is your mistake. Permit me to withdraw." He still spoke in Chelan, and he addressed the other as an equal, not as lord to servant.

He left, but not before I spat again, this time in his direction. His laugh floated back as he shut the door.

Hlanan left his chair and came forward, sitting cross-legged directly before me. He had wide-spaced brown eyes, and a thoughtful cast to his expression.

"Boy, I give you my name. It is Hlanan Vosaga." He said it such a way that I suspected there was a part missing. Though I was not certain, because I did not yet know his rhythms of speech, and also, naming can differ from place to place. But his tone? That I knew. He wanted me to trust him. Hah! "I want you to realize I mean you no harm. There are others who do. Who, if they find someone like you who can cast illusions, enslave them to cast evil illusions at their masters' will."

He waited expectantly. He'd been pleasant enough—for a captor—so I decided to answer him. But not give him what he asked. "I've managed to avoid the slavers for many years. And there are ways and ways of cheating a person."

"I trusted you with my name."

"Then you are a fool."

He surprised me a second time by sitting back and blinking at me, with no trace of anger in his face. I watched carefully, with no expression—except the scowl—on mine.

"What do they call you?" he asked finally, in a more cautious tone.

"My name is Lhind," I sneered. "And don't see any trust in the telling. Enchantments on names don't work unless..."

". . . unless you've the cooperation of the victim, however unwitting."

As soon as those words were out I saw the real trap. I jammed my teeth down on my lip in disgust. This is what I deserve for blabbing! I, who had spent my life guarding my secrets, had blundered like any village yokel first time in the city.

"Or, put another way," he said with an interested air, "if you expect to be enchanted, then you permit it. But there are not many who know that. Who is your tutor?" His steady gaze searched my face as he waited. I just glared back, unblinking.

He stood up. "Well. I can see you won't talk to me at all now. I want you to think over my words, and these. If you permit, I can help you make a better life for yourself. Safer, too. Till you decide, I'm afraid I must leave you tied up. Illusions cast aboard the yacht would be regrettable, to say the least." He gave me an apologetic smile, went out and shut the door.

I inspected the cord around my ankles. It was woven silk, very thin and not uncomfortable, but unquestionably well tied. The knot looked like a slip knot; if I pulled, it would tighten. The cord around my wrists felt much the same. No chance of wriggling free. I needed a cutting edge.

I thought with disgust of the dagger in the waistband of my knickers. It was right in front, just where I couldn't possibly reach it. *Remember this for the future, too*, I told myself.

I looked around the little cabin for a substitute. Against the far wall was a built-in bunk, and below it two cabinets, opposite a table with three fine carved chairs. Above the table shelves had been fitted, whose various objects were held in place by a carved guardrail.

I'd just finished my scrutiny when the door opened abruptly, and in walked the Strutting Root-Mold Rajanas. I had just enough time to give him a welcoming glower and to tense my muscles in readiness. He kicked the door shut behind him, then reached down with that deceptive slowness to grab the front of my tunic and straighten me up.

"I thought I'd better make the time to give you these words, my foul-smelling little thief. Hlanan is a friend of mine—"

"Pity him," I started.

He cuffed the side of my head. My cowl and hair were thick enough to cushion any sting, but I yelled "Ow!" anyway.

"Shut up," he said evenly. "He's also tender-hearted and idealistic to the point of rashness. I expect three things of you, and if you comply you will be cut loose in the first harbor we come to, with a coin for your pains. The first is: in the morning he will probably ask you where you came from and how you came by your ability to cast illusions. You will tell him. And when he offers to take you up and further train you, you will refuse. I do not believe you learned that trick by accident, but whatever incompetent fool of a sorcerer thought fit to teach the likes of you that spell is not going to learn anything of Hlanan that can be used to harm him. Or if you have escaped from your master then I do not intend to see you set free with any information to sell to the nearest practitioner of the dark arts. Do you understand me?"

He paused, and I tried to work up a good spit. He smiled suddenly. "The third thing is: you will improve your manners from this moment henceforth, or I will bestir myself to thrash some into you. Do you understand that?"

I gave him my deadest stone-face. He stared at me out of pale eyes, a paleness accentuated by his brown skin, and then, with that faint smile, he turned away. "You may as well remain here for the night. You have already rendered this cabin unfit for civilized company—" He smiled a little wider as he opened the door "—and your presence would probably shock said company right off my yacht." Laughing softly, he shut the door.

I snorted. "You don't frighten me, Offal-Faced Littermate of Skunks," I shouted at the door. I added a few more imprecations, then came the comforting thought that I'd had fair warning. That gave me all night to concoct a plausible lie.

I pushed myself against the wall and stood up. My head was light—though not nearly as empty as my belly—but I still managed to judge the rhythm of the water under the ship and hop over to the little window over the narrow table. Being somewhat short, I could just barely see through it, but what I saw was enough to convince me I was indeed on a very fine yacht, with no land in sight. A swim, then, was definitely out.

Not much of the yacht was in view: part of the gangway, along which two people in splendid dress strolled slowly. Beyond the rails, the water reflected sunset colors, and above marched a line of heavy clouds. Rain was coming.

Fine. If a storm was due, I wasn't going to spend it on the floor just because I'd been put there. I reached the bunk in two hops and a somersault dive. Glad to find my balance still good despite my dizziness and my hair and tail being confined, I wriggled around until I was as comfortable as those cords would allow—and then I sank into sleep.

Within an unknown stretch of time I woke up again, to find the ship rolling and pitching. Outside the wind shrieked, and under me the wood groaned like a live thing. My stomach lurched queasily, but I tightened it, thinking, *Quiet, gut. Not enough in you to make a fuss.* Curling up, I slid into more uneasy sleep, dreaming of ghost-riders in the thunder.

Nothing happened to me, though—that is, nothing until my door opened. I woke to see pale morning light slanting across Rajanas's angry face, and gleaming on the naked blade of the long knife in his hand.

TWO

Still hazy with sleep and hunger, I brought my feet up to make a last try at defending myself.

"Hold still," he said curtly, swatting my ankles aside. He reached down and grabbed the neck of my tunic, then flung me over onto my face.

"The yacht seems to have become separated from the other ships by the storm and the fog," he said. "We're about to be boarded by pirates."

He was interrupted by a long scream, followed by sudden shouts and clangs of weapons. I tried to sit up.

"Even a little rat of a thief deserves a chance to fight for its life," he said grimly, shoved me back down again, and sawed quickly through the silken cords binding me.

"Here." He pressed the blade into my hand, then dashed through the door. From outside came the sounds of cries and the clash of weapons.

I jumped down from the bunk and shook my head, trying to get my scattered wits to focus as I moved to the door. What do I do now?

Rajanas shouted a command, then he himself appeared a ways down the deck, running toward a knot of struggling people as he pulled a sword free of the sheath across his back. He turned his head and snapped more orders at the sailors swarming up from below-deck.

I looked up. The air was thick with swirling mist, making it hard to see the sails and rigging. Apprehension chilled me: this fog carried the taint of magic. I shivered, looking again along the length of the yacht. Most of the fighting I could see was going on at the front end of the ship, beyond which I could just make out the outline of another ship.

At the main hatch a few steps from me, a pirate yanked hard on a violently struggling woman half-wrapped in a cloak. He pulled her to the deck, one hand on her arm, one scrabbling at her neck. She flung away the cloak and something gleamed in her hand. The pirate struck at her. She whirled out of his grasp and stabbed him in the side. He stumbled away, howling, then more figures appeared, everyone fighting furiously.

I crept out. The deck was wet, cold, and slippery beneath my bare feet; forward, all the fighters were having a hard time keeping their footing as high waves splashed down one side of the yacht, foaming over the rails.

I leaped to the ropes leading upward, and when the yacht rolled away, I slung myself onto the masthead.

Now I could see more of the deck, through the rigging and the forward storm-sails.

A cloud of fog thinned momentarily, revealing individuals more clearly. I picked out Hlanan and Rajanas fighting against several pirates wearing scarlet tunics slashed up the side, with black trousers and shirts beneath. My throat dried. Those scarlet tunics were worn only by the Skull Fleet, one of the worst pirate federations plaguing the entire Azure seacoast. I had crossed them twice before—which was two more times than anyone needed to encounter the likes of them.

Think, I told myself, shaking my head again. I knew these pirates would not stop fighting until everyone was dead, unless someone was worth a great deal of ransom money.

I could make a shimmer. But how would a mere illusion help?

Rajanas's voice came back to me: "The yacht was separated from the other ships..."

A shimmer might help if it's big enough, I thought, rubbing my clammy hands down my tunic. Well aware of the penalty for trying magic in Thesreve, I hadn't dared try anything but small shimmers for a long time, ever since I'd crossed the border. Now, with aching head and empty belly, was not the ideal time to try more magic, but I did not seem to have any choice.

I tucked Rajanas's heavy-bladed knife into my waistband and raised both my hands, holding them palms out. I concentrated, whispering magic-gathering commands that I seemed to have learned in dreams. I was repeating words I did not understand, I only knew what they were capable of. As I muttered the litany, I pulled all the magic to me until my hands tingled and burned. When they began to pulse, I gathered the internal heat.

Sound! A horn—

A sudden, clear, low belling, like a hunting horn, rang out. My head buzzed warningly, but pride surged in me. Sound magic was so difficult, but I'd done it!

I threw all the rest of the power into the biggest shimmer I had ever tried. Snap! The spell finished, my fingers tingled so hard they were almost numb, but I watched in satisfaction as a black silhouette of a huge three-master slid close and noiseless near the yacht.

I laughed for joy. It looked real, cutting menacingly directly behind the stern of the yacht. Cries of fear and astonishment rose from the front of the yacht.

I stretched my fingers out again.

This time my hands did go numb, and I knew I wouldn't be able to gather and hold this much magic but once more—if that.

Fear helped me concentrate. Snap! Weak sunlight glimmered off half a hundred steel helmets, shields and drawn swords along the rail of my ghost-ship. The fog swirled close, masking the lack of detail that I did not have the power left to make.

But it was enough. My shimmers were aided by the pirates' own fog.

The pirates shouted and howled with rage, anger, betrayal.

My arms were heavy, numbing fast. But something more was needed.

I aimed my thumbs, and grappling lines snaked through the air toward the yacht's rails. My head pounded like twenty boulders had fallen on it, but I kept my arms locked and still, my attention focused just beyond my fingers. Then, with the last of my strength, I clapped—and a massive surge of water rose up to give the yacht a single, heavy lurch, as though the lines had snagged us and took hold.

An angry, raw-voiced command cut through the mist.

The pirates began to hack their way back toward their vessel. I spotted Rajanas's black head as he chased after, inviting death until the last moment. I sent my three-master heeling against the wind in the direction of the pirates, hoping the fog would cover the increasingly indistinct lines. The grappling hooks winkled into oblivion.

A sudden, hoarse cheer rose behind me. The pirates had cast off, and sail after sail billowed aboard their vessel as they began to run.

I let the shimmer fade into the fog, and as I released control, all the soreness of my head and limbs settled on me. Get back to that cabin! Pretend you were too scared to fight! I climbed back down the rigging.

When I dropped onto the deck, I was startled by a voice inside my head.

Hrethan! It was a call of recognition.

Who is that? I thought in fear, and as the presence entered my mind again, I shouted "Get out!" so loud I thought my skull would split. The voice and the presence disappeared.

I grabbed at the rail, fighting against the worst headache I'd ever had. Rajanas's knife clattered down beside me. Long years of never leaving a free weapon lying around made me bend instinctively to retrieve it. When I tried to straighten up, the deck rose to meet my face, and I had to give in to the dark fog that closed in on my thoughts.

When I woke I was stretched out on the bunk again. As I turned my head the sharp twinge of sore muscles ran along my arms, and my fingers twitched under my back. I was tied up again. A sigh of disgust escaped me—then my gaze fell on Hlanan.

He knelt beside the bunk, watching me intently. Behind him stood Rajanas, looking disheveled and tired, and next to him an unfamiliar, bearded man. I smelled something pungent: mulled wine. At the thought of anything wet and drinkable, I swallowed convulsively, and my tongue, which felt like a long-dried-out stocking, moved thickly in my mouth.

"Want some?" Hlanan smiled encouragingly. "I hoped the aroma might bring you around."

He slid a hand behind my hood and lifted my head, then held a cup to my lips. I tasted spicy hot wine. After a moment, vertigo faded and I felt a little more awake. Unfortunately, I was also very thirsty.

"Can I have some water?" I croaked.

"You're still thirsty?" Hlanan asked.

"It's only been three days..." I began.

Hlanan's dark eyes widened in surprise, and he gave a wince of regret.

"Maybe four...five..." I added in a pitiful voice, hoping to make him feel worse.

Instead his lips tightened. A smile? The quirk of his eyelids gave him away as he turned to the bearded man. "Captain Hucharwe, may I—"

A gruff voice from the captain: "I'll attend to it, Scribe."

Silence fell, and I shut my eyes, remembering that voice inside my head. *Hrethan.* I knew that word, but it, like the magic words, were buried in my past, difficult to retrieve except in shards of images, sounds. Once in a while a familiar smell.

Trying to think made my head feel worse. I opened my eyes as the hand slid behind me again, and this time I tasted water. Ahhh! I sucked it up until I couldn't breathe.

"Halt a moment, Lhind," Hlanan said. "Not too much at once."

Behind him I heard a noise of disgust—from a female. I opened my eyes again, to see the cabin crowded with several unfamiliar faces. One of them was a young woman with a beautifully shaped but sulky mouth. Her oval face was framed by a coronet of jewels bound into her curling yellow hair. She was dressed in beribboned peach and green silk, embroidered with gold—a gown more gorgeous than any I had ever seen in Tu Jhan, and her face was rigid with distaste, her chin lifted with assured arrogance, as she stared at me. Here was someone used to everyone else getting out of her way.

At her shoulder stood another young woman, with a pug nose in the middle of a round, smiling face. Her wide-set eyes were grayish-brown, and a coronet of reddish-brown hair framed her face. This was the one I'd seen fighting with a knife. Her air reminded me a little of Hlanan, that steady, intent gaze with the slightest tilt of head, conveying an air of question.

"Where did this creature come from?" the yellow-haired beauty said in one of the Southern languages. "Is this your idea of a little jape at our expense, Alezand?" She turned a sulky shoulder toward Rajanas.

He said, "He's a thief we saw in Tu Jhan. It seems he followed us aboard, and stowed away."

Stowed away? Indignant, I tried to rise, but the headache hammered me, and I fell back. The pug nosed woman pressed a gentle but firm hand against my shoulder, as if to stay me. Or protect me.

The doorway darkened, and a tall figure appeared, handsomer than the statue of King Bessemar the Just in Dunleth's capital. His long, ruddy-tinged blond hair lay waving on broad shoulders exquisitely molded in his velvet tunic of darkest midnight blue, edged with gold. His thin brows rose as everyone fell back, save Rajanas, and the lazy eyes turned my way.

Then the slack, bored expression hardened into disgust. He turned to the pouting princess. "Really, Kressanthe? You really want to be in the same breathing space with this noisome creature?"

"I want to know if that disgusting stowaway somehow got those pirates after us," Kressanthe demanded.

"Throw the worthless offal overboard, then you need worry yourselves no further," Prince Copper-Hair drawled.

"Since stowaways usually risk their lives to hide from danger, I am going to assume that he would not summon it, even had he the means," Rajanas said ironically. "You'll have to seek some other cause, Kressanthe."

"I'm already bored to death. Kressanthe?" Prince Beautiful-but-Evil lifted a velvet-molded, perfect shoulder, and left.

As the golden-haired princess hovered uncertainly, Rajanas said, "Of your courtesy, Kressanthe and Thianra, we would like to question our little thief, and I think it would be best if fewer people were present. The rest of you," he raised his voice slightly as he looked at the sailors crowding at the door, "have things to do, have you not?"

With a shuffling of feet and a whispering of skirts, the crowd dispersed. Then Rajanas shut the door and stood with his back to it.

"Stowaway?" I demanded. "*Really?* That is such a lie it hurts!"

"I'm very sorry about the lie. And the ropes, Lhind. These things are a backhanded turn for your saving us as you did, but the method you used has made us very uneasy," Hlanan said seriously. "Lhind, we need to talk about that magic."

"Wasn't me," I said the first thing I could think of.

"It was the pirates, of course," Rajanas murmured, smiling faintly.

Hlanan gave him a quick look, and Rajanas half-raised a hand, a gesture meaning he'd stay quiet. Hlanan turned back to study my face, which by now I had squinched into my sourest grimace.

Hlanan said steadily, "Lhind, magic is exceedingly rare in Thesreve. Any practitioners come from outside the country, and few dare to risk the stake and fires of Thesrevan law by practicing magic openly. Most of them are there for a reason just as deadly—to act as spies, for powers such as Dhes-Andis in the West. I promise I will not give you over to Thesrevan authorities. Indeed, we are past the border now. But I must know who your tutor is. That illusion was too large and complicated for most sorcerers' prentices. *I* wasn't able to construct anything suitable, and you can believe I was trying."

It was obvious they would not believe continued denials. So I muttered in my most grudging voice, "Wasn't any tutor." That much was the truth. But then, to protect myself, I added a lie, "I stole that spell."

"What?" Hlanan exclaimed.

"A good thief can steal more than just money," I pointed out.

Hlanan sat back on his heels, looking at me in silent amazement. Rajanas laughed softly.

Determined to ignore him henceforth, I gave Hlanan the story I'd concocted before I fell asleep. "I was sitting on a roof over on the Street of Doves. A lot of wealthy merchant folk live there, and the houses are close together and easy to break into. Anyway, I was waiting for a jewelry-maker and his wife to leave for a party. Their house was next to an inn." I stopped.

"Yes, go on," Hlanan urged.

"Some water first? Those long, dry six days...No food for at least a week before that...Then being jumped and tied up like a turkey for market..." I said pitifully.

Rajanas rolled his eyes upward, but Hlanan's brow puckered. "I'm sorry, Lhind. Here's the water." He held the glass to my lips, but when I was done drinking, he went right back to the topic. "So you were next to an inn, in the Street of Doves. Please continue."

"Was last summer. The attic window of the inn stood slightly ajar. I heard voices. A man, talking about illusions. I didn't really listen to the side-talk, but I sure liked what the spell could do. So I shifted over, and peeked in. He was talking to a sniveling fellow whose strength went into growing, not brains, because by the time he stumbled through the words and gestures, I had it all by heart. I thought it would be a great aid in getting take for my friends. In the Thieves' Guild. Who will be looking for me."

Hlanan listened with an air of courtesy, but didn't answer any of these hints.

So I sighed, and continued my lie. "Anyway, that magic tires you out so—and you have to be careful not to forget your surroundings. But when I stole that spell, the harbormaster, who runs the Thieves' Guild, you know, was so happy with me I went back to the inn next day, but a family of weavers was staying in the room. So I robbed the jeweler that day, instead."

Hlanan listened without interrupting, his brown gaze never wavering. When I stopped, I scowled again, hoping he'd believed me.

He didn't look skeptical or even angry, but when he spoke his words froze my gizzard: "I wish we could get you a bath, Lhind. I would like to see what you really look like."

"His looks might be just as repulsive as they are now, but it's bound to cure the smell," Rajanas said, grinning. "How long have you been wearing that cowl, boy? Since you first learned to walk?"

I snarled a couple of choice curses, adding heartfelt detail when I saw Hlanan's eyes narrow as he studied my cowl.

"We dare not spare the water until we find out where the storm drove us, Lhind," Hlanan said at last. "But you might enjoy it. Except, we would have to get you some new clothes. I don't think anything short of burning will do for those you have, and we have no one aboard who's small enough to provide a rough fit—"

"Call those a fit?" Rajanas interrupted. "I've been wondering why you weren't able to steal something closer to your size. Those, ah, knickers, look like they were last owned by that yellow-smocked bruiser you robbed."

"Easier to hide the take in," I said disgustedly. "And if you don't like my smell it's your problem! I didn't ask to come on this ship. Since I can't abide your looks, why don't you free me and we'll both be happy?"

"Manners, boy," Rajanas drawled, flashing a smile of amusement. Him, I understood. Though neither of us had the least respect for the other, he no longer saw me as a threat, nor did I see him as a threat. Hlanan was far more unsettling because I didn't understand him at all.

I snorted explosively.

"Why were you so reluctant to tell us how you got that spell?" Hlanan asked, gentle but persistent.

"Because you already grabbed me against my will, for doing nothing," I said promptly. "I thought if I told you I stole that spell you'd hand me right off to the mage-burners."

"Would you like to learn more magic?" Hlanan asked, leaning forward as if proximity would enable him to see inside my skull.

"No! One spell's enough for me," I said promptly, avoiding that steady gaze. I looked down at the crust of the rotten onion that I had so carefully smeared over my smock to help keep people at a distance. My stench, made up of smears of the stinkiest foods and spices I could find (plus vintage horse sweat when I sneaked into stables to catch some sleep) rubbed into my unwashed clothes, was a work of art. "I just want to get back to the Guild. They'll be worried about what's happened to me."

"You mean, what's happened to that purse you stole," Rajanas put in helpfully. "You still have it on you?"

I tensed, bringing my knees as close to my stomach as I could.

"Cease your fret," Rajanas said, with a lazy wave of one hand. "I haven't any desire to put my hand near that clothing to find it. The question was inspired by the repellent notion of having to sleep on a bag of coins...but you probably have a number of other oddments secreted in those garments as well, don't you?"

I worked up another good grimace.

Rajanas's smile flashed. "I never imagined housing a thief would be so entertaining. Shall we risk turning him loose among the company, do you think, Hlanan? Half of them have already seen him lying there on the deck by the galley, and I mislike locking up someone who very probably saved our lives."

"If he'll promise not to use the spell against the passengers," Hlanan said slowly. He frowned up at Rajanas, who met his look with a faint shrug. Turning his gaze back to me, he added, "And Lhind. This is even more important, and we must have your promise. To protect you, not just us. I've told the others that it was I who managed that spell. It really would be best if you did not mention you had magic."

"Better add that he cannot rob them, either, at least until we reach port. After that they can fend for themselves," Rajanas said with a dismissive flick of his fingers, and I understood that he didn't particularly care for all of his guests.

"I won't," I said, inwardly rubbing my hands. While I had no interest in the reasons for Rajanas's dislike, I wanted to find out who'd earned his ire. These would be my targets. *Also* my targets. He still owed me for grabbing me in the first place.

Hlanan gave me a grateful smile. "Good. I'll feel much better to see you free. Tell me, are you hungry?" He laughed. "Save your breath! If that was not a look of sheer appetite then I've lost my wits entirely. I'll fetch you something right away."

Rajanas stepped lazily away from the door and Hlanan disappeared. For a long stretch he seemed to stare right through me, giving no hint to whatever thoughts went on behind that bony face.

"How about untying me so I can eat," I suggested with some hostility after what seemed three forevers.

Rajanas blinked, his focus returning to the present. And to me. "From the looks of you you've never used your hands to eat before," he commented, his tone amused as he pulled a thin-bladed dagger from the top of his boot.

"Ha ha," I snarled, turning my back on him. "Are you going to keep your promise and turn me loose soon's this bucket hits a port?" As soon as I felt the cords ease I jerked my hands apart and rubbed my wrists through my sleeves. My feet were free next, and I rubbed my ankles as well, enjoying the faint disgust that curled his lip when he stared down at the mud flakes that fell off my filthy feet.

"We shall see," he said, straightening up. "Ah. Here comes Hlanan. Watching you eat will probably be a spectacle I'd rather miss." He sauntered out.

I made a rude gesture at his retreating back, then followed to the door, casting my gaze over what part of the yacht lay in immediate view. I could not see much damage. This was surprising. The Skulls were famous for destroying what they couldn't steal, and they usually made quick work of their victims by doing all at once.

That is, when they were attacking for their own purposes. Some of their captains hired their ships and crews out from time to time when normal pickings were lean. The lack of destruction pointed to the possibility of either slaving or hostage-taking missions. Attacking ships belonging to lords was a very risky business, and tended to cause the sort of thorough revenge-seeking that only the rich relatives of lords could afford—unless one of those relatives had hired the ship in the first place. Hostages? Or—?

Hlanan appeared, carefully bearing a tray. My eyes and nose welcomed lentil-and-tomato soup, and two wheat-cakes, and a thick, creamy pudding covering a fruit tart.

"Here you are," he said, smiling. "I suggest you eat and then sleep. You've earned it. We'll talk more after you've rested."

The way he carried the tray so carefully indicated he wasn't used to performing this task. The best way to get rid of nosy people, I'd found, was insults. And the quickest insult was against status. "For a servant you sure are slow," I said as I picked up the soup bowl.

"Slow at what?" he asked, his tone inviting me to explain.

I slurped in the soup, partly because it was hot, but mostly because slurping was supposed to be unmannerly.

"How am I slow, Lhind?" Hlanan asked again. "I'm trying to learn."

"Just slow," I said in my surliest voice.

"I beg pardon," Hlanan said, inclining his head. "How could I forget? Six days without food!"

I didn't like having my lies remembered. Safer not to talk at all.

So I ignored him and concentrated on the food, which was delicious. I ate as messily as I could without actually wasting any. That meant making lots of noise, grunting, slurping, and snorting. When I dared a peek at Hlanan, the smile was pronounced—he was enjoying my disgustingness! Flames of Rue, how was I to get rid of this person?

"Go away!" I snapped.

"As soon as you are done," he said gently, indicating the tray.

At that point I was thumbing up crumbs. His gaze followed my hand. Alarm thrilled through me—was my fuzz showing? No. I'd sewn my cuffs tight to my wrists, and my fuzz was thin and sparse at my wrists. None showed, especially under the coat of grime.

I shoved the tray away so it almost fell. He caught it up, the dishes sliding as the ship rolled the other way. Not a word of annoyance, or even a flash of anger escaped him as he steadied the tray, one elbow against the bulkhead. Then, timing his movement to the roll of the ship, he got out the cabin door, and closed it gently behind him.

I didn't bother to check and see if it was either locked or warded. Exhausted, full for the first time in days, I stretched out on the bunk.

I don't remember falling into sleep.

THREE

The cabin was dark when I woke, starlight glowing in the little window revealing a stone jug of fresh water. I drank most of it, then got up and stretched. Now was time to have a look around, without nosy servants, or mage-students, or scribes. Whatever Hlanan was.

I don't care, I thought. *I just want him and his questions out of my life.*

I reached for the cabin door with one hand, the other going to the loop in my waistband where I kept my lock-picking tool, but to my surprise the door opened. I slid noiselessly out. The night was clear and warm, the stars pale lights overhead, and one of the moons lay in a golden crescent just above the horizon.

A couple of sailors noticed me, but went about their business. I spotted a wide hatch with the honey-hued glow of lantern-light spilling out, and ghosted near as voices floated through the open space.

Someone strummed fingers along the metal strings of a tiranthe.

The notes shimmered in the quiet air, high, down to low, sending an echo to shiver through my bones and sinews, down into my brain to stir very old memories that I still couldn't quite reach. Once, surely, I knew music. Why else would it come so often in my dreams?

A flicker of brightness, no more—the Blue Lady holding out her arms to me—then the image was gone, like the sparkle of the sun on water.

The images wouldn't come back, but the feelings lingered. I slipped down the stairs as if compelled by some spell, knowing it was stupid. There was no reason for all these useless emotions of sadness and longing.

A thief has no time for music. After all, you can't steal it or spend it. I remembered the time, two or three kingdoms away, when I'd stolen a tiranthe. But when I got it to a place where I could try it, I found out fast that listening and playing are two vastly different things.

I laughed at the memory—but my feet wouldn't move on.

A male voice joined the tiranthe's glissades, a clear, warm tenor, and I oozed up to the open cabin door and peeked in. Lounging on a bunk, the center of attention, was that copper-haired fellow in velvet. The soft firelight made art of his fine cheekbones, the curve of his generous lips, the cerulean blue of his eyes as he sang a ballad in a tongue I'd never heard before, but as always the words formed into patterns, and the sense seeped in after.

Eugh! There I was, doing what I had vowed never to do again, admiring someone just because nature had been generous with his looks. But not with his nature. His single glance at me had been one of utter disgust, his humane suggestion that I (being offal) be tossed overboard. And here he was singing about love.

Love! Romance! Poets and bards all claimed love and romance were all-powerful as well as eternal, but really, what is either but attraction, as ephemeral as a sleet storm, and about as comfortable? No, attraction was more like a disease than a storm.

I recalled that contemptuous glance of disgust, the indifferent suggestion that I be tossed to my death, and turned away, but I couldn't scold myself into a comparable indifference.

Somewhere, somehow, I had formed the belief that beauty ought to be joined to the qualities I thought beautiful: kindness, compassion, truth. I scrambled up the steps to the deck, but the melody pursued me as relentlessly as memory. Two inescapables, memory and music, as imperceptible and yet as powerful as any magical enchantment.

And both as untrustworthy as beauty, love, and romance.

Music, I could not make. Memory, I could not command.

There I stood, unable to recover my own past. The memories I could call up were mostly the kinds I'd rather forget, like a certain lantern-chinned player in the ancient city of Piwum, where—for the first and last time—I'd actually managed to earn an honest living, as a theater mage. My illusions made those plays look better than they sounded, until I found myself watching that fellow instead of my cues, in hopes my cowled, disguised self would gain another smile.

He was handsome, but also loud, arrogant, tight-fisted with a coin, and disloyal to everyone except his own comfort. But did I see that? No, all I thought about were his beautiful black eyes, the cleft in his chin, the rich and sonorous sound of his voice, and I found myself using my powers to steal little things for him ("Just little things, it hurts no one," he said winsomely)—fine slippers and velvet cloth and gold ribbon for his hair—just to win a smile, to hear those pretty words.

I debated removing my disguise, just so...I never did define what was going to happen after that, except there'd be a glorious ending like the most romantic songs. Then, late one evening, I returned backstage to fetch my rain canopy and encountered him murmuring the exact same pretty words to the girl who sold fruit, before the two went off to be alone.

I left that city that night, and for the past three years, my strict rule had been to leave as soon as I learned anyone's name.

So here was this beautiful blond nobleman warbling this song about a couple of witless people wasting their time longing for each other and letting other people and weather and things deal them nasty blows without their doing much about it, except complain in metered rhyme.

Beauty, pah! Love, faugh! Romance, I spit upon thee!

Glad to be completely disease free, I thought scornfully that my shimmers had more substance.

I retreated to my cabin to hoard up on sleep.

I woke up in the early morning when Hlanan entered with another tray.

My mood was foul.

Hlanan's wasn't. He grinned like he'd just heard a rare joke, and I wondered if that Rat-eyed Rot-Nose Rajanas was above putting some sort of mouth-frying spice in the food. I'd certainly do it to him, had I the chance.

"Good morning, Lhind," Hlanan said.

Ignoring him hadn't worked, because he studied me with even more interest than he had the day previous. I didn't want to be studied any more than I wanted to be questioned. What to do? Ask the questions, and be as boring and annoying as possible.

"What are you laughing about," I snapped. "We *finally* nearing the shore so I can get off this garbage scow?"

"I'm happy because my aidlar returned this morning."

"What's that?" I retorted.

"It's, well, a talking bird," he said as if I'd asked eagerly and politely. "It travels with me. Went off yesterday to find out where we are, so now we are able to steer in the right direction."

"The wind picked up," I said. I could feel it. The ship rolled as if alive. "It's making me sick. Where are we, anyway?" I demanded.

"The storm blew us a ways north. The right direction, as it happens. We just outran the other ships we'd been traveling with. We should reach port by tonight." He set the tray down before me, then sat on one of the trunks with the air of one who intends to have a good, long chat.

So I forestalled his questions. "How'd you and the Slime-Slurping Night-Crawler happen to be there when I did that spell after the chase, in Tu Jhan?" I whined, then jammed wheat-cake into my mouth and chewed as noisily as possible.

"Sli— ? Do you mean Rajanas? We were spending time in the marketplace, waiting for some of his party to finish shop-visits, when Rajanas saw you rob that unpleasant man in the yellow dyers' smock. The man was bringing quite a bit of attention to himself, calling that apple-woman a cheat."

"*He's* the cheat," I snarled.

"So that's why you provoked a chase? To get him away from the woman? Is she a relation of yours?"

"She's my great-auntie. She'll be desperate, looking for me," I moaned pitifully.

"She did not seem unduly concerned when the chase began. No doubt she had her reasons," Hlanan said, his head tilted at more of an interrogative angle.

"Auntie counts on me being home soon's I can," I said.

"Home being…" He began.

"You don't need to know where her house is."

"True. Beg pardon." Hlanan inclined his head. "Anyway, it was your taunts that intrigued me at first. You called him a…What was it? A stinking scum of a sweat-sack. I wondered if you were bidding fair to become the gutter-poet of Tu Jhan."

"The what?"

"A reference to the Gutter-Poet of Akerik, who made himself famous in the Shinjan War. It's a long story. You don't read or write?"

"No," I snarled, and then whined with as much affront as I could muster, "You did all these rotten things to me just because I mouthed that bullying dyer instead of cutting and running?"

"You sound outraged." He grinned. "Well, partly that, and partly because you are so young. It made no sense, sorcerer's apprentice and thief. Especially in Thesreve. I wouldn't dare to do any spell in that country." He gave me a quick, lopsided smile, but his gaze remained steady and observant.

"That's exactly why I don't want any more magic than the one spell I stole," I said, and crunched into a piece of bread. "Yum!" Crunch, crunch, slurp, smack!

"Do you like being a thief?"

I shrugged. "It's an easy enough life, if you're fast."

SHERWOOD SMITH

"Your family are thieves as well?"

"Yep," I said. "Whole family. Both parents. Grams and gramps. Gotta get back quick."

"Do you never spare a thought for those you steal from?"

"Ha, ha!" I laughed, proud of the spattering of bread I sprayed. "It's always them't never been hungry, who say that."

Hlanan's brow creased thoughtfully. "Who has said it to you?"

I shrugged again, sharper. "I never saw that anyone was the happier for being honest. Take Auntie! Honest, but still Yellow Smock cheated her, saying he'd protect her, but he didn't. And as often as not she went hungry. So I decided, why not do something? It would be fun."

"Fun? Even though you were pursued and your life threatened?" Hlanan's eyes narrowed. "Why don't you want me to think you have loyalties?"

"Because I don't have any," I retorted. "I do what I like. I go where I like—" I began, then remembered the invisible Grams and Gramps and family, so I moved on quickly, "Loyalty is weakness, setting yourself up for another betrayal." I waved a slice of peach. "Loyalty to freedom, and fun, yes. Not to *people*. As for Yellow Smock, I robbed him because he's a vile bully and a cheat and it was fun to make him bellow in front of the entire street. The old apple woman, that is, Apple-Auntie, she isn't worth cheating because she's got nothing worth taking."

Hlanan leaned forward, clasping his hands between his knees, and said again, "Why do you wish to deny you have loyalties?"

I snorted, louder than a den of slumbering drunks. "It's the truth, for whatever that'll getcha in gold."

He tipped his head the other way. "To return to what you said earlier. As it happens I have experienced hunger, in a limited sense. I know someone who went hungry for longer, at much the age you are now. He worked to reverse the misfortune he'd been dealt."

I grinned at him. "So he's rich now, is that what you're saying?"

"He has recovered his birthright—"

"Good. Then point him out, and I'll do one lift without worrying about how he'll manage if he goes hungry again."

Hlanan sighed. "I've offended you. I'm sorry," he said directly, rising to his feet. "I'll go."

"Where'll I put this tray when I'm done?" I asked, suspicious at how easily he'd accepted his defeat.

His answering smile was as gentle as always, but his gaze had gone absent. "Take it down to the galley. Thanks." He walked out.

As soon as I finished eating, I nipped to the cabin door and threw the latch. A fast search through the trunks disclosed a small hand mirror under a load of cloaks. I pulled it out and tilted it desperately, examining as much of myself as I could see.

I had to make certain it was really the magic spell that had caused this spate of questions. I didn't want him finding out any of my secrets. It was possible he might guess I was really a female. That had happened a few times, as I couldn't help my size.

In some kingdoms it didn't matter, like Thesreve, in spite of the laws against magic. The secret that I didn't want anyone to guess was what *kind* of female. That is, that I wasn't like the humans that surrounded me. I'd not yet met anyone like me, and I'd learned the hard way that letting others see me as I really was brought nothing but grief.

I hadn't seen my own reflection since the beginning of autumn, when I'd found these clothes. I'd been certain then that nothing was wrong. The weather was now warming toward spring, but plenty of men and boys were still wearing cowls that hid shoulders, neck and ears, and many of those wore caps over the hoods. In heatless houses it was the only way to keep warm.

My tunic was a plain, heavy, shapeless homespun brown— what little of it could be seen beneath half a year's accumulated dirt and grease. I had sewn several pockets on the inside of it for quick stashing, and to fill out my shape. Underneath it I wore heavy black man-sized knee pants, which came down to my ankles. These were excellent for hiding bulky stash in. Below the knickers were my bare feet, coated as were my hands and face with brown nut-oil and weeks worth of grime. I turned my hands over, and found no challenge to the anonymous brown of dirt. So I tipped the mirror up and peered at my face.

An anonymous face, I thought. Small nose and mouth, like my short stature and thin frame, made me look much younger than I was, but what in that would cause interest? My eyes were wide-set, my brows dark with the nut-oil, and I'd seen plenty of people besides me who had eyes this same shade the color of honey. There were also plenty of people who had more of a slant to their eyes and brows than I did.

I threw the mirror back in the trunk in disgust. Who would have thought that doing one tiny spell would cause this much bad luck? *Just count yourself lucky you weren't seen by a Tu Jhan magistrate.* I recoiled from the memory of the stake, and a figure writhing in the flames.

Time to stop this and go do some spying. Maybe you'll learn something of use.

I returned the tray to the galley, swiping an apple on my way out in hopes that Hlanan would get in trouble for forcing me on board. Munching on the fruit, I returned to the deck and oozed along the gangway, keeping a wary eye for dangers—and Hlanan.

The wind had come up strong in the bright, clean air. Several sailors clung to yards high above, calling to one another as they unreefed the sails, which bellied out in wind-filled curves. Near the base of the tallest mast a grizzled man bellowed orders in a voice that would frighten a stone. Yet not twenty paces from him two well-dressed females stood at the rail looking out to sea, as if they were alone on a terrace at some castle. The sailors paid them no more attention than they paid the sailors.

When I was five paces away, the ladies turned from the rail, one's skirts billowing out like the sails above. Their faces changed, and I laughed aloud at the contrast. The yellow-haired one in the fancy gown looked affronted, and ostentatiously drew away from me as if I was a giant slime bug. The short-nosed one was Thianra. She gave me a welcoming smile, and started right in with the questions. She had to be related to Hlanan!

"Good morning, Lhind. Have you ever been aboard a ship before?"

"No." Since hers was an easy question, and she hadn't forced me onto the yacht, I made her the sort of grand bow I'd seen some of the merchants give the Mayor on First Day of the Spring Fair. She laughed and made a dainty curtsey, incongruous in her unremarkable blue jacket and riding trousers. "And, good morning yourself."

"Thianra, you *aren't* going to speak to this revolting creature," the other managed to drawl and sigh at the same time.

"He is a guest, Princess, as are we," Thianra asserted gently.

"Next time maybe the pirates'll take her with them, if she prefers their company," I said promptly. "Would serve the pirates right."

The princess gave me a sour look and stalked away. Thianra turned an observant gaze my way. "Princess Kressanthe isn't usually quite so rude. She's slept badly since that frightening attack."

"No matter." I made a grand sweep with one hand, dismissing the Princess of Pouters. "I'm sour myself, having been forced onto this yacht entirely against my will."

"I'm sorry," she said contritely. "It's just the unlikely combination. Thievery, and Thesreve..." She looked around. "And magic," she added quietly. "Hlanan, who's an old friend of mine, did tell me about that."

"Thieves can steal a lot more than gold," I said.

She tipped her head pensively, her air once again reminding me of Hlanan, though in every other way they were different: he tallish and slender, she medium height and roundly compact, he very brown, she with paler skin and lighter eyes. Well, maybe there was a slight resemblance in the fact that both had wide, thoughtful brows. "I think he wished to offer you a chance at a better life."

The brow could be accidental, and so could the air of question, as well as their manner, as if we were equals. Disgusting as he was, I understood Rajanas's behavior better, and beyond avoiding him I did not have to waste a thought on him. These two made me uneasy. "Hlanan's related to you, isn't he?" I asked.

Her brows arched in surprise. "Yes, but few know that fact. Can I ask you to keep it to yourself?" She was not only assuming equality, but trust.

I hated that.

But I liked her.

So I shrugged. "No harm done. I'm mum. Anyway, you won't be seeing any more of me soon's we hit port."

She began to say something else when a shadow darkened the corner of my vision. I ducked, keeping my back to a mast as Thianra turned and smiled up at Rajanas. He'd come up as quiet as a cat. I oozed to her other side, keeping her between me and the Rotten Road-Apple.

"Hiding behind an unarmed bard?" he inquired pleasantly.

"Why not?" I retorted. "And she's not unarmed, she carries at least one knife. Also, I wouldn't have to hide at all if someone hadn't forced me on this tub."

His eyes narrowed as he smiled. "Interesting that you noticed. Few do." I gulped inwardly, disgusted with myself, as he made a suave gesture. In annoyance I mentally priced his rings. That ruby alone would feed me for three seasons.

Thianra surprised me then by putting a protective hand on my shoulder. "Kressanthe has been complaining to you, has she not? Don't be angry with Lhind. The princess was horribly rude." I had no idea what game Thianra and Hlanan were playing, but at least their rules seemed to be fair.

"She has indeed," Rajanas said. "But I guessed what had happened, and I stand more in her disfavor than this little thief does, for informing her that she got what she deserved. So I can hardly chastise him for angering her." His tone to her after his words to me was like winter to spring. "So I am not here as executioner, but as emissary. Hlanan thought the boy might like to see the aidlar, and sent me to fetch him down."

Thianra smiled. "Oh, yes. You'll like Tir, Lhind. So beautiful, and very rare this far south."

She walked away, but before I could run, Rajanas snapped out his hand and closed five steel-band fingers around my arm. In spite of his lazy air, he could move pretty fast. Disgusted with myself for not keeping well out of his reach, I went along without fighting.

When we got to the stairway leading below, he stopped and held me against the wooden rail so that I had to face him. He said in a low voice, "It's clear you've a past. That doesn't bother me. I've one as well. But understand this. There will indeed be no retribution for your conduct toward Princess Kressanthe, but I warn you against further baiting of her. You can contrive to stay out of her way until we reach port."

I shrugged. He must have considered that agreement enough; he loosened his grip and with a mocking air of deference, indicated for me to precede him downstairs.

FOUR

Several doors opened off a narrow hallway. One of the doors stood open, and we went in.

This cabin was larger than mine. Paintings graced the walls, and Hlanan sat cross-legged on a wide, spacious bunk, next to neatly folded counterpanes. Behind him the little window they called a scuttle stood open, and salt air blew in, ruffling his fine brown hair.

When he saw me he smiled a welcome, and gestured toward one of the carved shelves near the painted ceiling. There perched a long-bodied bird with brilliant white feathers tipped with dark gray shading to black, a seed-picker's beak and eyes like the ruby in Rajanas's ring.

"This is Tir, Lhind," Hlanan said, pride warming his quiet voice.

"Good mor-row, good mor-row," the bird croaked.

Staring in fascination, I entered slowly. Memory stirred in me, just as it did when I heard certain kinds of music. Had I ever seen such a creature? I was instantly sure I'd dreamed of one.

The bird fluttered its wings, then flew from its high perch to the edge of a chair near me. It looked at me from one eye then the other, and without warning a voice said inside my head:

Hrethan!

The same voice that had spoken in my head the night of the pirate attack. This time, the voice radiated recognition.

Yes, you hear me. You are Hrethan, in false guise—

Though I had always been able to hear the thoughts of creatures, never before had one contacted me. And no one, ever, had questioned my disguise.

I clapped my hand over my ears and backed away. When I saw Hlanan react with alarm, I realized he hadn't heard the words—he'd been startled by my movements. His smile faded into question, and Rajanas's eyes narrowed intently.

I dropped my hands and pretended to stumble against the strong yawing of the yacht. Turning my eyes to the bird, I answered in my mind: *I deny I am anything but what I appear.*

You are Hrethan, the bird answered, flapping its wings agitatedly.

Afraid it would squawk its words out loud, I shouted in my mind, *DON'T TELL THEM.* And, because I was frightened by this totally unexpected attack from an unexpected source, I tried to force the other mind out. Something flicked down inside my brain, like a little door or an inner eyelid, and once again I heard only my own thoughts.

The bird promptly shrilled in distress.

"What's wrong, Tir?" Hlanan asked in a soothing voice, his eyes wide with question, his manner evocative of surprised wariness as he flicked glances from the bird to me and back again. Holding out his arm, he murmured, "Lhind is our friend. Don't be frightened." He spoke like one would quiet a frightened baby.

So he and the bird didn't talk mind to mind. He had no idea what the bird thought— how much the bird knew.

I edged toward the door as the bird settled on Hlanan's arm and croaked, "Lhind good! Lhind good!"

Hlanan's perplexity eased to a tentative smile, but his gaze was still speculative as he said, "There. Whatever happened, it's all right now."

But it wasn't. The bird kept flapping and trilling.

"Must be his smell," came Rajanas's dry voice—from right behind me. Even more quiet than I, he'd moved to block the door. "The distinctive aroma of vintage thief would upset anyone, obviously even a bird."

"Rather smell than have the face of a wart-nosed slime-dweller," I retorted under my breath.

"What's that you're muttering?"

"I wish you'd take that cowl off, Lhind," Hlanan interrupted Rajanas's laughing challenge. "It rides so low on your brow I find it difficult to read your expression. Perhaps you aren't really scowling as much as it makes you look—" As he spoke, he reached toward me, as if to help me take it off.

"No!" I said, and I dove under Rajanas's arm toward the door.

At once those steel-band fingers closed on my arm, and Rajanas pulled me back in. I twisted around and kicked his shin so hard I bruised my toes.

Giving a grunt of surprise, Rajanas thrust me further inside the room and let me go. So they wanted a fight? Backing up so I could keep them both in view, I whipped out my knife and crouched, waiting.

"What? Where'd he get that knife?" Hlanan said, looking from the flapping bird to me. "Tir? What's wrong?"

Rajanas sank down onto a stool bolted to the bulkhead, eyeing me in faint surprise. "Probably has a dozen of 'em in those clothes," he said with a soft laugh. "So you think the prospect of a bare head is a matter for steel, eh, my noisome young miscreant?"

Hlanan sighed. "Put away your knife, Lhind. I am sorry. I should have remembered that even an underage, half-starved thief has a sense of dignity. If you object so strenuously, then we shall allow the subject to drop."

Rajanas laughed, waving a hand lazily at me. "As well. Doubtless whatever he hides is sufficiently loathsome if he prefers that grimy item as a mask."

"Loathsome toe-mold yourself," I snorted, walked slowly past him. He did not move, merely watched. Keeping a suspicious eye on him, I reached the doorway, then ducked out, slamming the door behind me.

SHERWOOD SMITH

I headed for the deck, limping on my numb foot, but when I reached the stairway to the open air, I faltered. Nobody was following me, and I knew the only way to get answers to some of the questions crowding my mind would be to catch the cause unawares. So I sneaked back and listened at the door.

They were not speaking in Chelan.

"—slippery little bug," Rajanas was saying.

"And his remarks and actions remind me very much of us when we were that age," Hlanan returned. "You should know as well as I do that people with lives balanced between hunger and danger grow up a lot faster than most."

"Or they don't grow up," Rajanas acknowledged, with one of his sardonic laughs. "So what are you thinking now? You know your thief has led a thief's life. He's entertaining, but useless."

"No, that he's not. Have you forgotten his illusion when the Brotherhood attacked us?"

"His one trick. And it is a good one, I'll admit. But of what use to us? The sooner you give up this foolish plan of yours, the sooner we can get back to matters of real import, such as Dhes-Andis's prospective fleet—"

"Or what to do with Kressanthe," Hlanan replied calmly.

"You invited her aboard, you entertain her. You have no title, so you're safe enough from her designs."

"Ilyan, we couldn't have left her stranded in Tu Jhan."

Ilyan? Had to be a private or inner-family name. Nobles had them, and others who had public faces, I'd discovered. Ilyan for intimates, Rajanas his family name, and that nasty princess had addressed him by a territorial name, as if his importance was measured by what he owned.

For a delicious moment I imagined binding magic onto all three of his names while he was present, so that, oh, every time he tried to speak, snakes would fall from his lips, or he'd fold his arms and cluck like a chicken, but he'd probably find the snakes funny, and Hlanan would give me one of those looks, partly question, partly puzzlement, maybe a little sad. I *hated* that...that expectation that I had a better nature.

"Why not?" Rajanas said, blithely unaware of my fulminations. "Kressanthe has plenty of money, a powerful father to keep those thieving City Magisters from touching her, and I still maintain she only came to the regatta to nose around. The question is, for whom? We really should have left her on the dock. She could have bought her own ship."

"But she appealed so directly," Hlanan replied with a sigh. "I could not turn her down, not in any way that would not register as offensive when the reasons were conveyed back to her father. It is beyond necessary that no more attention be called to your activities than would normally accrue to a nobleman on a pleasure cruise. It's bad enough we're forced to carry Geric Lendan with us, but at least he'll find nothing of interest aboard the yacht. And carrying her ought to kill any rumors about our being on secret missions."

"Perhaps. But she'll repeat everything that my dear 'cousin' Geric gets these lackwits to say over drink." He gave the word cousin some extra drawl. "And she'll even carry back tales of this accursed mudball of a thief you've thrust on us. What a pleasant cruise we're having!"

Hlanan laughed, sounding free and boyish. "But Kressanthe's gossip is all to the good," he said. "Isn't it?"

Rajanas replied ironically, "Yes, I'd momentarily forgotten how valuable it will be to have us laughed out of the Imperial Court once the tale of our cat-and-mouse game with one undersized thief gets around. How better to keep up the appearance of a couple of bumbling wastrels?"

Hlanan laughed again, then said, "Come. Halt your gloomy mood with the midday meal. Let's find Thianra. Maybe she can sing you into smiles again. I heard her picking out some new pieces."

Quick as thought I hopped up the stairs to the deck.

The problem with eavesdropping, I thought aggrievedly as I massaged my throbbing toes, is that you can't take revenge for insults that you were not supposed to hear.

Limping swiftly back to my own cabin, I thought over what the two had said. What did it mean? And how could I use it against that Rat-Spawned Rajanas?

I felt the sun warm on the back of my cowl, and fought the urge to lift the hair that lay squashed against my spine. Scratching crossly, I reflected that the only bad thing about taking a bath every year or so is the itching in the warm weather. Each year I forget how much I hate summer until it threatens to come again. The sense of being smothered in all the thicknesses of my disguise nearly overwhelmed me.

Nasty as it was, it was also safe.

Fighting against a mood worse than any Rajanas could be suffering, I jammed my hand inside my trousers to shift my gear around more comfortably, and my fingers closed on Yellow Smock's money bag. Why, I'd almost forgotten it!

I thought angrily that this just showed how unsettling this adventure had been—imagine letting a take go this long before being explored!

First I went back to the cabin door and threw the bar, then I opened the bag onto my bunk. The wealth of glittering coins improved my mood with a bounce. Counting carefully, I came up with half a twelve of silvers and three-twelve and four lecca. More money than I'd seen at one time for quite a while.

Raising my eyes to the window, I saw a startling sight.

The horizon was no longer a flat blue, water dissolving into firmament. A line of dark mountains now stitched sea to the sky.

I moved toward the scuttle, as if pulled by an invisible thread. Mountains! It had been several years since I'd seen any. The sight inspired both fear and longing. In my earliest memories the fear had driven me to run away from mountains and hide. Those were my earliest distinct memories.

Restlessness itched at me, worse than that on my skin. I scratched irritably at my hood, wishing I could tear off my cumbersome clothing and loosen hair and tail. The itch subsumed the fear, freeing a desire to break through the fog of half-memory and puzzlement that surrounded my early years, and figure out who I truly was, and wherefrom I had come.

I glanced back at my wealth on the bunk. Whatever I'd said to Hlanan, I knew I was done with Thesreve. It was time to run again.

A knock at my door caused me to sweep the coins back into the bag. I got the bag stashed in my trousers again before I unbolted the door.

To my surprise it was Hlanan, bearing a tray of food.

"I thought you might like a noon meal," he said, coming inside.

"Doesn't it bother anyone, your waiting on me like this?" I asked.

"I have not asked. Does it disturb you?" he replied.

"Well, yes," I admitted. "A few scraps thrown my way would be more in keeping with what I'm used to. This makes me feel something bad is about to happen."

"I cannot ask Rajanas's servants to wait on you, and I am not the sort of person who flings scraps. You'll have to do with me. I noticed yesterday that you do not eat either chicken or fish." He looked at me questioningly as he set the tray down on the little table.

I shrugged, uncomfortable with any kind of personal questions. "Disagrees with my innards," I muttered, and filled my mouth with food so I wouldn't have to talk.

"And," he said, when he saw I was not going to amplify, "I wanted to have a chance to talk to you alone. I have a proposition for you."

"Prop—" I coughed on a wad of bread.

"—osition," he finished encouragingly. "Business. For which you'll be paid. Well, I might add." His voice changed to question, his gaze narrow and watchful. Whatever was about to come out was clearly important to him.

I scowled at him. "What."

"There is an ancient book of spells I would like more than anything to have in my possession. I need someone who knows a bit about magic as well as about the, ah, mechanics of stealing."

Relief whooshed through me. Now, at last, he made some kind of sense. "So you nobbled me because you need a thief," I said.

He smiled a little. "Well, yes. In part. The main part," he hastened to add.

"But a book? Books don't bring any kind of price."

"A book of spells," he repeated. "Very powerful ones. And I would reward you with six crowns. Uh, empire-struck gold crowns, not the silver-mixed ones used in the islands."

I calculated rapidly. "Six? But I can't read. What if I find the wrong one? I never go back to a house, especially some magician. I don't want to end up as a footstool."

"Ah yes, I'd forgotten that you can't read." His eyes narrowed slightly. "Then I will teach you."

I frowned, aware that he'd offered those golden crowns mightily easily. Whole houses were bought and sold in Thesreve for about that price, and to look at him there in his plain clothes one would have assumed he hadn't ever seen two together.

Setting aside this incongruity for later mulling, I went into bargaining mode. "Six..." I said, letting the word stretch out doubtfully. "That's not much when you add in all that sweat-work and time wasted learning a thing I won't have any use for in the future..."

"Double, then," he said promptly. "To cover the time you waste learning to read."

"Done," I said, before he could back out, and I actually felt a brief twinge of remorse. He was too honest to be a good bargainer, and I figured he'd regret this bargain when he'd had time to think it out. *Well, let him learn a lesson now. Maybe it'll save him some real grief later.*

"Good," he said, dropping his hands to his knees, and looking well pleased with himself. "We will be sailing into Letarj in the morning. We will leave from there straight for Imbradi, where we will form our plot. Our lessons shall begin on the way. Right now I'll tell Rajanas that you'll be accompanying us to his capital."

I snorted a laugh. "Better you than me," I said. Irritating as the thought of more of Rajanas's company was, it was cheery to reflect that his disgust on hearing the news would be at least as strong as mine. And in his capital, I would feel no compunction whatever about embarking on a strenuous quest to increase my wealth.

Hlanan left. I wandered back to the scuttle, pleased—and somewhat relieved—to have a plan of action. The sight of the mountains woke up that old yearning, and daydreams? Memories? Images flooded my mind, strong currents of air over deep, shadow-hidden valleys. Snow gleaming on rocky peaks in pale light. Gliding, high and wide . . .

That bird-voice sheared into my thoughts. *Hrethan, hear me! I would rather die than harm you. Hrethan spared our kind again and again in the past. They alone of your kind share the skies with us. Any aid I can give you I will, now and until breath is still, and all time stands before the Maker-of-Life. Command, and I hear.*

What's Hrethan? I cried back.

You, the bird returned.

Are there others? I asked cautiously.

Yes. Far and far. And then, to my surprise, the bird caused me to see again those mountain peaks and valleys.

I turned away, my heart hammering with fear, wonder, and questions, the foremost being: if these were memories, when, where, and how did I end up where I was?

You are like, and yet different, Tir amended.

And so I was forced out, is that it? To wander about on my own, to guard my own life or lose it, and no one to watch or care? Is that it?

The bird had no answer.

Old grief lay right under the memory-stirrings. I squashed it down again, and busied myself with rearranging my stash, and recounting my coins. Those, at least, were solid. Understandable. Real.

FIVE

That night they had a party. The quiet, efficient servants strung lanterns along the standing rigging. The night being balmy, food was brought forth and laid on folding tables on the deck. Musicians gathered around the binnacle, Thianra in their midst, wearing her bard's robes of blue, her hair shining with coppery highlights in the lantern-light.

About twelve people comprised Rajanas's company, not counting servants. (And they wouldn't count the servants.) Most of them were male, and all of them were young. Four young ladies, including that obnoxious Princess Kressanthe, vied with laughter and flirty fans for the notice of one of the young lords. All had dressed in their best finery, floaty panels and velvets, with ribbons and lace and jewels glittering and gleaming in the candlelight. I caught the random, blood-glow flickers of two rubies braided into Rajanas's long black hair.

The one who was the focus of the most attention was tall and slender, slightly older than the others, and marvelously dressed with moon-sapphires shining in his pale locks. He was exactly the type to arouse admiration and desire; once even mine, but I rejected the impulse to linger, and I looked only to despise.

They laughed and talked, switching back and forth between two or three languages. I could understand all the words, of course, but I sure didn't catch many of the references, and the laughter sounded more heartless than humorous. I noticed Hlanan, plainly dressed as always, standing on the perimeter looking pensive.

Taking my cue from him, I stayed up on the masthead, out of sight. Battles and chases I could handle with little thought, but there was a cruel edge to that laughter, especially when Kressanthe led it, that I deeply misliked, especially since what they said rarely made sense. I knew I could think up insults as quickly as any, but that was defense. Little as I wished to find attraction in Pale-Hair or his smooth-faced, glittering friends, still less did I wish to serve as target for their wit.

So I stayed only to nab some of the eats, and when the music started, stirring up old emotions and half-buried memories without much sense, I retreated to skulk in my cabin.

Not that I could entirely escape. Over the next watch occasional breezes wafted scraps of music into my cabin—which, I discovered, actually belonged to the yacht's first mate, who was now housed down below where the toffs stayed. The music played on and on, often blending with the sweet, silvery rise and fall of Thianra's voice.

I had worked hard to build a stone wall around my heart, but music always seemed to put cracks between the stones, through which useless emotions leaked out. I resented this weapon. I wanted hurtful emotions locked safely away so they couldn't, well, hurt.

I stayed high up until one by one the instruments and voices fell silent, and all I heard were the occasional calls of the night watch, the creak of rope and wood, and the endless wash-slap of the sea against the hull.

Next morning, I discovered the yacht swarming with activity. At first I saw none of the toffs, just their servants.

Then I spotted Hlanan moving quietly among the soberly dressed men and women laboring to bring up big trunks and bulky receptacles of various sorts. He spotted me at the same time, and his thoughtful expression lightened to a smile.

"Lhind," he said. "Just the person I need. Would you take this box down to Thianra?" He gestured toward the other hatchway, dropping a small wooden cask into my hands at the same time.

I looked down at it, surprised that my hands had taken it. When I looked up again, he was deep in conversation with several toffs, all looking off at the coast.

The cask was heavy, and it smelled like one of those good woods—rose, cedar, taurein. Twining figures of animals and flowers carved at either end. Heavy. It made a chinking sound as I moved it in my hands, and I wondered if it was loaded with coins. Maybe those gold crowns he'd offered me so easily?

He gave it to me? I stared down at it as I worked through a succession of reactions: amazement at his lack of forethought in handing coins to a thief; scorn for his neglecting to think I wouldn't lighten the load first; last, a twinge of discomfort when I recollected his words about how even a thief has a sense of dignity.

Then I remembered my easy promise before they first untied me. I could break that promise, but I found that I was reluctant to.

Here I was, divided between two instincts: the first, to take what I could while I could, the second to...not.

I didn't like this dilemma. It was unsettling, like I'd been bound by some invisible rope. But then practicality reasserted itself: they'd have only to check the cask and they'd know I'd messed with the contents long before we came into port. Of course they would count! At least once. I certainly would.

And so, as I had no desire to see how Rajanas carried out his threats, I continued down into the middle deck, where I found Thianra bustling about a tiny cabin strewn with clothing before two heavy chests, and a helpless-looking lady wringing her hands as she glanced about in despair.

Giving me a quick, preoccupied smile, Thianra bent to cram an armload of lace and silk into one of the boxes. "Lhind," she cried breathlessly. "Would you kindly sit upon the baroness's trunk so I can do the latch?"

"Hlanan sent me with this." I held out the cask.

"Just set it on the bunk there." She waved a hand, standing expectantly next to the trunk.

I climbed on it and crouched down. She shook her head and I hopped off. After much shoving and grunting and finding corners of flounces and frills hanging out the side, we finally got the latch to thunk into place. She straightened up, wiped a strand of hair from her brow, and began moving purposefully toward another chest. I slunk out.

Retreating to the masthead, where no one could see me and load me with their chores, I bestowed a moment's brief pity on those people with all their chests and boxes and dunnage to be dragged about. The only way that made sense was to have one set of clothes, and when they either wore through or itched one beyond bearing, one snaffled some new.

A strong breeze blew the yacht right down the center of the harbor. The yawing bow rolled and pitched in the deep blue of the sea like a horse galloping for home, sending sprays of saltwater high into the air. The river sparkled a lighter blue under the brilliant sky, marking where brine ended and fresh water began.

Even from our distance, Letarj appeared different from Stormborn Harbor back in Thesreve. It was built along the mouth of a wide river. The shoreline angled inward until we sailed into the river itself. On hills rising to each side the whitewashed and golden-brick buildings of the harbor city gleamed. A very rich city, this. But the thief gangs were tough and numerous and did not look kindly on independents, Thesreve rumor had it.

I sighed as we sailed past all that wasted wealth. And what a variety! I saw everything from beautifully decorated, fast yachts like the one we were on, to big old weather-beaten round-hulled trade three-masters. Twice we were passed by exotic and sinister-looking red-sailed Shinjan galleys moving out to sea. The slaves in the galleys dipped and raised the long oars in a matched rhythm one would have thought impossible to achieve, and the red sails looked like stains of fresh blood against the sky. I remembered some of the stories I'd heard about Shinja, and shivered in the strengthening breeze.

Farther and farther in we sailed, past anchored ships of all kinds, from all over the world. There was a long line of piers, next to which lay big traders or very fancy ships obviously belonging to royalty. Along the wharves lay goods from all over the world: gigantic wine barrels from the inland hills, crates of blood oranges from the islands, their aroma sweet above the brine; bales of wool from the high mountains, cloth, wood, even baskets of almonds, islanders in fringed vests bargaining loudly with dock merchants with their counting beads.

As we sailed slowly along, little rowboats fast splashing out of our way, it became apparent from the various flags that went up and down the foremast rope on the yacht, and at the harbormaster's on the hill, that we were to get a pier to ourselves.

Then I heard noise below. A shrill, sarcastic voice: ". . . if you *think* you can manage this without further damage—"

Princess Kressanthe stalked the length of the deck, yelling the while at a string of heavily burdened servants. She was gowned in some kind of shiny silk and so many diamonds hung round her neck, on her wrists, and in her hair, that it hurt the eyes when the jewels caught the strong sunlight and flung it back in shards of liquid light.

She halted in the middle of the deck, and tossed her hair back with an angry gesture, then ran her fingers through the curls flagging in the strong breeze. My scalp itched anew as I watched.

Nobody seemed to be paying attention to her. The princess scanned the deck, her eyes narrowing when she spotted Rajanas and the captain standing aft behind the wheel, talking.

Kressanthe turned her head sharply and shrieked at someone right behind her, "MUST you be so SLOW?"

The men remained at the taffrail, gazing at the shoreline.

The maidservant she snarled at ducked her head and ran back for another load, stumbling among the sailors heaving on sails as the yacht drifted up to the pier.

Thianra appeared, her face anxious and her hair loose. It flew about her in the wind as she rushed straight to Kressanthe and began talking very earnestly.

The ship shuddered and wallowed; the yards braced round, tight as the sailors could get them. The crowd of servants milling about staggered after one violent surge. One skinny maidservant burdened with a bulky receptacle of some kind lost her balance and lurched against the princess, who turned and slapped her ringingly across the face. The servant girl fell back, dropping her burden, which smashed on the deck and spilled its contents: jewels, rings, brooches, and necklaces.

We're now in port, I thought as I slid down a backstay. *Here's my chance.*

Snaking into the group of reaching, grabbing, exclaiming servitors, I went to work: a foot behind another foot here, a shove there, and a yank on a skirt—and the off-balance group fell down in a satisfying tangle of thrashing cloth and flailing limbs.

This kind of thing is an art, and I'd gotten mighty good at it.

Kressanthe was on the bottom. She lay there without moving, shrieking for her maids. I eeled out from the pile, snagging take as I went. A package got thrust into my nose and someone's elbow caught me hard in the stomach, but still I managed to nip three rings and two bracelets. My big prize was going to be the long string of faceted diamonds, right from Kressanthe's perfect neck, but I was distracted by sharp fleeting light at the edge of my vision. I took a look, and gasped when I saw more diamonds, much bigger, better diamonds, half-spilled from an embroidered cloth bag. The light didn't just reflect and refract, it seemed to gather in them, radiating pinpoints of ferocious sun.

I bent, whisked them up, and retreated to my cabin where I stashed them hastily in my knickers.

Then, gloating inwardly, I reflected that the best thing was that Rajanas, in ignoring the princess, could not possibly have spotted me making the pinch.

The instant my clothes were straight I strolled innocently out to watch the servants picking up scattered belongings and disentangling Kressanthe from the mess.

Her rising voice caused Rajanas to cross the deck. He bent to give the princess a hand up. As he pulled her to her feet, he glanced about, giving me a narrow-eyed glance. I edged discreetly back, and gazed off at the shoreline as if nothing was amiss. But I peeked sideways to keep an eye on things.

The sails were brailed up by now, the ship tied fore and aft. The crew extended a gangplank to the dock, which dropped with a bang, to be instantly tied down by dock workers.

Kressanthe snatched her hand away from Rajanas's arm, and marched toward the gangplank with her nose high in the air. I didn't hear her parting shot toward him, but it must have been a good one, as his brows rose in mild surprise, and Thianra turned away, her hand covering her face to hide laughter. My heart warmed toward Kressanthe—too late.

Kressanthe was the first to sweep down to the dock. Hlanan appeared at Thianra's side, both of their faces wearing twin expressions of concern. Rajanas, smiling faintly, moved to talk to them. I would have kept my distance, but Hlanan looked about, spotted me, and gestured for me to join them.

I took my time, catching the end of Hlanan's murmured words; he was talking in one of those languages I'd heard once or twice on in the southeastern reaches of the empire. ". . . I wish it hadn't happened because it will only sound the worse by the time the story reaches Court."

Rajanas shrugged. "If you believe for a moment she'll tell a story on herself, then by all means worry."

"It will not be the truth that her father hears, but the emotions propelling her words will be genuine," Thianra responded softly.

"You're right." Rajanas brought his chin down in a definitive jerk. "No time for our errands in Letarj. We'll make straight for Imbradi." He turned away, beckoned to one of his stewards, and began giving orders.

Below us on the dock, Kressanthe had dispatched harbor runners to fetch vehicles for hire. As I watched, three pair-drawn coaches rolled up and the harassed maidservants began loading trunks and cases into one coach. The servants then climbed into the smallest one, and from the largest—into which Kressanthe had stepped the moment they rolled up—a few coins spun, glinting, from the doorway to land at the runners' feet. Then the same imperious hand that had flung the silvers waved with another imperious gesture and the coaches rolled from the dockside with a great cracking of whips and pounding of hooves.

Hlanan said, "We must disembark now." His brown eyes were distant, his expression pensive.

Wondering what he was afraid of, I said, "Still want that book?" I was poised to run, but twelve golders?

"Book?" he repeated, brow furrowing, then he nodded quickly. "Oh yes, Lhind, I do indeed. I thought you knew that. Tell me, shall you mind a somewhat hasty journey? Rajanas wishes to travel fast."

"Well of course I'm used to kingly comfort," I said promptly.

A rich laugh behind me told me that Thianra had heard. "You stay to help Ilyan," she said to Hlanan, in Chelan. "I shall take Lhind with me to yon inn, and enjoy a bite and sip on firm ground."

Hlanan gave her a relieved smile, and I wondered what was going on that was not being said. Hoping to get a hint from Thianra, I followed her to the inn she pointed out.

Once again she was dressed in a fitted minstrel-blue jacket and riding trousers. Her tiranthe hung in its embroidered cover (much finer than her own clothes), and below that, a simple knapsack.

One glass of tasty brown cider and a big cheese pie stuffed with wine-braised onions and tomatoes went down to warm the inner Lhind, but during that time I gained nothing from her aside from a respect for her story-telling ability. She talked a great deal, mostly about traveling.

Once or twice I sensed she was watching me for signs of familiarity with the places she mentioned, but she asked no direct questions, and she answered the ones I asked her with friendly ease and humor. I also saw those browny-gray eyes flick toward the door each time someone came or went, and I noticed her hands, when resting, in reach of where I guessed her weapons to be hidden, but her smiling face never changed.

The inn we visited was as colorful and varied as her stories: not just for gentry, though several fine-dressed people passed us by, nor just for harbor folk. People from several lands sat at the rough-hewn tables around us, even four Shinjans, noticeable for their pale skin and eyes, and though they didn't actually have red hair, as most Shinjans are rumored to have, they wore red somewhere about them. The aromatic air was thick with the clatter of many tongues.

We were on our second glass, paid for with great cheer by Thianra, when Hlanan entered quietly and came to our table. "All the guests have departed." He spoke in Chelan.

"Then we may do the same," Thianra said. "Ready, Lhind?"

I looked from one to the other. "If we're definitely still on for those twelve golders."

"We'll be planning that as soon as we reach our next destination," Hlanan said, palm raised in the universal sign for *I vow this is truth.* Which I know is scarcely worth the air around it, but he hadn't lied to me yet. That I'd caught, anyway.

Thianra and Hlanan led the way outside again. The yacht bobbed at its pier. Despite its furled sails, its long, low lines made it look as if it were still skimming over the water.

I paused in the yard and thought about how splendid the yacht felt moving under full sail, once I'd discovered the mast heads, and I wondered how one of these might be pinched. *Maybe you could snaffle the boat, but how about the crew, dolt?* Grinning to myself, I walked on.

Hlanan and Thianra stood before a high-slung carriage with four restive horses pawing the cobbled street before it. The carriage was newly painted an imposing black, and I recognized the device on the side as the same that I'd seen stitched on Rajanas's tunic. Next to it an open chariot waited, with a matched team being held tightly in check by one of the stewards. Two high-bred horses, their reins held by other servants, danced and tossed their manes nearby. In back a big cargo coach, piled high with luggage, was also ready to roll.

Thianra and Hlanan stopped near the chariot, clearly involved in some kind of disagreement.

Thianra shook her head, and I barely heard her voice, using some language I remembered from long ago, but didn't have a name for: ". . . entertain Kressanthe, and I have. I told you, I heard rumors of new Kitharee folk patterns up in Barsk, and I need to hear them myself—"

Hlanan's voice was too low to make out as his back was to me, but I heard Thianra's answer, "Hlanan, you know where my true interest lies. But just this once."

"Thank you," he said. I heard that much.

And they both glanced at me.

Did they think I didn't understand them? I waved. They smiled, Hlanan friendly, Thianra more troubled.

Meanwhile, six men whose bearing and purposeful movement indicated they were warriors, despite the plain tunics like the rest of the servitors, mounted inside and atop the carriage. Rajanas appeared from the other side, waved languidly, and the carriage-driver cracked a whip. The horses started out.

The easy days of sailing plus a good meal had made me unwary. When a steely hand grabbed my shoulder, I jumped, then wrenched away and glared up at Rajanas. He tipped his chin toward the luggage coach.

The driver of this vehicle was a big, beefy-looking man with a rocky, scarred face and a purple nose. He had small, squinty eyes with an expression like a brick-pile falling on somebody's head, but his bristly brows indicated curiosity. If I was to ride with him, maybe a suitable story would win his sympathy—

"Arbren," Rajanas drawled, "this repellent scrap is a thief, hired for some obscure reason by the Scribe. I want those trunks to arrive in Imbradi intact. You are to see that he has no opportunity to inspect their contents."

Arbren's glance congealed into a glare that would have scared a weaker soul right off the coach. I contemplated cutting and running, but then Rajanas tossed me up onto the seat beside the driver.

"Haw!" Arbren gave a knowing guffaw that lost none of its sneeriness despite a complete absence of teeth.

Rajanas mounted the chariot, and Thianra climbed in beside him. Hlanan swung into the saddle of one of the horses, a steward mounted the other, and our cavalcade set out at a gallop.

SIX

It soon became fairly obvious that Arbren had at some point during the day imbibed a goodly quantity of ale and he apparently had not sullied its purity with any food. For a short while he treated me to what he considered to be his rare wit, dredging up a lot of stories about what happened to thieves he'd helped to catch, or had seen caught. I think he made most of them up. I don't care how practiced the town executioner is, people's ears do not stretch out so one can tie them into a knot.

At any rate the sun beat down upon us, making my head and neck warm and sweaty. Arbren had recourse to a very aromatic flagon that he did not offer to share. His purple nose got more purple, and after a time he fell silent, squinting between the plunging lead horses as if he had a lot on his mind. Like the weight of a good-sized headache. Settling back on my seat, I silently wished him well of it.

We rolled through increasingly wild country, scarcely checking our pace at turns and crossroads. The grassy hills gave way to rocky inclines, streams and then patches of thick forestland. We passed two or three villages, stopping once to change horses, then again, much later, when a white shape appeared overhead, cawing and flapping.

Hlanan's horse caracoled as the Scribe hailed the bird. Rajanas signaled a halt, bringing his chariot up. Slowing our heavy coach, Arbren muttered an oath under his breath. I hunched down, ready to clap my hands over my ears (as if that would keep its thought from invading mine), hoping the bird would not see me.

But the bird never looked my way. It cawed at Hlanan, fluttering its wings in agitation. Hlanan edged his horse near the chariot, and bent down to talk to Rajanas.

After a short colloquy, Rajanas turned our way. "Arbren! Pass Khiam. We'll ride until nightfall, and chance a roadside inn."

We rolled at once, Arbren muttering under his breath about blighted birds giving all the orders, and if a body is looking forward to the ale at the Helmtree in Khiam he has a right to be getting it.

Rajanas signaled for a much slower pace as these horses would not be changing at Khiam. Even so, somewhere along one of the sharp turns through a wooded area we lost sight of the third coach.

This didn't bother me in the slightest, but it apparently perturbed Rajanas, whose glances backward toward the empty road became more dire.

It was just before nightfall when he and Hlanan apparently decided the horses had had enough. For some little time I'd been hearing the horses' thoughts getting steadily more tired, and I sensed the animals nearing danger. I'd learned long ago that horses are the kind, like dogs, who will run until they die, if that is what pleases their human masters. Which is why I'd seldom risked making friends with horses.

These were not near death but they were tired and desperately thirsty. Just about the time I began wrestling with the prospect of having to make the horses' need known—without letting on how I knew—we drove through a village, and on its outskirts neared an inn half-hidden under a copse of very old trees.

Rajanas flung up his hand again, his fingers pointing into the brick-paved courtyard, and even Arbren muttered with unfeigned gratitude as our diminished cavalcade pulled in, slowed, and stopped, the horses blowing and steaming.

Stable hands ran out, some bearing streaming torches, and Rajanas stepped down from the chariot, apparently sublimely unaware of being as mud-spattered and wind-tousled as I on any of my worst days.

I peered through the gloom at the long, rambling building with its ivy-covered brick facade. It was one of those places only those with coin, and plenty of it, could stick a nostril into. No thief markings anywhere in sight, which didn't surprise me. Some toff places would assiduously scrub off any markings, even warnings, as a deterrent.

All the windows had good, broad glass, not the pattern of tiny, warped and rippled panes you usually saw. I decided if I was not to spend the night hungry outside (for in these places even the stables are guarded, much less the food) I'd have to stay close by Hlanan.

The innkeeper came out himself, drawn no doubt by the commotion that indicated a customer of means. He very quickly picked out Rajanas as the target for his blandishments, and bowing and smiling, he offered everything he had as his "poor best." I disliked this man on sight. I knew him immediately as the type of falsely humble innkeep who would rather burn scraps than allow hungry vagrants, such as myself, a chance at them.

As Arbren busied himself bullying the stable hands who were even busier taking care of the animals, I hopped down and drifted near Hlanan's side, keeping him between myself and Rajanas. Just in case.

". . . and we boast well-appointed bedrooms. Adequate, I trust, for your honors. I will send someone up to light the fires in all the rooms, if that is your wish, and we will serve supper within the hour..." The innkeep's round, shining face, tucked with the dimples and lines of a very broad smile, never turned away from Rajanas as he led the way upstairs to a private dining room.

"Don't bother with fires in the bedrooms. It's not winter. But we'll take the food as soon as is possible." Rajanas waved carelessly at him and walked off to talk to Hlanan.

The innkeeper took this airy dismissal with an even bigger smile, and bowed to Rajanas's back, then to Thianra, who said, "I should be glad to play for the company, if you wish. No charge."

The innkeeper smirked and bowed, and utterly ignoring me, turned to leave. In fact, he ignored me so completely I was able to see the smile drop from his face like an extra skin from a snake.

I retreated to a corner near a cheerful new fire to wait and watch. If that innkeeper served the food then I was going to wait till someone else tasted it before I ate any. And I hoped that if it was poisoned, it would be Rajanas who found out. Either him or Arbren.

A servant appeared with a tray of cold punch and three glasses. Rajanas poured out the punch, handing a glass to Thianra.

"Thanks," she said. "A sip or two, then I will fetch my tiranthe and tune it. I offered to play."

"That gives us an excuse to sit in the common room," Rajanas said. "Maybe we can overhear something of interest. Can you sense them with that thing?" he said over his shoulder to Hlanan.

"It doesn't work that way." Hlanan was studying a dark-stoned ring on his finger, a pucker of disquiet creasing his brow. This was the first time I'd seen him with any sort of ornament beside the cheap-looking ring he wore on his smallest finger. After a long pause he looked up, smiling a little as he accepted the glass of punch Rajanas held out. "No sign of them," he said.

"I mislike this train of events." Frowning, Rajanas sat at the end of the table, and Hlanan and Thianra took chairs on either side. I crouched on the hearth, making no noise, and wondering when I might snitch some of that punch. I was thirsty, and I could see that the punch was nicely chilled. Moisture-drops formed on the sides of the heavy jug.

"First those accursed pirates singling us out for an attack," Rajanas said, "just after we happened to get separated from the rest of the convoy. Second, their having managed to sneak up on us so neatly through that fog without the slightest warning."

"I apologize for having fallen asleep," Hlanan said. "I could have determined if the fog had been raised by magic."

"Coastal fog banks are normal this time of year." Rajanas shrugged. "You remember. And now this quiet disappearance of my supposed entourage, both on the road and by magic trace. Maybe I'd better ride back tonight and see if I can find them."

"If six of your Guard fell afoul of someone I don't think you'll be able to do much besides provide a bigger prize," Thianra said. "Hlanan or I should probably go." And with a sigh, "I suppose I may as well, though when I think I could be halfway to sitting around a campfire listening to Kitharee tritones..." She sighed, glancing toward the door. "Which room is which? I want to find where the servants put my tiranthe."

Hlanan said, "I wish Tir had a bigger vocabulary." He glanced toward the window, and murmured in a softer voice, "I wonder where Tir is."

Rajanas didn't seem to hear that last. "I am the one Geric surprised in the act of inspecting the ship-works at Jira-Jirai. It is possible he believed my tale of having another racing yacht built, but only if he thinks I'm stupid enough to mistake warships for pleasure vessels."

"Unless he knows that Dhes-Andis is having those ships built," Thianra put in softly. "Which means he was there precisely to see who might want to take a look at them."

"But he could not possibly have arranged an ambush so rapidly, either this one or the pirate attack," Hlanan protested. "He was on the yacht with us. We saw him off scarce moments before we left ourselves, and Keprima is no more his territory than it is yours."

Thianra shook her head. "The more I consider, the surer I am that it was not whim that brought him aboard your yacht, any more than he was there to court Kressanthe."

Geric. Wasn't that the tall, handsome fellow on board the yacht, the one with sapphires bound into his pale apricot hair?

Then I thought about all these mentions of Dhes-Andis. Everyone in the world knew of the wicked sorcerer-king of Sveran Djur. Was he mad at these three for some reason? I got that neck-gripping chill of danger. If my theft job had anything to do with that sorcerer, even twelve gold pieces wouldn't keep me from running.

Thianra added dryly, "I did put a great deal of effort into deflecting him."

"Unless he suspects that you are more than just a minstrel," Rajanas said, saluting her with his glass.

"Then he would be quite wrong," she retorted, but she was smiling in a way that made it clear the suspicion was nothing new.

Hlanan prowled along the wall to the window and back to the door as he said, "Then there's Kressanthe, who may be as stupid as she appears, but who is certainly rich enough and vindictive enough to aid anyone who wants to make mischief. Which puts us back to our question: which of them is the enemy this time, and which of us the target?"

Thianra said, "Geric Lendan cannot possibly have traveled any faster than we have."

"What worries me is why Geric never commented on the magic Lhind did, and I remember how interested he was in magic…"

I got that stomach-dropping feeling, like missing a step one hadn't known. Only in this case, I'd missed a danger I hadn't suspected.

". . . and how angry when the Council of Magicians turned him away and refused to teach him." Hlanan rubbed his eyes, looking unhappy. "Well, I just hope Dhes-Andis isn't involved, that's all."

Rajanas shook his head. "If he'd marched on Alezand we would have heard about it in the harbor." He smiled. "Despite its modest size he'd have no easy victory. Kuraf would have seen to that, if everyone else had failed." He leaned forward and struck Hlanan on the shoulder. "Cheer up! You're too tired, and you're seeing shadows brandish knives. You and I have been in much tighter spots than this one."

Hlanan shook his head. "Maybe it is just tiredness, but I feel warning all about me."

That makes two of us, I thought, edging close to the table. The punch jug sat untouched near Rajanas's arm. Perhaps they were too tired and hungry to drink much, but I was thirsty.

Hlanan went on slowly, "And while it's true we've been in tighter spots, somehow it was easier then—"

Rajanas gave a crack of laughter. "If you think sweating our bones out for that shark-teethed Shinjan taskmaster was easier, you must be tired."

"But then I was responsible only for myself." Hlanan stared down into the fire.

Rajanas and Thianra exchanged a look. Rajanas's expression wasn't scornful or even disinterested and amused. I was surprised to see concern shaping his steady gaze, in his softened mouth.

Then Thianra brought her palm down flat on the table. "All right," she said. "I'll stay with you until Imbradi, then either you go to Court, Hlanan, or I. Someone has to report all these disparate signs. If Dhes-Andis is involved with any of our recent bad luck then all three of us are marked anyway."

"I'll keep trying to signal your Guard," Hlanan said as he slid the ring off his finger and dropped it into a pocket. "I'll try again anon. As soon as Tir comes back. Perhaps I'll be less tired after a good meal."

"Where is the aidlar?" Rajanas said, looking up—just as my fingers snaked out and made the pinch.

I backed away hastily, raising the jug to my lips for a hasty swig. His expression went from intensity to surprise, and I think he was going to laugh, but he never got the chance.

The door slammed open. In dashed warriors with drawn swords. Their leader paused for the barest instant, then headed straight for Rajanas.

As if released by a spring, my arm snapped out. The jug sailed through the air and smashed squarely on the leader's helm.

"Good throw, thief!" Rajanas called, and laughed. He sent his chair skidding in the way of the attackers and whipped sword and long knife free of their scabbards.

The leader staggered back, ignoring the ceramic shards and punch all over his mail-shirt. His lips pulled back into a snarl. "Kill that one," he ordered, pointing his sword at me. "The other three we take alive."

Warriors converged on us, blades menacing. Rajanas and Thianra (who had pulled out two long knives) spread out so as not to interfere with one another's defense. Thianra placed herself before Hlanan, who was not armed.

Hlanan cupped his hands, muttering fast. Fire formed into a glow above his fingers. A harsh voice croaked something, and a curtain directly behind Hlanan ripped as a hereto hidden door slammed open. The warriors had spread in a circle, and one dashed in and smashed his fist across the back of Hlanan's head half a heartbeat before Thianra's knife came down on his arm. The Scribe, who'd been involved in some kind of incantation, staggered. The soldier warded Thianra with his shield and clouted Hlanan again with the hilt of his blade.

Hlanan slumped as Thianra, fighting desperately against three foes, blocked him from my sight.

A soldier headed my way purposefully. I shoved my shaking hands into my waistband for my knife, but a kind of swift, sick certainty stayed my hand: in the past I'd used my blade only for escape, or for dramatic effect. I'd never been able to kill any living creature. I knew these fellows would not be stayed by the brandishing of a blade—so I decided desperately that it was better off hidden.

But I had to act fast. I leaped to the table, and when the soldier jerked back, startled at the height of my jump, I kicked his elbow with a whack that cracked on the air. Pain shot up my leg but he dropped his sword, and I spun around, grabbed up the punch tray and swung it, just in time to deflect a blow aimed at the back of Thianra's head.

Smash! Everyone looked up when Rajanas crashed a chair into two warriors. Wood splinters flew in all directions. Five warriors tried to hem him in, but his whirling blades kept them at a distance.

A blade whizzed at my knees. I leaped, somersaulted down the table and came up with a punch glass in either hand. I potted the warriors nearest, clapping as the glasses shattered on their helms.

"Ho! Hey!" I yelled.

Ze-e-e-em! A blade cut the air beside my head. I flipped backward, landing on my hands, and used the momentum to kick both feet into the swordsman's chest, sending him crashing back into another soldier. Then I flipped again, landing on the floor as they fell in a tangle of arms, legs, weapons and chairs. Two more converged, I leaped again, kicked a helmed head and spun past a waving blade.

"Oh, good one!" Thianra gasped, backing desperately from the pressing attack.

Behind her, Hlanan lay on the floor, his hands limp. Anger flushed through me. Ranging myself beside Thianra, I sent the third glass at a soldier's face, wishing the innkeeper had brought up more food.

Why waste it on the betrayed?

That was old instinct, you could say my head. Fast as lightning flashed an answer from my heart: *Because I like them.* I didn't have time to scold myself for a sentiment that no one felt for me, because—

"Kill the beggar!" the leader roared. "NOW!"

Rajanas's blades, whirling vertiginously, disarmed two warriors in a row, and he leaped toward us. "Out," he shouted at me, his chin jerking toward the window.

I stayed at my place beside Thianra, trying not to get in her way as she fought against yet more converging attackers. They were closing in steadily, though as yet her speed and skill kept them at a distance. A big, burly fellow rushed me. I met his knee with my heel and ducked under his arm, jabbed my fists into a broad belly on another, and leaped clear over the table, just barely avoiding a deadly arcing blade.

Pausing beside the window, I looked back in time to see Thianra step back to avoid a hard swing, and stumble over the remains of a chair. Two warriors landed on her.

The rest advanced toward Rajanas, too many for me to do anything against—

I'm the one with a death sentence. I smacked the window wide and whirled through, scrambling onto the low roof. A running few steps, then I was high into one of the big, shady trees.

A shimmer! I thought then. Of course! But what? An army of hideous ghosts? Or . . .

Through the open window below I heard a mighty cheer from the soldiery. I knew what had happened: they'd finally brought Rajanas down. I was too late.

So there I was, safe in a tree, and the people who'd taken me prisoner were now prisoners of someone else.

SEVEN

So now I had a choice. Either I cut my losses and lope for safety, or I try to find out what was going to happen to them—

The glow of torches and the sound of harsh voices from the courtyard caught my attention.

"Can we take the rings off this one, at least? He cut up Raban and Kemm pretty good."

"This ruby will fetch a good price."

"I don't care, just be quick about it," came a voice of command.

"I think this one's only a servant. One ring in his pocket, and something tight on one finger. No stone in it."

"That one's the scribe-mage. Don't touch anything on him. Your nose will fall off. Or something worse."

"Aw, that old ring doesn't look like it's worth a tinklet anyway."

I edged along my branch and peered cautiously below as the warriors marched out in pairs, carrying Rajanas, Thianra, and Hlanan. Talk, the clank of weapons, the clatter of boots and hooves echoed up the stone walls of the court as they stuffed the three into a waiting coach. Warriors crowded

Rajanas as they stripped him of the jewels that I had mentally claimed as my own. Hmph! Then out came their own wounded, who got thrown over the backs of horses if they weren't on their feet.

After that the warriors mounted quickly and ranged themselves in formation on either side of the coach. The leader wheeled his horse and flung down a bag of coins at the feet of the cringing innkeeper. Then he rode out at a gallop, the rest following behind in a cloud of choking dust that rose as high as my tree.

A betrayal. They'd been expected, and the innkeeper had been bribed.

It's not your problem, weasel-wit, I told myself.

I knew that. But I still sat there, remembering Hlanan's words about dignity. Thianra's kindly interest and flashes of unexpected humor. I tried to harden my heart, to think instead of Rajanas's cold sarcasm and ungentle hands, but even he had given me a knife during the pirate attack, when he'd had no hope of escape.

Meantime, there was that bag of coins . . .

I swung down hand over hand through the tree, and dropped onto the ground near the kitchen windows. Like many kitchens this time of year, they were partly open to let out the heat of the ovens.

Next to one of the windows an ancient vine grew. I pressed my face into it so the leaves would hide me as I peered between the casement and the wall.

I could see one side of the kitchen, a huge fireplace, and two or three big tables covered with rows of crockery. A tall woman with a face like winter was giving orders to a young boy with a loaded tray. The boy hefted the tray and disappeared. The woman started laying pastries onto the crockery.

I was about to turn away when I heard the innkeeper's voice: "Why are ye standing around, ye lazy scum? Get to work!"

Two pairs of unseen feet scuffled away, then the door slammed.

The woman looked up from her pastries at the innkeeper, who was now in my view. He smiled at her in a fatuous and cringing way and dramatically dropped the clinking bag on the table. "So much for your fears, Runklia. I told you it would be an easy fortune." He hooked his thumbs in his belt and rocked back on his heels, puffing out his cheeks.

She stared at him stonily, totally ignoring his swagger, and shoved the bag to the very edge of the table with her tray. "Fool." Her voice was low. "If any of them had escaped you'd soon be dead. What about the servants?"

The innkeeper's mouth dropped open. Clearly he hadn't thought about them. Then he shrugged, his eyes flickering around like bugs in a high wind. "Who cares? They can do nothing."

"They can talk."

The innkeeper squinted at her uneasily. "Talk? What do you mean?"

"I mean, you stupid slug, if you are going to serve such as she whom you bargained with today, you must make sure you think of everything. Those servants will get back to that young lord's home and they will talk. If he lives near, then we'll have trouble the sooner, because *she* won't defend us, you can count on that."

The innkeeper pursed his lips.

The woman went on, soft and venomous, "You will have to kill them. And quickly."

Just then my ears caught the faint sound of jingling and horse hooves disappearing down the road. *That's Arbren and the others, or I'm the Emperor of Shinja.*

"But I never...we shouldn't have to...ourselves," he protested.

"If you are the blowhard coward I take you for then you will have to use some of that—" She nodded at the bag of coins. "—and hire someone to do it for you. But first you will have to lock them up. In the cellar, where they cannot be heard."

He stood there twitching uncertainly, his sweaty face none the prettier as he wrestled with his choices, then abruptly went out.

The woman picked up her pastries again as if nothing had happened.

One thing I knew for certain: these two stinkers were not going to enjoy the contents of that bag.

The woman filled a tray, then turned away to set it on another table. In that moment I hoisted myself noiselessly over the low sill, and crouched against a cabinet, keeping the edge of the table between me and Runklia's face. I watched her feet come back to the big table. I heard the soft thud of pastry dough falling into crockery, then she turned to heft another tray away.

I shot my hand up, grasped the bag tightly so it would not clink, and my heart pounded as I crouched there under the table while more pastry thudded into crocks. At last she turned to heft another tray and I flipped myself through the window into a crouch on the ground just as the big door opened again.

The innkeeper said, "Well it's too late. They put their carriage to and lit out while we were talking. So if I get asked, I'll just say—ho! Runklia, where'd you put my money?"

"Didn't you take it with you?"

I didn't wait to hear her answer. Within the space of five breaths I was through the trees and out into the open fields, running my fastest.

I couldn't remember the last time I'd been both well-rested and well fed; I ran without stopping until the moon was high. Reaching a secluded little grove beside a stream, I dropped into long, sweet grass and lay panting, staring up at the jewel-bright stars until I caught my breath.

When my heart settled back into its accustomed tread, I reviewed the fight. Rajanas had held some of those attackers from blocking my way to the window. *Even a little rat of a thief deserves a chance to fight for its life,* he'd said when the pirates attacked. He was a warrior, rough with his hands, caustic of tongue, but in his own way he was as fair as the scribe and the bard.

Except for taking me against my will at the outset, all three had been fair to me by their own code.

So...what about my code?

No, my mind wailed back. *I'm free, and for the first time ever, I've got enough take to live in comfort for two seasons.* Oh, the places I could go...the freedom that was now mine...but then treachery returned, in the shape of memory: Hlanan's considered words, as if our conversations had mattered. As if *I'd* mattered.

Thianra's laugh, her lovely voice drifting through the soft evening air.

Even a little rat of a thief deserves a chance to fight for its life.

Well, one thing I'd learned during my years of wandering: don't stay mad at yourself for long, otherwise you're at odds with the only ally you've got.

I finally admitted that I wasn't going to run off and leave them to their fates, though every practical instinct clamored for me to do just that. I knew I was going to find them, and free them, if I possibly could.

If I could.

Of course I could outsmart a parcel of boulder-witted warriors!

All right, so I'd think of it as a challenge.

I rolled over and splashed water over my hot face, wondering how I'd go about finding them —

As soon as I thought it, *Hrethan,* came the inner voice of that bird, straight into my head. *I am with them, and I will help you.*

I fought against surprise—or more correctly the fury that attends surprise—and managed not to lock Tir's thoughts out. My instinctive reaction of distrust dissolved when I remembered what the aidlar had vowed about never harming "my kind": one thing I'd found about creatures other than human was that they never lied.

So, *Where?* I sent the thought back.

No words came in answer. Instead, a mental picture of moonlit fields, as seen from the sky. The black coach and its guard, still riding in two militarily straight lines, was moving westward at a trot.

Westward: back toward the harbor.

We need to act now, or they'll reach Letarj before morning, I sent the thought to Tir.

I felt its agreement—and the confidence with which it awaited my plan. For Tir was a bird, and planning was up to humans. It had patiently flown with the carriage, and then when that was attacked, it flew to warn Hlanan. Too late. That much I gathered from the swift flow of images.

So then it followed the cavalcade that had captured Hlanan and the other two, loyally waiting for me to remember the three and concoct a rescue, just as would others of its kind.

That thought made me feel queasy.

You stay with them, and I'll find a way to catch up, I sent.

Again I felt Tir's unquestioning acceptance, and I got to my feet, wondering how I was to accomplish this. Their captors were riding steadily back down the river toward the harbor again. Running all night—which I couldn't do—wouldn't catch me up with them before they reached the harbor.

I walked slowly to the top of a little rise, breathing in the soft breeze that had sprung up. Wisps of fog drifted some distant hills; above, soft clouds rolled silently over the stars, blocking them from view. I sniffed the air, sorting the scents. Water...almond blossoms both sweet and bitter...citrus...cedar...and the pungency of horse. Horses?

As I crested a hill, I saw a farm nestled alongside a stream Clumped under some trees stood horse-shaped shadows, heads drooping. When I took a few steps, a few heads came up, ears alert.

Rejoicing, I ran down toward the fenced pasture.

Stealing horses has always been easy. I send them friendly thoughts, and the first one that responds, I climb on, hold the mane, and ride. When I'm done, I always send them in the right direction for home. Soon I was on the back of a frisky, freshly-shod young mare who was ready for a good gallop. She cleared the fence in a leap that left several hand-spans to spare.

The horse knew a path that paralleled the river road. She galloped happily, slowing when we encountered slowly drifting fingers of fog rising off the river. We cantered over the countryside, Tir sending mental pictures of the prisoners' location from time to time. The aidlar's position remained in my mind like a fixed star, and I guided the horse steadily toward it.

As I neared them, I wondered how I was to effect a rescue. I had myself and a bird, and against me were twice-twelve warriors, all armed. Rajanas, Hlanan and Thianra could not be counted on for anything; I did not even know if they were awake. Hlanan certainly had not been when they dumped him into that coach.

The obvious course was to use my shimmers somehow. But how?

My next thought was, I needed more allies. *Tir? Can you find Arbren and those other servants?*

I cannot hear their thoughts as I can yours. I see no other humans near.

So the servants were out. I figured they'd probably ride for home. As I recalled, none of them had been armed. But Rajanas's six guards had been armed. Where were they?

I remembered Hlanan's worry about losing trace of them, and I decided I'd better discount them.

All right, then. No human aid. Perhaps as well. No questions, that way. How about non-human?

I was near enough now to listen without ears or eyes. Digging my hands into the horse's mane, I sat as steadily as I could and spread my thoughts out ahead, sensing...and I saw little lights of many colors, most but not all dim, as though asleep. Then I found Tir and the others, and near them, the red mental presence of a warren of snakes.

Snakes?

I opened my eyes, fighting the moments of nauseating vertigo that always clawed at my insides after that kind of exercise. As I scanned the black line of forest that the swirling mist nearly obscured, a plan formed. I nudged the mare into a gallop and dashed through the fields adjacent, until I had passed by the gradually slowing cavalcade. *Tir! Can you fly ahead and show me the road?*

The bird riding high overhead did just that.

Very close was a bend perfect for my needs. It meant I had to act fast.

SHERWOOD SMITH

I called to the snakes, much the same way I did the horses. They came at once, making me uneasy. Always when I used a creature this way, I felt honor-bound to assure its safety. That was part of my own code. It was always much easier to risk only myself.

When the snakes were in position just ahead of the bend, waiting in mild curiosity, I slowed my horse and slid off into the tall grass. Ramming my hands over my eyes, I stretched my hands out toward the road.

Tir! Road!

I saw the road below me, and the cavalcade moving steadily. Directly ahead of them, where the bend curved, I shimmered a straight section of road, blurring the real road.

The first pair of warriors rode without hesitation onto my shimmer-road. Their pace checked slightly when they encountered rough field, but they saw road, and mist swirled about them, so they kept going.

My heart fired with triumph as I ended the false road. I sent a wordless command to the snakes. A heartbeat after the coach trundled past them, moving slowly down the real road, the snakes rose up on either side, hissing and waving their heads. The horses who'd been following the coach reared, whinnying in fright. I heard the surprised shouts of the not-distant warriors.

Shutting the distracting sound out, I obscured the snakes so they could retreat into the grass and not be trampled, then I hid the coach with shimmer-trees and made a false road again, this time bending inland, away from the river alongside a feeder stream in a valley. The warriors raced along it, trying to catch up with the rest of their group—and the coach was now alone.

Not for long. I got up, fighting dizziness, and ran flat for the bulky shape ahead.

"Hey! Where are you going?" the man on it shouted after the last of his escort, but the thunder of hooves drowned his voice. He leaped down, opened the door—

I don't know what he would have done with the prisoners, and maybe just as well. I launched myself into the air and landed on his back. We both fell onto the floor of the coach, off-balance. The heavy man managed to muscle me down onto the floorboards. He pulled back a fist about the size of a melon—and then Rajanas's boot heel whopped the man's head with a solid thwack.

The soldier fell slumped unconscious to the floor of the carriage, and I rolled free. "Come on!" I said. "They'll figure out the dodge soon."

"Thank you, Lhind." Thianra murmured, her voice warm with gratitude.

"Here." I reached for the nearest pair of hands, sawed at the rough rope with my knife, then I pressed the knife into one of the palms I'd freed. "Here. I'll loosen the coach horses while you cut their ropes."

I jumped out again, pulling the driver's sword from its sheath.

Cutting the harnesses free was easier than trying to deal with ties and buckles. As I finished, the other three emerged from the coach, ghostly forms in the gloomy fog. I called my mare to me, and she came trotting out of the mist.

Rajanas started to speak, but Hlanan murmured something softly, and he fell silent, handing me back my knife.

Hlanan and Thianra mounted on one coach horse, and Rajanas took the other. We turned back upriver, and began to ride.

EIGHT

I called more horses when we passed another farm, for ours were tired. Six responded. A good number, I thought. They'd look like a herd let run loose, for I did not want Hlanan and the others to know I'd called them.

The three seemed to accept the sudden appearance of unsaddled or bridled horses as lucky chance, for Rajanas shouted to the others to block them quickly. Thianra gave a pleased cry, and Hlanan said nothing. He kept rubbing his head.

We let the tired coach horses go. Once they were out of sight I sent my mare toward home.

As Thianra and Rajanas cut out three horses, Hlanan walked up to me. He was still rubbing his head. "The outriders. How did you do it? Your...your shimmer spell?"

"Yes. Told you it comes in handy."

"How far did you extend the illusion?"

"Can't do it far at all."

"Thank you," he murmured.

Rajanas loomed up, a silhouette against Big Moon, low in the sky. "Can you ride?"

"Of course," Hlanan said. But he didn't sound so sure.

Rajanas didn't say anything, but he rode behind Hlanan, leaving Thianra to ride point. I rode alongside her, figuring she was least likely to ask questions I didn't want to answer.

Nobody spoke much as we rode through the night. The sun came up as we made our way down a ridge above the river, which had widened considerably, moving placidly over a shallow, rocky bed.

Rajanas kept his hand on the hilt of the sword I'd taken off that coach driver, his eyes moving constantly back and forth, back and forth, as our mounts waded slowly across the rushing water. Thianra sat, grim and unsmiling, and Hlanan held tightly to his horse's mane, his eyes squinted against what must have been a fearsome headache. The bleak morning sun revealed an ugly bump on the side of his head.

But nothing happened. If pursuit there was, it did not find us. When we climbed dripping and tired up the ridge on the other side, it was within sight of a small town. We rode in not long after, and there we found Arbren and the other servants, and most of the baggage; Thianra pounced on her tiranthe with a glad cry. The servants had been in the midst of trying to raise some kind of search party that would be willing to recross the border.

By then I was so tired I thought my head would fall off my body and roll away somewhere. We stopped at an inn, and I sank onto a bench and watched Rajanas deal with his frightened, excited servants. If he was tired he hid it, and his voice was amazingly patient. Hlanan went outside to watch for Tir, who had been flying overhead, but then vanished.

Thianra sat down next to me, her instrument safely tucked over her back. I remembered that innkeeper's wife saying *She whom you bargained with.* "Do you know who sent those hired swords?" I asked.

She gave her head a single shake. "Gear unmarked with anyone's device, and they spoke Chelan to us, and among themselves. Someone local's private force, on hire for just one capture. Possibly in disguise. That would explain the lack of pursuit."

"They'll just go home and report it as a bad business?"

She lifted a shoulder in a faint shrug. "They might not have known anything more about us than we did about them, except that one of us was a scribe who could do magic. There are several people who could have told them that much."

"Is that unusual? I mean, scribes who are mages, or the other way around?"

"No," she said quickly. Her voice dropped a tone. "In certain areas, scribes are even expected to learn some limited spells. Hlanan got interested in magic, and left scribe training, so he knows more than most. But he still works as a scribe." She fought a yawn, and rubbed her eyes. "What I wonder is, what happened to Rajanas's own Guard?"

She did not answer her own question, and as I had no answer, we fell into silence until Hlanan appeared before us. "We've food waiting, and fresh horses."

Thianra got up stiffly; I shook my head, unwilling to move.

Hlanan smiled, then winced as if his head hurt. "Come, Lhind. You cannot part from us now."

"You don't understand," I said hoarsely. "You mages might not feel anything. But when I make a shimmer it tires me."

A flicker of surprise lifted his eyelids, but he said only: "I've something to add to our tea that will help. And we're riding just for a time. This town is still too close to the border."

"Our puny thief lost his puny strength?" That was Rajanas, of course.

I managed to produce a medium-loud snort. "Just tired of the company."

Rajanas's lips twitched.

"Bravely said, Lhind." Thianra chuckled huskily at my shoulder. "Come." Her warm, gentle hand on my shoulder somehow made it possible to stir once again, and I followed her into a private dining room.

Hlanan had ordered a splendid hot meal, and true to his word, he'd quietly added some kind of spice to the steaming tea. Warmth and wakefulness coursed through me at every sip.

No one spoke much during this meal. Afterward we trudged out front to find four new horses awaiting us.

We didn't ride long. Hlanan led us down the road into a very small village built up against a cliff. He took us to a cottage, and we were met by a smiling old woman.

By this time the effects of his herbs had worn off, and I could hardly think for the sleep-longing. So I followed the others inside the little house, and when pointed toward a loft I somehow made it up the ladder, onto a straw-stuffed pallet, and dropped gratefully. I was too tired even to arrange my take inside my clothes. I curled into a ball and slept.

And woke, eventually, to the sound of voices drifting up from below: Rajanas's, Thianra's and a high, pleasant voice I did not recognize. Looking about me, I saw an empty pallet and one with a long figure on it. I sat up and glimpsed part of Hlanan's face within the protective curve of one arm. As I sat back down some of my coins clinked. It was not a loud sound, but it was enough to cause Hlanan's eyes to open.

"Sorry," I said.

His sight was clear. He was one of those, like me, who come awake completely. It made me wonder a little about his background.

"I suppose you don't know transportation magic?" he asked.

I shook my head firmly. "Remember? I stole one spell."

"Ah. I'd forgotten." He rubbed his eyes, then felt his head with care, wincing and grimacing. Then he sat up.

Below, Rajanas said, "They're finally awake, I believe."

"We are," Hlanan called with unimpaired good humor.

I followed him down. Rajanas lounged by the door, his fingers moving with absent restlessness on the hilt of his sword. His eyes were shadowed beneath. He probably hadn't slept.

As soon as he saw us, he spoke. "My harbor Guard caught up with us—or five of them, anyway. You were right. They'd been ambushed as well. They were searched and stripped of weapons and your tracer-ring."

"Well, my other seems to have either fallen out of my pocket or been looted while I was incapacitated," Hlanan said with regret. "They escaped?"

"Yes. Left Nian behind. Took a wound in the fight. Three of them will go back for him. The rest are on their way back to Letarj to guard the yacht. Meanwhile, we have not been followed, and the Mistress says she senses no magical tracers on us. Shall we go?"

Hlanan rubbed his eyes again, his body tense. "Mistress?" he turned to the old woman.

"I will help you. Do you have a Destination—"

"Don't use it," Rajanas said abruptly. "If there's trouble in my city, the Destination chamber in the palace will be ringed with waiting guards."

"Right." Hlanan gave a short nod, and ran his hands down his tunic. "Outside the gates. That's open area. I feel better about that, being as tired as I am." He glanced at the window. "I hope Tir knows where we are going."

I was about to ask where we were going, and how, when the old woman they'd addressed as Mistress said calmly, "Take hands. Stand in a circle."

Thianra's slim fingers wrapped warmly about my hand, and on my other side Hlanan gripped my fingers almost tight enough to crepitate. Then he and the Mistress muttered strange words that made my ears sing in a not-unpleasant way—

—And colored fog swirled about us, then cleared.

We stood in an open field with blossoms nodding peacefully around us.

"Ho," Hlanan murmured, letting me go and sinking down onto the grass. "Did it."

Thianra shivered, and sat down also. Rajanas's face was pale as old cheese, but he only turned, swayed once, then wrenched himself erect. "I'll spy out the situation," he said shortly, and walked off through some trees.

"What's wrong? Are you sick?" I asked. "Should I find some water?"

Thianra looked up wearily. "It's that trans—"

"Never mind," Hlanan said. He lifted his head and opened his eyes to gaze at me. His expression was very hard to define: sort of bemused, and a little sad. "We'll be all right. I just hope Rajanas's correct about no one attacking his city."

SHERWOOD SMITH

"Is that where we are?" I asked. Intense curiosity stirred up questions like bees swarming when a stick hits their hive. "So that was real send-magic? Hoo! That's a handy thing..." I stopped.

Thianra grinned at me. "Don't even ask him. Besides, those who use magic to get away from thievery tend to get traced, and you wouldn't want any of the Magic Council on your trail."

I shook my head hard. "No-o-o-o-o-o. Not me!" I said quickly, though I wondered if it was possible to actually steal such a spell. Only how would I manage, even if it was? Everything I did was by instinct. "One spell's enough, and besides, half the fun of a good take is the getaway. It was only a thought."

Hlanan looked away, his mouth strictly controlled. Thianra laughed silently. I saw again their resemblance, and said, "How are you related?"

Have you ever walked into a room and felt the floor drop away? Well, I must admit I haven't had that actually happen to me, but that's what it felt like. I'd asked what I thought was a harmless question, then watched in amazement as all the laughter bleached from their faces.

Thianra's gaze narrowed speculatively. "How did you know that?"

I shrugged. "I...see it."

"You are very observant," she said, and in a lower voice, "and so am I."

"What do you mean?" I asked uneasily, poised to run, tired as I was.

"Nothing ill." She leaned toward me, speaking so softly that only I could hear. "It is just that I wonder why you wish to be taken as a child, when there is that in your face that indicates experience." She caught Hlanan's gaze, straightened up, and smiled. "Ah, but your secrets are yours to keep. As for ours...we share one parent. We don't talk about that, though."

"Why not?" I asked, unsettled by her question. I gabbled fast to get her thoughts, at least, away from what she'd said. I wasn't sure he'd heard her. "Got caught and thrown in jail?

• 84 •

Afraid nobody will hire you to sing if you've got a thief for a parent?"

Hlanan touched my arm. "It's something like that, but we're not ashamed of our background. We are who we make ourselves to be, whatever our parentage. Still, we don't talk about it, which I suspect you can understand. Can we ask you to keep that between us?"

"I'm mum," I said, spreading my hands. "Does the Rat-spawn Rotter know?"

Thianra turned away, laughing soundlessly. Hlanan said, "Yes. Rajanas knows. But he's really the only one. He and I have been friends since we were small."

"Gate's opening for us," Rajanas's dry voice broke into the conversation.

We got to our feet and followed Rajanas through the trees. When we emerged from the copse, we faced a good-sized walled city. As we approached it, the mighty gates began to swing open. Rajanas and Hlanan did not seem to notice; having gone a little ahead, they were involved in a low-voiced conversation.

Only that Rajanas would have the crust to walk, alone and on foot, to a guarded wall to see who was in possession, I thought.

"You're smiling," Thianra observed from my side. "At what prospect?"

I pointed my finger at Rajanas. "He's crazy. I would have waited and snuck in at night."

"It's his city, and his principality—Alezand," she said. As if that should have explained it.

Well it didn't, not for me anyway, but I forbore questioning when I saw some riders come galloping through the gates toward us. They led a string of four riderless horses. Presently we were circled by a group of guards wearing sky-blue tunics with a black device. We mounted fine-bred chargers, me with some difficulty, for I'd never managed with a saddle and reins before. Seeing my hesitation, a woman with looped yellow braids dismounted and tossed me up into the saddle with one strong movement.

SHERWOOD SMITH

The leader saluted Rajanas, received a lazy wave in return, then the guards formed in two lines behind us. I exchanged a grin with the guard who'd helped me, then our cavalcade set off through the streets.

Busy people crowded the streets of Imbradi. Absent were the usual signs of poverty I'd come to expect in a city. No beggars, no shabby open markets. The shops were built close together, the buildings steep-roofed with stone and even brick fronts. Ironwork decorated stair-rails, signs, and door latches, and many of the buildings had ivy growing up the walls. Age-smoothed stones paved the streets, the canals whose bridges we rode over looked and smelled clean, and I saw no piles of refuse anywhere.

The people wore brightly colored clothing, of cloth and design more flowing than what I'd been seeing in Thesreve. I saw none of the short tunics so popular with rich men in Tu Jhan. Those who didn't wear long robes wore long tunics slit up the sides where one could see loose pants stuffed into the tops of boots—like Rajanas's clothes. There was more embroidery on everyone's clothes than I'd seen anywhere, and not the geometric patterns I was used to seeing, but flowers, vines, leaves. I also saw every kind of headgear, from feathered caps to veils and turbans.

This is a dream city, I thought. I wonder if they have thieves.

Of course they have thieves. If you have people and goods you have thieves. But I took in all those knives and swords worn at people's sides, and wondered how easy a thief's life would be here, in spite of how comfortable things looked.

As we rode slowly through the streets, people parted, some looking on us curiously. Salutes were made to Rajanas, hands lifted, palm out. Some bowed; Rajanas nodded to right and left.

Up ahead the streets broadened into a wide green park. Through a gate and we were surrounded by well-tended trees and shrubs, and when those gave way, we rode into the courtyard of a huge marble palace.

At once stable hands in sky-blue and black livery came running out. For a moment confusion reigned as everyone dismounted and the horses were led away. A tall, impressive servant emerged from an impressive door and Rajanas walked back inside with him.

Hlanan appeared at my shoulder, his mouth smiling but his eyes quirked with tension and question. "Want something to eat?"

"Does a horse have feathers?" I joked. My mood was good. It seemed, amazingly enough, that I was going to be invited inside this toff palace. "Always. I am always ready to eat."

"We'll go straight along to the kitchen, then. I'll leave you there, and send a messenger to retrieve you when you're done. Thianra, I'll take you up to the Residence wing after we've left Lhind with the food."

Thianra returned no answer. She studied Hlanan, cast a glance my way. Her lips parted, then she gave her head a little shake, and walked away.

That was odd. "This way," Hlanan said, before I could frame a question. I wasn't even certain what to ask.

Hlanan led the way down a corridor with whitewashed walls and clay-tile floors. Wonderful smells soon wafted their way toward us, getting stronger at every step, and I couldn't think of anything but the yawning emptiness inside me, which seemed to reach right down inside my toes. Cinnamon—bread—baking fruit. My stomach rumbled.

We rounded a corner and passed through a large archway, then entered a huge room with five large ovens and a whole wall of open fireplace. There must have been six or seven long preparation tables with people at every one cutting, forming, filling, kneading. At the far end stone steps led down into a cool-room, and people bearing trays were going up and coming down.

As we entered a tall, thin man wearing a clean white apron came toward us. "Good day to you, Scribe," he said.

"Good day, Master Cook," Hlanan returned. "This is Lhind, and his highness has asked that you give him whatever he wants to eat. I'll send one of the pages along to fetch him. Lhind," this to me, "stay here and enjoy your meal. I'll see you again soon."

Once again I saw question in the faint quirk of his brows, his quick glance that lowered to his hands when I turned his way, but I knew by now that whatever was going on inside his head wouldn't harm me. I smacked my hands together, rubbed them, and grinned. "Don't hurry that messenger," I said.

He turned away, not before I caught his expression. A wince? Then I remembered that knot on his head. Maybe he was going to lie down. I wished him well of his rest, as I took in the delights the kitchen offered.

The Master Cook picked up a plate. "Here you go." His gaunt face was no less friendly now that Hlanan was gone. "Help yourself, just don't break up the whole pies."

I offered fervent thanks and made a fast circuit of the room, grabbing one or two of every tart, pie, and dish that looked good. I got a slice of vegetable pie, several tiny apple pastries, and a jug of cream to pour over anything I wanted. When the plate was piled too high to add anything more, I sat down on a low bench along one wall, and settled in for a long and blissful meal. An assistant brewer brought me water, and two kinds of freshly squeezed fruit juice.

I was just polishing off the vegetable pie when a cheerful brown-faced boy in a clean sky-blue-and-black livery tunic thudded onto the bench beside me. His eyes were the color of berries and he had teeth missing. His brown hair stuck up in shocks.

"Good day," he said. "I'm Mardi, third page. The Scribe told me to stay with you till you were done eating, then bring you to the Gold Suite."

"Good," I said, pointing to the food. "Prepare for a wait."

His eyes rounded as he surveyed the empty tins and the pile waiting to be eaten. "Will you eat all that?"

I shrugged. "If I don't, I'll stash it for later."

"Later?"

"Sure. Never know when you'll eat next."

His surprised face told me not only had he always known when he would eat next, he also thought it a very dull arrangement. He looked at me again more closely. "Whose 'prentie are you, and what d'ya do?"

"Nobody's," I said, taking a huge bite of a chocolate tart. "I'm a thief."

His gaze ran over me again, this time with a kind of wary respect. "What have you—"

"Ask me when we leave. Now I want to eat. Tell me about being a page."

He shrugged a shoulder impatiently, still eyeing my filthy Thesreve-style clothes. Then he straightened up, and I knew that, poor as the job seemed to him, he was going to do his best to impress me. "I'm third page this year. Residence and first floor runs. Next year, perhaps, council and then throne room runs. And then equerry, with my own horse. *And* already I have half the map memorized," he added proudly. "And I speak a lot of Chelan, and some Elras." He blinked. "The Scribe told me to speak Chelan, but you seem to know our language—Allendi."

I shrugged, fighting the alarm that was quick to bang at my heart whenever someone seemed to think I was outside whatever they regarded as normal.

It's all right. I'm safe now, it seems. "Picked it up once. So you'll be a messenger, is that it?"

He nodded, going on to disparage some of the other pages, illustrating with mistakes they'd made in delivery or protocol.

As I listened, I considered the idea of becoming a messenger. After all, I was good with horses and I could speak any language I heard. That would be an honest living, and a fun one, if I decided to retire from thievery someday. And I wouldn't have to stay around any one place or person long enough to be betrayed.

I think I'll ask Hlanan about it. I know he'll be pleased.

This idea delighted me so much I decided to put it into action at once. "Let's go," I said, sweeping the remains of my meal into my already-greasy tunic pocket for later.

His eyes widened at this, his approval now vast. But he said nothing, striding out briskly so that I had to hop to keep pace. He was maybe half a head taller than I and his legs were much longer than mine.

We left the servants' area with the whitewashed walls and clay floors and entered the marble-floored, elegant palace. Air moved along through wide archways decorated with carved vines, above each one a cartouche with Rajanas's stylized wheat sheaf in its center.

We hustled past tapestries and mosaics, Mardi naming the official functions of impressive state chambers, then we galloped up a long, curving marble staircase and down another hall.

Finally we entered a room with a huge carpet of ivory, brown and gold vines twined together. Overhead hung a crystal chandelier as big as a chair, and the furniture was all thin curving legs with inlaid gold. At one side six tall windows let in streams of slanting light, which reached the carved door opposite.

Hlanan stepped through that door, his face calm but his eyes more serious than I'd ever seen. "Thank you, Mardi," he said. "Lhind—" He indicated the door behind him.

"I just got a great idea," I said cheerily as I preceded him into a small room. "From Mardi. It's about what I could do that's perfectly honest—"

On that word, something strong but invisible closed an icy vise around my heart.

The door clicked shut behind me.

I whirled around, but the invisible bands pulled tighter, leaving me gasping for air.

I was trapped.

NINE

What had I just been thinking about trust? My inner voice wailed.

I hadn't so much as tried to escape, just walked right in, expecting anything but outright betrayal.

Through the black dots swimming across my vision I cast a desperate look around me. About two hand-spans in from each corner of the small room, forming a kind of square, tall white candles sat in silver pots. I knew they were somehow involved with magic—more magic than I'd ever felt in one place, at one time. With each movement I made, some kind of strong binding spell dragged at me from inside.

I turned again, slowly, and found Hlanan. He stood outside the square, between two windows, with his back to a wall. Except for that awful bruise visible between locks of hair straggling on his forehead, he was pale as death, still dressed in his dirty clothes from our run.

Hlanan stood there watching me intently with a thin silver wand lying across both his palms. The wand had a jewel at either end, each gem a dizzying swirl of colors. He'd obviously come straight up here and spent all the time I was eating in setting up this trap.

SHERWOOD SMITH

Just for me.

With my last breath I struggled to save myself. Instinct prompted me, and anger gave me enough strength to shout with all the magic will in me, "Open that door!"

The words came out like I'd yelled under water, but the effect on Hlanan as he stared into the flaring jewels made him go paler. "Voice cast, too," he said softly. Then he raised unhappy eyes to me: "I'm desperately sorry, Lhind, more than you'll ever know, perhaps, but I *must* know who taught you that magic."

"No one," I wheezed, my breath even shorter.

"You did not learn those spells on your own, Lhind. It takes a long time to master them, particularly without aids. Please don't lie any more. You're bound in what we call a shren-square, within which you can do no magic."

I raised my hands, trying to bring a wind to blow out those candles. My fingers tingled and glowed strangely, but no wind came. Hlanan's brows went up as he watched, but he said nothing, only waited.

The attempt closed the vise even tighter. My hands dropped to my sides, impossibly heavy. I lifted my gaze past Hlanan to the window, for I wanted to see the light before I died.

"Lhind," Hlanan spoke again, moving the wand slightly. "Is this another pretense?"

The vise eased a tiny bit. I sucked in a heavy breath, though I feared it would crush my chest from the inside. Desperate, I forced my anger and misery to harden and narrow into a thin, red-glowing arrow...

I knew his range—and I saw, then banished, the old memory of the last time I did this, that figure writhing in those terrible flames in Thesreve.

And I *thrust*—

And instead of striking out at Hlanan, a pain like a knife with a fire-blade lanced behind my eyes. I yelped and dropped to my knees, pressing against the increasing wintry heaviness with shaking fingers.

"Lhind," Hlanan's voice came, husky with emotion. "Mind cast too? Lhind—child—I'm desolately shamed, but I cannot loosen this square until you name your tutor!"

"I. Don't. Have. One." I ground the words out past the ice slowly freezing jaw, brain, lips.

"I'll try another spell," he said slowly. "To sense how you— Lhind?"

No longer able to bear my own weight, I fell forward, sprawling on the cream-colored carpet. Another few heartbeats and I'd be unable to move at all. I managed to look up at him, and I said, "I saved. You once. Beg. You don't. Kill. Me. By...fire." *Like they do in Thesreve*, I thought, unable to get another word past my lips.

My words seemed to hit him like my thrust had back-lashed at me. His cheeks actually blanched to a faint greenish shade. "I'd never—" He choked, clearly horrified, then he shook his head in perplexity, looking as miserable as I felt. "This is just a shren-square," he said. "Are you really so distressed, or is this another act?" He flung the wand away and knelt at the edge of the square, looking down at me with distress that echoed my own. "I knew this would be bad, but I did not think—" He'd begun in another tongue, switched to Chelan, then he stopped and stared at me. His expression changed again and he said in the earlier language, "You understand me, don't you?"

But I was beyond speech. The ice was slowly leeching away the pain, leaving me numb. Behind Hlanan the windows grayed, and began to darken.

"Lhind?" he said again, reaching toward me. My blurring gaze was caught by his silver ring. In the light, the irregular bumps on its face formed a pattern, suggesting almond-blossom petals. "Lhind," Hlanan whispered.

My eyelids, now heavy beyond control, closed. Just before consciousness slipped away entirely I heard an choked exclamation, and suddenly the terrible weight lifted.

Rolling over, I lay flat, enjoying the sweetness of being able to breathe freely.

I heard the rustle of cloth, and Hlanan knelt beside me. "Lhind? I lifted the square."

I got my eyes open. My lips were still numb. I worked them, but got no words out.

Puzzled brown eyes studied me from under a brow shiny with sweat. "Why did the shren have this effect on you? It merely binds—*magic.*" He whispered the last word, then cleared his throat, but his voice shook as he asked, "Lhind, who *are* you?"

"Lhind." I got it out all right—strength returned with each breath, each wonderful, expansive, sweet breath.

He wiped his hand across his brow, then sighed, short and sharp. "I shall have to send you directly to the Magic Council unless we can come to some kind of understanding. I promise on my life I would *never* murder you, but you must understand that someone with all these skills..." He lifted his hands. "You look so confused, but you must know what I am saying."

I shook my head, just a little, for the headache was not quite gone. "I'm alone," I whispered, too wretched even to lie. "Nobody taught me. That I can remember. Don't remember everything."

His eyes widened and he sat back on his heels. His distracted gaze went from me to the window and back to me again. "That magic is in you, is that it?" he began cautiously.

I nodded. "But I don't know why, or wherefrom. It's just always been there. That bird said..." Danger seemed to curl around me, making it difficult to think.

"Tir?" he prompted gently. "Said what?"

"Called me something. Mind to mind," I managed, though my voice was nearly gone. "If whatever put it in me is bad...I promise...not part of it...been alone since I was small..." I gave up.

He touched my cowl. "Thianra says that your clothing is a kind of disguise. Is she right?"

I didn't see how denying it would help me any. He could put me back in that square any time he liked. So I nodded.

He sighed again, this time with decision. "Tell you what. You can go and change, get cleaned up, rest, whatever you want, and when you come out, I invite you...I entreat you, but in no way wish to constrain you to tell me everything you remember. Or you can go, and nobody will stop you," he said quickly. "I owe you that. I owe you more than that." He ran tense hands through his hair, making it wilder than before. He grimaced when his fingers encountered that knot, then he dropped his hands and stepped away, gazing at me with mute appeal.

I was trying to find my voice. No, I was trying to find the thoughts to send to my voice.

To fill the silence, he said quickly, "Or I could send you to the Council. They are not just a punitive group, not when there's a mystery." He smiled slightly, a funny, lopsided sort of smile. "Or not! Lhind, no one will guard you, or watch you. I expect you'll never trust me again—and I don't blame you for that. I don't know when I've ever made such a terrible error." Another deep breath. "So run off if you must, and we will not stop you. But remember, you cannot run forever, and next time your magic might be noticed by someone a lot more harmful than I must seem."

He extended a hand, and after a hesitation I took it, and he pulled me to my feet. Once again he gave me a funny look, but without further speech he opened the door to the big room with the six windows and the chandelier.

Rajanas was seated in one of the carved chairs, drinking from a golden goblet. The room smelled pleasantly of cider and with a hint of cinnamon. "So what did you find?" he addressed Hlanan.

Hlanan drew in a third unsteady breath. "Lhind seems to know as much magic as I do. More. In certain skills, anyway. And speaks Allendi. Beyond that, we know nothing."

Rajanas gestured toward me with his goblet. "I'd suggest you search him, but judging from that fight at the inn, it would take six of you to tie him down. Perhaps you'd do better to obtain his cooperation first. Well, thief?"

I looked from one to the other. What did I have to lose? I could run, but Hlanan had said no more than the truth when he'd threatened that someone worse could always catch up with me.

At any rate, he seemed to be done with threats. So if I stayed, at least for a little while, I might find answers to some of the questions that had shadowed me all my life. "All right," I said.

Rajanas set down his goblet. "Then I suggest—for the good of my household, if nothing else—that you begin with a bath. And after that, join us for a meal."

"I'll take you to the bath chamber," Hlanan said, looking more relieved even than I felt. He led the way out, then murmured with some embarrassment, "I take it that Thianra was correct about your masquerade. But that doesn't solve the magic questions." He actually blushed.

I grinned, a little energy returning. "You mean you've guessed that I'm not a boy?"

His gaze turned to the opposite wall, as if he'd just discovered a treasure there and if he looked away it would vanish.

I chortled. "If you have to guess anything, you're supposed to guess that I'm just a female in disguise. You're *supposed* to think that's my only secret." And when he looked at me in puzzlement, I said, "I switched when I reached Thesreve. Because, well, I was tired of being a girl. There were reasons. I've switched back and forth several times."

He looked if possible more embarrassed.

I shrugged, trying not to laugh. "So you're asking me about clothes. I'd like one of those tunics, the ones slit on the sides, with the billowy trousers. I don't wear shoes."

He wiped his brow again, now plainly relieved. Then he stopped and opened a door. "Here. Through that door is the water. I'll have someone bring things to this room." He hesitated, then went out abruptly.

I sighed, rubbing my tired eyes. As I'd said, I was just as comfortable as a boy as a girl. The one thing I had always been careful to hide was what kind of girl. Which they would see when I came out of that bath.

But I could always run.

I took in the rooms. The outer chamber was tiled, with two arched windows. A fireplace set in the wall opposite. Beyond it was another room, also with a window. These rooms formed a corner of the palace. Into the middle of the second chamber's floor, which was also tiled in a pleasing pattern of blue and gold and brown, was built a long pool.

I walked up to the edge and stared down into the water, which rilled to the edge of the tiles. One end was very deep, and the other shallow; at the shallow end a low fountain sent a steady stream of gently steaming water pouring into the pool. How did it not overflow? Pacing to the other end again, I saw a hole at the bottom of the pool. The water must run continually in and out again.

Suddenly my entire body was one giant itch, and I flung off my clothes, only taking care that my tools and take did not get jumbled with the food I'd stashed, then I dove in.

My hair and tail stretched in the swirling warm water, and I gloried in having them free for the first time in close to a year. I swam down to the bottom and stretched out, letting my tail and spine hair wave in the current. It was exquisite.

When I came up for air I saw two mounds of soft soap lying on shells on a tile tray. One was yellow and gritty and smelled of streams and sun-washed herbs. The other soap was soft, gray, and smelled of some kind of perfume. I scooped up a handful of the yellow one and used it to scrub myself all over.

When I was done I swam about happily for a time. At length I climbed out, and shook myself. Water flew off in all directions, sparkling in the afternoon light streaming in the window. My hair lifted and settled several times, until it was a damp silver-blue cloud around my head and body, barely damp.

Going back into the other room, I found a big towel laid on the bench, next to some folded clothing. I used it to mop up the worst of the puddle I'd made in fluffing myself, then I turned my attention to the clothes.

They were made of heavy watered silk, a pale spring green embroidered with almond and cherry blossoms. The trousers had wide legs. I pulled them on backwards, so my tail could poke through the hole where the tie-string tied. Then I yanked on the tunic, which settled like a silken weight against me, reaching down below my knees. I wore this backward as well, so as much of my spine hair as possible came free of the open neckline. After the confining heaviness of my Thesrevan clothes, this was like wearing air. Last I tied loosely about my waist the wide, silky sash I'd been given, and I surveyed myself with satisfaction.

The only problem, I realized very quickly, was the lack of pockets in which to put my stash. So I rolled it all into my old clothes and tucked them under my arm.

I turned toward the door, but when I reached it I stopped, my nerves chilling. When was the last time anyone had seen my hair and tail free? The last time came very clearly—which made my stomach curdle with fear.

You can always run, I told myself. *Look at this as a dare.*

I slipped out into the hallway, and retraced my steps, back to that big room where Mardi had first brought me.

I heard them before I saw them, and I paused in the doorway, looking in. The three of them were there, sitting at a low table covered with fine porcelain dishes. Hlanan had changed and bathed, tying his wet hair back neatly off his high brow. He looked like a scribe again, his slim form mostly obscured by an open gray robe. It was the scribe's summer garb, the robe sleeveless, worn over a loose-sleeved shirt of undyed cotton-silk, and gray loose trousers of the same fabric as the scribe robe.

Rajanas no longer glittered with gems. He'd dressed to fit his status, but his burgundy-colored tunic was only tied with a gold sash, without embellishment. Beneath it, he wore a silk shirt of black, and dark riding trousers stuffed into his boots.

Thianra had gotten rid of her toff clothes and had donned her bright minstrel-blue robe, worn over floating trousers not unlike what I wore. She had braided her hair and bound it around her head. When I saw her, my scalp lifted in memory-protest, and my hair swirled around me.

It was then that Hlanan looked up, and his jaw dropped.

Thianra turned, her eyes startled. Rajanas lifted his brows and said wryly, "If you are indeed Lhind, that was a *very* effective disguise." He turned to Thianra. "I congratulate you on your powers of observation."

I felt strange under their triple gaze, so I held up my roll and said, "I've got nowhere to put my stash."

"That's your Lhind, all right." Rajanas's voice was ironic, but his gaze was not unfriendly. He saluted me with his goblet, and added, "Come join us, Young Mistress. I never thought I'd entertain someone quite so...ornamental."

"I only guessed a part of your secrets, Lhind," Thianra said apologetically. "Well, two parts. But *that*, I had no idea," watching as my hair lifted, clouding around my head and shoulders.

I flexed inside and forced it to settle, but my spine twitched and up it all went again, as if my hair, so long confined, gloried in freedom as much as I did.

"Hrethan," Hlanan murmured.

The word seemed to take shape in the air, making them all fall silent.

Rajanas was the first to speak. He rubbed his jaw, frowning, then said, "Correct me if I'm wrong, but I understood their...their fur and hair to be blue. And blue eyes."

Thianra nodded slowly, her gaze steady. "That's true. But Lhind's hair is the silvery blue of the Snow Folk. They are nearly invisible against the blue-white snows of the heights. Just as the darker gray-blue of the island Hrethan make them difficult to see against the water if they don't want to be seen." She looked puzzled. "Though I've never seen one with eyes the color of honey."

"My fuzz's the same color as my hair," I said, yanking up my sleeve, and showing them the fine short silver-blue hair that covered me from my neck down to my wrists and ankles.

They stared at my arm, so different from the browns and pinks and bronzes of humankind.

Hlanan still gazed intently at me.

"Stash?" Rajanas repeated belatedly.

"Yeah. Knife, burglar's tools, herbs, food. And, uh, money and jewels."

Rajanas slid a hand over his eyes, his shoulders shaking with silent laughter.

Thianra's eyes quirked, shining with a liquid gleam—tears had gathered along her lower eyelids. "You're still our Lhind," she said with a breathless chuckle. "I think Ilyan will give you a room, and you can leave your things there. No one here will touch them, I think I can safely promise."

Rajanas turned to Hlanan. "Well? Is this what you expected in addition to the—entirely understandable, considering Thesreve—swap of female mage for male thief?"

Hlanan just shook his head, then he frowned and tossed off a glass of the cider in his golden goblet. "All right," he said, taking a deep breath. "The first thing, I think, is to contact the Council. They can send a message to the Hrethan. Yes, I really think that's what we should do. If you're willing, that is, Lhind."

"But what about—" I snuck a look at the others. "The job?"

Hlanan shook his head. "I think that's impossible now."

To my surprise, Rajanas said, "Why? Shut your eyes to the vision before you, and think back to the fight in the inn. We've merely exchanged a dirty thief for a clean one. If Lhind still wants the job, she can disguise herself again. In fact I think that might be advisable."

Hlanan was rubbing his thumb over the bumps on his ring, a restless gesture. "Impossible because now that I have had a little time to consider, I believe that Geric Lendan got to that book first. The more I think about his insisting on joining us on the yacht, the more suspicious I am. I do know that someone used magic to summon those pirates, but I cannot prove who or how, merely that it was a fairly powerful spell to break my wards." He turned my way. "But that is a matter for another time. Lhind, you say you don't know wherefrom you came. What do you remember of your origins?"

I shrugged, and this time they all watched my hair cloud, then settle down my back. "Not much." The desire to have my questions answered was nearly as compelling as the wish to be free of the confining cowl.

And yet, I was still afraid. Secrets had been as much a part of my armor as the cowl. Perhaps even deeper was my reluctance to mention the Blue Lady. Maybe she wasn't a real memory. She might have been no more than a dream I'd made up to be comforting when times were bad.

So I began with the memories that I was certain of.

"I was with some people. Traveling ones. Cotton harvesters. They first dressed me as a boy, and I got used to it, I guess. They got angry when I tried to take the clothes off or stretch my hair, or my tail. And the first shimmer I made, the man—I don't remember his name beyond that he wanted me to call him Papa—beat me so bad I was in my bunk for four days. Later I wondered if in off-season they were slavers, or sold slaves once in a while.

"Anyway, I felt danger whenever any of them talked about me. After the shimmer he started tying my hands at night. So one night during a very bad storm I ran away. That part was easy. Figuring out how to live wasn't, and I ran into a lot of trouble along the way. But I learned." I shrugged. "I found I had only to hear other tongues and I could speak them, and I could call animals to my aid. One winter I spent with a den of wolves. They didn't eat me because I could make fire-shimmers, and I didn't want their food. I guarded the cubs. They let me be part of the pack, but it was very hard to get enough for me to eat, because I couldn't abide their food. So I left in spring, and went south."

"What brought you to Thesreve, of all places?" Thianra asked.

"Running. After I left Piwum, I got chased by some poke-nose who saw my shimmers and wanted my magic. Decided I was best off in a place where magic wasn't—well, looked for. Liked being a thief. Was good at it, I'm fast, I can jump, and I didn't have to talk to anybody."

"But you can't be a thief for the rest of your life," Hlanan protested earnestly.

I grinned at him. "Well, I was about to tell you my idea when you stuck me in that nasty magic-trap. I think I'd like to be a messenger. I like horses, and new places, and I can speak any tongue I want to. And it's honest." I finished triumphantly.

Rajanas laughed, and Thianra smiled, but Hlanan looked serious.

"Maybe," he said. "But first you must go to the Hrethan."

"So tell me," I responded. "Who are they?"

TEN

Hlanan seemed nonplussed. Rajanas merely raised his goblet again, and studied the fine etching along its edge. It was Thianra who answered me.

"They are people, kin to the humankind we see in greater numbers." She pressed her fist to her chest, and opened her hand toward the two fellows. "It is said that they came from another world centuries ago. They live in the mountains beyond Liacz, and on Starborn Island, far north in the Sea of Storms where snow falls most of the year. Other people of great magic live there as well, according to report. I know no one who has actually been to the heights, we only know the ones at the Summer Islands, as they are called, for Hlanan studied magic there. They are known by several names. Hrethan is just one. Snow Folk is another common one. They are supposed to have first settled Charas al Kherval, according to legend."

Hlanan rubbed his eyes again. "How long have you been on your own?"

"Not certain," I said. "I've tried to figure it out, but you know, everyone counts the years differently in every country."

"Do you remember what happened to you?"

I shook my head. Impossible to tell what was really memory, and what was just vivid dream. I felt it safest to say little. "I remember snow," I said. "Music. Deep blue sky...wind."

"Any people?" Hlanan asked.

"Don't know," I mumbled, thinking of the Blue Lady, and of the single image I had of a tall, smiling man with long yellow hair. Those images always came with a stir of intense emotion, too strong to talk about. I was unsettled enough by all this...truth. As their eyes took in who I really was.

"Do you remember any major events from Charas al Kherval or any of the other kingdoms on this end of the continent?" Thianra asked.

This was much easier. "I remember the year Aulin Crown died," I said, thinking back. I was careful to use the proper name: on the streets of Piwum on Dunleth's side of the border, the old emperor had been known as Aulin the Ugly. And worse. "That was the spring after I stayed with the wolves. Everyone wore mourning white in the capital. Crushed flowers on the streets."

Rajanas whistled softly. "Eleven years ago. You were right again, Thianra. Lhind is older than he—she—looks."

Thianra said, "At least twenty, probably a couple years older. I knew she was no child. The Hrethan are reputed to be very long-lived—"

At that moment Rajanas looked up at the doorway. "Kenned?"

The tall steward who'd met us in the courtyard had quietly appeared. His long face lengthened into incredulity at the sight of me, sparking my instinct to hide. I longed for the safety of my cowl, and the huge knickers that disguised my tail.

At the sound of his name the steward started, then bowed swiftly. "Kuraf is here, your highness," he said.

His second glance at me was quick—and covert.

"Tell Kuraf I am on my way."

The servant bowed again and left.

Rajanas got to his feet. He frowned slightly, then gave his head a quick, sharp shake.

"Must you leave this moment?" Thianra protested. "I think we need to decide right away what should be done about Lhind."

"One of the promises he made when he signed the treaty with Kuraf was that she has immediate access to him whenever he is in residence," Hlanan said. "And you may be sure she knows exactly when he appears."

Rajanas smiled. "Besides, she never comes into town but for a reason. Usually something I'd better hear right away."

As he walked out of the room, I turned to Thianra, who was pouring cider into the third goblet. "Who's Kuraf?"

She looked in question at Hlanan, who said, "Leads a band in the northern forests. Started as a thief under Ilyan's grandfather, who was not a good ruler. Later Ilyan and I joined her band..." Hlanan smiled, then he gave a tremendous yawn. "It was great fun, but a long story that can wait. They became allies, and she protects the northern marches, specifically the Idaron Pass that leads down into Alezand. Her daughter's in the Guard. In fact, you were riding with her."

"Kuraf sounds like somebody I'd like to meet!" I chortled.

A bright spot flickered, and Tir swooped into the room through one of the open windows, flew around Hlanan's head. "You found us," Hlanan exclaimed, and yawned again. Even with his watering eyes, he and the bird made an appealing picture, creature and human, each so intent on the other. "Welcome back, Tir," Hlanan said. "Do you see Lhind here, do you recognize her?"

I could have told him that Tir paid almost no attention to things like outer appearance, but I still wasn't ready to talk about mind-speech. I had revealed enough secrets, and I was still braced for a nasty result.

"Lhind! Lhind!" Tir shrilled, and lighted on the back of one of the empty chairs. Then the bird flew out again.

Hlanan touched his forehead gingerly. "Somehow I suspect Kuraf would either recruit you or challenge you to a duel." He laughed, then gave another jaw-cracking yawn. "Maybe Rajanas will invite her to stay. For now, I think we had better get you situated, and I need desperately to get some rest. The events of the last day, including that cursed transportation spell, have given me a headache the size of a moon, and I can scarcely keep my eyes open."

"Perhaps you'd better arrange a room for Lhind first," Thianra murmured. She also yawned. "The one adjoining mine?"

Hlanan looked from her to me, blinked, then nodded. "I think that would be best. I'll see to it now. I need to move. That cider must be harder than it tastes." He rose, blinked rapidly, passed his fingers over his eyes, then walked out.

Thianra set down her empty goblet, then leaned forward. "I understand it's probably offensive, and so I apologize, but I so badly wish to examine your hair. It looks so much like..."

She reddened. I shrugged. My scalp twitched in response and my hair drifted away, then returned and a few strands settled across her wrist.

She turned her hand over, letting the strands draw across her palm. "It is! It really is feathered!" she exclaimed in delight. "That's why it looks so cloudy."

"So's my fuzz."

I stuck out my arm, and she bent close to my wrist, saying slowly, "It's like down."

"Thick up here," I pointed to my scalp. "So it can lift. Helps me balance when it's free."

Because we were alone, I gathered myself—for a little strength had returned—and sprang to the back of the chair opposite the one on which Tir had perched. I balanced on my toes, my tail and hair moving to keep me upright. Thianra's eyes rounded. I couldn't help showing off, and did a flip right there, landing on my hands, my toes pointed upward. Then I pushed and somersaulted in the air before landing.

Thianra clapped lightly. "No wonder you were so nimble during that fight at the inn. How could you bear to have your hair bound under that cap?" she asked sympathetically, as she poured herself more cider.

I shrugged. "Just remembered what happens to magic-makers in Thesreve. Magic-makers and anyone who's different."

Her eyes narrowed. She knew what I was talking about. She said, "Please pardon if the question is impertinent, but why the disguise? No, I understand the swap between male and female, for convenience, but why a child?"

"I don't disguise myself as a child," I said. "I just let people think whatever they want to. Less trouble for me, that way."

"Trouble?" she repeated. "I should think there would be more. Unscrupulous persons always taking advantage of the young, the ignorant, the weak, for preference."

"And those I know how to avoid. Trouble with...other kinds of things," I said evasively.

She was giving me that steady gaze again, the minstrel searching for the exact line to sum up a character in a song. Only I didn't want to be summed up.

"Would your reason be related to why your disguise was so determinedly pungent?" She gave me a conspiratorial grin.

I had to laugh. "Yes! Amazing, how a convenient stench keeps everybody at a healthy distance!"

She rubbed her eyes again, but before she could speak, Tir flew back through the window and circled overhead, keening on a high, weird note.

As I looked at Tir's glittering ruby eye, an image flickered into my brain—

"Trouble," I said. "A long line of warriors, just beyond a hill."

"How do you know that?" she demanded.

"Mind to mind communication," Hlanan said from the door, even more hoarse than before. "Hrethan are supposed to be able to do that. Though not everybody knows it. Rajanas just sent for me. Kuraf says that we've got an invading force of some kind on the northern border. He wants us to get out of the city as fast as we can, and take Lhind with us. He and the Guard are securing things here, then will ride upland to seal the Idaron Pass, and Kuraf is going to hold the city."

Thianra rubbed a thumb against her teeth, frowning furiously. "If only I wasn't so tired," she muttered. "My mind feels fogged. I can't think! Who's out there?"

Hlanan shook his head. "They couldn't see details, but no banners."

"Can we leave by magic transport?" Thianra said.

SHERWOOD SMITH

Hlanan winced. "Only if we have to. Without a fixed Destination, and with the possibility of tracers by any sorcerers they've got out there..."

Whatever that meant, it was enough to worry Thianra. "I'll fetch my gear." She rose to her feet, stumbling against a chair. "Ho! I'm more tired than I thought. Where do we meet?"

"Here," Hlanan said after a dazed look around. "For if we must use a magic transport, our own Destination makes it somewhat easier." He pointed toward the door to that little room where I'd been imprisoned by magic so shortly before. Hlanan then turned to me. "Will you accept a suggestion? I think you should wait here. Since you do not know your way around the Residence. Then we three will depart."

Thianra gave a quick nod and sped noiselessly away.

Hlanan lingered, studying me with a sort of absent perplexity that indicated he was working on some kind of knotty problem. But when he spoke, all he said was: "I shall return in just a few moments." He rubbed his eyes again, as if that would clear his head, and exited once more.

Tir left its perch, and sailed out the open window into the bright air.

I expect you'll never trust me again. His earlier words came back to me, along with the regret I'd seen so plainly in his face. His care to make a suggestion—as though he had no right to tell me what to do—was as puzzling as how important it seemed to him to be trusted. Why would anyone want to be trustworthy? Unless you planned to use those who trusted you?

Well, one thing for certain, I had most definitely underestimated the power of trust. I'd lived without it so long, and yet I'd come to trust Hlanan with an ease that could only be termed stupid. That trap of his was a good reminder about what happens when you trust other humans.

I picked up Thianra's empty goblet and poured out the last of the cider, admiring the sparking golden liquid splashing into the burnished gold of the cup. I wasn't really thirsty, having enjoyed that wonderful meal so recently, but one thing I did trust was my belief that I should eat and drink good things while I had them at hand.

I was in the act of raising the cider to my lips when the door to Hlanan's magic room opened. I set the goblet on the mantel, wondering how someone could have got past me to enter that little room, whose only entrance was five paces from me.

Four figures emerged. Oh yes, wasn't that room what they called a Destination? A place where people could use transfer magic from one spot to another.

The first one through the door moved with a characteristic, arrogant lounge. Tall, long loose hair coppery gold, handsome, dressed for war in an elegantly cut battle tunic, gauntlets to match his tall boots: Geric Lendan. Whose last words in my presence were his suggestion to toss me overboard.

He was followed by three warriors wearing undyed battle tunics, with no markings of house or kingdom to identify them.

Geric's light blue eyes widened in surprise—a surprise with no recognition. Then he gave me a slow smile of appreciation.

And he bowed, as if I were a princess.

He gestured his three silent companions toward the outer door. "A highly unexpected honor, Hrethan," he said to me after the last warrior closed the door. "I had not known Alezand counted your folk among his friends. May I present myself, since no one appears to be nearby to perform that office? Geric Lendan, Prince of the Golden Circle." And he bowed gracefully, hand over his heart.

I still had not spoken, and Geric waited, his expression changing to one of speculation. "Is it possible," he said slowly, still in the language the others called Allendi, "you are new to our lowland tongues?"

Though I did not know this fellow, all the little clues of face, of manner, convinced me that he wanted me to be ignorant of the local language. That suited me very well, because how can someone question another who cannot understand the language?

I spoke at last, faking a preposterous accent: "Ze worrrdz...oh, zzzo hhhard..." I waved my hands, then gave him a big smile.

And he smiled back, with the smirk of one who knows himself master of the situation. Bowing again, he said slowly and distinctly (as if that was going to create understanding in someone who didn't know the language), "Where is your host, Honored One?"

I spread my hands, my hair lifting. I watched him watch it, his eyes widening in appreciation. When he wasn't smirking or talking about offal and throwing people overboard, he was very attractive. My heart pulsed with the sweet power of attraction. Even stronger than magic spells was seeing my attraction mirrored in his gaze.

For that moment, the entire world closed to the prince and me, poised on the brink of endless possibilities.

I could have told Thianra that I wanted people to think I was an urchin because then I could pretend moments like this didn't exist, except that they did. And I knew they did. The thing I needed to learn—I was barely able to think at all—was that my ignorance about such matters made me defenseless.

But I wasn't entirely brainless. This is the same fellow who wanted me tossed off the yacht to drown.

Indignation sparked. *Was* I really going to let myself be inveigled by that handsome face?

No, I was not.

The door to the magic room opened again, and four more warriors emerged, these ones dressed in gray surcoats, with deep hoods thrown back over their shoulders. They spread out, swords drawn.

Geric made a curt gesture and they sheathed their weapons. With a glance at me he said, in some other language, "Swift and silent. We are not expected. And send in something to drink, two cups," he added.

The four went out quickly, their mail tunics chinging sinisterly at each step.

"Who izzat?" I asked, smiling brightly again, and pointing after the four men in gray.

"Merely my honor guard," Geric replied, coming forward slowly. I noticed that he—possibly by accident—stood directly between me and the outer door. "Will you drink with me, Honored One? And, how should you be addressed?"

What kind of names did the Hrethan have? I thought desperately, thinking over what little had been said about these mysterious people. "Ah, in my tongue I am Bird Of Ze Snows," I said cautiously.

And he took it without a blink. "A beautiful name, O Beautiful One," he said, saluting me.

One of the warriors reappeared at the door. "My lord prince," he began, holding out a tray with two silver wine glasses on it, and a carafe cut from crystal.

Geric gave me a quick look, then moved forward to take the tray. I looked out the window, trying to seem as if I was absorbed in high and noble thoughts. Tir had disappeared again.

"All three have been secured by the Steward, all asleep."

"Ah yes! Give Kenned his money, then...see him off. You will know how." Geric's voice went soft as a snake's back. "Or, have the others do that. You must find the thief, kill him, and bring me everything he carried upon his person. Everything, missing out no coin or jewel. Am I understood?"

The soldier bowed. "As you will, my lord prince."

Geric turned toward me, and once again he smiled, then enunciated slowly in Chelan, "It seems that I shall be entertaining you for a time," said he. "My servant reports that our hosts all seem to be occupied with other matters, and bid us wait. I wonder how this might be brought to advantage us both?" He brought the tray forward, and set it down on a side table.

He moved to block the tray from my view, and made a flourishing act of pouring out two glasses of cider. Ice burned along my arms and down inside to pool inside me. I leaped high and noiselessly, peeking over his shoulder as he opened a ring and emptied a pinch of something into one goblet.

I landed, my hair swirling gently, as Geric brought the cup, bowed, and put it into my hands.

I held it up as if admiring the craftsmanship. *Secured—asleep—Find the thief, kill him.* If the traitorous steward, Kenned, came in now, he'd be able to point me out as The Thief.

SHERWOOD SMITH

Geric bowed, the other glass in hand. "Drink, my honored guest. I will propose a toast—to our excellent hosts, and may they find the future they so richly deserve."

I raised my glass to my lips, and took a sniff. On the surface was the pungent smell of very good cider. But underneath, the unmistakable tickle of liref in my nostrils: not a smell so much as a sense. Liref. Not poison, but an herb that sent people into sleep.

What to do, what to do?

"Do you not drink?" he asked, still smiling, but question began to quirk his eyes.

"Yess!" I watched his gaze lift to my swirling hair as I walked toward him. Deliberately, while his gaze was distracted by my hair, I slid on the rug and then stumbled against him. I tried to dump the cup, but his fingers shot out and steadied my hand so only a little of it spilled. His other arm clasped around me and held me against him.

His grip was strong. I knew I wouldn't break it easily, and struggling would give me away, so I let my hair whip into his face as I exclaimed, "Oh! My! Bad, me!"

He let me go, laughing a little. "Bad me, for I must say, I wouldn't mind you falling into my arms again."

I set my cup on the tray as I made a business of brushing off my clothes. "Oh! Bad!" He was watching me lazily, so I spread my hands.

Now what? A small shadow flitted past the windows—Tir was back! That gave me an idea.

I let out a shrill cry. He looked up quickly, wary and dangerous. I pointed at the window, gabbling earnestly in what I hoped sound like a Hrethanish language, and when he strode to the window to peer out, I switched the silver cups. And when he leaned out, I snatched the goblet from the mantel behind me and topped that evil potion just for good measure.

I set the golden goblet behind a side table a heartbeat before he turned around and said with pardonable exasperation, "It was just a bird."

"*Evil* bird? Scare me. Red eyes!" I sent a mental apology to Tir, in case the aidlar was listening to this exceptionally witless masquerade.

Geric might want to flirt, but only when convenient for *him*. He signaled his intent by picking up what he thought was the drugged cup and pressing it into my hands.

I lifted my goblet, saluting him. As I'd hoped—he mirrored my movement in his pretense of politeness—and when I gulped down my wine, he took a good drink of his own.

Another gulp—he drank—he set his goblet down, and so did I.

"Shall we take a tour?" he asked, holding out his arm to me. His smile showed the edges of his white teeth. "Perhaps this is the way to become better acquainted, ah, with not only each other, but with the...altered circumstances now obtaining—" He stopped, and frowned.

My eyes flicked to my bundle, resting beside my stool. Among my tools was a little bag of liref, enough fine-ground leaves to knock half an army out for a week. I knew how fast it could act, when added to any distilled or fermented drink.

Geric took a step toward me. His eyes narrowed, and his teeth showed again as he said, "Magic or mere trickery, Honored One?" His speech slowed, but somehow he forced himself to continue. "We shall—"

And I heard the finishing thought as clear as if he'd spoken: *We shall meet again, I promise you that.*

Then he stumbled to a chair, his head thrown back, his hands clenched into fists as he fought against the double dose of liref, but his limbs went loose, his eyes gradually closing. When his breathing deepened, I sprang forward to search him. My time as a pickpocket made me good at that: I relieved him of his knife, two rings, and from an inner pocket in that beautifully tailored battle tunic, a curiously carved piece of bone that made my fingers tingle warningly.

I threw all this into my bundle, tucked it under my arm, and faced the doorways, uncertain what to do next. Rescue Hlanan and the others? That was the instinctive response, for though my trust had been broken, I could understand why Hlanan had done what he'd done. He really had not intended to hurt me, I understood that much. This Geric, his reasons seemed both mysterious and far more threatening.

I had no idea where to begin my search, but maybe Mardi would. Surely I could find that kitchen again—

The curtains stirred as a white bolt shot through the window. *Flee! Flee!* Tir's voice in my head was nearly as shrill as sound would have been.

"What about Hlanan? Shouldn't I do something about them?" I asked.

Tir's thoughts were confusing, more image than words, then I remembered that order to 'kill the thief.' And Kenned knew what I looked like as both thief and Hrethan.

All right. Time to get away and plan.

I crossed to the window. Tir flew out again as I peered around. The tree branches stretched welcomingly near; an easy leap, another, and a short time later I stood on the ground in a lovely park, wondering what to do next, as Tir was a mere dot against the sun, wings beating as the aidlar fled northward.

ELEVEN

From somewhere beyond a tall stone wall horse hooves drummed in the pattern of a trot. I crossed a hedge and leaped to the top of the wall, lying flat, and watched a double column of gray-clad, armed riders gallop into the park.

Rajanas and the others had landed themselves into a nasty quagmire. Maybe it was related to the same quagmire we'd escaped before.

I slid off the wall again, and crouched behind a thick dark green shrub. Unrolling my bundle, I stared down at my wrinkled clothing. Grease stains, dirt, and the remains of many hastily-eaten meals met my eye; the herb-scented air of the park was overwhelmed by the odor I'd cultivated for a year.

Though I'd been perfectly content in those clothes until noon, I found that I was distinctly reluctant to resume them now. And they wouldn't be safe, anyway. That traitor of a Steward had seen me before I changed as well as after, so the searchers would have both descriptions.

The alternative was a third disguise. My new tunic and pants were common for these parts. Assuming I could hide my tail and hair, maybe I'd get by. Except I still had my old problem: where to put my stash?

When in doubt, wear it. I'd learned that long ago.

Working fast, I separated into three piles my burglary tools, my take, and the bits of food I'd stashed. Remembering the variety of headgear I'd seen on the citizens of Imbradi on our ride into the city, I wrapped the tools tightly into a corner of the sash. I flexed my scalp and neck so that my hair twisted tightly into a knot on my head. Around this I wrapped the other portion of the sash, making a turban. The jewels and rings I strung on the cord from my old knickers, and I slung this around my waist inside the tunic. My tail had to go inside the trousers, my knife in my waistband, and I resolved to get a cloak as soon as I could.

Last thing, I buried the old clothes and the bits of stale food that I'd stashed. Though once I would have cherished every bite, I'd eaten so well these past few days that the mashed, dirty bits no longer looked appetizing.

I slipped over the wall and ran toward the town, hiding every time I heard a horse approach. Twice gray-clad warriors rode at a flat gallop either to or from the palace. And when I reached the city, I heard far off the shouts and metallic clashes of fighting.

The streets were nearly empty. Once again I'd be conspicuous, unless I went to ground, and quickly. But where?

I tried to think over what Hlanan and Thianra had said about this city. Not much. *Tir!* I squeezed my eyes shut and yelled in my mind. *Tir? Where are you?*

At once a flash of mental-image entered my mind: myself, seen from high above. I looked up in the sky, and just barely made out an indistinct bird-shape against the white of sailing clouds.

You are sought, came Tir's mental voice.

Who? I sent back, ducking fearfully through an archway into a narrow street.

Kuraf seeks you. And these.

Again I 'saw' from the bird's view: not one, but three separate search parties. Two were groups of those gray-clad warriors, one of which moved perilously near. I waited, crouching behind someone's wash strung between walls, until I heard the clash and jingle of their mail and weapons as they marched by.

The smallest group comprised two men and a woman, who worked their way steadily down a street from the other direction. They stopped every so often to talk to the increasingly rare citizens passing by.

Question: were Kuraf's folk friend or foe?

Tir?

Their words carry no danger to you.

This decided me in favor of the three searchers. Maybe Kuraf's folk would give me some idea what was going on.

I vaulted the wall behind me and ran along it until I came to a low roof. Leaping onto that, I ran lightly over the rooftops, springing from one to another until I reached the end of the row.

Then I jumped down directly behind the three searchers. They whirled around, hands going to weapons.

"Looking for me?" I asked, reaching up to pull the turban free—taking care to keep hold of my tools still bundled in the sash.

They watched my hair cloud as from all sides a small crowd of people emerged from the shuttered houses and stepped into the street to ring us. One of the searchers bowed to me, and said, "Will you join us, Honored One?"

"Happy to," I said. "Lead on."

The three silently closed ranks around me; the people who lived on the street withdrew into their houses, shutting doors and windows. No doubt watching from behind the shutters.

Led by my new companions, I began a fast journey through the twisted, narrow streets of the inner town. I was soon hopelessly lost, and we moved too fast for me to try contacting Tir to find my position.

Abruptly we halted at a nondescript house in the middle of a row of such. One of the men remained on guard outside the door as the other two led the way inside.

We went up steep steps, and entered a small room with low furniture made with the same pleasing lines as that I'd seen in Rajanas's palace, though this was much plainer. Two people waited quietly, a man and a woman. The man was young, the woman old. It was to the woman my guides turned.

"Here is the Hrethan. She comes freely."

"Good." The woman nodded, gestured to me. "We will have food brought, and drink."

"Will someone tell me what's going on?" I asked.

The woman smiled briefly. "We wait for nightfall. Then we go to Kuraf. She will answer your questions—and ask you some, I expect."

She stopped talking as someone brought in some steaming tea, and several plates of food.

They tried to make me comfortable; I was never really sure whether I was a guest or a prisoner. Somehow I was never alone and couldn't try that door. And Tir had flown out of range of my thought-reach.

At nightfall we left again. Entering another house, we descended to a cellar. There, hidden cleverly in the brick, was a secret door. This opened onto a tunnel. Silently my guides led me into this, two before me and two following behind. While we walked in the utter darkness, I used the opportunity to tie my stash securely under my tunic, hoping it wouldn't bulge when light found us again.

When we emerged into the cool night air, I smelled rain on the way. We stood in a thick wood, and horses were brought. Still in silence, we mounted up and then rode for some time.

I could see little of the path ahead. The darkness was not absolute but very near it. Still, we did not stop for quite a while, and that was only long enough for the lead rider to light a torch. By then the rain had begun, soft but steady. The cool, wet air woke up my tired mind, and excitement coursed through me. I tried hard to follow the sense of our path, but all I could see was the uneven red flicker of the hissing torch, and smoke streaming behind.

Judging by my horse's labors, we rode a distance upward into mountains, then at last descended a narrow path into a valley. Steep cliffs blocked the clouds on either side. The rain had lessened by the time we dismounted, and I was bade to climb.

"Climb?" I repeated. The darkness was thick, and the torch had been put out.

"This."

Rope, a rope-ladder, was put into my fingers.

"Up," the anonymous voice added.

"Right." Curious—and a bit afraid—I pulled my way rapidly up this rope-ladder, which went quite a distance. A breeze stirred about me as the ladder swayed, and my tail twitched instinctively.

"Here," someone said, and I stepped onto a wooden platform, moving inward as those who'd followed me up the ladder crowded behind.

Then a spark was struck, a lamp lit, and I looked around in amazement at a series of platforms and ladders built into the branches of a mighty tree. Huge, broad leaves curtained the sides of the platforms; far above, the smaller platforms creaked and swayed in the wind. My toes spread and gripped, knowing their job by instinct, and my tail fretted at its confinement.

I found myself surrounded by about a dozen people, all observing me with various degrees of interest.

"Seem a bit like home?" one addressed me, a tall, strong-limbed woman with iron-gray braids bound closely about her head.

Caught by surprise, I tried to speak, but nothing came forth.

The woman laughed, a short, soft sound. "Never mind my rudeness, Hrethan. I'm Kuraf, and I never learned court manners. Come up, and welcome. We have much to discuss." She stood aside and gestured to one of rope ladders. "What shall we call you?"

She's not asking for a real name. "Lhind," I said anyway, scrambling up the ladder to yet another platform. This one had a low wall built round it, and furniture made it comfortable. "This is wonderful!" I exclaimed as Kuraf appeared behind me. "No wonder Hlanan said he had fun when he joined your gang."

Kuraf laughed again, and waved at one of the low pillowed chairs. "Are you hungry or thirsty?"

I shrugged. I wasn't, but in my experience you didn't turn down free food just because you didn't happen to need it right then. "What I am," I said, "is confused beyond measure."

The leaves rustled, and a white shape swooped down and landed on the back of a nearby chair.

"Tir!" I cried.

"Lhind help, Lhind help," Tir croaked, walking back and forth and studying us from one eye then the other.

Kuraf studied the bird in return, her eyes narrowed. Finally she said, "I'm confused as well, I'll confess." She smiled. "Alezand spoke only a few words about you, but those were right curious. Add to that your not recognizing the style of this place, and add again the Scribe's aidlar, who I'll swear has never been far from him until this day. Let us essay this: I'll ask you some questions, and then I'll try to answer yours."

"But first tell me what that Rot-faced, what Rajanas—that is, what your, uh—"

Kuraf burst out laughing, and this time it was real laughter. She clapped her hands on her knees and rocked back, strong white teeth gleaming in the lamplight as she crowed.

"It's also the first time I'd wished I was away from my homeland, and aboard his pleasure ship when you were taken, young Hrethan," she said, wiping the back of her hand across her eyes. "Your rot-face is the rightful prince of Alezand, the land we sit in now. He owes allegiance to Aranu Crown, and one might say that it was on her business that he and his companions were of late employed."

"He did say Alezand was the land name and his title."

She snorted a quick laugh, then said, "If you make it to the capital, and I'll talk with you about that anon, you'll find that these nobles address one another by their various titles. There's insults and praise to be found in how they use their many names, young one, or merely in a bow, and the rest of us might study years and not always catch every shade of meaning, or innuendo, they intend. Enough on that. Those of us oath-sworn to the land of Alezand use his title proudly, for he's been a good ruler."

"All right," I said when she paused expectantly.

"As for his words on you: 'And we spent some goodly time chasing a small rat of a lying thief at the Scribe's behest,' he told me. 'And it was goodly time because our thief turns out to be Hrethan, lost to her kind, and possessed of considerable sorcery. Saved us from a pirate attack that we now suspect was instigated by Geric Lendan.'"

"So Hlanan said. I don't get that. Geric Lendan was with us on the yacht," I said.

"Did you see him fighting?" Kuraf returned.

"N-no," I said, thinking back. "That's true. I didn't. But I didn't see that sniff-nosed Princess Kressanthe fighting, either. Several of those toffs on that yacht were hiding below, I think. I figured they didn't know how to fight."

"Lendan knows how to fight," Kuraf replied. "He has a reputation for dueling, and winning. I haven't met him—though apparently I came mighty close today. And that's what we need to talk about." She shifted position, stretching tiredly. "Nill! Some hot cider," she shouted upward into the tree, then she looked back at me. "It's been a long day, and looks to be a longer night. First, tell me what happened back there at the Residence. You did meet Prince Geric?"

I nodded, unsure how much to tell about that meeting. Long experience made me decide to skip over the fact that I'd robbed him, and I said merely: "He came out of that magic-Destination room, he and some warriors. They went into the other part of the palace and he blocked me off from the door and introduced himself. He ordered cider with liref, but drank the wrong cup."

"Just drank it, eh?" Kuraf snorted a laugh.

"After I switched 'em," I admitted. But she didn't look surprised. "Anyway Tir told me to run so I hopped out the window, tried to disguise myself, and Tir led me to your searchers." I pointed at the aidlar.

Kuraf smiled ironically. "That disguise didn't last long: by now, I imagine, it's all over the city how the silver-haired Hrethan dropped out of the sky. You'd have done better to have kept that hair covered." She shrugged and rubbed her neck. "Ah well. What's past is past—" She paused as feet appeared on the ladder overhead.

A thin boy not much taller than I descended rapidly, carrying a bottle and carved wooden mugs. He set these down, gave me a brief, curious look and a grin, then he scrambled back up the ladder again.

"My grandson Nill," Kuraf said, jerking her thumb upward. "Apparently you met my daughter this morning. In the Guard. Granddaughter, Kee, you'll meet anon."

I remembered the friendly young woman who'd helped me onto the horse when we first entered the city. It seemed a week ago.

Kuraf poured out gently steaming pear cider into the cups, pushed one toward me, then said: "You want to know what's toward. Here's the simple version." She paused to drink. "Lendan has taken Alezand. At least, he's got us while he holds his highness as hostage. We dare do nothing against him."

"Hlanan said something about you holding the city and Rajanas riding away. That was before he disappeared. The apple cider that they'd been drinking was full of liref," I added. "I gather that this two-faced Steward Kenned did that."

Kuraf pursed her lips. "Might have saved their lives, actually. I wonder if that's what he intended all along?"

"What? You mean, Kenned didn't sell them out?"

"He did indeed. But..." She frowned, staring into her cup. Then she blinked and shook her head. "Perhaps he'll have his chance to explain himself, in time. The matter at hand is more important: Lendan came himself to supervise. We need to figure out why."

Surprised, I said, "But isn't it obvious? I mean, if you are going to throw someone out of his home and take it over, it seems only practical to oversee it yourself."

"Maybe in the world of thieves. Not in the world of nobles and their games. Lendan is a kind of cousin to our prince. He would much prefer to appear to watching powers to be rescuing the situation, and holding it for his absent cousin—or dead cousin—after everything is settled."

"I don't understand," I said.

"Then let me put it more simply. Those mercenaries in the gray tunics with the hoods are the Wolf Grays of Thann, who some say were contracted by the King of Liacz—who has plenty of warriors of his own, though he is currently overreached—and the more disturbing rumor is that the contract was actually paid by Emperor Jardis Dhes-Andis of Sveran Djur."

"Isn't Sveran Djur a huge island somewhere in the western seas? Why would he want a bunch of soldiers here, paid or not?"

"Everyone knows he has designs on the fertile valleys between the mountains. Eventually he might even wish to challenge the empire, who knows? Back to our situation. They attack, and capture his highness, and hold Alezand. Lendan would then ride in leading a force wearing his colors, "defeat" them, and "hold" the land for his absent cousin. His friends at court know that he is in some wise allied with Dhes-Andis; his enemies at court also know that, but as he's here under a semblance of legality, they can do nothing overt without causing a war, unless his highness appears and asks for help. Apparently Lendan made a public show of friendliness and kinship while on the yacht. To all appearances, he is Alezand's ally."

"That makes sense so far," I said. "So why should it matter that Geric came early? Nobody but his toadies saw him—" I stopped.

"Except you," she said wryly. "And you got away."

"Oh," I said, remembering those two parties of searchers. I took a big swig of pear cider. It was delicious, with a touch of honey and ginger root.

"Then," she said, "there's the matter of what brought Prince Geric here early."

I remembered his words: *You must find the thief, kill him, and bring me whatever he carried . . .*

"Oh," I said again, choking on my cider. I set my cup down and blinked my watering eyes, to find Kuraf's shrewd gaze on me.

"And now we come to you," she said.

TWELVE

"Ah?" I croaked, wondering if she intended to kill me outright, or have me searched and *then* killed.

I sidled glances to either side, assessing my chances for escape as she leaned forward to tap one of her scarred hands on my knee.

"You have got to go directly to the capital and report to the Empress what has happened," Kuraf said calmly. "You have magic to aid you, you know the situation, and being Hrethan, you will even be granted an audience whereas none of us would ever pass the gate. Then, once you are there, you can be put in the way of finding your own folk. I know the Snow Folk do maintain an embassy in Erev-Li-Erval."

Sheer relief made me dizzier than twelve glasses of fermented cider could have. "Capital? Right. Most certainly," I said hastily, the stash under my tunic weighing against my flesh.

Kuraf gazed at me with her brows slightly raised and her mouth quirked. Instead of saying anything directly to me, though, she tipped her head back. "Kee!" she shouted.

"Right here," a young voice answered from just beyond the foliage overhead. "Heard everything."

"Good. Saves us some time," Kuraf said. And to me, "She'll see you safely there."

A rustling sounded overhead, then a figure swung down by a small branch, and—disdaining the ladder—dropped lightly in front of me.

I looked up, and found myself being surveyed critically by a pair of keen gray eyes under a crown of heavy pale blond braids. Kee was sturdily built, not yet fully grown. She had the rounded cheeks of a child, but those eyes were just like her grandmother's. As they studied me from scalp to toenails, their expression did not say Magic Person, but Thief.

Trying to remember what was proper, I said, "Well met."

"Well met," Kee replied politely, holding out her hand for a clasp. Her grip was strong, her palm callused.

"Show Lhind a bunk, see that she has what she needs, then you get some sleep. We will talk further in the morning, before you depart."

"This way," Kee said, waving toward the ladder.

She went before me, at a smart pace. I had to scramble fast to keep up —but keep up I did, even when she took off from a platform and scampered down a narrow branch to a smaller platform. I paused only to whip my tail free, and I followed easily, my balance as sure as if I'd been born running in trees.

The platform she led me to had three hammocks suspended from high branches, and three trunks lined one edge. The whole was lit by a lamp swinging high above the top hammock.

"Want some sleeping gear?" Kee asked.

"No. I sleep in my clothes," I said. "You're always ready to move that way."

She grunted, head cocked to one side consideringly. "True. Well, we'll do that on the road. Faster."

She flung her tunic off and pulled a long nightgown from one of the trunks, then she pulled herself into the highest bunk. Pausing to look over the side at me, she said, "Either of those is free tonight."

"Right," I said, catching hold of the bottom hammock. Before I could get into it, she blew the lamp out, and darkness closed on us.

I felt my way carefully into the hammock, feeling nervously aware of the platform's edge somewhere nearby. Once I was lying flat, though, with my stash arranged safely across my stomach, the hammock swung gently, and I stared up through the thick leaves toward the moon-silvered clouds sailing silently overhead. I had just enough time to register how peaceful it all was, then I fell heavily asleep.

I woke only once, when rain whispered through the leaves overhead. Somehow none fell on my face, and the soft sound put me right back to sleep.

When I woke up next, cool green light bathed the platform. I breathed deeply of the leaf-scented air, and swung out of the hammock onto my feet. I'd slept well, and felt more refreshed than I had in recent memory. Refreshed and even cheerful. Must be something about sleeping in trees, like the birds.

Don't you think so? I sent the thought toward Tir—but I did not find the bird's mental presence.

"Tir?" I said out loud, wondering if it was still asleep.

No answer.

"You awake?" Kee's head popped up from the other side of the platform. "Food's ready. Let's get going." Kee disappeared.

"Coming," I called, hastily looking around.

No one in view. I yanked up my tunic and untied my sash. My idea was to rearrange it more securely, until I could snag some better clothes for hiding things in.

But my gaze was caught by Princess Kressanthe's diamond necklace lying there in the jumble of tools, coins, and rings. I hadn't really looked at the thing since I'd pinched it. I stood staring at it now, a sense of vertigo tugging at my vision. I found it difficult to look away from the winking lights in the faceted stones. The longer I stared, the more distinct became the gut-curling sense of warning inside me.

I wrenched my gaze free by squeezing my eyes shut. I folded the sash, to hide them, the stones clicking against that bone carving with a sound like ice crunching against teeth.

My neck hair lifted, and I shook myself to get rid of the eerie sensation. Pretty as it was, I'd be glad to sell that loot and be rid of it.

I found the ladder going down, and soon had joined Kuraf, Kee, a grinning Nill and several others on the big platform. We ate an excellent hot meal of cakes and baked fruit, then Kuraf cleared everyone out but a tall, dark-haired young man, Kee, and myself.

Below, her followers gathered on the grassy turf, with targets set on the opposite side of a clearing. And there, in the dappled sunlight of early morning, they began practicing, some with swords, and some with quarterstaffs. Kuraf seated herself at the extreme end of the platform so she could watch them below, yet see me.

"We'll discuss your route," Kuraf said, "but first some straight talk, young Hrethan." Her eyes narrowed to points of cool gray scrutiny.

The tall young man moved to flank me, his hand on the hilt of a long knife. Sidling quick glances from side to side, I noticed at least two possible escape routes. Escape through the trees, that is. I wasn't about to take on all those drilling warriors below.

But trees were my old friends. I could move very fast in them.

I turned back to Kuraf, who said, "If a Hrethan has become a liar and thief there's a reason, and don't think I am unsympathetic. Howsomever. His highness's life depends not only on your speed, but on your completing the journey even if it's difficult. His cousin may not dare to kill him now, but that will last only until he's sure of his hold on Alezand. We're going to be spending our time harrying his forces, to keep that hold unsure—but we must know that someone goes to the capital. You agreed mighty quick last night, and you have not been Alezand's partisan."

"A blood-oath will get her there," the young man said quietly. "And will enable a sorcerer to trace her if she doesn't."

"Maybe so. Maybe so. But even for a good purpose, blood oaths are too close to blood magic, and I will not use such. Yes, I know they are legal, but there are different sorts of law, one might say. Though I bow my head to the old laws of the land, it is this law I obey first." She thumped a fist against her chest, glanced down at the warriors as the clack of sticks and the ring of steel echoed through the glade.

The young man flushed, made a gesture of peace by pressing his palms together, and sat back.

Kee crossed her arms, giving me a scornful glance; we were eye to eye, and it occurred to me that she assumed I was her age. "I can make it alone, Grandmother," she said. "I don't see the need for any of this. Or for *her*."

"You would make it," Kuraf confirmed. "But you'd never get into Erev-li-Erval."

"Try me," Kee retorted. "I can get into any city."

Kuraf smiled. "I make no doubt you could sneak in, child, but that is more likely to earn you a stretch in a dungeon than an audience with Aranu Crown. And you cannot risk speaking to any of the toadies who hold audiences for lesser folk: any of them could be under Lendan's pay, and you'd not know it beforehand."

"So he's part of the empire?" I asked. "He called himself a Prince of the Golden Circle. I've traveled a lot of places, but never heard of that land."

Kuraf called down, "You four, there. Archery now. The rest of you, keep drilling."

Then she turned back to me. "How much do you know about inheritance in the empire?"

"Nothing," I said, biting back a *And I have less interest.*

Her smile increased briefly as if she could read my mind. Below, arrows twanged. "Did you know that the emperors and empresses choose their heirs?"

I shrugged.

"In some lands, it's the eldest child. In the empire of Charas al Kherval, for the past couple of centuries, the ruler chooses whoever he or she thinks is best suited. Usually, but not always, among their own children. The ones unchosen were given the title 'Imperial Prince or Princess of the Golden Circle,' which doesn't come with any land or holdings, but means they had precedence directly after the rulers at court."

I gazed in surprise. "So Geric Lendan is the empress's son?"

"No, he's descended, third generation, from a prince who was not chosen. Now, as the generations went by, the sons and daughters of the Imperial Princes and Princesses of the Golden Circle were also called Princes and Princesses of the Golden Circle. Not *Imperial* Princes and Princesses, which meant they still had precedence over dukes and the rest, but behind their parents. Unfortunately, as you might imagine, by that third generation there were rather a lot of Princesses and Princes of the Golden Circle cluttering up court, which was fine, but some of 'em inherited a sense of privilege along with their fancy titles, and no sense of service. Unlike the rest of court."

"All right, so back to Geric Lendan," I said, as arrows thudded into the targets below.

"I'm coming to him. So Aranu Crown, who spent a lot of time among privileged, spoilt Golden Circle princes before she came to the throne, decreed almost first thing after she put on the imperial crown that henceforth, the Golden Circle will be reserved only for the empress's children who are not chosen as heir. And their children will carry no titles, unless they marry them."

"So Geric Lendan is not really a prince?"

"Oh, he's a prince, but he's the last generation who will have that title, outside of Aranu Crown's own children. Any children he has—and I find that a daunting thought—won't inherit land or title. Unless he annexes land. So that's what he's trying to do."

Thud! Was this display an everyday occurrence, or a hint?

"Now. To you." Kuraf's hand waved between me and the dour young man. "My son wants your oath. But as I said, I mislike forced oaths, with or without magic. I ask you, therefore, to tell us now: do you go to the capital, or shall we give you your freedom and food for a day's march?"

I hadn't really thought of the future. That was not my habit. I had always dealt with each situation as it arose, with my independence of foremost importance. On the other hand, conflicting feelings pulled me toward the promise. I did not like the idea of Hlanan and Thianra captive, and I resented the contempt in Kee's face; amid the cloud of strong, but unidentifiable, feelings drawing me toward a yes was a distinct desire to make her admit she was wrong to judge me.

So I said, "The capital is where I'd find my folk, they told me. I guess I'd be going there anyway. Why not combine it with your errand?"

"There will be danger on this venture," Kuraf said. "Geric Lendan will have all roads east watched."

"I've seen danger once or twice," I put in.

Kuraf smiled. "Yes, I'll wager you have." Her brows rose, and her face eased a little. "Then there's an end to it," she said. "Come here, you two. Let's discuss your route."

Her son grunted, and crossed to a low carved chest. He opened it, drew out a rolled paper, and spread it carefully on the table before Kuraf.

"Here we are," Kuraf said, pointing to a mountain area with letters carefully painted on it. "And, to the east, Namas Ilan—" She frowned up at me. "Can you read?"

I shook my head.

"I have the map by memory," Kee said shortly. "Erev-Li-Erval lies east. Which road is best?"

"None of the eastern ones," the son said. "Lendan will have spies on every road. You'll go west at first. You don't want to go south to Keprima."

I shook my head, remembering the disaster at that inn. I still had no idea who "she" was who had paid for us to be attacked.

"You'll have to get down to Letarj, and sail north," he said at last. "Then cross through Liacz—"

"But that land is very warlike, Uncle Coran," Kee protested.

"Most of Liacz's warriors seem to be south of their border these days. If you are circumspect, you ought to be fine. The most important thing is, that route will be unexpected, lessening the chance of your being hunted by any of these contract soldiers in gray. Cross the mountains, drop southward and enter the capital from that side."

"That will add weeks to our journey," Kee said.

"Not as much as you'd think. The sailing is a matter of days, and by crossing the Kertean Mountains in the north, you avoid having to cross the Anadhan range, which is much fiercer."

"And no one can hide in the plains," Kuraf added. "You must make haste. But we will do our best not to allow Lendan the leisure to plot pursuit, I promise you that." She turned to me. "Questions, Hrethan?"

"What about Thianra and Hlanan?"

"We will try to rescue them, of course," she said. "If we hear any word. But Lendan has little use for a scribe or a minstrel." She shrugged.

Lest I think that a good thing, the dour-faced son rumbled, "If he hasn't killed them outright, we'll spring 'em."

Hlanan—Thianra—killed? The idea hurt so much that I was taken aback.

"We know they can take care of themselves. We shall act as if they have." Kuraf folded her map with a quick gesture. "Anything else?"

"Only this," I said, pointing to the green silken tunic Hlanan had given me the day before. "Feels good to wear, but I don't want to travel in it—"

"I'll trade you!" A moment later Nill, who'd obviously been listening from above, dropped down onto our platform, holding out a homespun tunic that laced up the front. "Take this. I'm almost grown out of it."

"It's a swap," I said.

Nill grinned, plainly thinking he was getting the best of the bargain.

Kuraf descended the ladder with the agility of a much younger person, and began lecturing her archers as I changed.

A short time later I watched Nill carry the silk up the ladder again, feeling an odd hollowness inside. Was this regret? I laughed at myself for this sudden and unwanted wish to burden myself with wardrobe just because something had been a gift. Or maybe it hadn't even been a gift, just something someone had left behind, and Hlanan had brought it because everyone else was busy.

Face the truth, I told myself. *Hlanan had been kind because it is his nature to be kind. It had nothing to do with you.* The surprise was my discovering that what he thought of me actually mattered. No, this couldn't possibly be the silly sickness coming on me. He was just a scribe, an ordinary fellow with ordinary brown eyes and brown hair, and a very nosy manner.

Kuraf turned away from her archers and called, "Those packs ready, Nill?"

"Coming," Nill shouted down.

"Let's go find your mounts," Kuraf said to Kee and me.

A short time later we rode away on the backs of long-haired, short-legged hill ponies. Each of us carried a saddlebag full of journey-food, and a flask for water. They'd also given me a heavy brown cloak. Kee wore a long knife at her side, twin to her uncle's. They hadn't asked if I needed a weapon, and I didn't mention the knife in my waistband.

Kee took command of our expedition from the start. "This way," she said when we departed, and she led her pony up a difficult trail out of that valley. The huge trees were very soon out of sight—and within a short time I had lost the valley as well.

Our trip around the side of the mountain was largely made in silence. I was happy enough for it to be so. The higher we rode, the happier I became: the air, crisp as new wine, the light pouring clear and blue down the mountainside, gradually deepening in shades of green, violet, and then a thousand shades of gray and black as the stars emerged so bright overhead I could have reached up to pluck them. And in the morning, the sunlight spilled, yellow as fresh-churned butter, over the distant peaks, gradually striking fiery glints in striated levels of multi-colored rock thrust up at slanting angles, some covered by growth, and some not.

That first morning, as we set out, Kee looked around, then said softly, "They say Charas-al-Kherval, the imperial city, is just like that.

"Is it in the mountains, then?" I asked. "I'd love to see that."

She gave me a quick look, her expression closing over, as if she regretted the friendly words.

Once again she sank into silence. So I turned my attention to the birds spiraling upward, the new and ancient rockslides, sudden springs and waterfalls, and the quick dash of long-legged animals of varieties I did not recognize.

"I'm thirsty," I said. "Shall we stop at one of these springs?"

For answer Kee looked around, then led us to a path under a rocky outcropping over which fell a trickling waterfall. Leaning out to catch water in my hands, I drank my fill. Kee knelt silently at the side of the bubbling stream and drank, then she stood aside while the mounts slurped noisily at the water.

When they were done, she mounted wordlessly and clucked at her pony to pick up its pace. I tried again once we'd reached a long downward slope that afforded us a view of gentle hills and wide valleys.

"Where are we?" I asked. "I'm lost."

"South," she said over her shoulder. "In Forfar."

"That I guessed, but where exactly?"

"That mountain back there marks the border between Zhin and Forfar."

"So we're not anywhere near Imbradi?"

"We are west of it," she said. Not surly, not friendly. Just— flat.

"So when will we reach Letarj?"

"If we reach the border by tomorrow tonight—that's the river Fara—we should make it to the harbor in three days."

"Do we have to go all the way down to Letarj?" I asked, recalling the lines on the map, and trying to calculate distance in my head. "I know it's a big harbor, but wouldn't it be quicker to follow the Fara and find some kind of transport at Fara Bay?"

She snorted. "Obviously you know nothing about Fara Bay," she said. "It's a terrible place, a pirates' haven."

She kicked her pony into a trot, and that was that.

I jolted along behind her, never quite catching up. The scenery changed slowly to a sameness of low brush and occasional copses of spreading oak. Twice gazelles sprang gracefully across our path, running toward the dark line of forest to the east. Kee kept her eyes forward and her mouth closed.

So I decided to use this opportunity to practice shimmers. I'd never been able to make them while doing something else—like moving—and my recent adventures had shown me that I needed them most when I was on the run. So I sat squarely on my pony, tried to shut out the grassy hillside moving slowly past, and made rainbow bubbles.

Two things startled me, making the bubbles blink into nothingness.

One: the colors were brighter and the sizes much bigger than I had intended, which was something I'd never experienced.

And two: something at my waist glowed warmly, like a shaft of sunlight through glass. Casting a distracted glance at Kee, whose back was squarely to me, I yanked my tunic up and pulled out my stash. I ran my fingers through the loot until they discovered a fading warmth in the diamond stones of Kressanthe's necklace.

I pulled them free and held them up against the sky. The half-circle of stones swung glittering from my fingers, the colors dancing in a curiously compelling way. It took an effort to pull my gaze away. I slipped the thing about my wrist and made another shimmer—and the stones against my wrist warmed.

I held the necklace up. Deep within each of the gems on the sides of the central big one colors darted, like crazed fireflies. The big one—the one you'd expect to throw the most rainbows of light—shone steadily like a prism on a cloudy day. Except the center, in which gleamed a tiny pinpoint of blue, almost like an eye.

As I watched the blue faded out. When I made more bubbles, the blue leaped into life, burned coolly and bright, then dwindled out.

So I tried a big shimmer, almost as big as that fake ship I'd made to scare away the Skull Fleet from Rajanas's yacht. A thousand butterflies swooped against the sky, all colors from pale lemon to velvet-black.

The pony took one look and shied, snorting fiercely.

I tried to catch myself, but the pony was too fast. I found myself looping through the air, the wind whistling past my ears. Instinct made me curl up in a ball. When I landed I somersaulted a ways down the path, coming to a stop in a prickly bush.

Fast hooves thumped near, stopped, and Kee's head blotted out the dizzily circling sky. "Are you all right? What happ—" Her breath caught, her gaze on something near my head.

I turned, saw the diamonds blazing with color a hand-span from my nose.

"What's that?" she breathed.

"Necklace," I muttered.

Her mouth opened, then her gaze hardened. "Oh. I see. Something you stole, no doubt?"

"What do you know about it?" I muttered, getting to my feet and trying to dust myself off. My limbs trembled like water had replaced my bones, but otherwise I was unhurt.

"Nothing. And I don't want to," she said. "I just know I'd rather starve than steal." And when I said nothing, she added flatly, "I'll fetch your pony."

She rode a little ways off, and I walked slowly down the path. My mood of experimentation had given over to a vast, angry discontent. Why was I here anyway? I didn't need this sniff-nosed girl, or her thorn-tongued prince either, for that matter. What's to keep me from cutting and running, I thought irritably as I restored the necklace to the sash, and made sure Nill's thick brown tunic was pulled well over it.

I stopped, and scanned the eastern horizon longingly.

Thus I spotted the speck against the sky a moment before a panic-driven mental flash blasted its way into my mind. *Slavers, the slavers will have Hlanan. You must go fast,* Tir's cry ripped through my aching head.

And both ponies shied when Tir swooped out of the sky, cawing in distress.

THIRTEEN

"The Scribe's aidlar," Kee cried, struggling to regain control of both ponies.

I ran to catch the dragging reins of my mount. Tir flapped about my head, cawing in distress. *Slavers! Slavers!* Tir's panic stabbed into my mind again and again. Frightened by the bird, the snorting pony reared, and Kee hovered nearby demanding to know what was wrong.

I dropped the reins and clapped my hands over my ears. "Tir! Kee! Wait a moment," I yelped.

Kee clamped her mouth shut and once again got the ponies under control. Tir sailed close by, settling onto a boulder. The ruby eyes jerked back and forth agitatedly. I sat down in the middle of the road, drew a deep breath, then said, "All right."

"What—" Kee started.

I raised a hand. "Tir's got a message for me. I can't hear *anything* else while I'm getting it."

Kee blinked, her eyes going round with surprise, but she kept her lips closed.

At once Tir's thought speared into my mind, and I saw a distorted, color-drained memory-view of Geric Lendan facing several humans in unfamiliar dress. On the floor lay Hlanan, unconscious, bound by rope.

The smiling prince spoke. *Take him at once. You can get him safely to Fara Bay before he regains his wits, if you keep him dosed with liref.*

The bird's image ended with the two men reaching for Hlanan's limp body.

"Slavers!" the bird squawked.

Kee said, "What is it?"

"I'm not sure," I said. "Tir saw something nasty concerning Hlanan." And I described the bird's memory-image.

When I was done, Kee frowned. "Were those men dressed in brown, short jackets, long boots? Pointed steel hats?"

"That's it," I acknowledged, nodding.

"Then Tir is right." She scowled. "Those men are agents for Fara's ruler, who not only sells all their criminals to Shinjans for use in their galleys, but will take—for an enormous fee—criminals from neighboring lands. They require official verification of the crimes, but," she enunciated with disgust, "that's somehow always easy to provide."

"Does Rajanas get rid of his troublemakers that way?"

"No," she said. "Nor does he trade with Fara. His grandfather used to, but that was one promise his highness made to us when Grandmother helped him regain the throne. Not that he wasn't already against them. Few know it, but he and the Scribe were on one of those galleys," she finished in a low voice. "I think..." She cast a quick glance at the aidlar, then shook her head.

But Tir shrieked on a high, terrible note. "Slavers! Kill!"

Kee sighed, her shoulders jerking up and down. "Then Tir already knows."

"Knows what?" I demanded.

"The Shinjans always put a tattoo on their galley-slaves. If any escape, and are later recaptured, that mark earns them an instant death." She looked very much like her grandmother as she added flatly, "A convenient way for Lendan, accursed be his name, to get the Scribe killed without being directly associated."

Tir flew up again, sailing back and forth before me. A barrage of images and words bombarded my mind until I forced that inner-eyelid down, and closed them out. At once the bird went into a frenzy, squawking and cawing.

"What is wrong?" Kee yelled.

"Wants us to rescue him," I cried back.

"But we can't," she said. "We have to get to Letarj, we promised—"

"WAIT!" I yelled my loudest. "Let me think," I added more normally, as Tir and Kee both fell silent.

My first thought was not about the problem at hand, but about Tir. I wondered if the creature had ever rested; it must have flown off directly from seeing me safely in Kuraf's tree hideout to Imbradi, to find Hlanan, and then from there to find me.

I remembered the vow the bird had made aboard Rajanas's ship. A vow of loyalty to my kind. But its feeling for Hlanan was much stronger. This sense came through very clearly.

This feeling the aidlar had for the Scribe was very close to the very emotions I so despised. Distrusted. Only wasn't this bird demonstrating the very essence of trust?

Lhind help, Lhind help!

I'll help, I'll help, I thought to the agitated bird.

But how? Short of magic—

"Magic." I rubbed my eyes. "Of course! Why didn't I think of it before?"

"We can't turn from our mission—"

"We can if it will speed us," I said.

"What?" she replied shortly, not hiding her suspicion.

"Hlanan is a magician of sorts. He got us from wherever it was we'd been ambushed, to Imbradi, with some kind of spell," I said, remembering the old woman who'd helped him to shift us from the river all the way to Imbradi. "*Transportation* magic. Wouldn't it save us lots of time if we went straight from Fara Bay to Erev-Li-Erval in an instant?"

Kee chewed a knuckle, her brow creased with thought. "Fara Bay is dangerous," she said. "Some say that they even allow pirates to trade there."

"Tir will find him for us," I said, "so we won't have to search. We just get in. Stay hidden until we reach him. I'm good at that. And as for danger, it seems to me we're going to find it anywhere we go. If you want to turn back..."

Her cheeks reddened and her chin lifted. "I will not turn back."

"So let's rescue Hlanan, and travel by magic. Everybody gets what they want that way."

She brought her chin down in a decisive nod. "All right." She shot a glance at the bird, hesitated, then clamped her lips shut on whatever she'd been about to say.

"Hear that, Tir? We'll get him out, but you have to find him for us. Soon as you can."

The aidlar flooded my mind with a bright splash of joy that sent tingles through me to my fingertips, then it sped off, soon to disappear against the clouds forming on the horizon.

Kee mounted her pony, then wheeled it toward the west. "The bay is this way," she said.

By nightfall we were riding in a slashing downpour. This didn't much bother me, but Kee's face in the sporadic flashes of lightning was pale and miserable. When I offered to find shelter so we could wait out the storm she spurned the idea with a curt "No."

I stopped talking, mentally resigning myself to an unpleasant journey unless Hlanan could get us to the capital fast. For something to do, I went back to trying shimmers, this time experimenting with wind.

My ready magic knowledge was limited to shimmers, and wind pushing, and the ones Hlanan had called Voice-cast and Mind-cast. Each of those last two I'd discovered in dire situations: the first when I was about to lose my life, and the second, one terrible day in Thesreve. They scared me too much to try practicing them. Easier to harness a hurricane.

But wind-pushing was easy, if impractical for much besides blowing out inconvenient candles. I couldn't cause much breeze—hardly more than a stir—and it didn't go much farther than I could toss a heavy stone. Still, it was this one that I tried now, aiming the push somewhere right over Kee's head, so the wind drove the rain either in front of her or behind. It was hard to keep it up, and my aim wasn't always good (for I had to aim each push), but after a time I not only noticed that it was slightly easier to aim, my pushes had more force.

Then I became aware of a steady, warm glow from the necklace.

The impulse to put the necklace on was purely for the heat. The air had grown steadily more chill, and although I much prefer cold to hot, and indeed rarely feel cold as long as my fuzz was dry, being soaked to the skin makes me feel chilled after long enough. And wet chill isn't comfortable for anybody, excepting maybe fish and sea serpents.

So I pulled the necklace free. Though the day was gloomy, the necklace sparkled with inner lights, almost as if eyes twinkled and blinked. I fixed it around my neck. The big diamond settled between my collarbones, an eerily perfect fit. Then I made my push.

Whoosh! The rain parted like a curtain for an instant, and I almost fell off my pony.

Do not be afraid, a voice said in my head. *I am helping your focus.*

What? Who? Only my experiences with Tir's mind-contacts kept me from squawking out loud.

I, Faryana. I am prisoned in the stone you wear. Usually I can only sense the emotions of the wearer. Your thoughts, when you make your magic, come clearly, and I have aided you as you cause no harm. Who are you?

Lhind, I thought cautiously.

Why do you fear to tell me? I cannot harm you. But perhaps I can help. And there came a projected image.

Instinct made me close down the inner eyelid. At the same time, a gasp from Kee brought me back to the here-and-now. The rain, no longer diverted, poured down on her in a sudden deluge. I flung up my hands and made the breeze again, scarcely comprehending as Kee looked around in mute misery.

Then I looked again at the image the woman had sent.

Faryana was small, wearing a draped cloth over her smooth dark blue fur. Her hair flowed around her head like water, sweeping down her back into a long midnight blue tail. Her eyes were a dark blue, same color as her hair.

SHERWOOD SMITH

She was a Hrethan—but she was different from me.

My breeze faded and I made another. Warmth spread from the stone swinging against my breastbone, and I glanced down into a fierce blue light.

Cautiously opening the mental barrier again, Faryana's thought flowed in, hurt and confused. *You do not trust the Hrethan?* she thought sadly. *I promise you I will not harm you.*

No, it's not that. It's just that I, ah, feel safer keeping my secrets. How did you get into that stone? I asked.

I was trapped by a young sorcerer named Geric Lendan, came the answer. *I was newly appointed guardian of a Protection, which he tried to take from me. When I circumvented him by hiding it he tricked me with lies and forced me into this shape until such time as I release the Protection into his control.*

That's nasty, I replied. *So you've also tangled with that yellow-haired swamp-fouler! But how did your necklace get into that pickle-faced Kressanthe's keeping? Don't tell me she pinched it?* I smothered a laugh at the thought of that princess turning thief.

Geric wore these stones for a time, to gloat and to weaken my resolve. When he tired of that, he gave me into the keeping of this princess you mentioned, knowing that the constant barrage of her ill-natured, angry and greedy emotions would also work against me.

Now I understood Geric's command to that soldier concerning me and whatever I carried.

So you're the guardian of something important, eh? I asked. *How can we get you out?*

Geric has the key to the enchantment binding me.

A real key? Or—

It is a figurative image only. You can bind together the spells that form an enchantment with anything: words, or an object, or even a time that is to come.

I plunged my fingers into my sash, and plucked out the bone-whistle. Holding it up against the stone, I thought: *Is it this thing?*

I do not know. Her distress was clear. *But I sense great power and greater danger in whatever object you brought near. It has touched my prison much in recent time, causing me terrible dreams.*

I thought of the necklace and whistle rattling among my stash since I left Rajanas's palace, but I didn't want to tell her— yet— that she'd been nipped by a thief.

So you dream when you aren't worn? I asked instead, as I slipped the whistle back into my sash.

I do.

"This looks like a good cave," Kee's voice broke into my conversation. "Darkness is falling, so we cannot go farther. I must admit I mislike the way the rain comes and goes so suddenly. It's very uncanny."

I looked around. Our trail had led us downward into a valley between two rocky hills. All around us scrubby trees and bushes grew, the trees all too narrow to afford much in the way of shelter.

Kee urged her pony under a rocky overhang carved by an ancient river. Now only a run-off stream burbled and raced down one side of the cliff and away. Kee dismounted. I followed.

For a time no one spoke as we cared for the ponies, Kee demonstrating and me copying whatever she did. When they were as comfortable as we could make them, drinking thirstily from the stream, we felt our way farther into the cave.

It wasn't very deep, just round, with layers of stone carved over the centuries by rushing water. Here on the dry rocky ground we found the remains of an old campfire, and some dry brush stacked. Kee had brought a sparker, so we soon had a small fire going. Kee changed her tunic and spread her wet one over a boulder to dry, then she crouched over the fire for warmth, closing her eyes against the acrid smoke rising from the brush.

I knew I'd be dry enough by morning, and the air was not really cold. It was I who brought out the flatbread and cheese we'd been given, sharing it out equally. Kee ate hers in silence, then she curled up in the wrinkled cloak she'd stuffed in her pack, and her breathing deepened into sleep.

Eating did not tire me. Quite the opposite. When I finished my share of the food, I felt restless. The steady rain discouraged me from going out and exploring. Finally I decided to examine my stash more closely.

SHERWOOD SMITH

First I took the necklace off. When I laid it aside, the stones faded to cold, glassy dullness, and the little blue light was gone.

Then I took the bone whistle from my sash, and turned it over and over in my hands. It was a pale, grayish white, very thin, about as long as my shortest finger. A bird bone? Or the bone of another creature carefully hollowed?

The idea disturbed me, even though I knew the creature whose bone it was no longer felt the lack. What kind of magic required a portion of a once-living being?

Dark arts. I remembered Hlanan using this term several times. Could these arts be any worse than the "justices" of Thesreve burning people who had done little bits of magic, whatever the kind?

I looked at the bone, studying the odd marks scratched into it and trying to make sense of my instinctive revulsion and wariness. I'd finally left the wolves because of the piles of fresh bones that regularly appeared outside our cave after the wolves went on a run; it was entirely a natural thing for them, but it never was for me.

So what was the purpose of this bone whistle?

I put it to my lips and blew lightly through it. The wind it made was an unmusical whisper, a soft hiss like dead leaves on ice. It was not a loud sound, but on the other side of the campfire Kee stirred, murmured fretfully, then sank back into sleep.

Nothing else happened.

So I put it up to my forehead—

And a voice said inside my head, *Lendan? Why have you disturbed me?*

I yanked the whistle away. Another prisoner in a magical object? I looked down at the whistle in surprise. Well, why not pursue this? Good or bad though they might be, I could hardly be harmed by somebody in a whistle. So I touched it to my forehead again, and the voice came: *You are not Lendan.*

Did Geric stick you in an enchantment, too? I responded.

For a moment I heard nothing. The silence was strange, a blank wall. Then the voice was back. *Who are you?* Its tone was curious, and amused. Very different from Faryana.

Who are YOU? I returned. *Besides a prisoner in a whistle.*

A sorcerer, came the answer. This time the amusement was more pronounced. *I take it you are one as well.*

Maybe, I thought, enjoying the sense of challenge this voice caused. *One thing I will tell you, I pinched you away from G—*

Before I could finish thinking Geric's name, a stab of pain lanced into my head. My inner eyelid shut down hard and I could neither think words at the voice nor hear it thinking to me.

Once again I yanked the whistle away, rubbing my fingers against my head. What was *that?* Nothing had changed in our cave. The rain poured steadily, Kee slept on, and nothing had dropped on me or leaped out in threat.

I put the whistle back to my head. *If that trick was you, it wasn't funny. I'll throw you away and not free you if you try it again.*

It was just a small identity spell, came the prompt reply, in a respectful tone. *I won't attempt it again since you are capable of warding.*

The shift in tone warmed me considerably. Before I'd sensed that—despite being a prisoner—the person in the whistle had been laughing at me. There was no laughter now.

You wouldn't tell me who you are, it explained.

I'm Lhind, I replied. *And that's all you need to know right now—except I don't mean you any harm. I'm not a conceited, cheating swanker like that Geric. So who are you?*

After the slightest pause, the voice replied: *Jardis Dhes-Andis.*

FOURTEEN

*H*oo! I thought.

That is, if this person is telling the truth.

How'd he get you into a whistle? I asked. *I thought you were supposed to be the most powerful sorcerer-king around these days.*

Very distinct amusement permeated the answer: *I will tell you when we meet.*

So you want me to get you out? I asked.

I don't think you can reach me, was the reply. *You don't have enough skill.*

I was about to slam back a fairly hot reply when the voice added thoughtfully, *But perhaps I could teach you. After all, you are handling this method of discourse with admirable ease, and I understand it is difficult for most people. It certainly was for young Lendan.*

I chortled. *Well, I do know a few tricks, and nobody taught me those. So maybe I'm not as unskilled as you think.*

Perhaps, came a gratifyingly surprised reaction. *What can you do?*

I was just about to launch into a description when a belated sense of prudence stopped me. I studied the whistle in the reddish light of the flames. It wasn't that the voice—Dhes-Andis or not—had scared me. I'd scared myself. Until recently, I'd exerted my strength and wits toward keeping my secrets hidden. Then Hlanan exposed them, catching me in a trap that I should have been on the watch for. I'd relaxed my usual vigilance because I'd come to trust him.

Now here I was, all ready to give everything away, and this time there was no trap and certainly no trust, except the sort of trust one gives to the boundaries when someone, enemy—or not—is caged. I'd been ready to give all my secrets away just to show off, to wipe out the laughter that seemed to be aimed not at the situation, but at me.

Did I really have the mighty and feared emperor of Sveran Djur, a land more terrible even than Shinja (which paid him tribute), in this whistle?

On impulse, I put it back to my head. *How do I know you are really Dhes-Andis?*

You don't, came the reply. *When you have need of greater skill, come to me.*

And then I sensed that black wall again. The person—I may as well use the name Dhes-Andis—had used his own inner eyelid, and had shut me out.

I dropped the whistle into my sash and reached for the necklace. I clasped it around my neck, made a shimmer, and when I saw the faint blue glow within the big stone, I thought: *Faryana?*

I am here, Lhind. Her 'voice' was cool and silvery and seemed tiny compared to the sense of vastness that had come from the person in the whistle.

What would you say if I told you that I've got Dhes-Andis imprisoned in that other object I showed you before?

Distress flowed from her mind. *Do not use it! Do not even communicate with it!*

It might not even be him, I scoffed. *I've pretended to be all kinds of people, and I've sure seen plenty of fakes.*

Anyone who would even make such a claim is too dangerous to be treated with, except by a member of the Council. You MUST surrender that object to a magician, as soon as possible—

Annoyed, I shut my inner eyelid, finding this easier to do each time I tried it. Then I yanked the necklace off and stuffed it into my sash. At least whoever was in the whistle had not yelled a lot of unasked-for commands at me. Faryana was a mite bossy for someone who'd gotten herself popped into a stone.

Arranging the objects carefully inside my clothing, I made sure they didn't touch, nor did they show. I set my sash on a rock for binding round my hair come morning, and resettled the rest of my take in my clothes. Even though Kuraf had given me that fine pack, old habit made me more comfortable hiding the take in my clothes.

Then I settled down to rest.

"That's the harbor," Kee said late the next afternoon.

We'd ridden steadily all day, making our way downhill through gentler hills. Our westward path took us in and out of great patches of forest. Kee had her hand on her knife hilt, her eyes scanning continuously, though no one disturbed us.

We stayed well off the main roads. Kee led us cross-country, and when we heard the sounds of anyone coming, we concealed ourselves behind trees or shrubs until they passed.

At length we sat aside our tired ponies atop a small rise, looking westward at a great bowl carved out of the coast. Fara Harbor was busy with a forest of masts, dotted here and there with many-colored sails as ships moved in and out.

"I think we should spend the night up here and ride in tomorrow," she said. "We will not sleep undisturbed anywhere near that place."

I didn't tell her that I could sleep in peace anywhere, once I'd found a secure hole. It was not the time to remind her that I was a thief well accustomed to crowded, sometimes villainous surroundings. I said only, "I hope Tir will be able to find us."

I needn't have worried.

We sheltered for the night under a close-growing shrub, and when we crawled out early the next morning, the aidlar was sitting on a mossy boulder nearby, preening itself.

As I looked at the bird I had a fleeting memory of a white shape drifting, questing, through my dreams. Was that how Tir had found me? The answer caused a sense of disquiet. Until this adventure I'd always felt securely locked inside my own head, but for the first time, that was no longer true. If a bird could locate someone this way, might not a human be able to? A human who the someone might not want to be located by? *I shall have to practice closing that inner eyelid before I go to sleep at night, and see if it works.*

Tir stretched its black-tipped wings and croaked a welcome. "Come! Come! Today!" And with the words came a vivid mental picture of a red-sailed ship being readied for departure.

"We've got to ride fast," I said to Kee.

She gave a short nod. "I'll get the ponies."

We were soon on the road. The hill ponies are strong and sturdy for mountain trails, but they don't run fast or for long. We kept them at a steady pace, and I scanned mentally back and forth until at last I found some running horses. They were curious and willing, so I yelled for Kee to stop.

She was considerably startled by the sight of a herd of horses pounding toward us from across a long field, but I didn't explain. As usual I had to fight the dizziness that comes whenever I do mental-travel at the same time as I'm moving. "These horses'll run us to the harbor," I said, husky as I fought the nausea caused by vertigo. "We can send the ponies homeward."

Overhead, Tir screeched exhortations to hurry.

Kee silently worked with me to exchange the saddles, but I noticed a frown between her straight brows. We soon cantered over the low hills, grasses and flowers of spring flashing by underfoot.

It wasn't until we'd begun to pass occasional villages and farmhouses that we slowed somewhat. Fences crossing the countryside forced us to seek a road, which soon brought us into traffic. When we saw riders we slowed to a sedate pace, waiting until they were well past to resume our headlong flight.

During one of these times Kee turned that frown in my direction. "You can bring animals under your will, is that it?"

I shrugged. "Sort of."

"Have you forced creatures into thievery?"

I blinked. "Have I what?"

"Animals don't steal, except to eat," she said, still with that watchful frown. "I suppose it must be easier to use them—"

"Here. Let's understand one another," I interrupted. "When I call to animals, they come if they want to. And if they don't, I don't make them. I don't even know if I could." I snorted. "And I never used animals to get stuff, except maybe a few times when I was little, and wasn't too good yet. But that, too, was just for eating. Birds to knock down nuts and fruit. That kind of thing. All my stealing I do on my own. No help from anyone."

"Morals?" she asked, her mouth curving in irony.

"Sport," I said, matching tone for tone.

Her mouth thinned as an angry flush darkened her cheeks, then her eyes widened. "I guess I deserved that," she said reluctantly, if no more friendly. "I apologize for passing judgment."

I was sorely tempted to say *Right, you shouldn't*, but I was aware that I pass judgments all the time. You have to, to size up whether someone is an enemy or not. The difference is that I usually don't mouth it out, expecting the world either to concur or to change to fit my ideals.

Still, I could see that it had cost her some effort to make this admission, so I just shrugged again and said, "Come on, we've got a scribe-mage to rescue."

Tir gave a long, ear-scraping shriek. Our horses sidled, and began once more to gallop.

Fara Bay made Stormborn Harbor in Thesreve look prosperous, peaceful and orderly. The better part of the city sat along the outskirts, around the rim of the natural valley. We passed by small, formidably built-up castles, most of them flying an array of flags.

"They boast their allies," Kee said, pointing up at the gate of one castle. We counted twelve different devices hanging on the wall over the gate. Between these were rotting heads stuck on poles. "The large number of allies is supposed to serve as a warning to any attackers," she said.

"Those heads would work for me," I said, looking away from a fairly fresh one with thousands of black flies circling about. My stomach clenched inside me.

"That's what they do to criminals," Kee said, looking angry. "A criminal being someone who has committed such crimes as stealing bread, or not getting a fully-laden cart out of the way of a galloping lord. To enemies, they—"

"I don't think I want to know," I said. "Seeing as we're about to attack one of their haunts in the port."

Kee laughed and shook her head. "In truth, I have no taste for the ways of this land. But I think it better to be warned."

"I don't know about that," I muttered.

We passed down the road, the steel-helmeted warriors watching us. They were everywhere now, wearing different House badges but much the same sort of gear. Like the unfortunates who lived in this land, we drew aside and let them pass. Several times we were appraised from head to toe by unfriendly glances, but we were not stopped.

I figured we were too dusty and mud-spattered and uninteresting to bother searching. Kee'd braided her hair and stuffed it down the back of her plain homespun tunic, so she looked like neither boy nor girl, her age impossible to guess— and as for me, I'd bound the mud-streaked sash securely round my head when I woke up, and I'd also turned my trousers around and hid my tail once again.

The poor folk we saw were ragged and thin. The local citizens who stopped their work and stared at us seemed think us something exotic, as if they saw travelers outside their area only seldom.

Not surprising, I thought grimly as I looked around. Anyone coming through here would have to be on business— probably something sinister.

The houses built up close by the fortresses were scarcely more than hovels. No one but the lords owned land. The people worked land in exchange for protection, Kee told me in a low voice as we passed between villages. Not that they were much protected, because the most frequent pastime of the great lords was to make war on one another, wars that often involved burning one another's towns and crops.

We knew we'd reached Fara Bay at last when the villages gave way to narrow, winding streets between rows of crowded buildings. The houses were poor and filthy, the ragged locals even more pitiful. Quite a contrast to brightly dressed bullies belonging to the various ships who swaggered about looking for entertainment. The smells were nearly overpowering. It was obvious local taxes were not wasted on the guild that wands away animal droppings.

Tir's crest ruffled, and the bird made stressful murmling noises from time to time, but it never left my shoulder. Not even when a drunken sailor made a snatch at it, roaring something about "Worth a few coppers."

When we reached the streets adjacent to the docks the locals eyed us, and our horses, with a kind of speculation I immediately recognized. I gave them back stare for stare, and usually the glances sidled away. Kee sat silently, her hand on the hilt of her knife, her expression stony.

Then Tir flapped and danced on my shoulder. *Hlanan near, Hlanan near*! The frantic stream of images while I was moving made me so dizzy I nearly fell off the horse; I clapped my hands over my eyes, barely aware of Kee catching the reins of my horse and bringing us to a halt.

I closed the inner eyelid so I could regain my balance, then cautiously opened my eyes. We'd stopped in a small courtyard surrounded by tiny hovels thrown up every which way, mostly of broken and weathered wood, mud, old sail and other oil-slimed detritus fished up from the waters. No one was in view, but I felt unfriendly eyes scanning us, which made me twitchy.

I tried a shimmer: on the street where we'd just come, I made a squad of those steel-topped warriors appear. From behind the dilapidated walls came the sounds of sudden scrabblings as the watchers made a fast retreat.

"There," I said. "Maybe we've got a bit of time."

"What was that?" Kee asked slowly.

"Shim—ah, illusion magic," I said. "Nothing real. You'll have to get used to it, because we'll probably have to count on it to get Hlanan free."

She flushed right up to her dirty hairline.

I turned my eyes to the aidlar. *Where's Hlanan?*

Inside human-building.

Tir projected an image. Seen from above, I identified the kind of house toughest to break into. It was a few streets over, well-guarded. Built around a central square with solid walls on the outside, it only allowed one in through the single door—or via the roof.

Hlanan here, Tir sent. I saw a corner room, with a tiny window looking onto the inner court. The next image was a distorted view inside, with Hlanan lying on the ground, bound with chains.

Can you send him thoughts like you and I do? I asked.

No, Tir answered, its distress clear.

Go find out what's happening. Come right back.

Tir soared upward and disappeared over the rotting roof of an inn.

"That pothouse," I said, pointing at a building across the street from our courtyard. "Let's go in and get something. Better than staying out here, inviting someone to jump us."

"We'll be poisoned," Kee muttered.

"So we order but don't eat. Let's free the horses."

Kee dismounted, pulling her gear with her. Since it was likely the horses would be stolen anyway if we tied them to the post, it was time to let them go. We'd find our way on foot from this point on.

Inside the inn, the smells of bad punch, old garbage, and unwashed humans made the place seem smaller than it was. A tall, strong-looking innkeeper with an elaborate hairdo of braids snarled pleasantly, "Let's see yer coin, bumpkins."

I flipped a Thesrevan copper at her, knowing from experience that port cities usually take foreign money—usually attaching an exorbitant "change fee." That copper was probably four times the going rate for the punch which we wouldn't drink, but I hoped it would buy us some time unmolested. The innkeeper stomped to the other end of the counter.

Kee sat down at a table overlaid with a greasy film that gleamed redly in the murky light of a smoky fire. "I didn't know you speak Faran," she murmured. "I know some, but—"

"Never mind that," I said, casting a quick look around before I sat down next to her. She'd been well trained; the table she'd picked placed us with our backs to a wall, and with a window conveniently close at hand just in case. "Don't keep looking around like something stinks—"

"But it does stink," she protested in a whisper.

"So pretend it doesn't. We don't need them to think us slumming toffs." I leaned my elbows in the grease.

Kee tried to copy me, but when her arms skidded she shuddered, yanked them back and put her hands in her lap.

"Now here's the plan," I said. "Details to be worked out when the aidlar returns. I'm going to make an almighty diversion at the door. When they get out to look, you slip in. I'll go over the roof."

"How will you climb—so what ship will you try for this time?" Her tone did not alter as two thick mugs crashed down in front of us. I had to admire her quick wit. That big innkeeper had come up as silently as a cat just back of my right shoulder.

"Sailors, huh?" the innkeep growled in heavily slurred Allendi. "Hah." She snorted and stomped away. Her steps now shook the house.

Kee glanced down into her mug, and grimaced when she spotted brown crusties floating in the dark liquid.

"We'll do it again," I said, hoisting my glass and pretending to drink. I'd had half a mind not to waste good punch, but the sight of a many-legged insect floating belly up in my mug inspired me to reconsider. I'd have felt more confident about the punch had the creature been swimming happily. "I create a diversion, you get across to the corner room—here." I sketched the general layout of the house in the table's grime, and when she nodded, I smeared it out with a shove of my mug.

"How do we get him away?" Kee murmured.

"Maybe he'll have an idea," I said, shrugging. "If not, the same plan. The place will be in an uproar, I can guarantee you that," I assured her.

Tide low, humans saying—Tir's thought speared into my mind.

"Let's go," I said.

The open door darkened just as we reached it, and we found ourselves staring into the faces of five or six big, overgrown louts. "Hey." The foremost one, whose potato nose and hanging brow-ridge closely resembled the innkeep's, sneered. "You forgot to pay your visitors tax."

Kee's eyes met mine, and we moved together. A kick in a knee, a punch in a soft belly, a shove so that one fell and tangled himself in the legs of his cronies, and we were out the door. They didn't chase us.

"Not bad," I said, grinning.

Kee grinned back, the first I'd seen. Then her head jerked up as Tir fluttered down nearby. *Hurry, hurry. They take the prisoners out soon.*

"We must act now," I said. "Much rather wait for dark, but looks like we don't have that much time."

Kee hefted her knife. "With the two of us fighting, maybe we'll have a chance," she said.

"Don't count on me," I warned. "When I do magic, I can't do anything else. Maybe real sorcerers can, but I can't. I'll help as I'm able."

"Right." She gave me her characteristic short nod. Before, accusing, now just accepting of the facts.

We made our way through a narrow alley to the street our building was on. When I saw the guards standing before the doorway, I motioned Kee back. She came without a word. I couldn't explain it, but instinct urged me to ready any aid I had to hand. Something was wrong—more wrong than the fact that two undersized rescuers were about to attack a storehouse full of armed guards.

Crouching behind a crumbling fence, I fished around in my clothing and retrieved my two caged magicians. The whistle I shoved into one of the sash-folds, just above my ear. I was careful to keep it from touching my flesh; I didn't want

Dhes-Andis to know what was going on unless I had to. I slipped the necklace around my neck and shoved the stones down the front of my tunic. As I fixed the clasp, I concentrated on "closing" my inner eyelid. Kee faced outward watchfully.

"Ready?" Kee asked when I straightened up.

I nodded and we separated.

She started walking slowly up the street. I silently congratulated her on her control. She never once glanced back, though she didn't know what I was going to do.

I took up a position just below the overhang of the roof, then turned my attention to the other end of the building. Drawing in a deep breath, I raised my hands and readied myself. I whispered my magic-gathering spells, once, twice, thrice, four times, each time my hands heating until they prickled with heat, then I turned them outward, pointing, and—

BOOM! A thunderous noise made the guards jump and look about wildly. I aimed my thumbs, and fake fire leaped toward the sky.

The men dashed into the alley several steps, peering upward and exclaiming in shock.

Kee sped up behind them and slipped inside the door.

I leaped up and caught hold of the tiled rain gutter on the roof, swung up, my tail twitching hard in an effort to help me balance. I scrambled over the curved red tiles of the roof to the ridgepole, and lay flat so I could peer inside just as Kee entered the courtyard. I was about to slip down and join her when my sense of unease resolved into two facts.

One: the guards had stood before an unlocked door.

Two: no one waited in that courtyard.

Trap? Let's see.

I made a shimmer of myself landing in the dirty courtyard. My shimmer-self looked around, then swaggered toward the corner room where Hlanan was supposedly kept.

Tir! Go to Hlanan. Be my eyes—

The bird's wings fluttered, and as the white shape spiraled down into the courtyard, I wondered if the prisoners had been removed while Tir was trying to find us. Kee eyed my shimmer-self doubtfully, then moved to join.

The corner door opened, and two more guards stalked out.

Kee went into action. I made fireworks to divert the guards; one soon lay stunned, clipped efficiently behind his skull, and the other ran off somewhere.

Kee and Tir sped inside the door, me trying to shut out the starburst of Tir's happiness at the sight of Hlanan lying on the floor. They'd stripped him of his scribe robe, and he lay there filthy in his plain shirt and trousers, hands bound tightly behind him, legs bound as well, a manacle affixed to his wrists as well as the ropes, and bolted to the wall. The back of his shirt had been cut with a knife, exposing some kind of symbol tattooed on his shoulder-blade.

Hlanan looked up, his expression miserable. "Get out," he said hoarsely. "Now. It's a trap."

Then an inner door opened, and, flanked by a dozen guards with their weapons at the ready, Geric Lendan lounged in, smiling a bright welcome.

FIFTEEN

"Seize the thief," Lendan commanded, pointing at my shimmer-self.

The shimmer-me clapped its hands and disappeared in a shower of sparks.

The warriors who'd started forward, weapons drawn, fell back in confusion.

What now? What now?

I grabbed the necklace.

Faryana! Help me do magic to get rid of these reekers?

I must know exactly what you are doing and why. And I must have your vow not to harm any living—

"Secure them," Lendan shouted at his troops, pointing toward Kee and Hlanan. "The Hrethan thief is somewhere about. We'll kill these two unless she surrenders now."

Kee crouched, ready to attack. Good as she was, I knew she'd be no match for the dozen or so battle-scarred veterans who advanced menacingly. As for Hlanan, he just lay there in those ropes and chains, his face—still seen through the bird's eyes—pale and hopeless.

I fumbled at my turban, and smacked the whistle so that it touched against my forehead. *I need magic help—*

Here's a fire spell, was the instantaneous reply. The voice carried warning, and beneath it, that ever-present hint of amusement. *You'd better be able to hold it, or it will consume you.*

Then words flowed into my mind, a kind of chant that caused my head to buzz and my hands tingled unpleasantly with heat. As I spoke the words, the sensations of burning and buzzing intensified, my grasp on here-and-now expanding to encompass the stream of bright fire entering my mind.

The end of the spell was difficult to get out because my thoughts rode high in a fierce wind, my mental-image hands gripping twin spears of lightning. The wind and the light raced headlong through a weird night sky, pulling power in streamers from the stars. Time dissolved into meaninglessness, drawing me outward as I struggled to control the heat and the wind and the wheeling stars.

Hrethan!

That was Tir. I found the aidlar, and held on desperately.

My mind spiraled down from the invisible skies, and there was my body, small and fragile. I poured back into it, and as I did, I recovered sense and sound and sight: my head ached, my hands stung as I gripped the roof tiles, the smell of smoke burned my lungs. I remembered Hlanan. I remembered Kee.

I opened my eyes. Swords and knives rounded the two in a fence of steel. I moved . . .

So slow! But if I cast my mind free I can grasp the sun and the stars . . .

I tried to move, but the now had stretched out into eternity. My hands were heavy as stone, vibrating with the sparking white light. My eyes lifted for an instant—and again I was riding through the sky, faster and faster, trailing light like a comet . . .

Hrethan!

Again Tir called me back, mind to mind, and this time I forced my eyes open and used all my strength, straining in every muscle, to clap my hands together.

Thunder rocked the building. Everyone below me staggered, and the warriors looked up fearfully. Aiming my thumbs, I sent spears of light to divide Lendan from Kee and Hlanan. Fire lanced down from my fingers and scorched the stone floor, one bolt almost at Geric's feet, the other striking the chain connecting Hlanan to the wall. Red sparks exploded outward, and the air filled with the smell of molten metal.

The men stampeded, Geric following, yelling for them to halt, to pick up their weapons. His face, blanched and determined, turned this way and that, until his chin lifted and he saw me sitting astride the ridgepole.

"*There's* the thief," Lendan roared. "Bring her down."

I sent another blast of flame. This bolt splashed up a wall, starting a blaze that spread hungrily over the old wood. Each time I used the lightning, more surged in me, pulling at my mind and promising speed and wind and a universe of suns . . .

I laughed, and played with Lendan's warriors, sending bolts among them until they had scattered fearfully hither and yon.

Geric alone stood his ground, and I saw his mouth moving: he was doing magic.

A distant sense of alarm steadied me. I aimed a bolt directly at him—and he leaped aside. Flames shot skyward, orange and blue and bright, from the place he'd been standing. Smoke plumed up.

Hrethan? The cry held a note of despair.

Tir?

Another voice whispered to me to ignore the bird. I shut out that voice. Hlanan and Kee were in danger. I had promised to back Kee up. I had promised the aidlar that I would free Hlanan. I—barely—controlled the torrent of light and heat within me. In moments, in moments, if I didn't do something...I'd fly apart . . .

"Get us out," Kee's voice caught my ear, tiny against the rush of wind singing through my veins.

Need pulled my focus back into this world.

I spread my fingers and gave them a pathway bordered with killing light. Kee had gotten Hlanan's feet free, and he stumbled, leaning heavily on her, but he was upright. They lurched and swayed into the courtyard then through the open door.

Then I lost sight of them, but the urgent need to save them was gone. Fire crackled nearby and a haze of red smeared my vision. Smoke boiled around me, but I scarcely heeded it. I had kept my promise. Now I could glory in the power and fire streaming faster and faster through my mind. I could hold it, I could! Bigger and brighter, I just had to spread farther, and faster...the lightning spread into a vast storm, sucking me into its vortex . . .

The deepest instinct of all, self-preservation, forced me to throw my hands skyward, and lightning crackled high into the clouds. Somehow I got my inner eyelid closed, and the magic fled, leaving me spent.

I collapsed back on the roof, shaking weakly.

Ghostly, mocking laughter caused me to use my last remaining strength to shove that whistle back into my turban so it didn't touch my flesh.

"Lhind? Lhind?"

The voices came from the street.

Wearily I forced my eyes open.

"Come! Come!" Tir whirred right above me, wings fanning my face.

Forcing my limbs to move, I got to the edge of the roof and rolled off, confident in my usual ability to alight in balance—and I was stunned when the filthy street met my face. Hands grasped my armpits, pulling me up. Somehow my feet fumbled under me, and while the world spun nastily in front of my dimming eyes, my body moved between two supporting hands until, at last, I slid into welcoming darkness.

"Lhind."

The word reached me from a great distance.

"Drink this."

I moved ice-numb lips, and felt warmth trickle down the cold well inside me. With the warmth came awareness, in slow and painful increments. I was lying on a hard surface, and I ached in every muscle and bone.

"Again, Lhind. A little more this time."

Obediently I swallowed. More warmth spread into arms, legs, hands, fingers, toes. I opened my eyes, and took in a long breath.

Kee's face, smeared with dirt and troubled in expression, hovered over me. Opposite her was Hlanan's equally dirty face. His tired brown eyes were steady, his mouth a thin line.

"We're alive," I croaked. "Good. But I'm hungry," I added, making another discovery.

Kee looked relieved. "I'll fetch the bread." Her head swung away.

Hlanan smiled at me. "We're alive. You almost left us, though."

My eyes and lips moved, but not much else. "You tied me up again?"

"Again?" he repeated, puzzled, then his eyes narrowed in a kind of rueful laugh. "Oh. Rajanas's yacht. Does that seem a lifetime ago to you, too? No," he went on. "You're just desperately weak."

"Are we safe?" I asked. "Geric?"

"We're safe enough for now," he said, but his expression sobered again. "Drink." He slid his hand beneath my head to lift it, his gaze watchful.

Such a simple movement, the kind of thing anyone might do for another. Humane, we call it, thought 'human' can mean so many terrible things as well as good. A humane gesture that made me aware of his palm cupping the back of my head, each finger supporting my skull. The way his thumb avoided pressing against my ear, instead resting gently against the line of my jaw. I didn't have a word for how it made me feel, except both good...and unsettled.

I shut my eyes as a cup gently bumped my lip. This time I tasted the tea that I swallowed. It was strong, with a heady summer-herb scent. My fingers and toes tingled pleasantly, and the warmth stayed with me enough to enable me to make an effort to rise, to sit on my own. I heard the shift of cloth as Hlanan moved away. With him went that sense of being unsettled.

"Here's some fresh bread," Kee said, appearing again at my shoulder, her manner—shoulders hunched, gaze averted—embarrassed.

"I know," I whispered. "You stole it."

She grinned, blushing, as Hlanan gave a quiet chuckle. "I didn't dare risk being questioned," she said with a look at Hlanan. "But it had to be me who went out. Prince Geric sent out search parties."

"I'm all right," I said, annoyed at my weakness; when I raised a hand, a sharp smell assailed my nostrils, making me sneeze. "Ugh!" I dropped flat again. "What's that stink? Is this place on fire?"

"You," Kee said. "Or rather, your clothes. They were smoking when you dropped down off that burning roof."

"That's how we managed to get away," Hlanan murmured. "The fire you caused had spread to three streets, enabling us to lose ourselves in the general panic."

"Here. Have some bread," Kee said. "I'll help you sit."

Hlanan studied the empty cup in his hands while Kee slid business-like hands under my armpits and eased me to a sitting position. I munched on Kee's bread, which was still hot from the oven. Halfway through my second piece, Hlanan gave me a troubled glance. "Can you perform transfer magic?"

"Ugh," I muttered. "I don't think I could do the smallest shimmer right now. And the only thing I can move is air. I told you that before."

"You told me a lot of things," Hlanan said gently, getting to his feet. "There ought to be plenty of rainwater in the cistern by now. I'll brew more tea."

He doesn't believe me anymore. It hurt, and I had no defense against that kind of pain. Intensifying the pain was the sense of moral outrage—I'd saved him. How dare he...what? Not be grateful? Question me? What did he actually owe me?

Kee held out another bite of bread, but I waved it off as questions I'd never considered before insisted on worming their way through my muddy, shocky mind. Physical awareness was returning slowly; I heard a deep, intermittent rumbling of thunder, and realized I'd been hearing it since I woke.

It was time to get up. I pushed myself up onto my elbows. My vision swam sickeningly for a short time, then slowly righted itself. I saw we were in some kind of room with dirt on the floor and a low ceiling. It was lit by a fire a little distance away. All around us piled rubbish made a fence. "Where are we?"

"Close by. Neither of you were able to move far," Kee said. "We're in a cellar under an abandoned building. I went back and got a flame from your fire, which we set to these rotting timbers here. He found the rain cistern and I found the cups and the pot in the debris upstairs, and that's my good Mist-flower leaf. Gran thought we might need it to revive us on long marches." She touched her pack. "Luckily they didn't get mine. You must have left yours on the roof."

"Hate to lose that cloak," I said. "I'm cold."

"Here. Take mine." Kee pulled hers out and cast it over me. "The Scribe says to expect fever," she went on. "Something to do with that magic you did." She shook her head. "I don't know what to think about that."

"Me either," I admitted. "Never done it before."

I hadn't thought Hlanan, who was out of sight, could hear me. His voice startled me when he said, "We'll need to be gone from here soon. I hear footsteps overhead more often now. Poor sods," he added. "Lendan must be angry indeed, to force them to keep searching through that storm."

"How long did I sleep?"

"Since yesterday," Kee said. "It's late in the night now. The Scribe only woke a little while ago himself." She looked troubled again.

Hlanan appeared, sitting down with a steaming pot. The grimy, torn loose sleeves fell back, revealing lacerated wrists. "Drink up. We all need it." He poured tea while overhead, an tremendous crash of thunder boomed and rattled. Dust sifted down onto us from the timbers. Hlanan glanced up, and shook his head a little. Then he looked at us and said, "Meanwhile we must discuss what comes next."

"I know what I have to do," Kee said. "Gran is counting on me. If the Prince of Alezand is still a captive, I still need to get to the Empress as quick as possible, and tell her what's happened in our principality."

"I don't know if he is or not," Hlanan said. "I was drugged with liref leaves until we reached Fara Bay, and I don't

remember much of anything after the last time I saw Lhind."
He gave me an odd look.

My face burned. "I didn't do anything," I protested. "That
Steward was the one who put the herbs in your punch. He was
bribed by Lendan. I just escaped being snaffled by that nasty
Geric myself."

"I know," Hlanan made haste to say. "What confuses me is
why Lendan contrived this plot just to trap you. Because that's
why he brought me here, as bait for a trap for you."

Because I stole his diamond-and-whistle prisons, I thought, but
things had become so very unsettled between Hlanan and me
that I did not want to talk about them. Did I still have them?

My fingers moved instinctively to touch the diamonds at
my throat, and I saw both Hlanan and Kee watching. *They
think the diamonds are just diamonds. They don't know about
Faryana. But they won't believe the whistle is just a whistle.*

I pulled the sash from my head, and they watched my hair
lift and swirl about my shoulders. Surreptitiously I dug amid
the folds of the filthy sash, then relaxed. I felt the familiar hard
shape of the whistle.

Hlanan said to Kee, "You might have a chance to get away
if you can manage to board a ship. I shall try the same. Lendan
will have the roads watched, I'm sure, but even he cannot
suborn the Harbormaster, who answers only to the Faran
king. Do you speak any Faran, and have you any coin?"

"A few words of Faran, and not much coin," Kee admitted.
"Just what my grandmother gave me against my stay in the
Empress's capital, which is supposed to be terribly expensive. I
can work, though," she stated firmly.

"What shipboard skills do you have?" Hlanan returned.

"None."

"What about me?" I protested.

"What about you?" Hlanan asked.

His emphasis was on the 'about.' In other words, I was
surprised that I was not included in their planning—and
Hlanan was surprised I expected to be included. At least, that
was the impression he was conveying with his tone and his
quizzical smile. His gaze, however, stayed watchful.

Whether covered in mud or silks, I was incapable of being subtle. "You don't want me? Is that it?"

"What do you want to do?" Hlanan countered.

Kee sat quietly as she studied her tea.

"What's going on here?" I demanded. "Here's me, practically crisped from nose to toes in order to spring you from somebody I'd not started the quarrel with—and no mention of reward—yet you act like I've just stabbed you in the gizzard when you weren't looking."

"I haven't forgotten, and I'm grateful," Hlanan said soberly. "Very. But I also remember you declaring your preference to be free of such things as loyalty, or truth. I can't argue with you anymore. I can't even out-spell you, since your magic is obviously much stronger than mine, though I studied for several years. I accept that you'll do whatever you want to."

He did not sound contemptuous or even accusing, just...tired. Disappointed.

I sat there with the bread forgotten in my hand, once again hurt by a weapon I could not see, could not even name.

Kee said quickly, "You can come with me, Lhind, and welcome. I think we make a good team."

I plunged my hands into my trousers and came up with my bag of burglar's tools. Flinging out a fistful of the jewels and coins I'd accumulated since this adventure had begun, I said challengingly, "Think that will get us passage on some ship?"

Kee gasped. Hlanan gazed at the profusion of treasure gleaming and winking in the ruddy firelight, his brows raised. "We could travel like kings," he said. "With your permission, I'll take this and see what I can arrange."

"Hasn't that stenchiferous wight Geric Lendan put out a description of you for his nosers?" I asked.

Hlanan smiled a little. "I'll avoid them. This grandmother of a storm will help hide me. And I happen to know Fara Bay fairly well, much better than Lendan and his friends, I've no doubt."

"If the searchers find this place—" Kee started.

"We'll find a new hole." I turned my thumb out. "And Tir will lead Hlanan to us."

"I haven't seen Tir," Hlanan said, his even voice betraying worry.

I listened inwardly, and located the bird. "Tir's fine. Hiding under the roof."

Hlanan gave me another of those odd, puzzled looks, then swept the jewels and coins up with one hand. He thrust them into the pocket in his filthy trousers. "I'll be back as soon as I can," he said, and departed.

I lay flat again, heaving a huge sigh. "I feel as if that house— and maybe a mountain or two—fell on me."

"Drink some more Mist-leaf," Kee urged. "It will help."

I sat up just enough to drink off the tea in my cup and reach for more. The freezing lassitude had faded, leaving aches in every part of my body, particularly my head. With Hlanan gone, the sense of hurt eased. As I considered what I'd done, the spell for the fire-magic echoed. I knew I'd never forget it. The thought of calling it again made me shiver and clutch Kee's cloak closer about me.

I did it. I really controlled it. Who says I can't learn magic? On impulse, I reached: *Faryana?*

No answer.

I touched the diamonds, and tried again. Still no answer.

That was peculiar, and I felt uncertain, as if I'd been abandoned. A pang of irritation replaced the uncertainty when I remembered what she'd said when I'd asked for help. So she was ignoring me because I got my help elsewhere? Well, let her sulk.

Stealing a peek at Kee, I pulled the whistle from the sash. Kee was sitting over her tea, her eyes focused worlds beyond her cup.

Hiding the whistle in my palm, I pressed it up against my head.

You there? I asked. Outside, thunder smashed, shaking the building.

I am here. Well done, my young apprentice, the voice came, smooth and vast. I sensed silent laughter beneath the words. *Why are you hiding? Geric Lendan cannot stand against your will now. You can walk the streets and fire anyone who attempts to molest you.*

I could, I acknowledged, and pride warmed me inside. I remembered the exaltation I'd felt while riding high on that magic wind, sending lightning to strike anywhere I wished.

Strike anywhere, but not anyone, I thought. *Never again.*

Show me. I could feel Dhes-Andis reaching into my mind to find the memory, but instinctively I flicked down the inner door almost all the way, leaving only enough room for word communication.

Some other time. And I'm not ready to do that magic again real soon anyway.

The sense of vast darkness withdrew behind its own inner door, but tendrils swirled and misted around the voice as it said: *Giving in to weakness? I am surprised.*

You wouldn't be if you felt like I do right now, I snapped back indignantly.

Laughter streamed toward me, bright and caustic. *I will teach you how to avoid the effects.*

How'll you do that?

Come to Sveran Djur, was the reply.

No thanks, I retorted. *I've heard plenty about that place, and none of it good. Also, I have a—an errand to see to first.*

My city is beautiful, beyond beautiful. For what is the use of great power when one cannot commandeer the most beautiful things in the world?

He offered memories, this time beckoning me within his inward door, and though curiosity was nearly overwhelming, for my love of beautiful things was strong, I managed to resist. He might not be telling me the truth, only what I wanted to hear. I'd used that tactic enough in trying to escape tight situations.

His voice was once again amused when he thought, *What errand is so urgent?*

I hesitated on the verge of unloading the whole tale. Why should I? It wasn't as if I was safe here. What if Geric did manage to get the whistle back from me, and he wrested the story from the trapped sorcerer? And yet...and yet.

You don't need to know, I said importantly.

The voice laughed again. *I am impatient to meet you.*

But wait. Why Sveran Djur? Is that the only place you can be freed from this whistle?

No answer. The voice had disappeared, leaving only the low mutter of distant thunder.

SIXTEEN

"I think you'll enjoy this masquerade," Hlanan said by way of greeting when he reappeared. He shook the raindrops off his face and hair, adding, "At least the storm has abated somewhat, though the streets are ankle-deep in muck. Hurry and change. The ship will depart just before dawn on the outgoing tide."

He pitched wads of cloth at each of us. I sat up cautiously, glad to find that my headache had diminished. Kee yawned, poking curiously at her share.

"Use the last of our water to get the soot off your face, Kee," Hlanan said with a smile. "Lhind, you're probably better off as you are. Luckily there are a lot of other soot-smeared servants down at the docks clamoring for passage for their master or mistress who wants to get out of the harbor today. So the soot will contribute to your disguise."

"We're going to be disguised?" Kee held up a splendid gown.

"You are now a noble scion—Lady Kieran of North Chur in Keprima—and her faithful lackey. That's you, Lhind. Faithful lackeys don't have names, at least on ship's rolls. And tutor, at your service," Hlanan said, bowing. "If we can get across the docks, we've berths awaiting us. But we've only got a short time. Dress up."

"Me? A servant?" I asked, delighted. "This will be fun! As long as I don't have to do any work." I shot Kee a warning glare.

Kee snorted, shaking out her dress. We changed hastily, me—with a groan of disgust—stuffing my poor tail into the shapeless mud-colored trousers Hlanan had procured. The tunic was a better fit, large and roomy. It had a hood, and Hlanan had also bought a plain cap. My hair fit under all that. The only thing I ignored were the shoes.

Or tried to ignore.

"Put those on," Hlanan said, pointing to the shoes.

"Flames of Rue," I exclaimed. "I can't bear shoes. They are hot, they pinch unmercifully, they slip and slide at the worst times—"

"You won't be climbing any roofs or fences. Put them on."

"But they hurt the sides of my feet, and did you hear when I said they are hot? Make my toes itch."

"And bare feet on a supposed servant will flag Lendan's scouts for certain. They know you're a Hrethan, and Lendan will have told them that the Hrethan almost never wear shoes."

"Oh." This discovery of a Hrethan habit that matched mine made me feel peculiar. Wincing and grumbling, I eased my feet into the soft cloth shoes that Hlanan had brought. At least they were not stiff, but I still loathed the sensation.

Kee watched me take a few gingerly steps, then grinned. "You'll catch notice for certain if you walk like someone put slugs in 'em."

I stomped in a circle. "Is that more convincing?"

"Let's go, you two," Hlanan murmured, obviously trying not to laugh.

Kee whirled around, fluffing out her gown. It was a high-waisted affair sporting lots of lace at the neck and sleeves, and with her long pale hair unbraided and hanging down in fine, somewhat stringy locks, she looked like a different person.

When she saw me looking, she said in an undervoice, "Until today I was proud of the fact that I have never told a lie.

Now I am about to be living one. I do not know what to think."

There was this urge to say, *Now you know what it feels like*, except I'd hated it when Faryana acted so morally superior to me from the inside of the necklace.

I fell in step behind her, carrying the pack like a good servant. Hlanan had found himself some nondescript clothes, and the gray open robe of a low-level scribe, but he didn't look all that different from usual.

Catching my eye, he said: "I'll go to the ship by a different route. Tir knows where it is. Stay with the aidlar."

"I can get us there," I began.

"Not over roofs. Not in this dress," Kee warned.

"And they'll be looking on the rooftops," Hlanan added. "We've got darkness on our side, and the aidlar. Let's move quickly." He paused to inspect us. "And in case we don't see each other until we're on the ship, Lhind, when you reach the docks you stay a pace or two behind Kee at all times. Don't speak unless spoken to. You're sleeping in her cabin, so don't take the gear to the hold where the lackeys go. Kee, walk like a lady, not like a ranger."

"But I am a ranger," Kee protested.

"You're a lady right now," Hlanan said, his lips twitching. "Little steps, minding your gown."

"I've never worn a gown."

"They wear them in Keprima, where you are now from, and noblemen wear robes. Little steps, and hide those hands. Nobles usually don't have bow calluses."

Kee tucked her skirts up so they wouldn't drag through the mire of the streets and we left.

The walk was not far, and Lendan's hired prowlers were apparently watching the roads out of the harbor. Twice we encountered foursomes of those warriors in gray. They studied Kee with intensity, but when they saw her hanks of yellow hair, already tangling, they dismissed her. They paid scarce heed to her burdened, shuffling servitor who fumbled along as if his shoes were too tight.

More than one ship was preparing to sail on the tide, and the docks were busy. Just as Hlanan had said, a lot of people wanted to get away.

Following the soaring, wheeling aidlar, we made our way past ships of every description until we came to a big, high-built caravel that had been given a pier, so we did not have to hire a boat to take us out into the bay. The aidlar flapped down and sat on the rail of the caravel.

Kee's shoulders relaxed as we walked up the ramp. I was so delighted I wanted to dance a little, but I remembered that I was a servant, so I dropped back and adopted what I hoped was a suitable demeanor. Kee stuck her nose in the air and announced to the waiting steward that she was Lady Kieran of North Chur Castle in Keprima.

"Any luggage?" the steward asked, bored.

Kee sent me a wild look. I was already carrying our bags, but clearly noble ladies had much more.

"Coming," I said, with downcast eyes.

"My lackey is in charge of that," Kee said grandly.

"All the way forward, starboard cabin," the steward said.

Kee nodded, her eyes bulging slightly as she looked at me. She obviously had no idea what they meant. I said quickly, "Shall I inspect, your ladyship?"

"Do that," Kee said, her voice strained; it was clear that she was rapidly reaching the end of her invention skills.

I took over, confident I knew the way. This ship was as different from Rajanas's sleek yacht as one could imagine, but I figured the basic directions on any ship are the same. I'd heard about fore, aft, starboard, and lee while eavesdropping on Rajanas's sailors.

I led the way down to the first deck below, where the passenger cabins lined the sides of the ship, the best one of course aft all along the stern. We walked forward (Kee whispering "Forward. Starboard," to herself) and reached the last cabin on the right before the forepeak.

The little cabin was empty, the bulkheads curving inward over the single bunk. As soon as the door was closed Kee collapsed onto the bunk with a sigh of relief. "I didn't expect questions," she muttered. "I really hate lying."

"Think of it as playacting."

She gave me a considering look. "Is that what you've spent your life doing?"

I grabbed my cap and pulled it off, allowing my hair to lift. "Going about like this was a disaster," I said. "But playacting is fun. It doesn't hurt anyone, and it keeps me safe."

She rubbed her forehead tiredly. The door opened then, and Hlanan came in, wearing a long robe with fancy folded sleeves. It made him look taller. "Ah, good. Any problems?"

"No. We're all here and we're safe," I said, clapping my hands.

"I won't feel safe until we sail," Hlanan said. He sounded even more tired than Kee.

"Where are you located?" Kee asked.

"Down below, crammed in with a lot of other poor sorts like myself, forward of the crew berth." He grimaced. "Stuffy and close down there, no privacy, but the other fellows seem to be good enough sorts."

Of course he would say that. He seemed to like everybody unless they actively proved themselves unlikable, just as he seemed to find everyone interesting. Thus his endless questions, as friendly as they were nosy.

There was a trunk against the bulkhead between us and the next cabin aft. Hlanan sat on this trunk so he would not have to stand with head bent. I put our bundles on the floor next to his feet and sat next to Kee on the bunk. We looked at one another wearily. Outside the single window the sun grayed the ragged clouds, and at last the ship began rolling majestically out of Fara Bay. Within a short time after that, Hlanan went below. I gave Kee the bunk and curled up on the floor. We were soon asleep.

By nightfall I'd figured out my jobs. It was expected that I'd take meals to the supposed Lady Kieran, and bring the dirty crockery back to the galley. I was also supposed to keep the cabin neat, but Kee kept her few belongings squared away, and I didn't have any besides my stash, which I wore.

This time I adjusted to the movement within a day. Kee did as well, but she found the masquerade onerous. Other toffs aboard seemed to expect her to converse with them, make music with them, and other aristocratic pursuits.

The musicians were more enthusiastic than expert, making it easy for me to keep a wary, respectful distance. Music was so elusive, so beguiling, but I hated the way it stirred up the wrong memories and emotions.

Kee tried to avoid these friendly meetings after the first one when they asked her to take a turn. She mumbled something about tiredness, and retreated to the cabin. She decided to fake being sick, though she hated being kept inside the cabin, which got quite hot during the afternoon, if the wind wasn't on the starboard beam and blowing in the window.

It was left to Hlanan to invent suitable stories about our background, because of course none of the toffs thought to ask a lackey, and I seldom saw any of the other servants. He matched their accents with an ease that impressed Kee and made me wonder even more about his real story. At least after she'd heard him spin tales about Castle North Chur, Kee stopped worrying about the ethics of playacting: she might still be ambivalent about me, but she had great respect for Hlanan.

So did I, but at the same time I was aware that he was a very deft liar.

Hlanan decided at the end of our third boring day at sea that he should really act the tutor. Maybe this was invented for Kee's entertainment; at any rate, he declared it was time for me to learn to read and write, and to count in numbers higher than sixes. He chose Allendi for reading so that Kee could participate in the lessons.

"Also," he said, overriding my excuses and protests, "it's close enough to Elras, the tongue and script of Charas al Kherval. You'll get that next."

"But it's boring," I moaned.

"Think of it as more playacting," Kee said with a challenging grin.

"Or a secret code," Hlanan added.

"You two are laughing at me," I snarled.

"Never," Hlanan said loftily, holding up his palm. "As I recall another person saying once not too long ago, I wouldn't want a cranky sorcerer to turn me into a footstool."

Uncomfortable with this 'sorcerer' talk, I gave in with a bad grace.

And at first the lessons were just as boring as I'd feared. Matching the little scrawls to various sounds seemed tedious beyond bearing, but after a day or two of practice I began to recognize some of them—and I will admit to a secret thrill when I first wrote out my name.

We spent the days on tutoring, while Kee read the books Hlanan had found on board for anyone to peruse, and at night, Hlanan entertained us with stories out of history. He knew a lot of history. When Kee commented on that, he seemed pleased, saying, "Well, when you are a scribe student, you copy out a lot of history while trying to perfect your handwriting and speed. So I thought I might as well read the books I was copying out of."

We continued like this for a few more days. The trip was pleasant and even the weather behaved.

One evening Hlanan appeared in our cabin a little later than usual, Tir riding on his shoulder. The scribe carried one of the crystal goblets that they only used to serve the toffs. He had filled it with water.

"What's that for?" Kee asked. "They think I'm thirsty?"

"I said you were thirsty." Hlanan gave her a faint smile as Tir sent me a silent greeting and flapped up to perch on an empty candle-sconce. Hlanan went on, "My modest gear—such as it was—having been left behind in Imbradi when I was abducted, I'm forced to try something innovative. I've never been very good at this kind of communication. Not many magicians are. But sometimes where one fails, three can succeed."

Kee and I watched as he set up the goblet between two candles on the little table. "What's it you're trying to do?"

"I'm going to try to scry Thianra the minstrel. Want to help?"

Kee shuddered. "I tried that once, with Nill. Because we'd been told not to. And all it did was make me so dizzy my stomach took a violent dislike."

Hlanan did not look at me, but I knew he was waiting. In fact, I sensed that he hadn't really expected anything from Kee at all.

I shrugged, trying not to stare into the water in the crystal. The way the light played on the faceted edges of the stone, winking . . .

I blinked. Looked at Hlanan, whose expression altered from intensity to question.

"So what do you do?" I asked.

His brows twitched in surprise, then smoothed out into blandness. "You look in, and think of her. Call to her in your mind."

"That seems easy enough," I said. "Do, uh, Hrethans do it a lot or something?"

"I believe they do, though of course I've never seen them at it."

Something was missing, I could feel it. "All right." I shrugged. "I'll give it a try."

"I should warn you first," he said, putting a hand over the crystal. "If you hear anyone else—anyone at all—then stop scrying fast. The problem with this kind of method, when it works, is that any magician who's practiced and who happens to be scrying might hear. It's a little like eavesdropping," he added for Kee, who looked confused.

"Those rings," I said. "The ones that got taken when we were ambushed on the road out of Letarj. Do those work for only people who have the other in a matched pair or something?"

Hlanan nodded. "That's right. The magic on them wards anyone who does not have one of the rings."

"Can't you do your screening magic on this thing before we start?" I asked.

"I don't know how," Hlanan said. "The rings were given to us by magicians much more powerful than I."

You sure don't know much magic for a magician, I thought. But then he'd never claimed to be a mage, just a scribe who'd learned some magic.

I was going to ask, but the tension in his shoulders, the tight line of his lips, made me uneasy. He was too intent on this scrying for questions, that much I was sure of.

I shrugged again, and remembered Faryana, who had not answered me when I'd tried to call her. Her diamonds lay among my thief tools. I remembered the whistle, which was tucked safely into my sash inside my shapeless servant tunic. *They won't hear us as long as I don't touch them.*

So I turned my attention to the candlelight flickering in the crystal-held water. The light swirled, became a scattering of stars in the night sky . . .

"You're drifting," Hlanan murmured. "Take our hands, and think of Thianra."

I gripped Kee's small, callused hand, but hesitated before taking hold of Hlanan's fingers. He offered them in silence, and I closed my own around his, which were slender for a male, warm, a strong, steady grip.

Concentrate. Obediently I called up an image of Thianra, and there she was in the crystal. She looked tired, her eyes startled. *Who?* Her lips shaped the word, though I heard no sound. Instead I felt it inside me, and then Kee gasped and I switched my attention to her.

"It works," Kee exclaimed, pointing. "I saw her."

"And we lost her," Hlanan said dryly.

"I'm sorry. I won't talk again." Kee flushed with embarrassment.

"Try once more, Lhind," Hlanan whispered.

I closed my eyes, fighting the curl of dizziness around the periphery of my vision. Again I concentrated on the memory-image of Thianra, and this time when she appeared in the crystal she looked calm and ready, her eyes focused slightly inward.

Oh, you're looking into a crystal, too? I thought.

Thianra smiled. *Is it you, Lhind?*

All three of us are here, Hlanan's thought joined, his fingers tightening on mine. *Kuraf's Kee—*

Kuraf is here with us, Thianra interrupted. *I'll be glad to report to her that Kee is safe.*

Where are you? Hlanan asked.

Idaron Pass, came the answer. *We've been holding it against the mercenaries.*

Ilyan is free then?

Oh, yes. He escaped before I did. Lendan's hirelings retreated into the city and captured a portion, making surrender-or-else noises. Kept us busy for several days, until Rajanas got the idea we were being diverted. So he sent Kuraf and the rest of us up here to hold the Pass while he chases the rest of the Wolf Grays out of Imbradi. So far it's mostly been maneuvering, and we still hold the Pass.

A pang shot through my temples. I almost lost my concentration, but I forced myself to listen.

This sending is remarkably clear, Thianra went on. *Where are you?*

Heading north and west into the Azure Sea, Hlanan answered. *We're going the northern route.*

Kuraf will be pleased, Thianra said. *I hope you escaped the vicious blizzard that hit us just days ago. Came from the south. You'd know better than I, but it seemed to have been magic-driven, if not magic-caused—*

A warning flashed from Hlanan to Thianra. No words, but it was distinct. Puzzled, I felt around in my mind for anything that might be wrong — and I sensed a familiar tendril of awareness, drifting near . . .

"*Dhes-Andis*," I breathed, shutting my eyes.

Dizziness smacked me from the inside: I could not tell what was up or down, and I fell back onto the bunk.

"Dhes-Andis? The Emperor of Sveran Djur? How do you know that?" Hlanan demanded.

I opened my eyes and tried to study his revolving face. "Ugh," I said, closing my eyes again. "Hey, it was you who sent that silent 'shut up' to Thianra—"

"That silent 'shut up,'" Hlanan retorted, "was because I didn't want it to get about that you'd been the cause of the havoc wrought on the region."

"Me?" I croaked, trying to rid myself of the dizziness.

"Did you really think that magnitude of fire-spell would not have a reaction?" he said with pent-up frustration. "Or have you been playing us for fools all along?" He took hold of my chin, forcing my head up. "Where is Dhes-Andis? How did you know he was scrying?"

"Well, I'm not sure, but I think—" I gabbled, trying desperately to think of some believable explanation.

"For once, Lhind," Hlanan as close to anger as I'd ever seen him, "no lies."

Just then a wild clamor of unmusical bells claimed our attention, followed by a distant cry of "All hands! All hands!" Running feet shivered the wooden decking, and Tir let out a squawk of fright.

Hlanan let go of me, and Kee sprang to the door. "Is that an alarm?" she asked, her face pale in the flickering candlelight.

"Yes." Hlanan straightened up, then sent me a troubled look, his mouth pressed in a thin line. "We'd better see what it is, then we will return to this conversation. Stay here," he added to both of us, and he went out.

Neither of us heeded his command. Kee beat me out the door by a nose, only because I paused to jam my hair under my cap, then we ran forward in silence. Torchlight flickered down the caravel's length, revealing the captain shouting hoarse commands to grim-faced sailors running about purposefully.

Beyond our ship, ghostly in the light of the new moon, a long, lethal shape glided through the water directly across our bow. And beyond that one, another similar shape. Warships. Fast ones—ones I recognized, causing a bone-deep shiver of fear.

Hlanan stood at the rail, his face drawn as he stared at the sinister vessels converging on us.

"What are those ships?" Kee whispered, pointing.

Hlanan didn't even seem to notice us. "Maker protect us," he muttered. "The Skull Fleet."

SEVENTEEN

"Hard alee!" the captain bawled.

The caravel slanted away from the wind, masts and timbers creaking—the only thing the captain could do was run and hope to outsail the enemy. Waves splashed up over the lee rail, sending water running down the deck. Passengers darted about, some slipping on the wet deck. A few ran with purpose to fetch weapons, but most seemed to be running around in a panic, hooting questions at the laboring sailors, as if they sought a comforting answer.

"We're carrying wool," one elderly man groaned to no one in particular as he tottered by. "What would pirates want with wool?"

"What about your magic?" I asked Hlanan.

"My knowledge is useless for this," Hlanan said shortly. "We'd better prepare for a fight." He ran to the hatch and worked to go down as others scrambled to the deck, adding to the confusion. Muttering fretful cries, Tir sailed around in a circle above the hatch, watching for him.

"Come on," I said to Kee. "Let's get ready."

We fought our way down to our cabin, shutting the door and breathing hard.

"I don't care if I ruin our disguise. I'm not fighting in this dress." Kee kicked her way out of her gown, and yanked on her old clothes.

I watched, wondering what to do. Kee's chin jutted determinedly but her hands shook as she braided her hair tightly and pinned it up. I didn't fault her. I knew what the Skull pirates were like. Whatever she'd been told probably wasn't nasty enough.

What to do? I already had my burglary tools on me. The only thing I'd stashed was my knife, which I now fetched from under the mattress on the bunk. I thrust it through my sash, then turned my attention to my booty.

Faryana's diamonds lay in my tool pouch. I hauled them out and put them on. The whistle sat safely in my sash, where I'd put it when we came on board. I'd avoided communicating with its imprisoned sorcerer until I'd thought out the fire spell experience a little. Except I hadn't thought it out. I'd pretended like it never happened.

There were fewer people below now. I ran to the ladder and swarmed up to the deck, catching hold of a shroud and pulling myself up so I could see. A third ship had slid out from behind one of the little islands we'd been threading our way through. A trap, I thought. Why else would three Skull cruisers just happen to be here in the islands—and why would they drop on a merchant vessel?

So if it's a trap, it means they're expecting someone. One of these other passengers?

Or maybe *us?*

I brought the whistle out and examined it in the uneven lamplight. It was a pale, long shape, with odd shapes etched on the sides. I rubbed my thumb absently over these, and felt that strange tingle again. Should I ask that sorcerer for help?

The fire spell had been a spectacular success on land, but I wasn't going to use it now. We'd all go down together, pirates and passengers alike. Ask for another spell? I was reluctant to contact that sorcerer unless there was no other option. Prisoner or not, he made me more uneasy every time we communicated.

The whistle was useless otherwise—

Useless? It was, after all, a whistle.

I opened my bag again, and carefully removed my little wallet of liref, which had broken down to a very fine powder. Still potent, though: an inadvertent sniff made me reel on my perch, as if a bale of cotton had bloomed behind my eyes.

Holding my breath, I took a big pinch and shoved it into one end of the whistle. I jammed an even bigger pinch after it, just in case. Then I placed the whistle into my sash, and put the bag away.

Blowing liref into an enemy's face wasn't much of a defense, but it was all I could think of. Shimmers would be no good against three ships, even if I could hold them long enough. *I won't use that fire spell*, I vowed to myself. *I won't.*

Kee and Hlanan joined me. He, too, had changed out of his flowing robe, into his worn gray tunic and riding trousers. He carried a sword he'd been given by a sailor. "If either of you can use one, they have a few extra," he said.

"I'm better with a knife," Kee said flatly.

A cry followed by wild sobbing yanked our attention away. One of the aristo passengers dealt her serving-woman a ringing slap across the face, and the servant abruptly subsided, covering her face with her hands." If you can't fight, get below," the captain yelled, advancing on the crowd of passengers and waving his sword.

One of the pirate ships maneuvered almost alongside, ignoring the rain of arrows being fired from the foremast by a group of defending sailors. Another cut across our bow, catching the caravel's bowsprit in the pirate's rigging. As we watched helplessly the grappling hooks were flung over.

"Repel-boarder parties for'ard!" the captain yelled.

Thick netting reached from the rails to the rigging; the repel boarder crew were busy with booms and other weapons, disengaging the grapplers as fast as they could, though here and there they gave cries and slumped, or fell into the water, from pirate-shot arrows.

The useless passengers had finally retreated below, presumably to hide, or to make a last stand in their cabins. A second set of sailors—the ones not working the sails—waited in silence, weapons to hand. Here and there an elegant sword gleamed in the jeweled hands of one of the well-to-do passengers, and several silent, grim servants stood with plainer weapons held ready.

The first boarders to come over hacked at the nets with well-honed blades. Sending up a cry, the sailors attacked them. These nets probably gave the defenders an extra edge in normal circumstances, but they hardly stopped the black-clad pirates, who struck net and foe down alike with cold-blooded ease.

In addition to the creak of sail and mast rose the clash of swords and cries and groans. My palms began to sweat. At my shoulder, Kee gripped her knife, shifting from foot to foot as she watched.

Then Tir's mental voice speared into my mind: *Look who waits.*

And, seen from the bird's perch in the rigging of the pirate ship next to us, Geric Lendan lounged against the rail, smiling expectantly.

On our deck, the pirates fought their way through the passengers, not slaughtering as is their usual practice—but searching. Short people specifically.

It's not us, it's me they want. I knew it with deadly certainty.

Quick as thought I leaped up onto the forecastle, and from there into the rigging of a mast. Swinging in the salty ropes, I felt my cap twitch askew then go spinning into the wind. My hair, now loose, helped me catch my balance. Realizing that disguises no longer mattered, I clung to the ropes with one hand and with the other used my knife to slit the back seam of my trousers so that my tail was free at last. I found a perch on the foresail yard, its sail snapping and thrumming beneath me and sending vibrations through my feet.

Below, sailors and pirates fought in furious knots all along the companionways. I saw three or four pirates chase passengers down the length of the deck, and I wished I had something to pot them with. Smoke drifted out of the hold, amid distant cries and clashes.

It was over quickly. Pirates began systematically searching the cabins, occasionally dragging out passengers. The pirates herded their prisoners aft, and relieved them of their weapons,

Kee among them. Most were short young women, but among those were wealthy-looking merchants, obviously candidates for ransom.

At last a plank was put across and the Skull captain and Geric strolled across to the deck below me. Longing for some itchwort to drop on them, I fingered the whistle in my bag and the hard lumps of Faryana's diamonds beneath my tunic.

Faryana?

Nothing.

Are you afraid of me? The familiar amusement swirled out of vast darkness.

I jumped, looking down at the whistle in my hand. So one could communicate by just touching it with fingers, and not head?

Why don't you ask my help instead of begging aid of a moral-prating hedge-witch who failed her first post?

Who says I need help? When in doubt, assume bravado.

Lendan sees you now, was the reply.

And from below came an angry voice, "There's the light-accursed Hrethan thief."

A ring of torch-bearing pirates encircled my mast, all looking up. Wishing I had a cauldron of fish gumbo to dump on them, I crouched in a small ball lest they throw things up at me.

"We're waiting, thief." Prince Geric appeared directly below me, his upturned face angry and triumphant, apricot hair streaming over one shoulder, shirtsleeves snapping in the wind. "Or we'll slit the throats of everyone here. Beginning with them."

He gestured and two pirates came forward, flinging a disheveled, bloodstained Hlanan down on the deck. He was unconscious. Another muscled Kee up next to the mast and yanked her head back, holding a knife at her neck. *No fire! No fire! What, then?*

A fire spell would be stupid, came Dhes-Andis's smooth voice. *The most effective defense is a mind-thrust. I can teach you easily.*

Memory-images shot into my mind, and I shoved them violently away.

But not fast enough. *So you do know mind-thrust, Dhes-Andis mused. You tried it once?*

This exchange was quick, hardly taking the time of one indrawn breath. Below, Geric Lendan and his pirates waited for my answer, all motionless as statues except for the wind playing through hair and clothing, and the streaming torchlight.

It was an old man, caught doing sorcery in Tu Jhan. The words—memories—flickered faster than my heartbeat. *He wasn't anyone I knew or even wanted to. He'd tried to ruin a rival's pottery by a rot-spell. The gang wanted to see the burning. How he screamed! I couldn't bear it. The guards, the crowd, all were enjoying it.*

So you attempted a thrust against the patrons of the spectacle? Acid amusement drifted through the dark stream of Dhes-Andis' thoughts.

No. I tried a thrust against the guards, to save the man. But I learned you can't do it unless you hear someone's range—and then only one at a time. Those screams. They gave me the old man's range. And when he kept begging for someone to finish him fast, I did.

Very effective. The voice conveyed cool approval. *If you do escape him now, Lendan will only hound you to death. You and those people you are protecting. Thrust now. I can give you his range, if you haven't it already.*

No.

"Thief. I will not wait any longer." Prince Geric turned to the pirate holding Kee, and raised his hand—

"If he touches her, I'll fling this thing into the ocean," I yelled, holding up the whistle. "And this, too." I pulled the necklace out.

Dhes-Andis' laughter flooded my mind. *Use it, child. Strike!*

I thought Geric was supposed to be your pal, I answered indignantly. *Great ally YOU are. He's doing this to get you safely back.*

The laughter increased. *He wants what I can teach him, and does not yet know that you have supplanted him as my apprentice.*

Who says I am anyone's apprentice? I shot back.

Too late, was the reply, amid stinging mirth. *I await you with growing impatience.*

He wasn't the only one.

"Try it and they die anyway," the furious prince snarled, head thrown back. Distractedly, I couldn't help noticing that he was handsome even when in a rage. "But I will take my time." Handsome but nasty through and through.

I had to act fast.

Glancing at Kee's pale face, I remembered our ride through the rain, and my use of wind—

Of course!

I recalled Kee's range, and tried something I'd never done before. I shaped a thought and shoved it at her head: *Hold your breath.*

And I put the whistle to my lips and blew. A fine mist of powder, almost invisible, floated out. Would my wind-shimmer be strong enough to spread it? No way to find out but to try. With a wave of my hand I directed the cloud of liref directly down onto the faces waiting below, making myself see it reach them all.

For a long moment nothing happened, then thud. One pirate slid to the deck. The one holding Kee fumbled weakly with his knife, then he too dropped, knocking Kee off balance. Prince Geric tried to lunge at her, and fell on his face at her feet. All around her the others toppled.

"Where are the rest?" I called to Kee.

She pointed behind her, her hand over her nose, her face rapidly turning red.

Two came running, faltered when they entered my cloud, and gently joined their brethren in slumber.

I hopped down. Kee followed me to the hatch, both of us sucking in lungfuls of air as the rest of the liref dust drifted out to sea. Through the opening I heard the sounds of cries and scuffling. I bent down, carefully blew the rest of my liref dust along the stairway, and used a shimmer to waft it through the passages below.

Presently we heard thumps and thuds, then silence.

"Oh, thank you," she exclaimed fervently. "What was that? Poison?"

"Liref."

"Then the Scribe will recover." She sounded thankful.

An interrogative shout from the second pirate ship brought both our heads around sharply.

"Do you have enough for them?" Kee asked, pointing shakily.

"I don't think I could control the cloud unless I was on their ship. Bet they don't know magic, though," I said. "Watch this."

I couldn't use the fire spell to aim at people, now that I knew its strength, but I could use it against the masts of a ship.

I braced myself with my back to the rail, then I dropped the whistle into my bag so I wasn't touching it. Gathering my strength, I ran through the fire spell. This time I was prepared for the rush of light and heat through my mind, and I took what I needed and let the rest slip by.

"There," I said, aiming my hands.

Fire slashed through the night, hitting the sails and rigging of the pirate ship. The caravel's bowsprit caught flame as well, and broke off with a shower of sparks. "You next." I flamed the second ship's sails.

"And there." I sent lightning toward the third pirate ship and soon its sails and upper rigging glowed red against the stars. Cries erupted from the ships.

Fighting the vertigo of reaction, I turned in triumph to Kee. "How's that?" I asked past chattering teeth. "No one hurt. F-fires should burn upward. B-but the pirates can't go anywhere, and they're too busy. To bother. Us."

She laughed, a gasping sound very close to tears. "It's wonderful," she said. "But liref won't have the pirates on our ship asleep forever. What shall we do? Tie them all up?" She asked doubtfully.

I pushed myself away from the rail, ignoring the ache that settled into my bones. "How about we drag them below, get their weapons, and lock 'em in. Then we get away as soon as we can."

Thunder muttered a distant warning. The sky blackened behind angry clouds.

"A storm coming," Kee shouted. "Let's hurry. Rain might revive them faster."

We sprang to the nearest pirate, and found that we could barely move him even with me tugging on his booted feet and Kee dragging on his limp arms. I sank down on my knees, breathless from the exertion. It was Kee who ran away down the deck and reappeared with a thick cape. After rolling the snoring pirate onto it, we dragged the cape toward the hatch. We repeated this again, finding it a less difficult method for hauling them.

Your work would be easier with a shifting spell, Dhes-Andis's voice interrupted me suddenly.

Startled, I dropped the end of the cap I was tugging, and Kee stumbled, casting me a reproachful look. *How did you do that? I'm not touching your whistle.*

Do you want a shifting spell? Or you could make the sleep last as long as you like.

I don't trust your spells.

But you just used one, child. It all gets easier with time.

I closed my inner eyelid. Had it worked? I waited a little, then cautiously listened.

His laughter at my futile hide-and-seek game scoured my mind. *You gave me your range when you memory-shared, my child.*

A hideously unpleasant thought occurred to me then: *You're not a prisoner at all. What is this whistle thing really for?*

A communications device. Necessary for some, but not for you. I shall teach you how to use that farsense gift—

Gritting my teeth, I concentrated on slamming my inner door—and my mind contained only my own thoughts.

I glanced up. Kee's face in the torchlight was worried. "You looked like someone in a nightmare," she said.

Lightning flared overhead, and thunder ripped the air. A moment later stinging rain slashed down at us.

I shook my head at her. "Let's finish," I shouted. "I'll explain later."

She gave a jerky shrug and we went back to work. The wet deck made it more difficult to drag people about, but as the water became more choppy, the ship pitched and rolled. We found our task more manageable when we waited for a wave to slant the ship in our direction. Our pirates rolled easier then. When it was Geric's turn I stopped long enough to rob him again. All I got this time was a ring and a small bag of coins.

The last two pirates muttered and struggled a little, but we got them below, Kee bumping them down on the cloaks. They'd probably be bruised up a bit, but after all, as Kee said, "They're pirates. They deserve some bruises."

We shoved them all into the big stern cabin, then I threw the last of my lief into the cabin with them and shut them in. We piled a giant barricade of barrels and furniture outside the door.

By this time the storm had broken directly overhead. The pair of ships bumped together, timbers creaking warningly. On the burning ships, the pirates were too busy fighting flames to bother with us.

Kee and I staggered up to the deck, exhausted and wondering we should do next. Passengers wandered around looking dazed; others who'd been caught in the lief cloud lay here and there, groaning. We found Hlanan sitting up groggily in the slashing rain. The torches had gone out, but we spotted him in a flash of lightning. He was looking around, and saw us in the same flash.

"You're all right," I shouted in relief. "We got the pirates locked up. And the others won't be attacking any time soon." I pointed at the red glow of the fires on the other ships.

Hlanan scarcely gave them a glance. He moved with slow, painful-looking steps to Kee's and my cabin, which still had candles lit in it. Kee sank gratefully onto the bunk, but Hlanan stopped me from following her and grabbed hold of my shoulders. "Lendan traced us here," he said. "By magic. Who have you been in contact with?"

By now I was shivering so hard I could hardly get my burglar's bag out. I fumbled the whistle from the bag and numbly held it out. Reaction was setting in fast. "I took it off Geric. In Imbradi."

Hlanan wiped his streaming hair out of his face and squinted at the whistle. "What's this?" he reached for it, but I yanked it away.

"Don't t-touch it," I mumbled. "He might hear you."

"Who?"

"Dhes-Andis." I braced myself for the angry tirade I expected and—I gulped—deserved.

Hlanan leaned his head back and shut his eyes. His hands dropped away from me, then he straightened up and eyed me in anguish. "Why?"

"It happened by accident. Here." I opened the window and flung the whistle out into the sea. Lightning flared, shining on the pale white shape spinning end over end toward the water. It disappeared without a splash. "He can't get at your mind now."

Hlanan's tired brown eyes narrowed at my emphasis on 'your.'

"We've g-got to get away," I stuttered on. "Dhes-Andis knows who I am, and he knows w-we're here."

"I've got to do something," Hlanan said softly, as if to himself.

"We gave those pirates more of her liref," Kee spoke up. "And we shut them in the big cabin that way."

"All right," Hlanan said. "That's a start." His face tightened with purpose. "Kee, watch out," he said suddenly.

I glanced at Kee, saw her puzzled face, then I tried to look back at Hlanan to ask what he was talking about.

I say I 'tried' because his fingers flickered, stars flashed across my vision—and it was my turn to crumple to the deck, dazzled by a spell.

EIGHTEEN

Someone shook me.

My head pounded in protest. I mumbled "Go away," and tried to dive back down into sleep.

"Lhind. Wake up."

I opened bleary eyes to find Kee's face next to mine. "Ow," I groaned. "Ache all over. What happened?"

She gave me a brief grin. "A stone spell. He said you'll feel heavy at first."

"Oh." I tried to stretch. "I remember that." With the memory came a flood of sadness, of regret. I swallowed fast a couple of times, then tried a casual voice: "So I'm back on the villain list, huh?"

She shook her head. "No, nothing like that. 'swhy I'm here, trying to wake you up."

"Huh?" I sat up, trying to ignore the clumsiness of my limbs. Feeling was coming back rapidly.

"They're up there, talking about what they should do with you." She pointed toward the ceiling. "I thought you should hear. So I came."

I rubbed my eyes. "Thanks, Kee. But what's happening?"

"Come on. I'll tell you while we go upstairs."

I got to my feet, and made two discoveries. The good one: my tail was free, helping me to stand despite the vertigo making my vision revolve gently. The bad one: my sash and its contents were gone.

Smacking my tunic pockets, I said, "My stuff?"

"The Scribe had my mom search you," Kee said, flushing. "Your things aren't in here."

"Hoo," I sighed. "Why? What happened?"

"Let's go," she urged. "You're supposed to be still asleep. And if they knew I was here I'd get into trouble."

I rubbed my aching jaw and followed her into a marble hall lined with arches decorated with vines and wheat cartouches. I'd seen them before. "We're in Imbradi. In Rajanas's palace, right?"

"That's right." She gave a quick nod, and picked up the pace slightly. "The ship landed off the coast of Liacz, and the Scribe found some mage who transferred us here."

"Then why didn't he take you to the Empress?"

"He told me that he was afraid there might be tracers on you, and he didn't have the skill to discover if that was true. I don't know what he told the mage, whose loyalties might lie with the King of Liacz more than with the Council." She rubbed her eyes, frowning. "I don't really understand high politics, and I guess I don't want to. And I'm glad I only had to endure one transfer. That hurts worse than a fall off a horse."

"But why did he put that horrible spell on me?"

"Hurts, does it?" she asked with sympathy. "So you didn't escape that, either. The Scribe said he wanted to keep that evil sorcerer from your mind, and that was the fastest way to do it."

"So the ship captain didn't blame us?"

"I guess he never figured out that we were the target, and the Scribe didn't tell him. After he put that spell on you, he spent a night and a day putting healing-spells on the bandages of the pirates' victims. That was good to watch." She gave another of her quick nods. "He's very deft with that kind of magic. This way."

We started up a long, curving staircase. "So we made it here safely," I prompted.

Kee frowned down at her feet for a few steps. "Yes. A while ago, this message came." She sighed shortly. "I'm not explaining this right. They've been fighting here, trying to hold the Pass."

"I remember that, from our scrying before the pirates attacked the ship."

"I guess there's a whole army on the Liacz side, an invading army of hirelings. That Pass is high, and most of the year it gets snowed in. As of last night, our prince and my grandmother agreed that if we can stall the army off until the snows start again, then king of Liacz won't want them sitting there on his side, and will revoke his grant of passage. Nobody wants an army squatting at their back door. Especially the Wolf Grays." She stopped, then quietly stepped through an archway into a round room decorated with curved couches in emerald green brocade, with an ivory and green rug on the floor.

I followed her through. "So what happened?"

"Sh-h." She frowned at me. "They're in that room," she whispered, pointing across the carpet at the door on the opposite side, then opened a door at her right.

I followed her through a small room dominated by a writing desk and several chairs, then through that room to a glass-paned door that opened onto a balcony.

Kee stopped there and whispered, "But just a while ago a messenger arrived. A Djuran soldier, right into the Destination. He had a message from Dhes-Andis. He said that if we give you up, Dhes-Andis will give the order for that army to go away. Otherwise, he will send them against Liacz, and say that it was our prince who paid them to attack so dishonorably. Everyone knows the Gray Wolves fight for the highest bidder. The messenger will return tonight for the answer. So now they're trying to decide what to do, and I think it's not fair. You should be there."

"Well, then I'll go in and tell them—" I started toward the window she pointed at, but she caught my arm.

"You are supposed to be safely asleep. It's because of what you said about Dhes-Andis being in your mind." She looked uncomfortable.

SHERWOOD SMITH

"Oh. They don't trust me anymore."

"I don't know what they're thinking." But she didn't look at me when she said it.

Instead she motioned me to duck down and crawl along the balcony under the windows of the next room over. We settled underneath the window that stood partially open. The voices from inside the room came clearly.

"I don't care what he promises." I recognized the lovely, musical voice of Thianra the minstrel. "Even if we could trust the likes of Jardis Dhes-Andis, which would be a stupid thing to do, I would prefer to take our chances at holding the mercenaries off, and as for the King of Liacz, I will go to him myself. If I carry a letter from you, Ilyan, I think he'd believe the both of us that Prince Geric Lendan had allied with Dhes-Andis over the fact that you'd suddenly gone mad and were declaring war."

"Or that I could afford the price of the Duchess of Thann's mercenaries." That was Rajanas's familiar drawl. "I'll go to Liacz myself, soon's I get rid of Lendan's wolf pack here. But that is going to take time."

"Which we do not have," Thianra murmured.

Rajanas said, "At least Dhes-Andis seems reluctant to send his own armies over here in force. Yet."

"He seems to be testing our strength. Everyone's strength. One thing I can attest to in my turn is the strength of his magic," Hlanan said. "I'll wager anything he smells a double-cross from either Thann or Lendan."

"The first is possible, but the second is almost sure," Thianra stated. "You are both ignoring tonight's time limit in favor of these longer plans. Does that mean you will surrender Lhind to him?"

"No!" Hlanan sounded hoarse. I wondered how much rest he'd had while I was quiet under that spell. "But when we say no, we had better be prepared for some consequences. There will be some. Their magnitude will depend on how important Lhind is to him. That's what we've got to figure out."

"How can we?" Rajanas asked. I heard the click of crystal on wood.

"We can't," Hlanan said. "We still have Lendan somewhere about, possibly in this very city. If I could find someone to transfer us, he can, too. Or maybe he can do the transfer himself. I am certain now that he got the book. He could never have managed any of that magic without it. Which is why I think we should call the Magic Council and surrender Lhind to them. She'll be safe with them."

Silence. My palms were damp. I pressed them against my sides.

"She won't want that," Rajanas said. "From our short acquaintance, I'd say our little thief values her freedom. If she wanted interference from your Magic Council—"

"Help," Hlanan interrupted. "And training."

"If she wanted any of that, she'd have sought them out herself. I'd say she's reasonably competent in getting what she wants."

"She's a walking peril," Hlanan exclaimed. "You didn't see her set fire to half a street. And the same thing happened to those pirate ships. Without any thought at all to the consequences. That was before I found out about the accursed communications device she'd been playing with. Bespelled device. Communicating not with just any evil sorcerer, but *the emperor of Sveran Djur.*"

"You think he suborned her," Thianra said slowly.

"I don't know. Not consciously, perhaps, but she's so...oh, so gallant, but so ignorant. Desperately so." A sharp sigh followed this. "Look, I hate to see any creature's freedom curtailed, but it's for her own safety. That accursed sorcerer has got to be after her for a reason, and I'll gamble my life he doesn't intend any good by her."

"Then I say we set her free. If she's not here, we can tell him she's not here. As for the other problems, we knew before we ever met Lhind that we'd be having them sooner or later." That was Rajanas.

"Can't you give her at least a start on the training she needs?" Thianra asked.

"I tried," Hlanan said dully. "And I've failed. Why do you think I insisted we abduct her in the first place? We make a vow before we ever leave the School not to leave any lone mages we find without trying to bring them to accept the Council pledges, if not the training. I don't know if I've done too much or too little, but I do know I've completely failed. Lhind is now more a danger to the world, and herself, than she was as a thief running around Thesreve casting illusions. She trusts no one—and we cannot trust her. Lying, for her, is..."

"A game," Rajanas said. "I distinctly recall a pair of escaped galley slaves who played that very same game."

"I call that a habit of survival," came Thianra's gentle voice.

Hlanan gave a sharp sigh. "The point is, I can't believe anything she says, though I want to. Maybe that is why I failed, because I want to...but that is my problem to deal with. Right now, we have Lendan and his book, Dhes-Andis and his threat, and the Wolf Grays up in the Pass. So I guess that adds the King of Liacz to our problems."

"That," Rajanas said wryly, "is nothing new."

Hlanan went on in a low voice, "I've failed in every possible direction. I think it's time to call on the Council's aid, and quickly."

Silence.

I knew what it meant.

I backed out from under the window and retreated into the next room. Like a shadow, Kee joined me, her brow furrowed.

I swallowed something about the size of a sun-fruit that had suddenly lodged in my throat. "I'm gone." I hated the way my voice sounded high. "Soon's I recover my stash."

"I know where it is," she said softly. "I'll show you."

We sped through more fancy halls to a small, plain room on the ground floor. On a table between the windows lay all my burglar tools, including my empty bag of liref, with Faryana's diamonds and the few coins and jewels I had left. I swept them up, hesitating over Faryana's diamonds.

Did they know what those were? I wondered if I should leave them, but instinct warned me not to. *I know you can't hear the others, and even though you won't talk to me I'll see what I can do to spring you,* I promised the silent diamonds as I dropped them into the bag.

"I can get you a cloak," Kee said.

"I'll wait here." I tried a jaunty smile. "I can go out the window when you get back. No one will see me. Thanks, Kee."

"Thank you." She didn't say what for, but departed in haste, her expression even more troubled.

I wandered around the room, trying to think over everything I'd learned. Everything I'd done. But my brain didn't want to work, and all I heard, over and over, was Hlanan saying, *We cannot trust her. Even worse? I can't believe anything she says.*

When Kee returned she put a thick, plain-colored folded cloak in my hands, and then she handed me the pack she'd carried on our shortened journey. "I don't think you'd do any magic to hurt any of us," she said. "But they're not asking what I think."

Without any thought to the consequences. "Are you going to get into trouble for this?"

She glanced down at her open hands. "Kuraf will hear me out."

"Well," I said awkwardly. Then, remembering the liref, "What happened to Rajanas's Steward? The one who drugged their cider?"

"He disappeared. Just ahead of Lendan's assassins, apparently. But he saw to it that his highness escaped first."

I remembered what Kuraf had said about waiting to hear his side before judging him. Kuraf, at least, knew that motivations were not all evil or good, or maybe that people might think their motivations good, but others would disagree.

I couldn't get that into words. Thinking that way was too new. So I stayed with the immediate. "I'll try to pay you back, Kee. I promise."

"If you find a way to help," she said, earnest as always, "there will be no debt." She didn't wait for an answer, but left.

I opened the window and breathed deeply of the cool, moist air.

Rain was on the way. I'd best find shelter by night, I thought as I swung out and dropped into the lacy shrubbery of the garden. Shelter, and a disguise to cover my hair and tail.

Planning for weather and these other details was better than hearing Hlanan say over and over *I've failed*. And *Lhind is now a danger to the world*.

Worst of all, what he'd said about trust.

I slunk through the garden. When I reached the fence I donned the dun-colored cloak, pulled the hood over my head, and slipped into the city. By midday I was plodding bent-backed behind a long line of carts going out through the city gates. The watchful Guards on the gate gave me no more than a glance.

The sun rested atop the highest of the mountains behind me when I crossed the bridge past the last stone plinth of Alezand. The next plinth, on a weather-worn ridge above the river that marked the border, said NAMAS ILAN, and below it, arrows pointing out names of villages or towns, none of which meant anything to me.

I remembered that Imbradi was situated in the northwestern portion of the principality.

I looked around slowly, past the slanting shadows cast by the long prairie grass. Where to go? Behind me lay Imbradi, I'd just stepped onto the western corner of Namas Ilan, which I knew nothing about, with the bulk of Liacz above it. South beyond Alezand lay Keprima, and eventually, Thesreve. Eastward were the nigh impassable Anadhan Mountains, and on their other side the legendary capital city of Charas al Kherval, Erev-li-Erval. Either west or east were mountains, among whose peaks it was rumored the Snow Folk lived. Should I try to find them?

Faryana, are there Hrethans in the Kertean Mountains?

No answer.

There are, but you will not find them, came Dhes-Andis' voice. *I have not, after considerable hunt.*

I jumped, staring around wildly. Then I remembered what had happened aboard the caravel before Hlanan woke up. *You have my range*, I shaped the words with care, keeping my inner door shut enough so that no thoughts or images escaped, only the words I meant to send. *That means you can talk to me this way, without any aids, clear from Sveran Djur?*

Acid laughter tumbled darkly through my mind. *I can, and you will, too. Come, child. I have been patient, a rarity that carried its own brief interest. You show all the potential and the prowess that I'd hoped for. Your ignorance is a little matter requiring time and attention. We will amend that very quickly.*

Hoped for? I stumbled forward on the road, unable to see the road around me. Images came with his words, the merest flicker. One a blue-haired woman, the other a tall pale-haired man. It was the vision of the blue-haired lady that caused me to stop in my tracks, unable to see, to breathe. "I know her! The Blue Lady." I choked on the words.

A triumph of an alliance, don't you think? Your remarkable gift for the arts comes from your mother. She was the best of her kind. But the prowess is part of our Andis-Sveranji blood.

My world had splintered. I clutched my head, remembering— remembering. "She was my mother?"

She also bequeathed to you her regrettable sentimentality, the cold, stinging voice went on. *But you will unlearn that weakness fast enough.*

Unheeding, I thought, *The Blue Lady. My mother. Where is she?*

She abandoned you and returned to her own world. You were lost, but now you are found again, and you are mine. Come to Sveran Djur.

Tears stung my eyes. I thumbed them away. "I don't care what you say," I shouted. "I loved those dreams of her, and I always will. I loved her. And I don't like you. I don't trust you."

Dhes-Andis's thought scoured my mind with scornful amusement. *Trust is the cry of the weak, and to heed it renders you equally weak. When I give a command my servant has a choice: obey or be destroyed. I have no interest in their puling opinions of me. Or in yours either, my ignorant young apprentice.*

I won't, I cried in mind. But still I listened.

You remember the fire spell, don't you, Lhind? he continued, giving me back my own image of drawing fire down from the boiling clouds, and shooting bolts at the frightened guards who moments before were ready to thrash me. *See? I permit you that absurd diminutive your mother insisted on calling you, which will suffice until you have learned enough to assume your real name, your place, your power.*

He must have sensed that leap of my heart at the words 'real name,' but he seemed to think my reaction was to the word 'power.'

Yes! You sampled power and if you are not afraid of the real truth you know you want more. You have the potential to have more. I will train you, and then set you on your own path.

With the words came images, compelling and fascinating: whole rivers set aflame; mountains smashed, sending boulders sky high; a vast army, glittering with weapons and chain mail, all kneeling and bowing their heads before me.

Your mother's blood gave you the ability to shape magic, but it is your Andis-Sveranji strength that will permit you to use it.

His projected images were so alluring that I envisioned myself as he wanted me to. But the grand view of me standing on a castle wall waving a hand and sending armies on the march only lasted for a heartbeat. Much more compelling were the memories of individuals. Hlanan on board the caravel fighting to protect Kee against pirates who singly more than outmatched him. Kee saying with inner conviction 'Kuraf will hear me out' —and me knowing this was true. And Rajanas pressing a knife into my hand and saying 'Even a thief deserves to fight for its life.'

When they work together like that, their strength as a whole is greater than any single part, I thought to myself. Maybe that's the strength in trust. When each depends on the others, knowing they will do their part. That's enduring power, because it gives. Doesn't take.

I'd always had to trust myself. Then came the thought: Even if I had all that magic Dhes-Andis promised, if I don't eventually trust somebody else, well, who would watch when I sleep?

Was this why that sorcerer had not left his stronghold in Sveran Djur to find me himself?

To him I thought, *You may's well get yourself another apprentice because it's not going to be me.*

I whirled about, and took the first running steps back to Imbradi. Back to the people I liked, and to my old, easy ignorance—

Stay. The voice cut into my mental turmoil with a compelling sharpness. *You cannot recross the border.*

I stopped so fast I tripped over my own feet and fell painfully on my tail. *What? Why?*

Why do you think I permitted the girl to let you slip out? I've just now bound Rajanas of Alezand's troublesome province in a barrier spell. When I am done with them Alezand will beg for the privilege of becoming a vassal state. In the meantime no one can cross the border and live.

"A barrier spell?" I whispered the words out loud. I had no idea what that meant, but I didn't think it was anything good.

I will send someone to you.

NO! I shouted that thought as hard as I could.

Do not try my patience too far. I am capable of teaching obedience in a manner you would bitterly regret.

When in a bind, lie, had always been my policy. Maybe that was my Andis-Sveranji blood. Hoo. So...how much of what he said is really true?

I guess I need some time, I hedged.

Once again Dhes-Andis' laughter rolled like thunder through my mind. I turned and faced south, thinking of Thesreve. Knowing he could hear my thoughts. Then I shut the inner eyelid.

I could almost feel him battering at my own inner barrier, but I knew I could hold him out—at least as long as I was awake—and I thought, *Time to run. But where?*

Looking back in the direction I'd come, I descried a greenish shimmer in the air. Stretching my hands toward it, I felt the warning tingle that I now associated with strong magic. I thought of Kee's forthright face; I thought about all of them penned there, waiting for a mage-war that they couldn't win. And I remembered my promise.

Who was strong enough to fight Dhes-Andis?

I wasn't.

Who, then?

I faced the east, where already the sky deepened toward nightfall. It was too late for mere military allies. Beyond those mountains dwelt the Empress Aranu Crown. She would have both the armies and the court sorcerers who could face down the Djuran invaders.

Rajanas's voice drifted through my mind, *Kressanthe will tell stories at Court of this accursed mudball of a thief...*I thought of Hlanan's Magic Council, all ready to pounce on me.

And I thought: *Is Dhes-Andis really my father?* Impossible, instinct said, except my old memory of the Blue Lady and the image he'd sent me matched. The tall, pale-haired man might be the sorcerer-emperor, who might be my father. I just did not know. Meanwhile, supposing someone at the Court does know, and it turns out to be true? Exactly how fast would it take them to sling Dhes-Andis' thieving daughter into the deepest dungeon?

The journey would be fraught with danger, all right. But then, my whole life seemed to have been one long preparation for danger. But there were always the rooftops.

So, the choice was made. All that was left was the method of travel.

A cold breeze sprang out of nowhere, and tugged at the hood of my cloak. *I will send someone to you.*

I shuddered so hard my teeth rattled in my head.

A *fast* method of travel.

I began to run through the grasses, listening to the world around me. Before too long I raced into the strengthening wind on the back of a wild, long-limbed prairie horse.

You are mine...You are mine ...

I pressed my knees against the horse's sides, riding hard, as if I could escape that echo in my head, until the sun sank below the mountains in the west, and my mount slowed and slowed to a drooping walk.

I slid off him to walk him until he had cooled, and let him trot off in search of water. The clouds had piled high into the sky, blocking the emerging stars. I had avoided any signs of habitation, but now I sought some kind of shelter. The land was too flat for caves. Maybe a barn?

The rain had begun before I found what I was looking for, a ramshackle corn bin on the edge of a big farm. This being spring, it was empty except for left-over seed corn, spiders, and a small nest in a corner. I was soaked to the skin, so I pulled off my clothes and laid them carefully over the nearest corn barrels. Oh, the glory of having my hair free! A couple flexes of my scalp, a shake as my fuzz ruffled up, and the rain shook off me, leaving me slightly damp. I hadn't thought to dig into the knapsack Kee had given me until that moment. I discovered not only an extra pair of trousers, a tunic, and a knit cap, but a fresh loaf of bread and a hunk of cheese. Such riches, better than diamonds, I thought happily as I pulled on the clothes, and then broke off half the loaf and the cheese.

When I'd eaten, I climbed up under the rafters, spread the cloak over the moldery hay left up there, set my weapons and the diamonds next to me and lay down, my hair settling over me like a warm cloak.

I lay back, exhaustion weighing me down as I listened to the roar until I caught a faint sound. A steady sploosh, sploosh.

Footsteps.

Sleep vanished. I sat up, reaching for one of my daggers as the door creaked, then slammed open, letting in a whirl of cold air and rain spatters.

The invader struggled to shut the door, making too much noise to be successful as a sneak.

I raised the dagger as I eased into a better defensive position—

Then lightning flashed, blue-white and shocking.

I recognized that silhouette in the doorway. "Hlanan?"

NINETEEN

L ightning flared again. He shivered, wet through. Blinking rain from his eyelashes—the drops glinted like Faryana's diamonds in the sudden flare—he stuttered, "You never looked behind you."

"I don't understand. Did you follow me by magic?" I asked as I flung all my weapons and jewels and food back into the pack, and climbed down.

"No. Can't do magic now. Dhes-Andis would be on us in a moment. You do know that?" His quiet voice, barely audible above the low rumble of thunder, laid emphasis on the 'do.'

"I figured that out," I said. "Too late. I mean, you know about the barrier spell he laid over the border?"

"Yes. But it is worse than that. He has to know your magical signature by now. I think he might know mine. Neither of us can do magic, even an illusion. He'd be on us in a heartbeat." Then, "How did you know about border spells?"

Thunder rumbled and the rain roared overhead. I wished I could see him, but I didn't really need to. I could feel his tension.

"He pounced on me not long after I passed the last border marker, and was trying to figure out where to go," I shouted against the rolling thunder. "Not in person! In my head! He can do it anytime he wants to. But I know how to keep him out, now. I think. I hope. Or...hmm."

Hlanan's voice dropped as the thunder faded away in fretful rumbles, "What did he say?"

"I'll tell you, but first, sit. You're shivering so hard I'm afraid your bones will crack. Here. Where's your pack?"

"I don't have one. Came away without." His voice stuttered. "Found you gone. My fault. I had to find you. Talk. Thought we'd transfer back."

I sighed, and pulled off my cloak. "Put this on."

"No, I can't take your..."

"Flames! My hair keeps me warm enough. Put it on." I flung it around him.

Abruptly the rain lessened to the musical sound of drips. Lightning flared again as Hlanan settled on an upended bushel basket, and as the thunder rolled away into the distance, he said, "Why did you leave?"

"Because you said you didn't trust me."

"I—"

"You did. I heard you. I was listening under the window," I said. "So I left. That explains me. Why did you have to find me? Did you think up some more accusations, or is this your plan for doing some nasty magical thing to me to take me prisoner for your Council?"

Lightning flared again, revealing his bent head. When he looked up, he'd gotten control of the stuttering, though his voice sounded gritty from the effort he made. "When I discovered you were gone. And Kee admitted to what she'd done. I scried you. Difficult spell. Focused on your location. Came alone. Dared not risk anyone else."

I remembered what could happen if transfer magic went awry, and my neck hairs stiffened, tickling against the back of the tunic collar.

"When I recovered. From the magic. You had gone out of sight. Was going to return. Scry you again. Discovered that the border was warded. Couldn't cross it."

He fell silent. All I could see was his silhouette, grayish against the inky shadows of the barn. Angry and unsettled, I waited.

Finally he said, "So I set out after you on foot. I hoped you might go east. I spotted you down-slope in the river valley, summoning those horses. I managed to catch up with them before you vanished over the far ridge. Rode after you."

"That explains what you did. Not why."

"I wanted to explain."

"Explain what? I think I heard pretty clearly what you think of me."

He shook his head. "You heard what I said, but not why I said it."

"'I can't believe anything she says.' Even someone as ignorant as I am can understand that much."

He flinched as though I'd struck him. "'Though I want to,'" he repeated, low-voiced. "Did you not hear that? Though I want to. Lhind, you don't know what's at stake."

"Oh, and now you've decided to tell me everything, when you accused me of not revealing my own secrets?" I could hear my own nasty tone, and squirmed. I did not like the way I was behaving, but I couldn't seem to stem the flow of bitterness.

"No," he said, his voice low. "Not everything. There are oaths to be kept. Others' secrets I have no right to divulge. Some of it unrelated to the problems before us now. And none of them as disturbing as the fact that you kept your connection with Dhes-Andis hidden." He burst out, "Do you have any idea how terrifying that was to hear?"

"I do now," I admitted. And so, because I needed to get it out, I told him what Dhes-Andis had said to me about magic, and about my origin.

Hlanan listened without interrupting. As I was finishing, another brief, violent band of rain came through, too loud for speech, but he seemed to need the time to consider. So did I, though my thoughts chased in a useless circle.

When the ran lessened, he said, "Is that it, then? No more surprises?" I could hear him trying to smile.

"Isn't that enough?" I retorted. And then, to make sure, I said firmly, "That's my budget of secrets. All of 'em."

"I'm glad you don't believe everything he says."

"So he does lie. I thought so!"

"Yes. No, not outright. It would be part of the game he plays to tell the truth, but not all of the truth. Using just enough of it to prod you into believing what he wants you to. For example, his being your father. I doubt very much that that is true. But you might be his niece, for there are rumors that his older brother married one of the Snow Folk. Dhes-Andis was quite angry about that."

"So that man with the pale hair. The Blue Lady. They might be my parents, then?"

"Perhaps." His voice was husky.

I said quickly, "I think we ought to sleep. Since we're here, and neither of us wants to trudge in the rain."

"Lhind, I apologize. For everything I have done wrong."

"All right. I don't like being mad, anyway. It's too tiring. Here. You can have the loft. It was slightly warmer up there."

He got up. I could almost feel his effort. He climbed to the loft, and I heard the little sounds of him settling down.

I looked about me in the flash of distant lightning, and spotted a stack of feed sacks opposite the corn barrels. I felt my way to them in the darkness. They were rotten with dust and dried-out mildew, but better than the damp ground. I dragged them out and curled up on them.

I'd just closed my eyes when a horrible thought occurred to me, and my eyes flew open. "I don't dare sleep," I exclaimed. "What if the inner eyelid isn't enough to keep him out? Can he get into my mind when I am dreaming?"

"It sounds like you've the right instinct. If it helps, think of your inner eyelid as a mind shield." Hlanan's tired voice floated down. "Try this. Imagine going into a little room with no windows, locking the door, and then lying down to sleep. That's how we are taught."

I did, and fell asleep secure in my mental hut.

I woke early, as always, and inspected the outfit that Kee had given me. The tunic was plain, undyed cotton-linen, the trousers egg-shell blue. Down at the bottom of the pack I found a broad silken sash of a bright, peachy orange, which I ran through my fingers, wondering if I ought to bind up my hair to hide it, or put it around my waist.

From the slow sound of his breathing, Hlanan still slept. I plucked the nice, clean cap from the knapsack. It would serve as a makeshift basket. The necklace had fallen into it. I was shaking it out when it coruscated with light that did not reflect from anywhere around me. I gripped it in my fingers, and cautiously opened the mental door.

Lhind?

Faryana! I'd forgotten all about her when I'd told Hlanan I had no more secrets, and grimaced as I picked up the necklace. I made sure that inner wall was closed tight around my thoughts, except for a tiny peephole through which I focused on the diamonds. Then I sent: *Why did you wait so long to answer?*

I slipped out of the barn and began walking, scrutinizing the hedgerows as I listened on the mental plane.

You have learned how to focus. By that I mean you have learned to block out individual farsensers, as well as the universal block you used once on me. I did not have the courage to communicate with you when Dhes-Andis might be listening, even after I was fairly sure you were not choosing to cleave to him.

Who says I was choosing any such thing? I snorted, scaring a bird hopping nearby into flapping up into the air, scolding.

It seemed a close run race there for a time, she returned with considerable irony.

I was about to sling back a hot answer when I remembered my delight in chasing Lendan's warriors about with fire bolts. Then I remembered how the power I'd played with so happily had nearly consumed me.

Is that what you call the dark arts? I asked.

The dark arts twist or destroy the world and the lives on it in order to achieve the magician's ends.

That sounds to me like a judgment on the user, I thought at her as I walked over a mossy stone bridge. *Magic is magic, isn't it?*

In some ways, that is true. But there are practices that are only used by sorcerers of the dark arts. Some of these practices are known to us, but we choose not to use them because of the harm they cause.

I can understand that, I thought.

Further, there are what we call the Mysteries—agents of magic, difficult to explain simply—who know the intentions of any user by some arts we cannot fathom and who choose not to ally with those sorcerers. Dhes-Andis and his colleagues will tell you that these do not exist, because they interfere so rarely. But that is part of the larger balance we vow to maintain. We must know when to interfere, and when not; when action is called for and when not, and always, always, we must consider the far-reaching consequences of our actions. Our most revered magicians appear ineffectual to the common world because they so seldom take perceived action but in reality they are on constant guard to protect and maintain the world's balance.

Do they call us Hrethans one of those Mystery things? I asked. Then I remembered that I'd hidden my Hrethan background from her. And then I remembered the other part of my background.

Sadness permeated her thoughts. *I guessed you are related to the Snow Folk, because I can hear you so clearly. And because you accessed magic so swiftly.* A whisper of thought—maybe her private thoughts?—came, *But you did not trust me enough to tell me.*

I was getting dizzy, trying to keep the pinhole tight and walk at the same time, so I stopped, and perched on an old fence. Then I shut my eyes. *Can you tell me a little about the Snow Folk, Faryana?*

You know nothing of the Snow Folk, yet you are related?

When I did not answer, she went on.

We are called one of the Mysteries by some. But our abilities range, as with the rest of humanity. You can learn more of these matters from others. One thing I must ask—

I waited cautiously, still holding hard on my little peephole.

The question, when it came, took me totally by surprise. *Have you shape-shifted yet?* With the question came a distinct image of a white bird soaring through the skies. Not an aidlar, but larger, with bright blue eyes.

I straightened up so fast that I almost fell off the fence. *So THAT's what Tir meant,* when it first named me Hrethan, I thought to myself. And to her: *Birds? How?*

When we reach a certain age, the ability is just there. One day you stand at a cliff's edge, feeling the pull of the winds, the impulse is there, like using your tail for balance, but inward. Then you take wing. It has saved us time and again from the likes of the Djurans, or the old-time Shinjan slavers, who tried to capture us and sell us as pets to the wealthy.

I wanted to ask her if that shape-changing extended to half-Hrethan, but that seemed a dangerous question. Maybe it's something that only happens to full-blooded Hrethan, I thought to myself, because I had perched on many a rooftop, but never once had I felt an impulse to take flight. A wish, yes. But I knew the difference.

A wave of dizziness blurred my eyes. The long contact was tiring me. *I need to eat*, I thought at her, and I felt her awareness close off as if she shut an inner door on me.

When the vertigo eased, I flipped over the fence to the far side, where I discovered a tumbledown cottage and an overgrown kitchen garden.

I scavenged food from the garden until the cap was full, then trod back to the barn. I found Hlanan sitting on the upended bushel, his head in his hands.

He looked up, his relief smoothing into blandness.

"Breakfast," I said, setting the cap on a barrel, then, out of habit, surreptitiously shoving the necklace back into the pack. Oh. Another secret . . .

Hlanan had been eyeing the snap beans, carrots, three kinds of sweet berries, and a gleaning of chestnuts and hazelnuts that the local animals hadn't found the autumn previous. I halved again the now-stale half loaf, and the cheese. "Got those from an abandoned garden. There's a stream not a hundred paces off, where you can get a drink."

"And wash the grime from my face," he said. "Thank you."

I picked up my dampish clothes that I'd draped over the corn barrels, feeling oddly off-balance. Of course it would be unsettling, I reasoned. I was not at all accustomed to going without my protective layers of disguise.

Before I could eat, I decided to get the worst over. "Um. Actually, I do have one more thing to confess." I pulled out the necklace.

Hlanan almost dropped his food. His eyes went round, then narrowed. "I remember that. Kressanthe's necklace. You were wearing it when you rescued me."

"Yes." And I told him everything Faryana had said. As I spoke, I braced for him to scowl, to scold, to try to take it away for my own good. Since it wasn't mine, I wasn't certain why I hated that thought.

He turned his palm up, as if he were about to demand it, or even plead for me to relinquish it to him, but then his hand dropped to his knee. He gave me a twisted smile. "One good thing, Faryana is better at explaining magic than I, and she saved me a lot of effort." His tone was apologetic. And a little bitter, maybe with self-judgment.

Since he didn't say anything personal, I didn't, either. "Can you free her?" I asked, leaping to my feet as I packed everything into my knapsack except the damp tunic and trousers. "I think we should eat as we walk." I couldn't explain my sudden restlessness.

He obliged, picking up the cap and following me out of the barn. "No. I don't know nearly enough magic."

"Then back she goes inside my clothes, where she's out of sight," I said, suiting action to words. I tied the damp clothes by sleeves and legs to drape over my knapsack so they would dry in the sun as I walked. Imagine, the riches of two outfits!

I ran the silky orange sash through my fingers, fighting the urge to glory in having my hair and tail free to lift in the breeze. Habit was strong.

Because no one was on the road, I tied the sash around my waist, and dared to walk out as I was, my hair and tail snapping around me as if resenting confinement.

Then I joined Hlanan, who was watching the muddy pathway as if wisdom of great import lay there. "Will you honor me by repeating your intention?" he asked at last. "I believe you told me last night, but my wits seem to have fled."

"Going east," I said. "Kee and I talked about it. She thinks Aranu Crown would listen if I told her about Geric Lendan and Dhes-Andis and that army."

"So you are not running away, you are running to someone."

"I've never thought about it that way before. Both, I guess."

"Something I learned from Rajanas, back when we first met." He lifted his head, his gaze reaching far past the dilapidated barn roof. "We were a pair of scrawny twigs, full of ideas, captured flat." He blinked, and gave me fleeting, whimsical smile as he poked among the beans for the last of the berries. "While we were chained together on the galley bench, Rajanas sometimes said that it took some mental twisting, but having a plan instead of mere escape meant, oh..."

"I remember. That if you just keep running, someday you will have nowhere to go." I took the cap back, which had a few beans at the bottom, and three small berries.

"I said that before, didn't I? Forgive me if I sound insufferable. And pass me the berries, would you? Unless you'd like to finish them off."

"You don't like beans? The crisp snap, the delightful smell of fresh green?"

"Not uncooked for breakfast, I must admit. Perhaps later..." He paused as though he was going to say more, but didn't.

"Later what?" I asked.

He opened his hands. "You tell me."

"If I knew, I wouldn't ask," I said. "Did you expect me to find more, then? I will, of course."

"Ah, so we will travel together?"

I stared at him in surprise. "Have we not so far?"

His smile was wry. "Until you left. Though the fault for that was entirely mine," he added hastily.

"Well, what else were you going to do?"

"I hadn't planned on anything but finding you, and asking you to transfer back," he said. "After which...but nothing I'd thought of doing is the least use now, not with that barrier spell. So, my next plan was to find the nearest town where there might be a mage connected to the Council. Try to scry Thianra, and failing that, apprise the Council of what has occurred."

"Sounds like a good plan to me," I said. "We can go together, and you can teach me more things. Oh. That reminds me. One more confession."

Hlanan looked askance, his brows lifting in a way that reminded me briefly of Rajanas. He was trying not to laugh.

"Not a secret," I said hastily. "I overheard it, at the inn. Before I stole the bag of gold the innkeeper was paid."

Hlanan coughed, still trying not to laugh. But when I was done repeating the conversation, all the humor vanished from his face. "So it was a 'she' who sent those hirelings," he said thoughtfully, before he popped the last berry into his mouth.

"You think she is Kressanthe?"

Hlanan gave his head a shake. "No. Impossible." He gazed up into the clear sky, as the cool, rain-washed breeze tugged at our clothes, then his expression changed. "I believe I know. And if I'm right, it answers a lot of questions."

"Geric Lendan acting through someone else?"

To my surprise, he shook his head again. "Geric might have sent a message to her before boarding the yacht. It might have been a condition of his contracting the Wolf Grays. But she would not act on his orders. Not at all." As he spoke, he lifted his head. In the distance riders emerged from a copse of trees and vanished over a hill.

"So who was it?"

We took a dozen steps. I was beginning to wonder if telling me broke one of those mysterious oaths he'd alluded to. Then he said, "The Duchess of Thann."

"Who's she?" As I said it, I thought, haven't I heard that name before?

"She's the one who contracts out the Wolf Grays. Some say she's getting them trained for a major political action, and making a fortune doing it. I can believe that, having run afoul of her. Twice, actually."

"You did? How?

"Really want to hear this old history?"

"Sure," I said. I'd always been interested in his past. "I like stories, and we've nothing else to do."

"Here's the most recent one, then. I was traveling on another matter entirely when I came to the river, and in seeking for a likely passenger boat, I chose the one on which Thianra was employed as a bard, thinking she might be able to tell me a little about the captains. I got more than I expected.

She'd discovered evidence that thefts along the river were not sporadic. We were curious enough to investigate. Discovered that the thieves were part of a ring."

"And so she reported them?"

"I did. She wanted to stay with the riverboat, because she wasn't satisfied we'd found who was behind the ring, so we decided she should lie low. We also wondered if the information would be forgotten, or worse. I made my report, and nothing happened. That was last winter."

He paused, his head turning. His intent gaze caused me to turn my head. I made out the silhouettes of horseback riders vanishing over a distant hill.

Hlanan turned back to me. "Where was I? Oh yes. This spring Thianra discovered that the theft ring was not only protected, but it was part of something much larger. Do you know where Thann lies?"

"No. Wait. Isn't that somewhere beyond Thesreve?"

"Yes. Mountains—hills, really, mining country, between Thesreve and Akerik, which had petitioned to become part of the empire. Akerik has been thriving since joining the empire's protection, and everyone has been happy except the Duchess of Thann, who has ambitions. She uses the wherewithal from her mines to raise and train the Wolf Grays."

He paused to glance around, then said, "The conditions in her mines are deplorable, as she wrests every bit of wealth she can out of them. The empire would like to..." He shook his head. "Listen to me ramble! It's walking in the sun like this."

"So this duchess is running the thief ring?"

"I think it's more that she's benefitting, and using the thieves as spies. And assassins, Thianra thinks. She had been looking for proof when an assassin team came after her. This is one of the reasons why Rajanas set sail as suddenly as he did."

"And here I thought Thianra was just a bard. Except she fights too well to be just a bard," I said.

"She would like to be just a bard," Hlanan observed, his tone difficult to understand. It was tentative, like he could say more, or should say more, but didn't.

Instead, he shifted so he was walking sideways as he peered out over my head. I whirled to look as well, but I wasn't tall enough to see over the hedgerow growing alongside the road, so I turned back, and nearly stumbled into Hlanan. I stepped back, distracted by the shape of his jaw, and the unexpected ruddy-gold glint of whiskers. I snapped my gaze down, my nerves jangling like one of Thianra's stringed instruments. I'd never felt that before, like I had walked uninvited into someone's privacy.

I sneaked a glance upward, to discover him regarding me speculatively. "You've another terrible surprise to spring on me?" he asked, the corners of his mouth deepening in the quirk that meant he was holding in laughter.

"You haven't done the spell to stop beard growth?" The question just slipped out.

He exhaled a laugh. "No." He passed a quick hand over his jaw. "I don't need the beard scraper but two or three times a week. I seem to have been remiss." And, the amusement pronounced, "It could be some day I might need a beard to lend me some presence. I am aware that, even when I am wearing my best clothes, I look like someone's junior clerk."

Perhaps because of Dhes-Andis, the subject of families was not far from my thoughts. "Does your father look like a clerk? You and Thianra are so different. What are your parents like?"

"My father looks like what he is, an archivist," Hlanan said. "On normal days you will find his fingers stained with ink, his robe dusty, and a feather quill or two stuck behind his ears. Thianra's father is an artist—ho, there they are." His eyes narrowed, and he beckoned to me, drawing me under a leafy tree near the road. "After we escaped from the galleys, Rajanas was determined to get military training, and though I didn't, I have learned a little from him. Such as, avoiding creating a silhouette on a hilltop." He gestured to the tree overhead. "And second is to understand search patterns. There are two search parties down there, faster than I expected. It's unlikely that they have anything to do with us," he said apologetically. "But they are too far for me to determine whose colors they are wearing. I'd feel easier if we considered leaving this road altogether, and cutting cross-country toward the nearest town, where it might be easier to get lost among the populace."

"Dhes-Andis did say he was sending somebody to find me," I said, my shoulder blades prickling as I scanned the peaceful countryside again, at least as much as I could see. "I tried to make him think I was going to Thesreve, in case he really could do that. Can he?"

"If he had riders along the border, he could. Even he cannot send armies hither and yon via magic."

"I wish Tir would find us." I dug the last bean out of the cap, sighed, and began stuffing my hair into it. If we were being chased, the sight of my hair would be worse than a beacon.

"I think I transferred too far for Tir," Hlanan said with obvious regret. I finished tucking my tail into my trousers, rolled up my now-dry second outfit (I still could not believe the profligacy of owning two outfits!), and tucked it into the knapsack, and turned to find Hlanan staring. "You better keep the cloak." And, "Which way?"

He blinked, then pointed in a northwesterly direction. "On that last hill, I caught sight of a trade town alongside a lake. From what I've seen so far, the searchers, if they are searching for us, are mostly looking to the east. Let's take an unexpected route."

"Shall I summon horses?"

"I think we're better on foot, though it's slower. We can hide if we're not mounted. And I'd rather not draw attention by an unexplained stampede of animals in our direction."

"Lead on."

TWENTY

We left the hilltop directly, and plunged down the wooded slope, following a stream until we found ourselves deep in a valley. Water trickled everywhere, unseen; slow-stirring air smelled of a thousand kinds of herb, shrub, and tree. On the steep slope of a river streaks of dirty snow remained, stippled with small paw prints.

We picked our way along the riverbank until the folds of land on either side of us gradually began opening as the river broadened. Presently Hlanan glanced at the westering sun and, "You should probably take the cloak back."

"Why?"

"Because we should begin seeing signs of habitation soon, and possibly a road. I'm afraid you'll catch the eye. It doesn't quite cover all your hair in back. Not many have silver-blue hair."

"Oh. Didn't think of that," I said. "Well, if we can get to yon town before the shops close, just let me get about for a bit, and I promise you, nobody will recognize me."

"It's those searchers who worry me. And anyone else who might pass by and be questioned."

I was about to retort that I was very good at avoiding possible pursuit, but then I remembered the first time we met, I was running just ahead of a howling mob. I jingled the coin bag hanging inside my loose clothes. "I can hide. And when we get to town, we've got this."

So it was.

The sun had just set when we drifted into town, me going first, and him a hundred or so paces behind. We agreed to meet in the town center at the next bell, and find a place to stay.

The lakeside portion of town was the busiest. A coin here, and trade there, and my nice new silken outfit vanished piece by piece. When I rejoined Hlanan, at first he looked right past me, gratifying me so much I chortled. Then he whirled around, and whistled. Then sniffed. "A very convincing urchin," he said appreciatively.

"There is nothing like a sprinkling of overheated horse and rancid onion to keep nosers at a safe distance," I said, flapping the front of my new tunic, a patched, tattered garment I'd traded the pretty orange silk sash for.

He peered down at me. "What is that sticking out of your cap?"

"Horse hair. I stopped by a stable, and pulled the hairs out of a curry comb. The splotches are just mud. Nobody will see any silver now."

"Excellent. Here is your apron," he said, handing me a sturdy canvas covering, with many pockets sewn on it. "We are now locksmiths."

I'd given him some coins before we parted. He'd been as busy as I was; his clothes were now worn, patched laborer's clothes of dull green and brown. Over it, of course, he wore the apron, with the guild stitchery over the top pocket.

He led me back to the poorer side of town, away from the lake, where he'd taken a room with a cubby off it at a rundown but popular inn. It catered to laborers and artisans' apprentices. The common room was jammed with brightly dressed people, four and five or even more sitting shoulder to shoulder around little tables meant for two or three at most.

We threaded through to a tiny table, covered by a clean cloth with cheerful bunches of cherries embroidered on it. This table was on the opposite side from the low dais, where an act with two singing women and a pack of dancing dogs performed with loud vigor. The crowd at that end was solid, loud, even roistering as mug-waving customers sang the chorus along with the two-legged performers.

Not long after we sat, a brawny young fellow set down two plates, two bowls, and two mugs of ale. The food was plain, but delicious: plenty of hot bread and cheese on the plates beside roasted bits of fish on skewers, and spicy bean-and-rice soup in the bowls. I put my fish skewers on Hlanan's plate. He inhaled them, licking his fingers after each bite.

When our hunger had abated some, I asked, "Do you know anything about locks?"

He grinned. "As it happens, I am pretty deedy with them. Not among the best, as I only spent a winter season working at it, but good enough to have passed through a few locked doors during my first encounter with Geric Lendan."

"Hah," I said, flourishing my bread. "Crime!"

"I am aghast at your insinuations. My movements were investigative. This untoward glee at my lapses in civilized behavior grieves me," he said soulfully, but he was mocking himself, as he knew, and I knew he knew—and he knew that I knew that he knew—that he had been in every respect a thief. Even if he hadn't actually purloined anything.

I was about to ask why a scribe would study both magic and locksmithing, when the door slammed open and tough-looking armed guards in dark purple surcoats stamped in.

Instinct was faster than thought. Between one heartbeat and the next I'd sunk under the table, my bowl and plate clutched against me.

"Hi, there," the innkeeper's deep voice rasped. "I'll not have my custom disturbed!"

"We are on orders directly from our king," was the accented response. "We seek a Hrethan who has been endangered. We are to provide safe escort."

"Hrethan!" the innkeeper exclaimed.

"Female, appears to be somewhere between fifteen and twenty-five years, brown eyes, not blue."

"There are no brown-eyed Hrethan here, or any other color," the innkeeper stated. "Hrethan not being part of our usual custom, whatever age."

His sarcasm raised a belly laugh from the avid watchers.

"Now get along, please. I've broken no laws, neither me nor my custom, and I'll thank you to send that to your king in Liacz."

The door slammed. The air promptly filled with voices exclaiming, cursing, demanding answers to questions. Above them all the innkeeper roared, "Where's our entertainment?"

A clash of cymbals, a tweetle of pipes, and the singing started up again, ragged but determined.

I oozed back into my chair, and settled my dishes on the table.

Hlanan's brows lifted. I was about to speak, but glanced around, and caught a puzzled look from a woman at the adjoining table. I scowled and crouched over my plate, breaking the last of my bread into pieces.

Hlanan said in the slurred accent we'd been hearing around us, "Mind your manners, rascal. No more diving for coins under the tables!"

The woman looked away again, and we finished our meal in silence, then Hlanan (who was fighting yawns) led the way out. I slouched after him, doing my best to appear the dejected young apprentice.

The room we'd been given was tiny, the cubby off it barely enough to spread out a blanket on the floor.

As soon as Hlanan shut the door, he muttered a spell and light sparked, catching on the wick of a very small piece of candle. He set the candle on the bare table next to a bed with a sagging middle, sat down, and gave himself up to silent laughter. "Under the table?" he finally said.

"Habit." I shrugged.

"Probably as well." He poked the sagging middle of the bed. The slats beneath groaned unpromisingly. "'Hrethan.' Well, we know at least one of their targets."

"Unless there's another Hrethan besides me running around. What was that about the king of Liacz? Aren't we in Namas Ilan?"

"We are. I take it you do not know the local history?" The candle light flickered in his eyes.

"Nothing. This is as far north as I've ever been. As I remember ever being," I corrected.

"A succession of terrible rulers resulted in a civil war after the last king died, and his descendants squabbled over the crown. After two years of the countryside being laid waste as this prince fought that princess and back again, the populace rose against the few contenders left, and appointed a council made of guild leaders and free-town mayors. That lasted about ten years, until the corruption disgusted the populace all over again, and civil war threatened. The last act of this council—as the people howled outside the old palace, wanting to hang the lot of them—invited the King of Liacz in to help keep the peace. He was very glad to oblige, and his warriors are still here. Nobody wants them, but nobody knows how to get rid of them. The kingdom is too impoverished to organize against Liacz."

"This inn, at least, seems to be doing well."

"I will venture a guess that most of that custom works for their bean soup and bread. You saw how little trout there was on those skewers." He glanced at the candle. "If you wish to change, I suggest you take that bit of candle into the closet before it burns out."

"Oh, no," I said. "I just got my new outfit. It needs at least six months of proper seasoning before I change."

"Seasoning!"

"Yes. If capture is likely, I might add a layer of vintage fish in aid of the rancid onion."

"A formidable threat. Do you want the bed?"

"I think that thing would smother me. I'll take the floor," I said. "I'm used to floors."

"At least have the blanket," he said. "It's chilly in here." He pointed to the open window high on the outside wall.

"All I need is the cloak." I pulled it off the bedpost where he'd hung it.

The candle was already guttering. Hlanan blew out the flame, and I listened to the rustle of clothing as he undressed, then the creaking of the bed as he settled in. Again I had that sense of intruding on his privacy, though I had often slept in a room full of thieves, many of whom had preferred to air their clothes at night, and I hadn't given them a second thought. I could not understand my reaction, which made me feel off-balance.

As I wrapped the cloak around me, I thought about how seldom in my life I had been on a name basis with people, much less exchanged as much information as I had of late. If you liked people, it made you vulnerable to attack—Geric Lendan had certainly known that, when he'd threatened to kill Hlanan. A vivid image of Hlanan lying there tied up, his shirt ripped baring that tattoo on his shoulder, and I resettled myself to face the other way, my mind wheeling too much for rest. The mud I'd smeared on my face and the backs of my hands itched, an old sensation that I found steadying. That, at least, was something normal.

"What are you thinking?" Hlanan said presently. His voice was warm in the darkness.

Usually I was quite ready to blurt out exactly what I was thinking. But I found myself reluctant, at least until I understood myself a bit better. "Can't anybody help the people here get rid of the King of Liacz? I mean, without sending another army in?"

"I hope the people themselves will do that. You noticed how most everyone wore a bit of red?"

"No, I didn't," I said. "I thought the room downstairs cheerful, but my habit is to watch faces for threat or question, and hands for weapons. What does the red mean?"

"The original flag was crimson with yellow oak leaves. The red is a gesture of, oh, resistance to outsiders? Maybe even a kind of loyalty, renewing itself after all the trouble. What they need is a leader."

"And then there's a new king, heigh ho, and it all starts over again."

"Not necessarily. Custom and habit are as strong as greed and ambition. Education can be..." His tone was musing. "Effective." He was taken by a yawn. "I beg pardon."

The pause lengthened into a silence. While I wrestled with questions, gradually I became aware that his breathing had slowed and deepened.

I remembered that he'd had little sleep before showing up on the border of Alezand in my wake, and I wondered how much rest he'd gotten the previous night while rain-soaked and chilled.

My body was tired, as I was not used to walking all day, but my mind was not going to let me sleep. So, instead of lying there while my thoughts hooted questions at me like a cluster of owls, I decided to seek some answers on my own.

A quick hop, a wriggle through the small window, and I stepped onto the rain gutter along the edge of the roof. From the hubbub of voices below, the common room was still occupied, though with fewer people. The town was slowly settling down for the night.

I stood up and looked around. In this end of the town, the houses were close enough together for me to leap. Very practiced at this method of travel, I sped along the edges of roofs so that my steps would not be heard by anyone sleeping in attics. I hopped from eave to eave, watching below in alleys and narrow byways for anyone in those purple coats.

In my experience, one seldom overheard important conversations while people were busy on a job. It was when they relaxed in their own quarters that an eavesdropper had the best chance of finding things out.

I finally spotted a patrol, and altered my path to run along above them. As expected, what chatter I could hear was mostly about names I didn't know, sour beer, stable problems, late pay, and observations about what they saw.

But I stuck it out, until (after what seemed forever) my patrol went off-duty. They led me straight to their guard-house, which was not only lit all along the ground floor and half of the upper story, but most of the windows were open to the balmy night.

SHERWOOD SMITH

Pulling my dark green knit cap down to my eyebrows, and safe in the knowledge that I'd mudded my face earlier, I ghost-footed along the roof, listening from window to window.

Dicing...an argument about a horse...two people angry at a third person called 'Morith'...discussion of a meal...three people complaining about some slacker...nothing, nothing, nothing.

I hopped down to the tiled awning over the back door, and landed in a tiny courtyard beside the stable, sending chickens squawking and scolding. I hopped their low fence and pressed against the wall. There was so much noise in the kitchen that no one seemed to have heard the chickens protesting my intrusion. So, watching constantly in both directions, I began slinking below windows . . .

. . . and heard one of the voices from upstairs join a group below-stairs.

". . . agrees with me, why should these wolves think they can order us around?"

A man with a deep voice said, "I've been asking the same thing. Since when does a duchess outrank a king?"

Duchess?

"Morith thinks she's a queen," a woman cracked, causing a room full of laughter.

The laughter cut off abruptly, as if someone had shut a door. I hazarded a quick peek at the corner of the window, hopping on my toes. The room beyond seemed to be a recreational chamber for the guards. Everybody in it faced an inner door, which had been opened.

Four people in gray riding tunics trimmed with dark red entered, fanning out in a row, hands to weapons.

"You had something to say about the Duchess of Thann?" the eldest, a gray-haired man with a pointy beard, spoke into the sudden silence.

"Whatever I said was not intended for any ears but those of my compatriots," a black-haired woman stated, her own gauntleted hand resting on the hilt of her sword.

"It is as well," Gray-beard replied in a slow drawl. "Or I might have something to say that is intended for all ears, which you might not care to hear."

"And if I do not," the woman retorted. "I know what I might do, which you might not care to feel."

The shivery sound of her blade sliding out of its sheath was broken by a new voice. "Now, now, my friends and compatriots! Are we not all enjoined to follow our chiefs' orders? Surely we can find plenty of brigands and criminals on which to practice our skills, rather than one another." And after a pause, the man said in a harder voice, "Can we not?"

"Yes, captain," the woman muttered, and rammed her sword back into its sheath.

"And my friends from Thann? I trust you will forgive any mis-heard words, like reasonable people, and join me in a glass of spice-wine? I happen to have a bottle of the best, set by for special occasions. Surely, your riding on your mission in our territory constitutes a special occasion?"

"Thank you. Permit me to gather the rest of my command, so that I might issue tomorrow's orders. Then we shall rejoin you." I leaped up again, to see Gray-beard make a hand gesture, then back through the door and turn to the left.

As a clump of grays who had hitherto been unseen started toward the door, watched covertly by the Liacz company, I hastily backed away from the square of golden light spilling in the courtyard, and scrambled up to the tiled awning just as the door opened below me.

I flattened myself on the top of the awning as a dozen pairs of riding boots clattered below. Raising my head cautiously, I peered down as Gray-beard looked from left to right, and the rest of them did, as well: wall, stable, fenced-off chicken yard. No people in sight.

Except me. But nobody thought to look up.

Gray-beard said, "Well, you've heard the reports. They insist our target isn't here."

His tone of irony caused mutters among his group, the most audible voice saying, "And they looked so hard."

"It is not their pursuit," Gray-beard stated, shrugging. "It's not to be expected they will match our diligence. So. This I am sure of: if our target is in this town, he will not want to stay long…"

He?

". . . Either he or the Hrethan."

"Do you think they are together, then?" someone asked.

Gray-beard shrugged. "It is possible. I received a communication this morning from Fara Bay that the Hrethan rescued the scribe from Prince Geric. So we can assume that they would travel together if they found one another." He began pointing at his people, dividing them into groups of three. "Therefore. Before dawn, you are to be watching the three roads out of town. I myself will watch the dock, in the unlikelihood they take a boat to cross the lake. Keep yourselves hidden, and refresh yourselves with the description. Stop anyone you have to, on any excuse you deem reasonable. The Hrethan is also a mage, so you'd better take her by surprise, and immobilize her without hurting her. She is worth a great deal, the duchess says, and any who find her will share in half the price." His voice changed. "The scribe, you may damage as much as you wish. The duchess wants him alive, but I did not get the impression she cares how much."

A rumbling chuckle ran through the group, then the leader nodded at the lone person who hadn't been appointed to one of the search parties. "You'll ride to Keshad and hand my report to the duchess. All right, people. You have your orders."

They parted, some laughing.

I lay where I was, terrified they could hear the pounding of my heart, until the courtyard was empty. Then once again, I slithered down, ghosted over the chicken wall, and away. As I leaped from rooftop to rooftop, I wondered if I should waken Hlanan.

But when I got to our window, I discovered steady light. I climbed in to find Hlanan fully dressed, with a new candle on the table. He was busy writing a letter.

When I slipped through the window, he looked up, his mouth a thin line, his eyes marked with exhaustion, his high forehead tense with worry.

His face lengthened in relief. "You're back."

"They're after us both," I said, and told him where I'd been.

At the end, he gave a short nod. "We'd better leave now."

"What about the search for a mage to transport us? Scrying?"

"While I was procuring our locksmith aprons, I asked questions here and there. According to local gossip, the town has several charlatans selling luck charms and the like, and only one real mage, mainly concerned with reinforcing rooftops and cleaning water. Doesn't scry. And even if he could, I'd have to find out what level he is, and if he is Council-sworn. If he's first-level, that is, the most common, there is a chance he could scry for us, then turn around and sell what he heard to whoever asks."

"So no scrying, then. Or should we get a water glass and try?"

"Do you think you can keep Dhes-Andis out?"

"No," I admitted. "Not sure at all."

He gave a short nod. "I think it's time to leave."

"Are we just running, or do you have a destination in mind?"

"We?" he repeated. "So you want to stay together?"

I shrugged, surprised. "Do you want to go alone?"

"Not at all. I like your company," he said, and he flashed a grin. "It's just that I don't want to assume anything on the part of a Hrethan who can kill me with her brain."

Surprised, I snorted a laugh. "Hardly. I've only done that mind-cast thing twice, and the first time made me sick for a day after. When I tried it on you, it made me even sicker. Maybe the other Hrethan are good at it, but I wouldn't say it's a skill I know well."

"Other Hrethan can't do it at all. Unless they are keeping it secret. I've been told that only a few have those talents. So, if you're with me, then let's get going. Keshad is at least a couple days away, if I remember the map aright."

"Keshad?"

His grin flashed wider. "The capital. Morith of Thann never leaves her citadel on the highest mountain in Thann. Or hasn't until now. Don't you want to find out what she's up to?"

I stared at him, distracted by the glint of ruddy gold along his still-unshaven chin, his tangled hair, unbrushed since it dried from the rain-washing the previous evening, the tunic he'd pulled on so hastily that the lacings hung loose, revealing the line of his collarbone on one side. He certainly did not look like a clerk's assistant now.

"Why not?" I said.

TWENTY-ONE

"Is your knapsack ready?"

I picked it and the cloak off the floor. "Ready."

He blew out the candle, and to my surprise, pushed it into my fingers. "Since I had to pay for an entire candle, we may as well keep it. I made up some story about a missing lock for which I had to search, but I could see they were suspicious. I wish you'd let me know you were going out to scout...but yes, I fell asleep. Well, well. Can you see now? Shall I take the first turn carrying the knapsack?"

"Sure," I said, to both questions, as I tucked the candle in beside the diamond necklace.

"Then lead the way," he said, shrugging the knapsack over his shoulders. "No, not through the door. We don't want anyone downstairs seeing us leave. In fact, if the innkeeper thinks we are still asleep, and keeps any search party down below waiting for us to descend, so much the better."

Moving carefully, because he was not as small or as agile as I, he followed me out onto the roof, along the edge, and down.

And then, as the rest of the town quieted into slumber—except for guards, thieves, and bakers—we made our way as noiselessly as possible to the east side of town, and then,

SHERWOOD SMITH

careful to move parallel to the road, we set out walking as Little Moon dipped low on the horizon, and behind us, half of Big Moon arced lazily on the other side of the sky. The balmy air smelled sweet; somewhere in the vicinity grew a citrus orchard.

As soon as the silhouette of the last house was well behind us, I said, "I can understand why that duchess wants me unharmed. Dhes-Andis won't give anyone a reward for a dead Hrethan. But the things they said about you make it sound like she is carrying a grudge."

"I suspect she is."

"Against you?"

"Against me."

"You told me what you and Thianra discovered, but you didn't tell me about your first encounter with her."

"It didn't seem important at the time."

"Now we have nothing but time. And a long trudge ahead, for I don't hear any horses in the vicinity. Not loose ones. How did you first know this duchess?"

"I was very young. Very callow. Thought I was smarter than anyone else. Subsequently I found out that the sort of fellow I was is her favorite prey."

"Prey?" I asked, sniffing the air. We were passing someone's garden.

"I met her by accident. I thought. This was when the Council assigned me to work my half year as an assistant, when I was almost seventeen. Harbor mage in Akerik, at Enlee Bay, on the east coat. Beautiful city. When I think back, it's embarrassing, how easy I was to beguile...she admired me so much, thought me so learned for my age, so comely. And, oh, she just wanted help with an old curiosity she'd happened upon. She was a collector of such, she said. Could I translate it? Sure I could, proud of my prowess, until I discovered that the scrap of paper she happened upon was a spell of blood magery."

"I don't know what that is."

"You don't want to know what that is," Hlanan said grimly. "But if you did know, you'd understand why Thesreve kills mages."

My innards tightened with bad memory.

He took a few steps in silence, as if he were thinking, too. "Anyway, in horror I earnestly told her what it was. She professed to be astonished, but I could see that she wasn't."

"She wanted you to translate evil spells for her?"

"I think she was leading up to that. At first I tried to make excuses for her, but it didn't take long to discover that she was wooing a young scribe at the same time that she had been dazzling me. He told me she thought him comely, and learned for his age, and he was so *very* clever, could he sneak into a Council archive?"

All I could see of Hlanan was his profile outlined against the brilliant stars, but I could hear an undertone, almost a roughness, like hurt. Then he laughed, as if it were no matter, so very long ago. "A salutary lesson! There are few things more gullible than young boys who enter the world thinking themselves comely, learned, and more clever than anyone else."

"Boys or girls," I said, uncomfortably remembering my handsome actor.

"To resume. He was young enough to like the risk, and she offered him a flattering reward. He was supposed to copy a page at a time, as it was difficult to get at the book for long."

"Why do they even keep it, if it's so dangerous?"

Faryana? I opened the mental door a pinhole. *Are you listening?*

I cannot not listen, as long as you wear my necklace. Her mental voice was wry.

Do you know what book he's talking about?

We are constrained from talking about that.

Of course she was. I shut the pinhole, as Hlanan went on, unaware of my quick mental exchange. "The Mage Council got involved in a...let's say an intense debate. Very intense. Some thought the book ought to be destroyed. Others that it ought to be studied to develop antidote spells, for they don't believe there was just one copy."

"Like there is never just one cockroach," I said.

He uttered a brief, soft laugh, then the humor faded. "Those who practice blood magic earn an instant death in most kingdoms. There were many in the Council who assumed it had successfully been stamped out a couple centuries ago, when the kings took the matter into their own hands, and began executing any accused of using blood magic."

"Thesreve decided to execute anyone doing magic, except licensed mages who go around and fix things, accompanied by armed guards," I said.

"Exactly. Thesreve was particularly hard hit many years ago, so they remained vigilant, but most had relaxed their concern. Other kingdoms permit certain spells, under tightly controlled circumstances, for what they consider justified legal or political reasons. Alezand is one, though I have been working on Rajanas to change that law. Anyway, about fifteen years ago, this book surfaced in the loot from Shinjan slavers who had been preying on islanders on the other side of the world. The duchess told this young scribe that the book was her family history, kept from her by some political trouble in the past."

"So he didn't know it was magic?"

"No. He thought he was copying out Ancient Shinjan records. Few scribes learn that language."

"He could just sneak in? They didn't guard it?"

"It was bound with wards. But she'd given him some kind of magical token that blocked wards, though he probably thought it was a luck charm. So he wafted right through, without knowing what danger he was in. How she got that..."

"My guess is that there's some young mage somewhere else who was bedazzled by a duchess who told him he was clever and comely and all the rest of it."

"No doubt. And now I wonder if that was Geric Lendan. Anyway, while the scribe was out with a party of friends one evening, I burned his pages, and left her house. I returned to Erev-li-Erval and reported what she was doing to the Council representative. I don't know how stiff a fine she paid, or what lies she told to the Council, but even though this was ten years ago, she apparently never forgets a grudge."

"Was this the book you wanted me to steal?"

"Yes."

"Wanted me to steal it from that Council?"

"No, not at all! I got word not three days before we met you that the book had gone missing, and the Council sent out warnings to all mages of a certain level to be on the listen for signs of it. You'll remember that Emperor Jardis Dhes-Andis threatened to be able to find you by a tracer spell."

"I haven't forgotten," I said. "I haven't made the smallest shimmer since I left Rajanas's city."

"Well, such a tracer spell was warded on that book, along with many other protections. Whoever took it transferred the book by magic to Finn, a small principality in the eastern mountains. It was near enough to Thann that I thought it might be worth investigating, in case the duchess possibly had anything to do with it. My thought was, you and I could travel as scribe and apprentice, and see if we could locate it. By then I hoped to convince you to go to the Council with me, where you could be safely enrolled in their training."

"Do you think Geric Lendan got on that yacht because he had the book?"

"I do now. And oh, he must have enjoyed gloating."

"That book is sounding nastier with every mention. And you wanted me to steal it?"

"I wanted you to help me search for it. After meeting you, I thought, if anyone can find that book, it's a thief who knows magic."

"We. You said we, a moment ago."

"Do you think I would have sent you alone?"

"I think you would not have trusted me alone," I retorted.

He said in a low, flat voice, "I apologize again for what I said the other day."

"That's not what I meant," I said in haste, and considered, saying slowly—finding my way toward the truth—"Though I don't know what I *did* mean. When we were on the yacht, I didn't like how you and Thianra were so ready to trust me. It made me uncomfortable."

"How?" His voice lightened a bit.

"Because it made me feel I ought to be trustworthy, of course. I hated that sense of...of invisible bonds. But when I overheard you say you didn't trust me, it felt even worse. And I know you explained. I understand everything, and yet here I was just now, trying to get you to repeat it all, as if making you repeat it would...make me feel more trusted? But that's not how to make trust, is it?"

"I sensed something of your dilemma by the second day we were together on the yacht," he said, the note of constraint gone. "Rajanas agreed, but—getting back to the book—he thought you would not be able to resist stealing it and then vanishing, to offer it somewhere else to the highest bidder. He added that he would have done that, when he was a street urchin, after his family was murdered in retaliation for some of his grandfather's excesses, and he found himself dumped on the streets of Fara Bay, when he was small."

"He's right about what I would have done to anything else, but he's wrong about the book." I shook my head. "That is, if you'd told me what that book really was, I wouldn't have been tempted to steal it for myself. And that wasn't a matter of trust. I would rather not meet the kind of people who would pay for such a thing."

I could hear the humor in his voice. "A practical attitude. As well as shrewd."

I had to laugh at myself for the sense of gratification I got from his words. "Is she beautiful, this Duchess Morith?"

Again he walked in silence for a time, then finally said, "Not sure how to answer that. Everyone is beautiful. Except when they are angry or hateful. Anger and hate are not beautiful. Looking back, I realize she didn't always hide either, but I was so bedazzled, I made excuses for her. Heh! What a fool I was!"

"Is it foolish to trust someone's words?"

"It is foolish to trust flattery."

"But how does anyone know it's flattery and not truth?" I exclaimed. "We all want to believe we're smart, comely, and deserving of..." I sidestepped naming emotions I still felt ambivalent about. "I am very sure I would not have talked to Dhes-Andis as long as I did if he hadn't almost said that he was my father. He certainly made it clear that he was family. He must have understood at once that I felt the lack, before I was aware that I felt it. So I can understand Morith of Thann using her wiles as the quickest way to get what she wants, though I hate her for it. Those feelings ought to be..." I thought of my cherished dreams of the Blue Lady. "Those feelings ought to be sacred." I glared at Hlanan after I spoke, daring him to laugh at me for sentimentality.

Hlanan walked, head bent, as a night bird cried faintly in the distance. "Love, or what one thinks is love, makes one vulnerable. Neither of us was the first to be so used, and won't be the last. Is that a hill?"

"Yes, and I smell..." I sniffed. "Horses!"

Within a short time we were on horseback, riding toward Keshad. We didn't slow until the stars glimmered and vanished ahead, the distant mountains emerging in the diffuse gray-blue of a summery dawn. When the first pearlescent rays of the new sun slanted down, picking out the roof tops and towers of Keshad, we set the horses loose. They frisked along the riverside toward home as Hlanan and I lay behind a hedgerow to snatch a quick rest before the morning traffic began.

I woke abruptly at the plodding sound of horse hooves and the creak of wood. Wagon! As I struggled up, panicking, I remembered that the Gray Wolf courier was to set out in the morning, and couldn't possibly be here yet. Sure enough, the first person on the road in the early light was a farmer.

I turned my gaze away, and froze.

Hlanan uttered a soft, happy laugh as, at the same time, we discovered the white aidlar sitting on a branch above us, ruby eyes glinting as Tir turned its head from side to side.

"Tir?" Hlanan held out his arm.

A squawk, a flutter of wings—the aidlar perched on his forearm, uttering little bird cries. I cracked open the pinhole in my mental shield, to be flooded with shrill mental cries, joyful and exhausted both: Lhind hear! Lhind hear!

Tir had undertaken a heroic search for us, flying for days.

Since I had kept my mental "door" closed, Tir had navigated by listening for Hlanan. This disturbed me until I remembered that, just as there is a magical 'signature' there is also a mental one. Though Hlanan obviously didn't keep his mental door shut all the time, Dhes-Andis didn't know him, and so couldn't find him in the realm of the mind.

Tir made it clear that joining us meant it was time for activity, not for flying up somewhere to tuck head under wing and snooze. The aidlar had already rested, probably more than we had.

Hlanan said slowly, "With Tir here, we can get twice as much done by separating, one to follow the couriers wherever they go, and the other to listen to rumors around the city. Count how many Gray Wolves are among the Liacz army. How the local people regard both."

I said, "I can spot and follow the couriers. I'm good at that."

Hlanan got to his feet and dusted himself off. "Yes, much better than I. Also, though I don't plume myself on my memorable looks, I can't count on who among Morith's most loyal servants might recognize me at a glance, even in this locksmith garb. It's important to be stealthy, silent, and unseen."

"Stealthy, silent, and unseen," I repeated.

"Especially by the duchess," he added, glancing from me to Tir. "She is dangerous and vindictive."

"Unless she lurks in the kitchens, I don't plan on ever seeing her," I assured him. "Kitchens are always where the good gossip is."

He cast a relieved glance up at the slow-moving sheet of little puffy clouds that meant rain, then said, "Tir will know where we are if there's trouble. Since Tir has joined us, I think I'll walk into town and ask for work. At the same time, count how many Gray Wolves are in the streets. Maybe the locals, or even the Liacz foot soldiers, will be complaining about them. I can also get us some breakfast, if you've any more of your ill-gotten gains."

"Ill-gotten? I would call my stash nippily-gotten! This is the cash the Duchess paid that innkeeper for our capture, so she really does owe it to us," I said, digging into the knapsack. "Here are some imperial silvers. I've heard everybody takes them, whereas I don't know about lecca this far north."

"Good thinking," Hlanan said, as I poured coins onto his palm.

By now the morning traffic had increased steadily, most of it people heading in to market. Hlanan slipped in among them. Before he was out of sight beyond a hill full of wildflowers, I saw him in conversation with a wool merchant and an aproned girl carrying a basket, Tir flitting high overhead.

Silent, stealthy, unseen, I reminded myself as the market traffic increased steadily. *No magic. Remember to make a pinhole so Tir can find me.*

As the morning light strengthened, taking on the peculiar white glare preparatory to a storm, I shifted uncomfortably on the grass behind my shrub. My skin itched, especially my hair, confined as it was in the cap. Why had I ever thought disguises were fun? My eyelids burned with tiredness as the heat became oppressive.

Midmorning, I was thinking about moving just so I wouldn't fall asleep sitting up when a pair of tired, foam-flecked horses appeared on the road, the man and woman riding them looking hot and uncomfortable. Between the pair, they carried enough weapons for half an army.

This had to be my courier and partner.

I got up, drifted into the crowd, and began to follow them. I remembered to make a pinhole long enough to let Tir know I was moving, then shut the inner door. I was far too tired to listen mentally and walk without getting dizzy.

As it happened, the journey was not long. Keshad was built along the curve of a ridge above a loop of the river. The royal castle took up a great portion of the riverside, built largely of limestone, which looked translucent in the glaring white light. Its roof was made of many-colored tiles.

The royal garden behind the castle abutted a vast square flagged in geometric patterns, around which were built many grand houses of three and four stories, each with carved balconies with fanciful vines and leaves and on the eaves, gargoyles to scare away bad luck.

The grays crossed the square to a singularly grand house. Surrounded by a high lime-washed stone fence topped by sharp ironwork spikes, this house was also made of limestone, with eight double chimney-stacks on the beautifully edged roof, two to each alabaster wall.

As soon as I saw the great gate with its gatehouse above, I knew there'd be no sneaking past that. Not without a shimmer, and I couldn't use my magic.

So I slunk along the fence until I came to a portion overreached by leafy green branches of a chestnut tree. There were gardens to either side of the house, crowded with fragrant fruit trees, and sky-sweeping chestnuts to further block the unsightly windows of the neighboring mansions.

By the time the couriers had passed inside the gate and dismounted at the stable, I had leaped up and ghosted over the wall. I light-footed through the garden and peered between sweet-berry vines in time to catch the couriers treading up stone stairs to the servants' entrance.

They vanished. I surveyed the kitchen court: water being hauled from the well, clucking and pecking chickens, a bored urchin about my size turned fresh fish on a spit over an open fire next to a bake house.

Another urchin, a girl, came out with a basket and trod to the henhouse. They definitely hired youths, then.

I pulled off my locksmith apron, leaving me in my dirty but otherwise unremarkable clothes not unlike what I saw in the kitchen helpers. I looked around, spotted the well, and walked out to grab a pail. I dipped it and carried it toward the kitchen, my heart pounding; everybody in a busy kitchen always needed more water than they had. I would carry that pail as long as I could, until someone noticed me. Maybe, with luck, someone would set me a task, and I could listen the more.

But I'd no sooner made this plan as I lugged my sloshing pail inside than I overheard a pair of apprentices, both wearing the red caps of bakers, complaining in a side room as they worked over a flour-dusted prep table.

". . . who she thinks she is, ordering Vilik around like he's a slavey? If she treats artisans like that, what will happen if she sees us?"

"We'll be put to mucking out the pigs, no doubt. What kind of a mage is she, anyway? You'd think anyone who knew real magic would be able to magic up her own food. What good is magic for, if you can't do something that simple? 'Fetch me a cold drink...fetch me hot bread . . .'"

Mage?

"Hush," the first speaker said, lowering her voice. "If *she* said we wait on the mage, we wait on the mage."

"I hear you," the second muttered. "Besides, with our luck, that witch'd turn us into doorknobs as soon as look at us. I've no doubt she knows how to do *that.*"

Mage? Why did the duchess have a visiting mage? Because 'she' had to refer to the duchess. The two didn't say the word with hatred, more like with the emphasis you give to someone whose words, interests, and moods are all-important.

I cast a glance inside the kitchen, which was frantic with activity. There seemed to be two sets of actions going on: the preparation of enormous amounts of food, and stacks of plain, shallow dishes. That had to be for the guards. At the far end, a man wearing the tall yellow hat of a master cook directed the finishing touches to a meal, with beautiful porcelain dishes waiting on silver trays.

Ahah!

I lugged my pail in, scanning the workers. Red hats: bakery and pastry. Yellow: cooks. Between the busy workers darted youngsters in gray tunics and trousers, with gray tasseled caps. Pages!

I dodged around busy people, and followed one of these pages until I spotted the linen chamber. Here were not only table clothes and napery, but aprons, hats...and gray tunics and caps. And, tucked under the shelf of aprons, several sets of servant slippers, all with quiet soles.

I plucked up tunic, trousers, cap, and shoes, ducked behind a cupboard of serving dishes, and hastily shed my old outfit. Using my water, I washed myself off as best I could, getting rid of my carefully applied rotten onion and horse sweat. Then I donned the page's livery, making sure to hide every vestige of my hair under the cap. I made sure the last of my horse hair (which I'd been shedding without noticing) hung down my back, covering my hairline over my neck.

I folded my old clothes and stuffed them inside the waistband of the gray trousers, which were too large. And then I slipped out, lurking beside the silver trays as the last dishes were set on them.

The master cook glanced at me, and made a shooing motion. "What are you waiting for? Take that up to the rose chamber before it gets cold! Do you want a flogging, boy?"

I gulped, and then a large hand reached past me to pick up one of the trays. "Come on, stupid," a tall, skinny boy said, his voice cracking. He frowned, looking at me a second time. "You new?"

I ducked my head in what I hoped was an obedient nod as I picked up the second tray.

"Well, come along, and don't dawdle. She hates loiterers." We sped up carpeted stairs to a beautiful hallway with climbing roses painted inside the archways, and beyond to a chamber overlooking the side garden.

We set our trays on a buffet, me copying every movement made by my guide. I dared a glance at the occupants of the great wing-backed chairs at either side of the two tall windows. In one sat a woman of about fifty, her gray-streaked dark hair plainly dressed. I sensed magic somewhere about her, but she could have been wearing some kind of spell-laden charm. She wore a simple gown of such a deep purple it was nearly black.

In the other chair sat a red-haired woman wearing paneled silk robes embroidered with cherry blossoms, her curling hair dressed with sticks of pure gold.

". . . the weather in the valley is quite breathless, Morith," Purple Robe was saying. "If you insist upon a demonstration so we can get on with this, may I suggest we get it done? I find this climate insalubrious."

Morith?

The red-head turned, and languidly snapped her fingers. "You, there. Open the windows."

She hadn't looked at either of us, but it was clear from her manner that she expected to be obeyed. That one was Morith, I was sure.

The skinny runner leaped to obey. The duchess said, still without looking, "We'll serve ourselves. Shut the door after you, and do not disturb us until I ring."

Stealthy and silent I'd managed as promised. Now to get myself unseen. There was no chance they were going to talk business with us there...but outside those two open windows was the chestnut tree.

I made it outside in the count of twenty. Three people had shouted orders at me on my way down. I'd nodded and bowed each time, and kept on running.

When I reached the tree, I climbed as high as I dared.

They were not speaking Allendi, but a language I knew by their clashing accents and their slow, considered speech was neither woman's native tongue. Later I discovered it was Elras, that spoken in the empire of Charas al Kherval.

". . . take Geric Lendan off the list, then?" That was the mage.

"Why not? As you see, I won." The duchess had a high, sweet voice, but anger revealed itself in the quick sibilants. "And before that, he did absolve himself with that information about Sveran Djur wanting the Hrethan. It is always good to get an emperor on your side. Especially with so easy a capture."

"Lendan said the Hrethan knows magic."

"Eh, they all do, but they don't use it to any discernible purpose," Morith said dismissively. "Or they would hold power now."

"Perhaps," the mage said, as silver clinked against porcelain. "Your local politics hold no interest for me. I promised you three lives bound as you will. Three only. And then the book is mine."

"As we agreed. But the demonstration lies outside of that," Morith said with a quick laugh. "I wish to see for myself that you can do what you say you can. Only a fool would not insist on evidence. And once you have completed what I ask, the book is yours. What use have I for such things? I cannot begin to read it."

The book? She had it in her possession?

I caught hold of the branch above, holding my breath lest I rustle the branches—or fall out of the tree. Shutting my eyes, I concentrated, made a pinhole, then sent the thought to Tir: *Book! Tell Hlanan, she has the book.*

Thunder crackled in the distance, nearly smothering the mage's calm, low voice. ". . . tell me whose blood to use, and we shall begin?"

A gust of cold wind whooshed through my tree, causing me to grip my branch tighter as it undulated.

In the room, the duchess said, "I intended to use Hlanan Vosaga's. He is still first on the list. For your demonstration, let us use one of my prisoners. I will send—"

Click. She had shut the windows.

Prisoner? Hlanan? List?

The only possible answer to those questions was: *I have to get that book.*

I looked around. The first spatters of rain hit the branches. A huge, cold drop splattered on my cheek. I slithered out of the tree, then dashed for the kitchen again. I'd gone inside two steps when someone smacked my head from the side, sending stars across my vision, and I fell to my hands and knees.

My cap was my first thought, but I hadn't been hit hard enough to knock it loose. As I got to my feet, a man snarled, "I told you to stack the cups!"

I thought wildly, and waved my hand toward the stairs. "I was sent to polish…"

My imagination failed me, but he was too impatient. "I don't want to hear it. Now, get those dirty dishes from upstairs. You know what will happen if she sees them sitting around."

I bolted upstairs, delighted with the order. The first room I came to had obviously just been vacated. From the smell, by a crowd of sweaty people. Dirty dishes sat everywhere. A girl of about twelve, wearing gray like mine, was busy piling dishes onto a big wooden tray.

She looked up, relieved when she saw me. "Oh, good. Master Dolaff said he'd take a stick to me if I didn't get this room done at once. They're having another meeting."

"Sure is busy today," I said.

She rolled her eyes as she picked up cups and I grabbed plates. "Are you one of the Thann pages?"

"Sure am," I lied.

"Is *she* always like this?" the girl whispered, leaning toward me. There was no hint of admiration in her use of 'she.' "It was so nice, before she got here. The bossiest of 'em was Captain Parkal, but he was all right if you remembered everything and were quick."

"Always," I said, nodding. "I could tell you stories," I began, hoping this girl would behave like most people, and be more eager to talk than to listen.

"That's what Vilik says! But he also says that *she's* always on the move. But has she budged? Not even outside, ever since she brought that horrible witch here..." The girl went on babbling in a fierce whisper as I began bringing all the dishes from the window sills and cabinet tops and side tables to the buffet.

I heard a lot about life in the mansion, but nothing about magic books, mages, or plans. When the tray was filled, I said, "How about I take it down, and you stack the rest. We'll be faster if it's all ready for the tray."

"Good idea."

I hefted the tray of dishes, and staggered out. What now? I paused, looking down that long hall, then spied a sideboard at the other end, under a window. A few painful steps and I eased the tray down, glancing at that closed door where presumably the duchess and the mage were still eating and talking about blood magic.

I had not seen anything like a magic book in that room, nor had I felt anything with strong magic, aside from the mage. She couldn't have had a book with her, though.

That meant the book had to be somewhere else, and now was the time to search, before that precious pair went looking for their blood victim.

I was about to try the nearest door when I heard the snick of a lock behind me. The duchess's room! I picked up the tray again, bowed my head, and scurried down the second staircase a heartbeat before she got the door open.

Downstairs, I entered a beautifully tiled vestibule, to be waved at by an older woman in livery. "Are you mad?" she whispered, her eyes wild. "You know she hates servants here, especially with *that*." She glanced at my load of dirty dishes, placed a hand on my back, and nearly shoved me through a narrow doorway I hadn't seen.

I found myself in a narrow hallway of plain plaster, that smelled of stale cabbage. From the other end came kitchen noise. Propelled through by another exasperated shove, I managed not to drop my tray, though it was a near thing. I reached a long prep table, where a pair of brawny teenage boys in Wolf Gray livery took my tray and began plunging the dishes into a huge water barrel. Magic flashed, and the dishes came out dripping but clean.

I picked up the empty tray, turned around to make another try for upstairs, when I glanced at the bread room and stuttered to a stop.

Sporting a red cap, his hair neatly braided, was Hlanan. He motioned a couple of pages, who were carrying little cakes, looked up, and in the most natural way, exclaimed, "A page! Just what I need for the berry toppings."

TWENTY-TWO

He'd gotten rid of his canvas locksmith apron and scrounged a baker's apron from somewhere, which he'd pulled over his grubby green tunic and brown riding trousers.

"They are searching for you," I breathed, the moment we got inside the bread room.

"I know that," Hlanan whispered back, motioning the other pages out.

"For blood magic," I added.

His eyes widened, and it was his turn to stumble to a stop. "I didn't know that."

"I overheard—"

"I found out—"

We spoke at the same time, then he said grimly, "Blood magic? You had better go first."

As he motioned to bowls and containers of ingredients, I handed them off and told him as quickly as I could what had happened.

He threw ingredients together in a gigantic bowl, stirring with a wooden paddle. "This is what I found out," he murmured, glancing once over his shoulder. "She's been hiring locals left and right. Soon's I discovered that, I came straight here, and all I had to do was mention baking and a harassed steward pushed me in here."

"Why is she hiring so many people? They are going crazy in there."

"I noticed. Understaffed, and a terrible lack of facilities. I overheard some grousing from a couple of guards sent to chase chickens for dinner. She's pulled in all her mercenaries not on contract, to this city. Headquarters in this house. I think they are all eating here, as she doesn't want the Liacz force, or the locals, knowing how many of them there are. The king of Liacz issued an order limiting how many armed followers any noble can have."

"What can be the purpose?" I asked, and then pointed to the bowl. "Is that a big mess, or do you know what you are doing?"

"Of course I know," he said with dignity. "Spent a very memorable summer as a pastry prentice, just before I got snatched by the galley slavers." He flashed a quick, distracted glance behind. "Stir the berries in after I get the sugar and the cream cheese blended," he said in a self-important voice, as someone entered and dumped down more cakes, steaming from the bake house. "Then you decorate the top of each cake....She's gone. As for Morith's purpose, I suspect she's going to make a try for the empty throne of Namas Ilan—"

"Hlanan, she is hunting for *you*. To use *your blood*. You have to get out of here, and let me—"

"Not leaving without you," he said evenly.

"She doesn't know who I—"

"Berries are in that container over there. Stir them gently, or they break and turn the icing purple." I knew from his change in tone that someone new had entered. Lightning flickered in the window, then the entire house shook under a crash of thunder.

Hlanan gave the topping a last stir, then motioned for the berries. As he gently blended them in, he said over his shoulder to the two kitchen helpers about to depart. "I need to see to the pastries. You two can top these cakes here, while the new ones cool. All you do is dip this spoon like this, and use this spoon to drop the topping onto the cake, then you swirl..."

In three steps, the little cake was perfectly topped. He demonstrated with three more cakes, set them on a plate, then handed a spoon to each page. He picked up the plate and started toward the door. "Eat the failures and hide the evidence," he said kindly, as the pages brightened. "But do hurry. You'll have a horde of hungry soldiers howling soon."

Another crash of thunder rattled the windows, followed by a sudden roar. The rain was here.

Hlanan bore his plate out into the kitchen, moving with an air of purpose. I trailed him. He looked around, then spotted one of the servant halls beyond a swinging door. We slipped inside, and he held the door shut.

He pulled off the red hat and we looked at each other. His gaze searched mine, eyes flicking back and forth, as if he wished he could hear my thoughts. He passed his free hand over his face, fingers tense, then dropped his hand. "We need to find that book."

"Before that mage does her demonstration," I said, and then the truth hit me, sudden as the thunder shaking the house. "You don't mean to search. You mean, go take it."

Hlanan's face was bleak in the shadowy light. I could feel him poised to action, to risk, no throw away his life, to prevent a greater evil.

"At least let me try," I said, pointing at my page's outfit. "I can poke my head in, see what faces us, and then we can figure out how to do it." I reached to take the plate of cakes. "This will be my excuse to go upstairs."

"All right," he said, relinquishing the plate. "And while you do that, I will scout a bit. The duchess cannot be in two places at once."

I didn't see what use that would be, as the book was our goal, and we were pretty sure we knew where it was. But I would have agreed to anything, as long as he stayed away from the duchess and her sanguinary plans for him.

I ducked through the door, mentally opening the pinhole as I made my way to the backstairs. *Faryana?*

That book must be captured and destroyed! I will help you. Call to me the moment you see it.

I ran up the front stairs to the main hall. Hlanan vanished in the direction of the back stairs.

When I got to the next floor, I found the hallway deserted, and all doors shut. I listened at the one where I'd first seen the duchess and the mage. No sounds.

I pulled my lockpicking tool from my stash, used it on the old-fashioned lock, then cracked the door open, ready to fling my plate of cakes if anyone charged at me—but the room was empty. And there on the sideboard were the trays, with dirty dishes still uncollected. Better than cakes! I set those on the sideboard, picked up one of the empty silver trays, and kept going, wondering which doors to try.

I found them by the feel of magic, a cold tingle that made me shiver in spite of the hot, breathless air that the storm battering the mansion had not begun to cool. I sensed the magic from around the corner and down a hall I hadn't seen before.

I paused at the corner and took a quick, furtive peek—and recoiled. Before a thick door stood a pair of heavily armed Wolf Grays.

Before I could dither more than a few fast heartbeats, the clatter of approaching footsteps emerged out of the muted thunder and the distant roar of rain.

I sprinted to the other end of the hall opposite the stairway, and ducked behind the sideboard under the round window as a new pair of burly Gray Wolves appeared, dragging a starved-looking, bruised, filthy young man between them, his hands tied behind his back. This had to be the prisoner who was about to be sacrificed. His greasy hair hung before pain-hazed eyes.

My heart tried to crowd up into my throat, and I forced myself to pop up and run behind them. When they halted at the door, I lurked behind the largest guard, holding my tray. I formulated an excuse—*Someone sent me to collect dishes*—as one guard gave a double-rap at the door.

The door opened and a guard peered out, then motioned the three in. She scowled at me, then looked inside at the duchess. "There's a page with a dish tray."

"Who sent a page?" came the impatient voice, tight with anger or stress.

"The steward thought there were dirty dishes to collect," I mewed.

"The morning parlor, idiot," the duchess yelled from inside, and the door closed in my face.

But not before I'd seen past the drooping head of the prisoner: two guards; the duchess, wearing riding clothes of gray and red, with vambraces on her forearms, and a gold-handled dagger at her trim waist; the purple-robed mage, and in her hand, a slim book.

Did you see that, Faryana?

Yes. If you see it, I can see it. Can you get closer?

I can't get in—oh, wait.

I knew where the magic room was, now. Beyond it lay the second garden. And though the storm still pelted down, it was the front of the building, facing the street, that was getting the worst of it.

I sped downstairs, clutched my tray against me as an excuse to pass unmolested through the kitchen, and used it as a rain canopy as I splashed out into the garden. The shoes were promptly ruined, so I kicked them off and ran barefoot.

Keeping below the sight of the windows, I ran along until I found the wall below the window of the magic chamber, then I peered up past my tray. No convenient tree, but the wall was festooned with aromatic honeysuckle, its tiny flowers glimmering against the dark ivy leaves it fought for precedence. The ivy, tenacious in its grip, seemed to be winning the silent war.

What to do with the tray? There was no help for it. I had to leave it behind. Shoving it into a bush in case someone came prowling around, I rubbed my hands, tested the ivy, and finding it firm, I swarmed up as quick as a cat.

The magic chamber had a bank of windows, the outer two of which had been set slightly ajar for air. Easing up to one, I peered inside.

The mage's voice was clear in the heavy air, a deliberate, sonorous roll of ancient-sounding words as the guards held the prisoner pressed to a table, his neck exposed. The duchess had pulled her knife. It seemed that she wanted the pleasure of slitting the prisoner's throat when prompted.

My skin crawled...and my cap nearly flew off. The hank of horse hair flapped around my face as I forced my hair to still.

She's creating the boundary, Faryana said. *Let's break it.*

My magic was all natural, which meant I drew by will on the same mysterious force that these mages called through their words and signs. Under Faryana's direction, I squinted into the room, perceiving a faint greenish shimmer around the table where the sacrifice victim lay. Imagining a sword made of sunlight, I cut through the shimmer . . .

The mage faltered, frowned, and the muscles in her neck tightened. I ducked before she could look up. I counted to five, then cautiously lifted my head again.

"The lightning must be interfering," she said. "Are you certain you will not wait for this demonstration?"

"We're here. And I'm bored," the duchess replied. "I want to see if this thing is worth what I paid to get it."

The mage began again, her voice even slower, her pronunciation crisp, her signs carefully drawn in the air, so carefully I perceived a faint train of greenish light trailing in the air after her hand.

Once again I imagined my sun-sword, and drew a circle around her hand.

The mage lowered the book, frowned, then once again, I sensed she was about to look around. "The magic breaking my spell originates from that window."

"So it is the storm, then?" the duchess asked.

The mage didn't reply. I counted to five again, looked up . . .

Right into her astonished face. Then her eyes narrowed angrily.

She's going to strike you, Faryana cried.

I could see that. Quick as thought, I hummed under my breath. The only way I can explain voice-cast is to compare it to singing a song. You hear the proper notes, and match your voice to them.

"*Silence*," I said, just as her lips parted. Though I'd heard very little from her, it had been enough to get her own distinctive personal range, and pitch my voice to smite straight to her nerves.

Her face suffused with color, then contorted with anger and fear. Her mouth worked, but her voice was frozen.

She is still dangerous, Faryana said.

"*Still as stone*," I commanded.

The duchess's face appeared at the window. Her eyes widened in fury. She slammed the window casement open so hard that it crashed into the wall, sending glass flying, and snatched at me.

I ducked out of her reach, my hands clutching desperately on the ivy.

She yelled over her shoulder, "Get that brat out of the tree!"

As she did, I lunged up, reached through the open window, and snatched the book out of the mage's hands. Then ducked down again, the duchess's hands grasping a hair's breadth from my head.

"Get my sword," she commanded, without taking her gaze from me.

"If you do," I said, brandishing the book, "I will set this on fire." As a herd of guards splashed into the garden below me, I added, "If they come anywhere near me."

The duchess motioned to the three guards who'd just reached the ivy and were about to pull themselves up. "Wait there." She smiled. "I can wait. Can you? Who *are* you?"

If ever there was a time for a lie, this was it. "I was sent by Emperor Jardis Dhes-Andis," I said.

Acid laughter rolled through my mind. Faryana was gone. I froze, witless with fear. I'd left the pinhole open too long! Dhes-Andis's mental voice, still chuckling, sounded like distant thunder on the mental plane. *I will back your efforts, my inventive little apprentice, as long as you keep hold of that book. I want that book—*

I slammed the mental door.

Think! I could make a shimmer, but that would not get me away from the ivy. Could I turn into a bird? I was desperate enough—as if to torture me with what I could not have, I heard Tir's frantic cry somewhere above the roof. I tried loosening my grip, but my body in its sodden clothing was too heavy. I knew I'd drop like a stone.

Then the shivery sound of a sword sliding from a sheath rang through the air, and the duchess said, "I am tired of waiting. Give me the book, and you can return to the emperor with my compliments. In fact, since you are obviously better than this fool, why don't you come inside and take her place? Give me what I want, and the book is yours. And as much gold as you ask."

She struck the frozen mage with the hilt of her sword, and the woman thumped to the floor, helpless to break her fall.

Idiot, I thought at myself. I cleared my throat, then hummed to get her register, but a warning tightening of my own throat caused me to wheeze in a startled breath. Curling one hand, I surreptitiously tried a tiny shimmer, a flower among the ivy leaves.

Nothing.

Dhes-Andis had done something to my magic. So that was why he said he'd help me—he wanted me relying on him for magic, and had gotten my register. Meanwhile, he was probably sending minions . . .

But he was a continent away, and my immediate danger was here before my eyes. What to do? What to do?

Lie my way out of it, of course.

Trying for as callous a tone as hers, I said, "I can drop you with a word. So no tricks."

The duchess gave a breathless laugh, and backed up. "All right, all right." She snapped her fingers, and a guard presented a gem-chased sword sheath. The duchess gave me an amused glance, and returned the sword to its sheath.

My fingers had nearly gone numb. I loosened my death grip, and climbed the rest of the way to the window, then slid inside, careful to keep my back to the open air. She and her three guards (one had been sent to fetch that crowd down below, getting rained on as they glared up at the windows) and the prisoner, still lying awkwardly on the table with his arms painfully bent under him, all watched me as I made a business of carefully opening the book.

I looked down...at illegible scribbles. While traveling on the ship I'd become proficient at the alphabet that Chelan, Allendi, and Elras shared, but this one? I had no hope of reading it.

Not that I would have.

"I need to make the boundary," I said in an important voice. At my feet, the mage uttered a faint groan. I feared that my spell was already wearing off.

I cleared my throat again, attempting to shape a voice-cast, but once again, my neck tightened on the inside. I coughed, and looked down at the book.

I opened my mouth to speak some gibberish, and the duchess snarled, "You fraud! That book is upside down!" She held out her hand. "My sword—"

I was about to dive out the window and take my chances with the ivy and the rain-soaked horde below, when the door slammed open.

The duchess uttered a harsh laugh. "Hlanan Vosaga? This *is* my lucky day." And to the guards, "Take him."

TWENTY-THREE

Hlanan had put on his red hat, and carried a tray of food. He dropped the tray on the big table beside the prisoner, who struggled to turn over now that the guards were not holding him down. Then, as two guards closed in from either side, Hlanan flung a pot of hot drink at one, and a bowl of soup at the other.

"Ahhh!" one yelled as steaming liquid splashed across his face.

"Unh," the woman grunted as she ducked the soup, bumped against the table, then crashed to the ground, sliding in the soup at her feet.

Hlanan tossed a plate at the duchess, who ducked easily, her teeth showing as she brandished her sword and advanced. But as she passed the table, the prisoner punched out with both feet, catching the duchess in the side. She stumbled, recovered, and lunged at Hlanan.

He staggered back, but not far enough. As my breath caught in my throat, the sword point flashed into the middle of his baker's apron—and bent.

Bent?

She shortened her arm for another stab, but this time I got my shivering joints moving. Vaulting over the table and somersaulting in the air, I landed on her shoulders with both feet, and we tumbled to the ground, with me on top.

Hlanan swayed back and forth, struggling with the third guard, who was trying to obey the order to capture him, yet his eyes strayed back to the duchess. I lost sight of them as Morith heaved me off, catching the side of my head in a clout that sent stars across my vision. I lost hold of the book, which I'd meant to use as a weapon.

So I tried to make a shimmer. Nothing. But there was the brass bowl, I guess intended to catch the blood of the sacrifice, rolling at my elbow. I picked it up and held it as a shield. Clang! The sword hit it hard.

The duchess had her back to the table. Mistake. The prisoner had struggled upright and now flung himself on her, using his weight to knock her to the floor.

I rolled out of the way, picked up the bowl, and cracked her a good one on the side of the head. Bong! She slumped, moaning.

I jumped to my feet, to discover the three guards frozen, two with looks of surprise on their faces, and one whose mouth distorted with pain from burns. Hlanan's stone spell!

Hlanan dashed to the prisoner and snatched up a fallen sword. The young man flinched back, a foot coming up, but Hlanan said, "Turn around."

The young man's bruised face cleared. He turned, and Hlanan cut through the ropes binding him.

I grabbed the book from where it had fallen, and the three of us ran out of the room. The hall was empty, a faint smell of singed wood on the air, like a fireplace had been lit somewhere.

I said, "Guards below the window. Waiting for orders."

Hlanan dashed back into the room, and yelled in the direction of the window, "He escaped! Quick, to the stable!"

Then he slammed the door, and wheezed, "That stone spell won't last long, I'm afraid. She was already stirring."

"Just needs to last enough to get us out," I said.

He jerked his head in a nod, and turned to the prisoner, who leaned against the wall, blinking rapidly. His face beyond the bruises was pasty, his once-fine robe encrusted with weeks of grime.

Hlanan said, "Are you Tolvar Vaczathas?"

A brief, weary nod.

Hlanan reached under his tunic, and pulled a sheaf of papers from the waistband of his trousers. So that's what had stopped the duchess's sword! "Here. I think your king is going to want to know about these." And as Tolvar took the papers, "Can you make it outside?"

"I'll make it."

"Wait," Hlanan said, and concentrated. He whispered, making signs with his fingers, and before my eyes Tolvar turned into a Gray Wolf. "The illusion should get you well away, as long as you don't touch anyone."

"Whom do I thank?" Tolvar asked.

"Don't thank. Act. You really need to look at those papers. It outlines Morith of Thann's plan to take this kingdom for her own."

Tolvar's illusory brows lifted, and he lurched away.

"Let's get out of here," Hlanan said to me. "They'll be after us sooner than later. I left the knapsack behind the chicken house..."

Did the servants' stairs seem smoky? A thin haze hung in the air, and I wondered which of the desperate cooks had let something burn, and what would happen to them.

Neither of us spoke until we got to the kitchen yard. As he picked up the knapsack, I tried another tiny shimmer. A flower popped open, and relief surged through me. So he'd only been able to block my magic inside that room, not permanently.

An angry shriek rang from wall to wall. Even if I hadn't recognized the duchess's voice, the way her servants froze made it clear who was shouting, "Get them! The pasty-faced page and the man in green wearing a baker's apron and cap!"

Then, from another window, "FIRE!"

"Ah." Hlanan's grin was fierce as he flung off the cap and apron. "Just in time."

"Fire?"

"Morith's suite."

The entire household began boiling out of the kitchen doors, as up above, flames glowed ruddy in two of the windows. "I had no idea how terrible she is," Hlanan said, squinting against the rain, which fell steadily now, drenching us both. "She had a collection of torture instruments."

"There they are!"

A patrol of Wolf Grays halted, spreading in a ring.

Hlanan looked down at his dull green coarse-woven tunic, grubby after three days of wear. "Uh oh."

"The page has the book."

Hlanan and I exchanged glances. "Shimmer," I said to him. "I'll run."

I whirled around, leaped to the top of the chicken house, and from there, another leap carried me over the iron spikes of the fence, one just grazing my ankle. I landed and rolled in the mud, then I was up and running, as overhead Tir squawked, swooping and diving.

I ducked between a couple of houses, my empty belly growling. A fine time to remember breakfast, I thought as I splashed up a pretty brick path, and skidded under a brick archway with a trio of matching gargoyles grinning down from the top.

I looked both ways along the street—in time to see a crowd of Wolf Grays dash out, spreading in both directions. I ducked back, but not before a couple of them caught sight of me.

Sploosh, splash, I dashed through the puddles pooling in the flagged street. On the opposite side, the mansions were slightly less imposing. Good. Away from the river's edge and the royal palace meant less noble housing? My best running grounds were always narrow streets and close-built houses and jumbles of fencing.

Two more streets, as the longer-legged guards slowly closed the gap between us, and at last I reached what I was looking for: houses built close enough together for me to roof-run.

A leap, a moment on a fence to catch my balance, and another leap put me on a roof, as the panting guards closed in below, round faces looking up at me. I turned away, ran across the roof, and leaped to the next house.

The Gray Wolves had no chance of catching me, for they, too, were sodden by the rain, and none of them could leap.

Roof runs were often exhilarating, especially in the rain, as lighting blued the distant mountains to the east, reflecting in the lake, and thunder boomed and crackled across the sky. Though I was hungry and tired, a little light-headed, like the day I first met Hlanan, the old thrill sizzled through me as if the lightning lent me some of its power.

The last time I'd roof run from chasers I was alone, not belonging anywhere, or to anyone. I'd preferred it that way. It was safer.

It had not been all that long ago, but in one sense it seemed another lifetime, for this time, I was running to somewhere, and I had a partner. A trusted partner.

Tir flitted overhead. I dared not open the pinhole, because I knew Dhes-Andis was waiting, but I didn't need it. I followed the bird, who led me gradually around in a half circle, past stables and houses and a clay yard and finally past a huge apiary, built against a small loop in the river, at the east end of the city.

I pelted down the pathway, with deep hedges to either side, frequently looking behind me for the pursuit that I'd lost. The rain smeared my prints almost as soon as I made them.

Tired, panting, I slowed up when I reached a little hillock behind the last of the hives, and there Hlanan waited, my knapsack at his side. As soon as I saw him I put on a last burst of speed—though I did not know why—but before I reached him, my foot caught in a half-submerged tree root and I shot headlong.

I didn't splat headlong in the mud.

Hlanan caught me under the armpits, I slammed into him, and his arms locked around me. I flung mine around him, and I clung, breathing hard, half-laughing, dizzy with emotions that swooped like Tir through the stormy sky.

Hlanan's grip tightened until I pulled back a little, to look into his face, his brown eyes mirrored my own emotions, and then—it felt so natural—I tilted my head and kissed him.

It almost went awry, my lips brushing the soft ruddy-gold beard stubble that he had yet to shave. A second try, both of us breathless with laughter, was more successful, firing my body with light.

Then he let me go, and looked at me with a rueful smile, his forehead under streaming wet strands of hair both puzzled and tense. "Lhind?"

"I don't know what that was," I said, and remembered something Thianra had said about hiding as a child. Maybe this was a terrible mistake, but it felt so right, unlike my foolish experience with that rotter of an actor. "I mean, I do, but I don't know...what it means. Except I do like it," I said wistfully, and when he gave me a quick, inadvertent smile, not all the evil mages and ravening warriors could prevent me from saying, "Let's try again."

He cupped his hand around my cheek. "I want to. More than anything, ever, in my life so far." His gaze was unwavering. "But the search is going to be out, and they will find us if we don't get moving."

"Tell me first how you got away."

"I made an illusion. It got me into the street, then I felt that mage trying to find me by tracer, and I ended it, just before I caught a ride on the back of a wagon. I hid among the barrels, and dropped off the road right up there. Searchers ought to be along any time, now."

"You'd better take this." I pulled the book from under my tunic, where I'd stashed it between roof-leaps.

I opened it, watching rain fall on those unreadable words. "So much evil. Why don't we rip it up and toss it into the river? Faryana said to destroy it."

"I'd love to destroy it, but with my respect, Faryana," he raised his voice slightly, "you know that is not my decision to make."

I did not dare open the pinhole to find out what she might say. "Dhes-Andis is also going to be searching," I said. He had to be hovering around in the mind-realm, waiting to pounce.

Hlanan's mouth tightened briefly. "I haven't forgotten. Neither of us can try magic again. I've no doubt that mage has my magic signature by now, and though we don't know who is talking to whom, or how much they are revealing, we can assume that Dhes-Andis will cooperate with anyone who nets him that book."

"I'll call some horses," I began, and then cold pooled in my stomach. "No. I can't."

You can, came Faryana's voice.

I nearly jumped straight into the air.

You are too tired—you are leaking thoughts, she sent, and instinctively I widened the pinhole as she began, *But I will teach you—*

The roar of thunder blasted my skull. Dhes-Andis!

I fell to my knees, my hands clutched over my head to keep it from flying to pieces as pain lanced through me, brighter and sharper than lightning.

But Faryana had learned my own range, and I 'saw' her as she reached...and took control of my mind. My hands. A hum resonated through me, soft and harmonic. My fingers braided signs in the air, making light shiver and dance, and—

The assault ended up abruptly.

Faryana released control of me, and I sagged, to discover myself in Hlanan's arms again. "What's wrong?" he repeated over and over, his voice high with anxiousness.

Faryana said, *We rarely teach that before a certain level of learning. But I know you well enough now to trust you. You have shut the Emperor of Sveran Djur away by magical ward. You can shut anyone out of the mental realm the same way.*

Thank you, I responded, and opened my eyes. It took a couple of breaths to get control of my shuddering, but then I explained what had happened, as Hlanan gazed at me with wide eyes. Then I said, "So now I can call horses. We'll soon be riding."

"We," Hlanan said slowly, "yes. But not together."

I gazed at him in surprise. "What did I do wrong?" My face flushed to my ears. "Was it because I kissed you?"

"No!" His hands came up. His smile was crooked, his voice ragged. "Besides, I think that was an impulse we both shared."

I grinned, heady with relief. Oh, yes, this new emotion could hurt worse than the cut of the sharpest knife, but the

SHERWOOD SMITH

possibility of happiness was also there, stronger than that sense of the sun just beyond a distant mountain at dawn.

Hlanan let out a short breath, then said, "It's this cursed book. And the fact that Morith knows me." He glanced worriedly at the road, which was still empty. "I want her chasing me. Not you. She doesn't know who you are, and I want to keep it that way. If I'm right, it won't be for long."

He looked back at the city, diffuse in the gray, watery light.

"Does your 'if I'm right' have something to do with those papers you gave that Tolvar fellow?"

"Yes. He's the nephew of the King of Liacz, sent to this kingdom as governor. I guess she couldn't seduce him, or buy him, or coerce him. I gave him her secret correspondence with certain nobles in this kingdom, who apparently can be seduced, bought, or coerced."

"Ugh." And, listening in the mental realm, which was blessedly free of any evil emperors, "Horses will be here shortly."

He gazed bemusedly at that evil book, his manner odd, as if he wanted to say something.

I tried to help. "I still don't see why we should separate."

He glanced my way, and his tense expression softened. "Because somebody needs to get to Erev-li-Erval, and report what happened at Alezand. That's at least as important as returning this thing." He flapped the book. "I've got an idea. If I'm right about how Liacz's king will react to those papers, all I need to do is get the Grays to chase me, but stay out of their hands long enough for Liacz to be raised. If that goes as planned, we'll meet..." He looked away, then braced his shoulders, as if he had come to a decision. "We will meet in the imperial city."

"Where?"

"Find the..."

The sound of hoof beats caused us both to look up sharply. Then, as one, we ducked behind the drooping willow growing along the river's edge, as a patrol of Wolf Grays galloped by.

Once they'd vanished into the rainy distance, I looked in the other direction, and here came a couple of frisky horses.

Hlanan stretched out a hand toward me, and when I didn't move, he touched my face lightly, his thumb stroking along my jaw. Sweetness and sorrow hollowed me inside, and I gulped, my eyes stinging.

He backed away. "Stay safe, Lhind."

"You, too. Do you..." My throat constricted.

How strange it was. Here's me, enthusiastically using stinks to keep the world at a safe distance, undone by the briefest touch of tenderness. "Need money?" I forced the words out.

"More nippily-gotten gains?" His smile was sweet, but also brief, a flash of brightness. "No. I'll be fine. Go. East by north, to where the mountains reach the sea. You can catch a transport at Halfmoon Bay, which will take you to the end of the peninsula, where you'll find the imperial city." His smile went crooked again. "This will give you a fine chance to invent some new disguises."

I couldn't bear to prolong the moment. *Is this what people who pair off live with every day?*

The impulse to ride and ride, never stopping until I'd outrun the hurt of separation—the vulnerability, the expectations—was nearly overwhelming. I threw myself on one horse's back, and turned my head to see Hlanan's horse fording the river, his shoulders tense, his brown hair, tied in a tail, dripping down his back. He was riding out in the open, waiting to be seen.

I turned away, and began to ride along the hedgerows.

A week and two days later, Little Moon had risen and the stars began wheeling toward midnight when my latest mount slowed to a drooping plod. Though my muscles felt unstrung and my bones as heavy as stone from exhaustion, the sense of urgency had not abated; so far I'd seen nothing, but I knew that I was pursued, and relentlessly.

I'd managed to scrounge food along the way, sometimes growing wild, occasionally from villages. I raided kitchen gardens, but paid for cooked food, when it seemed safe enough to indulge the luxury. I took brief naps high in the boles of trees, and once in an abandoned fox nest under thick brush.

Never enough rest.

I forced my attention to the ghostly stretch of fields ahead of me, and on the mare's moon-touched mane stirring in the breeze. Her hooves flashed among the tall grasses, slower at each step.

On my right, the jagged mountains created a silhouette against the hazy, thin clouds not quite masking the brightest stars. We'd turned northward that day, my intent to ride alongside the Anadhan Mountains until they guided me to the coast. Judging by the infrequent signs, I'd reached the last of the frontier that both Namas Ilan and Liacz shared. No one owned this land. The signs were all of nomadic travelers, or herds of animals ranging for grass.

I'd slowly sunk against the horse's neck, and forced myself upright. A tremor ran through the horse's muscles when I shifted weight. She was blowing hard.

Time for another mount. As I sat up, pangs throbbed behind my eyes, further fogging my mind. I had to be alert! I made an effort to blink away the fog, and scan the horizons.

Running forms caught my attention. Distant, fast. Non-human.

I called wordlessly, and they veered in my direction. My tired companion raised her head and whickered.

I saw their dust before I saw them. It clouded up, pale gold in the moonlight as it hung suspended in the air. I heard the thunder of hooves, then I was surrounded by a herd of long-legged, long-tailed plains horses. They galloped round and round me and my tired mount. One or two danced near and snuffled at the mare. From the center of the herd a leader mare trotted, tossing her mane as she eyed me.

A stallion circled, teeth bared. I sat where I was, unsure if these creatures meant peace or war.

So I listened—

And was buffeted by a strong mental voice: *I know some human words and ways. Why do you call us?*

I must be swift, I returned. *Danger follows me.* Remembering how effective Tir was with images, I turned and pointed westward, picturing the evil green shimmer that the emperor had created along the border of Alezand.

What makes the danger?

A human sorcerer, named Dhes-Andis. He has prisoned everything alive in that circle. I go to Erev-Li-Erval to seek aid.

The stallion pranced near, shaking his head. White rims showed round his great dark eyes. The lead mare stamped her feet and blew hard through her nose. *We know that name,* came the surprising answer. *It means death to land, death to those living on land and under it. I will bear you.*

I slid off my mare, and promptly fell flat on my face. As I got up, fighting dizziness, I sensed a ruffle of laughter in the beasts still circling round and round me. A whisper of thought came from one: *They are such funny creatures.* And from another, *This one smells much like a human, but also like the Animal-Friends.*

The mare lifted her nose, and the young stallion, her son, minced toward me.

I had to grab hold of the stallion's mane and pull myself to his back, but then he wheeled and leaped into a canter with a smooth, powerful gait.

I dozed on his back. When I next became aware of my surroundings, the sun had crested the mountains to my right. My stomach pinched insistently, reminding me how long it had been since I'd eaten.

I waited until we reached a river winding its way slowly toward the south. When the stallion waded across, I leaned over and caught up several drinks with my hands, then I dug some stale bread and a few crumbs of cheese from the pack, the remains of the food I'd bought from the last village I'd encountered.

The gray clouds began to pile high overhead, dimming the light. A cold wind sprang out of the north, buffeting my face and flinging dirt up into my eyes. I began to feel that knife-blade-between-the-shoulders sensation of being watched.

The horses running on either side seemed to sense it as well; their alert, flicking ears and their high tails revealed signs of nervousness. At an abrupt whicker from the lead mare, they veered in a group and galloped southward, leaving her son and me to continue on by ourselves.

For a time we continued on, utterly alone on the long flat plains, under a sky that occasionally sent rain slashing down. Thunder muttered far in the west and here and there brief, greenish flashes lit the clouds.

That sense intensified. I shut my eyes, and a bolt, green-white and deadly, lanced from the horizon of the mental realm to the other side. Whoever it aimed at, whatever its intention, it missed me totally. But I must have reacted, for the stallion missed a step and nearly stumbled.

Rain struck, hard and cold. My gray tunic soaked up the rain until it was a weight dragging at me, so I fought it free and let it sail behind me onto the plains, leaving me wearing the undyed cotton-linen tunic that Kee had given me. I had long since traded the confining trousers in favor of Hrethan-friendly ones, and removed the hated hat to the depths of the knapsack. Freed, my tail fanned across the horse's back, and my hair lifted, the rain streaming off.

Presently the clouds rolled slowly southward, and pale blue sky peeped out here and there. When the last rain departed, I saw that we were no longer alone.

The newcomers made a perfectly spaced line dashing out of the northeast at an angle that promised an intersecting path. The shapes resolved into silhouettes of separate horses with low-bent riders, and then into a group of grim-faced young nomads carrying wickedly pointing javelins.

When they neared, I saw eyes widen. I remembered my lack of disguise.

They split into two groups, running on either side of me and my still-racing stallion. Three flanked me on either side, the javelins held loose in strong fingers, parallel to the ground. The lead riders, a boy and girl who had to be twins, began to close in—

But then a sound not unlike thunder resolved into the distant beating of wings. Everyone looked up, including I. Soaring high overhead was every manner of bird I had ever seen, in numbers I couldn't count. As I watched two broad-winged hunting birds stooped, diving down toward us.

They dropped at terrifying speed, then snapped wide their wings and skimmed the ground, one at either side of me, between me and the riders.

No words were spoken, and if any signals were given I did not see them. The riders altered their course, the javelins shifted from the outside hands to the hands nearest me: now I had a protective vanguard, who could throw those weapons outward. All this accomplished in silence, except for the drumming of hooves and wings.

The horse's thought came: *They know your quest.* And then: *The birds have seen pursuers, humans in coats the color of stone, who bear the reek of evil magic.*

Gray Wolves! I tried not to worry about Hlanan.

The riders veered, galloping westward. To harass the gray-coated hunters, I hoped. After a time the birds, too, departed, all but a few who rode the air currents high above.

My stallion provided another mount for me in the late afternoon. Another herd appeared, and after I made the change the herd ran alongside us.

The sun had disappeared behind me when we reached the higher foothills leading upward into the Anadhan Mountains. I had thought to avoid the mountains, but my vanguard had carried me to higher ground.

The shadows stretched long and blue. The cool wind blowing down from the heights stirred my tired body, and from far, far back in memory a voice whispered, *Home.*

The fastest route lay directly north, but I found my heart lifting at the prospect of mountain heights, with their pure, clear air, the crisp winds, the long vistas. I felt safe in mountains, even moreso than on rooftop runs in cities, or even in trees. I was too tired to question anymore. I rode, figuring I'd deal with those snowy peaks above me when the time came.

A scattering of twinkling lights on one of the hills indicated a village. We passed by, giving it wide berth. Two more, come upon unexpectedly, nestled in valleys. The inclines began to steepen, and here and there thick forest obscured the slopes' contours.

The horses slackened the pace when we were enclosed at last in forest. For a time my mounts picked their way willingly along increasingly narrow paths, until one of them took a misstep, sending a shower of rocks down a long cliff. The mare recovered her step, but the alarm burning through me set my heart to banging.

Go back, I said to them in my mind. *I'll find my way from here.*

Go swiftly, was the reply.

I sent a heartfelt message of gratitude, and from them came, *Your quest is good.* How did they know that? I had no answers. All I could do was push on.

I stood on the trail and watched them disappear back down the trail. They were soon swallowed up by the night-cloaked trees. I turned and started trudging my way uphill, breathing deeply of the pine-scented air.

I heard a stream plashing its way down the mountainside soon after, and I picked my way to it, and drank until my belly was full.

It felt good at the time, but I discovered my mistake when my insides sloshed at each step I made uphill. I kept putting one foot in front of the other, but all my good feelings disappeared; the thick-forested beauty around me faded, leaving overwhelming awareness of the gnawing stomach of hunger and anxiety. Hunger I was used to. To counter the anxiety, I reverted to my old habit of concocting long imprecations, using every insult I'd ever heard, in every language I'd come across in my years of wandering, first attaching them to Geric Lendan, and then to Dhes-Andis.

I was on "Pest-bitten Gargoyle-faced Stenchifer" when I rounded a corner and found the trail widening. A little farther and I saw the lights of a village sprinkled down the slope of a mighty mountain.

I knew I should bypass it. I knew I should go back until I found another animal trail, and keep on climbing. But the aroma of fresh-baked berry pie wafted on the air, accompanied by the cheering sounds of clapping and music. My feet turned toward the welcome sounds and scents, and my brain was too tired to argue.

All right. Just this once. You should be safe enough now.

I paused to dig the cap out of the pack and shove my hair into it, then I started down the trail. I remembered my tail only when I nearly stumbled, swaying to stay upright, and I had to stop again in order to stuff it back into the mud-caked trousers.

My steps drew me to an inn as if I'd been pulled by an invisible rope, one woven of light, good smells, and happy voices. The inn was crowded with people singing and dancing between the tables, most of them wearing green ribbons, indicating a wedding. I peered in a window first, but saw no sinister-looking Gray Wolves. There were even a few free spots at some of the tables.

I fumbled in my stash bag and pulled out a few coins, then went inside. Warmth and the heady scents of fresh bread and braised onions filled the air. Steel-stringed and bag-fluted music skirled merry melodies. A smiling innkeep waved me toward a rough-hewn wooden table, and soon I had a plate of slow-cooked potatoes and vegetables and a mug of drink before me. I waded in until the plate was clean and I'd drained the last drop from the mug, and then I leaned back, my eyes closing . . .

A shriek cut through the dream. I gasped when a cat leaped up on me, clawing my arms. My eyes flew open and met the intense yellow ones of a big tabby. *Run! Run!*

"There." A loud, commanding, triumphant voice ripped across the noise of the inn.

I looked at the doorway. Two sword-bearing Gray Wolves moved purposefully in, both staring right at me.

There was only one possible response.

Sucking in a deep breath, I pointed at them and shrieked, "THIEVES!"

TWENTY-FOUR

Squawking a lot more nonsense about how they'd robbed my family of everything before they'd sacked my village, I got up and backed away.

With an outraged bellow, the massive innkeeper confronted the two. "Rob a little maid, will ya? I'll rob you!"

"Do not interfere—" one began in a commanding voice, but he didn't get far.

"Threaten my man, will ya?" an equally big, brawny goodwife grated. And she followed this up with a huge meat platter, right in their faces.

Swords whirred out, and the inn erupted in noisy fighting. Fists, furniture, and food went flying this way and that; from the enthusiasm with which the wedding guests piled in, this free-for-all was considered no mean part of the wedding entertainment. One of the men stayed, fighting off the barrage, but the other worked his way grimly in my direction.

I climbed on my table and leaped to another, pausing only to fling some cups of steaming mulled wine toward the grease-splattered Gray Wolf. He ducked, I jumped down, found a window at hand, shoved it open, and leaped through, onto the roof.

Sure enough, the place was surrounded by the rest of their hunting pack.

I leaped into a pine tree, and nearly missed, I was so tired. I crashed my way down, my nose singing with the sting of broken pine twigs, and I ran.

I heard my pursuers crashing behind as I made straight uphill to where the trees were thickest. Very soon I was too winded to make any speed. So I pulled my way rapidly up into the topmost branches of a tall tree. The searchers smashed their way toward my tree...slashed bushes below me with their swords...and then moved beyond.

I waited until the forest was absolutely silent. Made my way carefully down, pausing every now and then to listen for pursuit.

When I hit the ground, I hadn't gone four steps when a voice snarled triumphantly, "I thought you'd gone up a tree. Hey! Stop, you!"

"Catch me if you can!" I yelled over my shoulder.

Bushes crashed and thrashed just ahead, and another Gray Wolf appeared. I turned smartly to my right, and zipped under some low branches—

And gripped a fistful of needles, flailing for balance, when I found myself on the very edge of a high precipice. I could not see any thing but darkness below.

"Trapped," someone behind crowed.

"It's about time," someone panted.

"Watch it. They say she's quick."

"I'll show her quick," the first voice snarled.

"Just don't kill her. No reward for a dead Hrethan," the second voice warned grimly.

I shifted my grip, the air currents from below spiraling up to caress my face. I shut my eyes. I won't use fire. I won't do it.

Faryana said, *You're Hrethan! Ride the winds, child.*

I'm half Hrethan, I answered, despairing.

A gloved fist punched through pine needles and whuffed the air beside my head, clutching. I thought of Dhes-Andis and his threats. I thought of Hlanan, far away, and I hoped, safe.

And I let go.

My body fell end over end in the cold, piny air. The cold, clear, beautiful piny air. I drew in a long breath . . .

Ride, Faryana urged me. *Lift your wings, and ride the air.*

The wind whistling past my ears seemed to curl protectively around me. I couldn't see, but I was no longer afraid. Facing downward, I flung my arms wide, my body flashing with blue-white fire—

—And the air whooshed under me, carrying me up and away from the towering spires of rock just below. I sailed out into a wide valley, turning to look wonderingly at my white wings glowing in the moonslight.

I had changed to a silver-blue bird.

My clothes had fallen away, and with them my pack. I turned, rejoicing in how easy this was, and glided back. I found my pack ripped open on some rocks, and next to it my bag of stash. A little farther away Faryana's diamonds gleamed ghostly blue in the moonslight.

When I lit on the rock, the light inside me faded, and my human form pressed around me. I perched there on my hands and knees, breathing hard until the pins and needles sense faded. Then I sat up, shivering, my fuzz fluffed out. I stuffed the diamonds and my stash into the bag, put one of the shoulder straps between my teeth, and leaped off the spire again.

This time I changed quickly, soaring out over the canyons. Far to the north, I caught the gleam of moonslight on the ocean, a pewter gleam. To the east stretched the long peninsula, mountains marching down its spine.

The bag swung from my curved, nut-cracking beak. I lifted my long, elegant wings, and began the climb toward the snowy summits along that eastern spine.

All through the night I flew, riding warm currents of air down through the valleys and soaring over peaks. My tiredness lay somewhere just beyond perception, though it had not completely vanished. I scarcely comprehended the majesty surrounding me. I had become a creature in a dream, gliding tracelessly through a dream land, all emotions and memories as distant as the land below.

When at last I passed the highest crests and started the long descent toward the peninsula's headland, a thrill of regret ran through me, but hard on that came the exhilarating thought: I can be a bird anytime I want to!

As long as I was in the heights.

The sky-scraping snowtops had begun to diminish toward the headland, revealing the gleam of a city along the mighty cliffs at the extreme end, like Faryana's necklace of diamonds.

Erev-li-Erval had been built along those high cliffs. Unassailable from the land below, and protected by the mountains at its back, the capital of the empire had existed unmolested for centuries.

But it was not in the heights.

The sun was just rising above the dark expanse of the sea when I began to feel weight tugging on my wings and body. At first I thought it was my exhaustion closing in on me again, but as I sailed lower and lower still, I sensed that I was soon going to lose my bird shape, and thought I fought it mentally with my dwindling strength, I knew that transformation was only possible in the heights.

I flapped as high as I could, and rode the brisk morning breezes within sight of the white marble of the Empress' city, nacreous in the peachy light of dawn. When I came down at last, it was gently enough, but my human weight overwhelmed me and I fell headlong on to the grass.

You're almost there, I told myself. *Thianra and Kee and the others count on you telling them what happened.*

I swayed to my knees and pulled on my clothes once again. Last, I clasped Faryana's diamond around my neck. I was so tired the necklace seemed unbearably heavy, and I could not bring myself to pull on my cap. I would go as I was, without disguise.

I began the long plod toward the high gold-spired gates, fixing my gaze on them lest they slide away farther. What had seemed a short distance from the air seemed a day's march now, but I kept plodding, one foot, second foot, one foot, second. . .

I felt a brush of magic as I neared. I didn't know what it was, and didn't care. I just had to make it a little bit farther, a little bit longer. Step, step, step. Don't stop. Don't rest.

A noise caused me to lift my tired head. Three richly dressed figures on caparisoned mounts rode through the gate. My heart eased at the sight. Surely I could beg a ride from these, as my quest was so important?

I halted, swaying, when I perceived the riders coming straight for me. My gritty eyes rested with pleasure on the riders' sweeping silken cloaks and sleeves ruffling in the wind, the gems gleaming in the circlet on the leader's brow.

Then I recognized his long apricot hair.

I stared mutely up into Geric Lendan's triumphant smirk.

"What a fool you are, thief," he drawled, teeth showing in a contemptuous grin. "Did you really think you'd enter this city without my knowing?" He lifted a ringed hand and gestured to his companions. "Disarm and search this creature. No need to be gentle," he added with smiling cruelty.

They dismounted and came toward me—

But before they could touch me, a muted flash of light startled us all. Four figures dressed in unrelieved black appeared out of nowhere.

Geric's companions retreated in alarm. The angry prince forced his nervous horse between me and the newcomers.

"This is a thief," Geric said, "who has stolen something of value from me. I did not summon you, and I do not need your help. Since when do you interfere in a question of justice to be decided by a Prince of the Golden Circle?"

One of the black-clad newcomers silently drew a blade from its sheath, and warded Prince Geric's helpers back. Another also drew steel, which gleamed cold and pale in the morning light, and brought it down in a slow, warning movement before the furious prince.

His horse reared and backed. Prince Geric pulled hard on the reins, but the mount would not go forward.

The other two silent newcomers stepped to either side of me. I squinted up at a tall, shadowed face, wondering if by some miracle this grim person was here to rescue me? A friend of Hlanan's perhaps, or even Faryana's?

I felt a black-gloved hand close around my arm.

"How dare you interfere!" Geric snarled. "I shall go straight to the Empress—"

He was interrupted by an almost inhumanly disinterested voice, and I don't know if Geric or I was the more shocked at the baldly stated words:

"Hrethan. You are under arrest for the theft of jewels from Princess Kressanthe of Meshrec, by order of Aranu Crown of Charas al Kherval. You will come with us."

TWENTY-FIVE

Other than a brief, gloating laugh inside (I was too tired to utter it) when Lendan backed away in impotent rage, I went entirely numb. To have come so far, just to be caught by *that*? The irony—the *stupidity*—of it chased every other thought out of my skull and I stood like a seed husk, empty inside.

"Come." It was a command.

I could scarcely get my legs to move forward. My mind wasn't much better. Plans and counter-plans chased themselves through my brain like fireflies in a storm, to be abandoned and forgotten.

We walked through the gate and I caught a glimpse of pleasingly designed canals, curving bridges and white stone buildings amid flowering trees and shrubs, then my captors took me through an unobtrusive door in the wall. We marched down stone steps into a narrow underground chamber, followed along this for some distance, all in silence, that black gloved hand resting on my shoulder to guide me. We passed long corridors and doorways, to all appearance undistinguishable from one another.

The guards turned abruptly at one of these corridors. We climbed up a long stairway, coming out finally in another narrow hallway. This one looked exactly like the previous ones, but somehow I knew I was above ground again. The oppressive weight of the surrounding stone had eased slightly.

More halls, then at last a big, iron-studded door. We stopped and one of the guards struck the door once with her fist.

The door opened. Passing over the threshold, I felt a faint but distinct tickle of magic. My hair involuntarily lifted and one of the guards' eyelids flickered.

Now we were back in civilization: a wide white-marble hall with a blue-painted ceiling with gold stars overhead, and the floor covered with a mesmerizing mosaic pattern in various shades of blue and gold.

A tall woman dressed in blue and gold came silently from an adjacent hallway and beckoned to the guards. We followed her through two richly decorated anterooms, then she opened a door.

Another woman, stout, with steel-grey strands in her dark hair, sat at a desk beside a huge window that overlooked the white-bleached cliffs high above the sea, and the flow of a river into a vast, curving waterfall. Above it, there must have been a hundred types of birds dancing and diving above that glistening veil of falling waters.

I wrenched my gaze away, and turned to the woman, who waited in silence.

She, like the guards, wore severely cut black clothing. Her face was unremarkable, jowly-square around a short nose, her dark eyes steady and narrowed in a considering gaze as she studied me from dusty hair to filthy feet. Something in the shape of her brow, the curve of her wide-set eyes, seemed familiar, though I had never met her before.

"What is this about Prince Geric Lendan, Princess Kressanthe, and some diamonds, little Hrethan?" The woman spoke Elras, in a low, musical voice that again seemed vaguely familiar. Then she made a casual gesture and the guards silently withdrew.

A thick fog of exhaustion had settled in my skull, obscuring thought and memory. My gaze was drawn inexorably back to that window, and the braided swoop of birds . . .

"The diamonds?" she spoke again. "Do you still have them?"

Lhind? Faryana said.

"Oh, yes." The fog retreated a little. I turned to face the woman in black. "I can't give them to you, because they need to go to the Magic Council," I said. With those words, the sense of urgency returned. "But that's not why I'm here." I remembered I'd been arrested and added hastily, "Ah, why I came to the imperial city. I need to speak to Aranu Crown as quickly as possible."

"Why?"

"Because—well, first, who are you?" I said suspiciously, remembering what Kuraf had said about enemies all over Court.

The woman laughed, a rich husky laugh that was not unkind. "You are in a position to bargain, little thief?" A pause to wipe her eyes, then she said, "I am Aranu."

Enormous relief swept away any other reaction I might have had. "You've got to hurry," I said earnestly. "Dhes-Andis put a barrier spell over Alezand, all to try to catch me, and then he was chasing after this evil book..."

The Empress' eyes narrowed again. "Please, young Hrethan. Will you start at the beginning?"

I did. I started with Yellow Smock bullying the Apple Woman yet again, causing me to retaliate, and I'd reached the pirate attack on the yacht when she raised her hand, palm out. "Wait."

The floor seemed to dip under me and I swayed.

"Sit down," she bade, not unkindly.

I flopped bonelessly onto an embroidered chair.

The Empress got up and moved to what I'd thought was a dark mirror, framed by old silver scrollwork. She made a brief gesture with her fingers before it, and a man's startled face appeared.

"Your Imperial Majesty—" The man said, bowing.

"Have you received any word, or signal, from Alezand?" The Empress rapped the words out without preamble.

The man looked at something out of the range of the mirror. When he looked back, he said, "Nothing at all."

The Empress gestured to me. "Please begin again, young Hrethan."

The man in the mirror looked at me silently, and I told my story again. His expression went from puzzled to grim. He listened without interruption, even when tiredness caused me to get my words jumbled, and I kept having to go back to explain things.

But at last it was all done. The Empress said to the mirror, "I want you and the rest of the Magic Council to go to Alezand, lift this spell, and investigate. If there is any sign of Dhes-Andis or his minions, you have my permission to do what is necessary. You will see to it?"

The man's thin lips stretched into the tiniest, smallest hint of a shadow of a smile I had ever seen, but somehow I sensed that he very much looked forward to executing these orders. He bowed, and the mirror blanked.

The Empress turned to me. "From the various and surprising reports I've received over the last day, your story, amazing as it is, appears to be corroborated," she murmured. "In spite of his protestations, it also explains why Prince Geric Lendan risked my wrath by laying a forbidden identity tracer right outside my gates. Now, show me this necklace the Meshreci have been clamoring over."

I fingered the necklace out of my tunic, and fumbled the clasp open. The Empress leaned forward and took the necklace from my hands, then she lifted her voice slightly and said, "Morin."

The tall woman reappeared.

"Guard this room. Let no one inside. Officially this child is in the dungeon." She rose and touched my shoulder. "You will answer further questions, and have your questions answered, when you have rested. Sleep well, little thief! You have earned it."

She passed out of the room. The silent woman indicated a couch nearby.

I looked at the couch.

I moved toward it.

I dropped down onto it . . .

. . . And woke up much, much later in a room that was dark except for a candle burning steadily on a low table nearby. I lay still for a while, reveling in not having to move at all.

Presently I became aware of the soft sound of running water, and I got up and crossed the room into the next. There I saw a wide pool with water pouring down from rocks. Several lamps revealed a thick towel, waiting soap, and a long swath of silk embroidered over with flowers and leaves.

I hesitated about half a heartbeat, then my clothes flew in all directions and I dropped gratefully into the water. After a long bath, I felt truly awake again. When I was dry I turned to figure out the silk, which seemed to be an item of clothing. I held it up, inspecting it in puzzlement.

"That part you are holding is trousers, and those two portions hanging down go around your neck and drape in front any way you want," a familiar voice spoke from the doorway.

"Thianra?" I exclaimed, whirling around. She entered smiling, dressed as usual in minstrel blue.

"The Magic Council came and cleared off Dhes-Andis' spell. The Gray Wolves had already gone, some with Lendan, and others to the north. The senior mages brought us here." She chuckled. "You might as well get used to Hrethan clothes."

"Draped," I repeated. "So that's why the Blue Lady looked so different from—" I stopped.

"Here, and here." She demonstrated as though I hadn't spoken.

I pulled the slithery silk over my body and around my arms. A twist, a loop, and I was decently covered, yet my tail and my spine hair were free. "This is wonderful!"

"Hungry?"

I groaned and she said quickly, "I know. Does a horse have feathers?"

We both laughed, relief and hunger making me feel curiously light inside. I followed her into yet another room, where hot food had been set out on a low table. Pillows circled the table.

I was on the verge of asking her if she knew anything about Hlanan when I heard his voice. "May I join you?"

I whirled around. Hlanan stood in the doorway, his smile tentative. He too was clean, his hair ordered, his chin shaven. He was dressed in his customary scribe clothing.

"You're safe," I cried. "What happened?"

Hlanan grinned, looking more like his old self. "The King of Liacz has Morith, now. The Gray Wolves chased me until they found themselves surrounded by a regiment from Liacz. The king, it seems, is very fond of his nephew. The duchess, and those she suborned, are going to have a lot to answer for," Hlanan said.

"And that horrible book?"

"The Council has it."

"I don't suppose they caught that mage?"

"The Council took my description of the correspondence. It's up to them, now."

"How about Faryana?"

"No one knew she had disappeared," Thianra said. "Thanks to you, now the Council Members have her, and they are busy trying to find a way to free her."

"Lendan knows how," I said quickly.

"Yes, but he can use that to bargain. The empress does not want him in any position of power. There are complications surrounding Geric Lendan."

"But everyone is all right? Even Rajanas?"

Thianra nodded. "Busy with Kuraf planning defensive measures in case Dhes-Andis, or anyone else, tries any more forays."

The two exchanged a brief glance, then Thianra said, "I think I will go see what has happened to that breakfast."

The door snicked shut behind her.

Hlanan took a step toward me, then turned around purposelessly. "There's something..." He swallowed. "There is one. Other. Secret. But it has to wait," he said to the waterfall beyond the broad window. And then to me, after a short breath. "I was asked to explain some of the basics of magic to you. To help you for whatever you eventually decide to do."

"All right," I said, aware of the emptiness inside my arms. On my long run I had imagined our reunion in various ways, but never like this, calm and yet distant. "All right," I repeated, as if saying the words would make it true.

"Magic." He cleared his throat. "There's magic in and around the world, just like life. Your illusions don't take much magic, but changing things does. Not many magicians ever master enough to make changes, but apparently you've inherited a gift for just that kind of magic, the greater magics. You can do good or harm, just as you will, once you've learned to control your gift, but there's an effect. Not just on you but on the world around you. We call it a price. Dhes-Andis and his adherents think of it as a necessary part of magic. And that is why he must continually conquer new land."

"Is there something wrong with Sveran Djur?"

"Much of it is blasted and warped, nearly lifeless. Scarcely anything grows there, and the people, those who are left, are miserable. Long centuries of unchecked use of magic for military purpose has drained the area of life."

I winced. "He told me his city is beautiful."

"It is. Or was. I do not know, having not been there," Hlanan admitted. "But it used to be one of the most beautiful cities in the world. If it still is, Dhes-Andis probably expends a tremendous amount of magic to keep it that way—again at the cost of the land around. So by his reasoning he must conquer new lands, just to gain the magical strength he needs to sustain what he and his father before him have done. Back to you. Those wild storms in Fara Bay and over the ocean after the pirate attack were the result of your ripping magic into fire-shape and sending it through the air."

Appalled, I said, "So I've done terrible damage? With two spells?"

"Not direct damage," Hlanan said. "It's more like you stirred up a pond violently, but it's slowly settling back to normal, minus a little of the water that got splashed out. You could do damage if you kept at it, or if you learn and use more powerful spells."

I clasped my hands together. "I am willing to learn."

"I know," he said. "I told them that. But that brings me to the second thing. I was asked to prepare you for the formal—that is, the public—ah, interview come morning. A very serious interview. Before the entire court."

I remembered then how I'd been brought into the Empress' city. "You mean a trial? So I'm still under arrest?"

"It was the only way to get you from Geric's hands," he said seriously. "Meanwhile, Kressanthe's accusation still stands."

"So I'm still in trouble for snaffling Faryana's diamonds?" I was disgusted. "All I can say is, we're lucky I stole them."

"Yes," Hlanan said. "But that's something that cannot be said in public. Try to understand. When you stole them, you did not know they were enchanted, right?"

"No. Yes. No," I said, remembering. "I sensed that they were something special. I was about to take the ones from right off her neck, but these felt different." I frowned, trying to recall. "Besides," I had to laugh, "I was afraid she'd notice the ones she'd been wearing were missing and set up a squawk."

"Then you committed a theft."

"And that's a matter for an Empress?" My nerves shot cold.

Hlanan said swiftly, "You are not in danger from the Empress. But you are from Kressanthe's people. Here's what's going on. Lendan is trying to defend himself by making claims that you are secretly Dhes-Andis's apprentice, and he will use the magic spells you created as proof, as well as the theft. He's denying his own connection with Dhes-Andis, and with the Duchess of Morith. Don't worry about that. We've caught him in enough lies, and this is not the first time he has been in trouble."

"Oh yes. He was refused magical training, right?"

"Among many other problems. But he's also been wooing Kressanthe's father, the King of Meshrec, a known trouble maker, but whose command of the strait between the two continents makes him important in international circles. He is demanding you be handed over to him for justice since the crime was committed against his daughter in a port city belonging to one of his allies."

"But if we just tell them what Lendan did—"

"But we can't, "Hlanan said. "As far as the King of Meshrec—as far as the world outside is concerned, they are perfectly ordinary diamonds. Right now the set is being copied in secret by a very skilled jeweler. The new set will be handed over to Kressanthe tomorrow, and the Empress is going to claim that since she made the arrest in her city, and recovered the jewels, any judgment falls to her. No mention of magic will be made, and you can just wager that Lendan will not mention it, either, lest a line of inquiry gets opened that he would find it very difficult to answer."

"What happens if I just come out with Lendan's sneaky trick on Faryana?"

"The best preparation against a liar who is really an enemy is not to let him find out how much you know," Thianra said from the doorway, as she wheeled in a cart loaded with things that smelled wonderful. "If we are quiet about Faryana, Geric will go off to woo Meshrec in order to get the diamonds from Kressanthe. If he can. Kressanthe is pressing the matter purely for the attention, so she may or may not give them back, depending on how much flattery he can manage before he chokes." She paused, smiling ruefully.

I couldn't help laughing at the idea of Geric mooing soft words about glorious eyes and starry romance to the pouting princess, all the while trying to grab the necklace from her.

"Anyway, if he does get them, he won't know if we replaced them or broke his enchantment," Thianra said. "It gives us time."

"We need time, for a number of reasons," Hlanan said, shaking his head. "But since you know little of politics or magic, they can wait."

"So tomorrow I go on trial in front of these high and mighty nobles, and I confess and give them up, is that it?" I asked.

"That's it," Thianra said. She laughed and added, "Suitably humble and chastened, and we'll have to coach you on protocol. I assure you, it will be severely formal. But you won't have to say much, and it will not last long."

"And after?" I said. "What about after?" My gaze strayed to Hlanan, who was toying with his cup again.

"That's for the Empress to decide," Thianra said. "But I'm reasonably sure that whatever happens will be something you wish."

"All right," I said, trying to understand Hlanan's avoidance of my gaze. "Last question, since you two seem to know so much. Do you know anything about Jardis Dhes-Andis's family?"

"He's not your father," Thianra said quickly. "But apparently, and I just found this out myself, he is your uncle."

Our blood, he'd said. He hadn't quite lied. I made a sour face. "What happened?"

"Your people came from another world long ago." Thianra passed out plates, and we all began to load them with pastries, stirred eggs, little crispy potatoes of many colors, and fresh fruit. "They reappeared some years back. Dhes-Andis's older brother went to them as ambassador—actually to spy out their weaknesses—and ended up falling in love with your mother. What he didn't know was that love, or some other change of heart, had caused your father to completely foreswear the villainous plans they'd laid."

"The Council says they think Dhes-Andis expected that any children would be gifted in magic beyond the normal range. They were to be trained by the emperor, and used in his plans. When you were born, your parents tried to disappear rather than hand you over," Hlanan said.

"They disappeared from their allies as well, rather than endanger them, but Dhes-Andis is good at hunting people down when he wants them, and the Council thinks he might have caught them before they could do gate-magic and go to her world. They apparently tried to hide you somewhere, and separated to go to ground. No one knows who you were given to, or what happened subsequently," Thianra said, and bit into a tartlet. "Oh, that is superb."

"Everyone thought the three of you were dead by the emperor's decree," Hlanan said, toying with his fork. "He probably spread that rumor around himself, as he didn't want anyone finding any of you first. It could be that your parents didn't survive. But you did."

"I see, " I said, with an effort to be casual. "So that mystery is solved. Uh, will you two be there tomorrow?"

"I will, in my function as lowly court scribe," Hlanan said.

"But I'm just a minstrel, and so I'll not," Thianra said, smiling crookedly.

The door opened, and the Empress appeared. "Well, my children?"

"All caught up," Thianra said, rising to her feet. Hlanan had as well. So I uncurled my legs and hopped up.

"Except one thing," Hlanan murmured.

"We shall resolve that one now," the Empress said, and to my surprise, walked up and put a hand on each of their shoulders. "Lhind the Hrethan thief, very few people know this, but they insisted you be in on the secret: these two are my youngest children."

I stared. "What?" I remembered that one ought not to squawk questions at an Empress, and backtracked hastily. "So that is why you looked familiar! Um, Your Imperial Majesty."

The Empress's lips twitched as Thianra chuckled. Hlanan regarded his plate of food as if it had bugs crawling in it.

So that was his one other thing.

The Empress gestured for them to sit down. "All four of my children have different fathers. They have been trained well, without anyone knowing anything more than that I have children. This is our tradition. Hlanan is my youngest."

"And so...you are going to pick one as an heir?" I asked, remembering what Kuraf had told me. "Or is that already done? The older ones?"

"One of my older sons has striven for excellence as a commander, his goal to defend the empire as my heir," the Empress replied. "That decision has yet to be made. I have to admit that I favored Thianra from the beginning. Though there are exceptions to everything, I think women are better managers. Men tend to throw things when flouted, like armies. Thianra had the best training of them all, and she was ambitious enough to make me happy...until she fell in love. There's no gainsaying that passion."

"With someone?" I turned to Thianra, who laughed and shook her head.

"With music. Though she's dutiful, I can bring before her a gathering of the world's sharpest rulers and diplomats, but she spends the evening talking to the hired players about tri-tones and the differences in wood for instruments."

Thianra saluted her mother with a bite of egg. "Music, the great leveler. Far more interesting than armies and laws and balancing money exchanges."

I waited for Hlanan to say something, but he had begun to eat in an absent way, his attention distracted. I said, "Rajanas knows who you are?"

Hlanan had put down his fork and was twisting that silver ring on his little finger. "From our days together on the Shinjan galley. He said to tell you, by the way, that you are always welcome in Alezand whatever you decide to do. And Kuraf offers you a home."

He was facing me now, as if...as if the worst was not yet over?

The Empress clapped her hands to her knees and got to her feet. "My children, I wish I could stay and chat. Lhind, I want to hear more about your life. A lot more. But I have a chamber full of people waiting to talk to me, and I need to make certain that everything proceeds exactly as I wish tomorrow." She bent down and flicked my cheek. "Ask Hlanan to take you out to the waterfall. I think you will like it."

She walked out, followed by Thianra; the last thing I heard before the door closed was their voices, both sounding very alike.

"It's your foreheads," I said to Hlanan. "The resemblance is there."

He dropped his hands. "Can you forgive me?"

"Forgive you? For not telling me about that?" I hooked my thumb toward the door. "But it's traditional not to tell people. I learned that from Kuraf."

"For all the burden that comes with knowing," he said in a low voice.

"So you want to be the heir?" I asked, finally getting what he could not quite bear to tell me. As if he feared it would be a burden too weighty for me to bear.

"I think I do." He let out his breath in a short sigh. "I do." He up his hand with the ring. "We all had to go out into the world to experience it, and to learn. Used to hearing myself described as smart, and bored with the scribal training that my father had insisted on, I left a lot earlier than most. And almost immediately found myself on a Shinjan galley. The only protection we had were these rings. I could have used it to transport myself home from anywhere, but to walk out on problems without solving them would mean I was a failure."

"Did your mother go through that?"

"Some day ask her about working as a ship's cook in the fleet fighting the slavers away from the south coast countries." His grin flashed, then he was serious again. "I told you that once we escaped, Ilyan Rajanas and I each chose ways to learn to deal with the harsher parts of the world. He turned to the military, and I to magic." He halted, and gave me an uncertain glance.

"I remember that," I said. "I remember everything you told me."

"And everything I didn't tell you." He looked away, his hand turning his cup around and around. "Here's another truth. I don't know where we are going, that is, you and I. My only experience with women was that one time, with the duchess. Ever since, I've kept my distance. The boring scribe no one notices. I understand it's a kind of disguise, called hiding in plain sight. But it didn't prepare me for meeting...you."

"I probably have less experience than you do," I said.

He nodded. "The grime and the essence of fish. Also excellent disguises." He squared his shoulders. "So this has been my goal." He lifted his chin.

"Being chosen as heir?" I asked.

"If I can prove my worthiness to myself first," he said quickly. "The thing I learned on that galley is how much damage someone in power can do. How many lives can be lost as the result of one person's will. I believe a good emperor should not have to use armies. My brother disagrees. Maybe I'm wrong." He lifted his gaze to mine, then said in a rush, "I want to prove myself by taking down Jardis Dhes-Andis of

Sveran Djur, and freeing the Djurans from his evil rule. And I want to do it without starting a war."

I rubbed my hands. "Now that is a splendid plan."

"What do you mean?" he asked, taking a step nearer.

"I mean if you want to do that, let me help. Oh, I know I'm ignorant, that it can't be done today. But everybody keeps telling me I have potential. So if I meet these Hrethan, and assuming they don't throw me out on my ear for being a thief, they can teach me about magic. I think you and I make a fine team. Don't you?" I finished a little wistfully.

"Lhind," Hlanan said, taking another step. "I believe that you're probably the one person he's afraid of. But is that what you really want to do?"

"Right now it is," I said, and closed the distance between us. "This is what I know right now. I never felt so right until we were fighting side by side against that duchess, and then when we stood by the river. Maybe it was even before that. The first time we talked, you expected the best of me, because you expect the best of yourself, and you look for the best in everyone. I hated it at the beginning, because I knew you were right. Now. I think...I think I love that. I think I love you. As little as I understand love."

He took my hands, and there was the real smile at last. Crooked, but there. "You can't be more ignorant than I am, but we can explore that together. There's time, and yet the thing I fear most is that the expectation of my position might become a burden to you, who has cherished freedom above all things. I might become a burden. If we do succeed against Dhes-Andis, and I must return to state affairs."

The future emperor of Charas al Kherval, twenty kingdoms spread over two continents and countless islands, held my hands tightly, waiting for me to make the first move.

And so I did. "State affairs," I said, "can wait their turn. And so can evil emperors. About that kissing. Can we try that again?"

ABOUT THE AUTHOR

Sherwood Smith was a teacher for twenty years, working with children from second grade to high school, teaching history, literature, drama, and dance.

She writes science fiction and fantasy for adults and young readers.

If you want to read more books set in Lhind's world, they are listed at the beginning of this book.

http://www.sherwoodsmith.net/

ABOUT BOOK VIEW CAFÉ

Book View Café is a publisher and professional authors' cooperative offering DRM-free ebooks in multiple formats to readers around the world. With authors in a variety of genres including mystery, romance, fantasy, and science fiction, Book View Café has something for everyone.

Book View Café is good for readers because you can enjoy high-quality DRM-free ebooks from your favorite authors at a reasonable price.

Book View Café is good for writers because 95% of the profit goes directly to the book's author.

Book View Café authors include Nebula and Hugo Award winners, Philip K. Dick and Rita award winners, and New York Times bestsellers and notable book authors.

http://bookviewcafe.com

CPSIA information can be obtained
at www.ICGtesting.com
Printed in the USA
FSHW022109291218
54739FS